Momentarily dazzled, Athena worked to close her gaping mouth. However, before she could gather her wits enough to check both herself and him, Mike said, "I thought you looked fine then but I didn't expect you to be this gorgeous in person."

It might have been the way he dragged his deep voice across the word "gorgeous" that had Athena's lust-filled brain working overtime with the various positions in which she would like to hear him say that one word over and over again. But she refused to let herself be sucked totally under his spell. She pushed open the door.

"Thanks," she said, "that really means a lot coming from you."

She managed to check him with a cool eye and got, for the first time, a genuine response from the handsome playboy as he threw back his head and laughed.

SOUTHERN FRIED STANDARDS

S. R. MADDOX

Genesis Press, Inc.

INDIGO LOVE SPECTRUM

An imprint of Genesis Press, Inc.
Publishing Company

Genesis Press, Inc.
P.O. Box 101
Columbus, MS 39703

All characters in this book have no existence outside the imagination of the author and have no relation whatsoever to anyone bearing the same name or names. They are not even distantly inspired by any individual known or unknown to the author and all incidents are pure invention.

Visit us at www.genesis-press.com
or call at 1-888-Indigo-1-4-0

DEDICATION

To Eddie and Pearl

Thank You

ACKNOWLEDGMENTS

Hurricane Katrina made 2005 a particularly rough year. This book was born as a result of those difficult times. I hope people enjoy reading *Southern Fried Standards* as much as I enjoyed writing it.

CHAPTER 1

"I'm such a bad, bad girl," Athena Miles moaned as she bit into yet another of Thea's famous southern fried catfish cakes.

Smacking her lips in appreciation, she slid the remainder of her flaky reward into her mouth. After all, she deserved it. She had pulled off a fabulous impromptu after-work party. Everyone invited had arrived, on time, mind you, and as the champagne continued to flow more than two hours later, no one seemed to be in any hurry to leave.

It was the perfect evening, Athena thought, immediately crossing herself. She couldn't help it. She wasn't exactly superstitious, but she did believe in balance and humility.

"All good things come to an end," her daddy often quoted. Unfortunately for Athena, her life had proven to be a running testament to that.

For every great success in her life there was a sometimes greater failure right behind it, and, unfortunately, this time was no different.

As Athena tossed back the last of her apple martini, she tried to mentally unjinx herself, but it was too late.

She heard herself begin to wheeze before she actually felt the gag in the back of her throat as a huge wad of fish lodged in her airway.

Coughing loudly, Athena shifted in her seat to find a better position, one where she could actually breathe.

Refusing to let her unfortunate menu choice get the best of her, Athena gasped for air as her throat constricted. She had always known her poor diet choices would kill her one day, but she would be damned if it would be in Thea's kitchen.

"You okay, Ms. Miles?" A deep baritone voice wrapped in the tantalizing scent of Irish Spring boomed in her ears.

Athena looked to Kwame, the handsome six-foot-two linebacker turned social worker sitting to her left, forcing a smile as her eyes began to water. Yeah, if she could just lose the girdle, the one thing standing between her and unrestrained back fat, and, oh yeah, have men only a few years younger than herself stop referring to her as Ms. or worse, ma'am.

That's what she would have said if her throat wasn't on fire.

"I'm fine," Athena croaked as she attempted her best come-hither glance, working her hand beneath the waistband of her jeans. As she took a sip from her water glass, Athena slyly unbuttoned the top of her pants.

Whew! Much better, she thought, hiding her relief as her stomach pooched under her blouse and the fish and booze made their way to her stomach.

Much to Athena's dismay, Kwame had already turned his back. With his paycheck no longer in jeopardy, Kwame continued his conversation with Athena's newest hire, LaTonya Blessey, as if nothing had happened.

Damn, Athena thought ruefully, taking another sip of water, trying to regain her breath, feeling the sweat pop on her forehead. Did it take dying for a sister to get a little attention?

Peeking over Kwame's shoulder she couldn't blame him for his interest in LaTonya. A pretty young thing just graduated from Dillard University, LaTonya had been valedictorian of her class. If Athena didn't know better, she might think she was a bit jealous of LaTonya.

Athena mentally pinched herself for her train of thoughts. It wasn't LaTonya's fault she had drawn Kwame's attention—in fact, it was to be expected. They were both close in age and worked together forty-plus hours a week. Hell, they shared an office!

Of course Kwame would pay a lot of attention to the petite girl rather than his big-boned boss who could fire him at whim. However, if Kwame knew the number of times Athena had fantasized about catching him alone in the copy room or the boardroom or any room, for that matter, he would have been more leery about turning his back.

In fact, he would have handwritten his own sexual harassment case against Athena before running for the hills to protect his manhood. The thought made Athena giggle briefly before she began to shake her head at her ridiculous crush.

What made her think this chocolate god would be interested in her, especially in a room full of women younger than she and probably half her size? *Forget size*, Athena thought, brushing a hand down her now frizzy

3

shoulder-length raven hair. She had never had much patience with makeup and clothes, everything that got a woman noticed. Too busy keeping her nonprofit health center afloat, Athena had to admit she was not at her best looks-wise. Hell, when did she have the time? She was lucky she had inherited flawless skin. Smooth and clear, Athena's caramel-kissed skin was her best feature. It was the only reason she was able to get away without wearing makeup. With her high cheekbones and full lips, she was the perfect combination of her father's and mother's best features. Unfortunately, she had never taken the time to capitalize on what nature had given her. Besides, she could never be as beautiful as her mother, or even as charming as her baby sister.

Frowning at the crumbs left on her plate, Athena knew she had overdone it. Still, when the waiter placed another saucer of golden cakes in front of her, it didn't take long for her to give in to the temptation once again. Her downward spiral had begun earlier that morning after an overdose of Krispy Kreme and cappuccino. That much sugar that early would ruin even the strongest constitution and hers was habitually weak, so Athena knew she had to stay on watch. A cupcake meant a salad for lunch. A cheeseburger meant nothing but fruit for the rest of the day. An entire box of doughnuts? Well, there's always tomorrow.

Besides, what's a chick on a binge to do anyway? Athena knew there was only one choice: dial Thea's and jump into a plate of southern fried comfort.

Thea Roy, Roy's, or just Thea's for the locals, was named after Althea, a businesswoman from New Orleans and the original founder. The deed to the restaurant on the Back Bay of Biloxi had changed hands many times over the years and the restaurant was currently one of the best on the Coast. Athena's overworked staff had given her the perfect excuse to indulge. In fact, seventy-five thousand excuses.

Who'd a-thunk it?

Her crackpot crew had coerced an unheard of seventy-five thousand in donations from guests at their "Fun On The Bayou" fundraiser. Therefore she, uh, they, more than deserved a treat, right?

Well, of course they did.

Hypnotized by the bright lights and the possibility of seeing a local celebrity (big whoop?) or international one (whoopee!), her shiny-faced employees were awestruck.

Dinner conversation was sparse, but Athena was happy to see them happy. She couldn't help it. She had taken on a quasi-mother role when she hired them, many straight from college, and she was proud of them. Although sometimes it unnerved her to be twenty-eight and considered an elder of her company, it had some perks.

Her staff worshiped her.

For instance, Kwame, five years her junior, had designated himself as Athena's personal bodyguard, although she had to admit he was slipping, considering tonight he hadn't protected her from her own worst enemy—herself.

She really needed to cut back, she knew, rubbing the fullness of her abdomen. Unfortunately, Athena had never met a southern fried anything that she didn't like and she doubted that she ever would.

As far as Athena was concerned, diet belonged with those other four-letter words. She had abused some of the best genes in town, but she chose not to think about it, especially since dessert was coming.

However, considering that Kwame, like most of the men in her life, treated her like his daffy old aunt instead of the sexpot she knew she could be, Athena should have responded to the clue that maybe her image could use an overhaul. But no, she was far too busy with work to care, wasn't she? Or was she?

Athena sat back in her chair to give her jaw and her belly a rest. Compelled, her eyes turned to the massive brick fireplace and the poster-sized picture of the current owner of Thea's above it. Aileen Miles, Athena's famous and glamorous mother, in her patented sex-kitten pose, wore a foot-long smirk that said, "You're not going to eat all of that, are you?"

Never Mama, Mom, or God forbid, Ma, Aileen had a long-running feud with Father Time and food despite being considered one of the best chefs in the country.

Under Aileen's watchful eye Thea's had weathered gentrification and the arrival of the casinos and had grown from the rundown takeout restaurant it was two decades ago to a five-star dinner club, launching Aileen's monstrous career into the stratosphere as "the Southern Honeybee."

A loving (in her own way) mother, she had never minded being pregnant nor having children. What she minded was the fact that her two children had grown up despite her own Herculean efforts to remain forever thirty-five.

Looking down at the crispy crumbs left on her plate, Athena could imagine what her perpetually size-four mother would have to say right now.

"Honey," her mother would drawl, smiling sweetly, "honeybee, we must be aiming for the look of a hump-back whale tonight," she would have said loudly, play-fully pinching Athena's burning cheeks, red despite the fact she had heard a variation of that same theme practi-cally her entire life.

Nonetheless, ever mindful of her mother's public image, Athena's only comeback would have been to smile ruefully as her table was magically cleared of the various deep-fried dishes, replaced by a large salad—naked except for a splash of red wine vinaigrette.

Her mother was only trying to help, she would repeat over and over to herself as she would have to laugh along with her awestruck dinner guests, even adding a joke or two of her own as they realized her mother was "the" Aileen Miles, celebrity chef and best-selling author.

Of course, that's what good Southern girls do after all—grin and bear it in spite of the nausea and vomit.

That's what would have happened if her mother had been there, Athena thought, looking towards the kitchen, waiting for the doors to open and a puff of smoke to emerge, followed by her petite mother. However, when neither occurred, a genuine smile began to form on her face for the first time that night.

Her mother would not be here tonight, Athena remembered. The Southern Honeybee had gone to Atlanta with her baby sister, Sheree, for a sorority meeting. Inside, Athena shrieked, "Yessss!" and pumped air with a closed fist a la Tiger Woods, but to her fellow diners she remained the picture of serenity.

Exhaling, Athena made her decision. Raising one hand to call the waitress over and carefully tucking an inky black strand of hair behind her diamond-studded ear, Athena didn't try to hide the grin exploding on her face as she placed a double order of crispy crabcakes.

Unlike Athena, who had over the past year bargained her way down to just once a week, not counting today, of course, Aileen rarely missed a night at Thea's. However, she just couldn't miss this sorority meeting, she had told Athena about a month ago between plane rides to L.A. and New York—L.A. for a magazine cover and New York to meet with her publisher.

When she was younger, Athena had hated every time her mother got another phone call or fax or telegram calling her away at a moment's notice. She knew it was ridiculous but because of her mother's perpetually booked schedule, Athena had never felt close to Aileen.

There had been no cookie baking, unless there was a camera nearby; no story time, unless recorded for posterity; and no Girl Scout meeting, unless, you guessed it, there was a reporter trailing. Video or still, it didn't matter as long as she could share it with her fans. Through it all, Athena pretended she understood. She was the oldest, after all, but she and her mother had just never clicked.

This probably explained why she had done something she was opposed to. Even though she had cringed at the thought when an undergrad, Athena had recently started the process of joining the Sigma sorority as an adult member, much to her mother's delight. In fact, if it weren't for the responsibilities of her position at work, Athena was sure she would have been attending the convention this weekend since she had, as her mother put it, "finally come around."

Although as CEO of a growing nonprofit she could use all the publicity she could get, Athena's time was limited now that she had begun construction on a much larger office space for her twenty employees. Also, all that god-awful neon pink and yellow and the secret greetings that sounded like dolphins in heat was really not her scene.

No, even though Athena knew the connections the association would bring were priceless, she just was not up to it, at least not this weekend.

That would be her mistake number one.

If she had only known what was to come, Athena would have flown the damn plane herself and parachuted her way into the convention in a neon pink and yellow bikini. Well, maybe a one piece with a wrap, but nonetheless she would have been anywhere except sitting in her favorite booth, bloated and clueless.

Startled by a loud crash in the hall, Athena turned with the rest of her table in time to see trouble walk through Thea's rose-framed French doors. A vision in plaid glided through the seating area.

Diminutive in stature, the new arrival shimmered with a confidence that caused something fat and sharp to crawl its way through Athena's belly pudge and burrow into her deepest, darkest thoughts.

Dressed in a skintight scarlet and green plaid pantsuit, the new arrival sashayed past the irate hostess and other waiting would-be diners to the back of the packed room, finally coming to a stop a few feet from Athena.

Despite her urge to do otherwise, Athena forced herself to heed her grandmother's home training. So instead of ignoring the woman's presence, Athena smiled and extended her hand.

That was mistake number two.

If Athena had known the she-devil's evil plan, she would have forgone the effort and directed the waiter, who was a third cousin by marriage, to stop the intruder's butt cheeks from touching the seat.

Considering her loyal workers were chomping to get out of cubbyhole hell into a promotion that included walls and a door, Athena was sure they would have lent a hand as well, but instead, she ignored her every instinct, squared her shoulders, and spoke.

"Well, hello, Celina. It's so nice to see you again."

Lying had never been Athena's biggest strength, but what else could she say? "Get thee back, Satan?" Required by Southern law, Athena maintained her manners at all times.

Besides, at the time, Athena didn't know the vile woman's heinous plan. At that moment she was just walking irritation wearing a pretty mask.

"Atheeeena," Celina cooed, slapping at Athena's out-stretched hand as she pulled her into a crouched hug over the marble table as rain dripped from her slicker, wetting Athena's silk blouse.

When she let go, Athena fell back in her booth, relieved, that is, until Celina tossed her coat on the bar and slithered into the empty space.

Damn it.

At that point, Athena had no choice but to make the introductions, and like any good Southerner, offer her last crabcake, along with something cool to drink, hiding her curses behind a smile when Celina accepted both.

This wasn't the first time the two women had met. Athena had run into Celina Figaro at several social functions over the past few months. However, the extent of her knowledge of Celina was that the chic young woman was a recent transplant from Atlanta and the newest television producer at the local TV station. Athena should have suspected her demonic ties from the studio affiliation alone, but unfortunately, she didn't.

To say the least, Athena was shocked when Celina not only singled her out at Thea's, but also begged her to appear on an upcoming show of *Delilah in the Morning*, a half-hour program at WPTL.

Of course, Athena refused immediately. Athena was looking for press for her company, not herself. Athena usually had to chase people down and convince them to hear her message before she could get them to open their pocketbooks.

SOUTHERN FRIED STANDARDS

Not many people wanted to hear about what they should be doing to stay healthy or the growing AIDS program she had started at Regent's, the community center she owned. However, despite the health center's efforts, Athena wondered if the community had changed in any way. No, they would rather continue their bad habits—they were so much more fun, of course.

In other words, they wanted the hot and sexy, as Sheree, Athena's little sister and part-time Yankee, often said, and Athena dealt with the not so hot and sweaty.

"I'm just trying to educate women," Athena would often say as her sister rolled her eyes at her. "Don't you realize that women make up the fastest growth in AIDS cases?"

Her sister of course knew this already and Athena realized she could have saved her breath. Sheree was an editor for one of the largest publications for women, *Tawny*, out of New York, and was as socially aware as they come. Regardless of that, however, she chose to feed her causes with her pocketbook whereas Athena was always the one to take action, sometimes to the irritation of her friends and family, especially when she recruited them.

Still, Athena liked it that way, and it was her passion that made her effective while providing her with a healthy bank account. This was the sole reason Athena refused Celina—initially.

If only she had held firm to her refusal to appear on the *Delilah in the Morning* show.

Unfortunately, it was the little squirt of optimism born out of guilt at her ill-mannered thoughts, spurred by a chronic case of "good girl-itus," as Athena's best friend, Mel, termed her need to please, that caused her to change her mind before one of her shifty-eyed cousins could clear their table.

"What could it hurt, Ms. Miles?" Kwame had asked, chewing on a hot wing. As he coughed from the peppery sauce, Athena asked herself the same thing. When Celina promised a personal hair stylist and makeup artist to make her over just for the show, Athena could not think of a single reason not to take a chance just this one time.

5 A.M. one week later at WPTL studio . . .

Athena's instincts had told her to run after she found out that her promised "personal stylist/ makeup artist" was actually a secretary with a two-way mirror and a bag full of frosted pink lipstick, but she didn't. Athena was determined to maintain her hard-won professional image even in the face of the waves of irritation rolling her way. Then it happened. As she reached for her complimentary coffee and one packet of sugar, Athena's eyes fell on a piece of paper highlighted in neon pink.

It read:

Guest #1, Segment 2, Life Choices and Regret. "Athena Miles, the angry, bitter single woman!!!"

Nausea began to rise in Athena's stomach as she blinked with disbelief at the producer's set pages.

Celina, who had yet to show up, had described a much different show. She had said the show was to be a positive take on the infinite choices of local modern women in the twenty-first century. When nothing changed after the second reading of the note, Athena felt her blood pressure rise as denial gave up the fight and truth seeped in.

"So everyone in the studio thinks I'm coming on *Delilah in the Morning* to talk about the pitiful pool of men these days, and how it's so hard to find an eligible, straight man," Athena said to the nervous young stage assistant, who trailed her to the brightly lit set.

Chatty earlier, the fresh-faced woman now avoided Athena's stare as she attached her microphone, holding her breath until she could dart offstage. Considering she was breathing like Darth Vader with asthma, Athena couldn't blame her.

Angry single woman. Hell, yeah, Athena was angry. No, strike that. Angry was too small a word for what she was feeling at the moment. Athena was freakinfurious— with five exclamation points.

Athena had accepted the invitation to appear on the show to talk about how fabulous her life was as a successful, independent businesswomen, not end up in a three-ring circus like the *Ricki Lake Show* or some other bad version of trash talk TV.

"Well, I'll show them," Athena thought.

At least, that was the plan until she caught sight of Delilah. Even more beautiful in person, Delilah was a prettier, tanner version of Angelina Jolie. Instantly, Athena felt transported back to middle school when she had big feet, cystic acne, and a cowlick that could not be tamed.

Without a second to spare, Delilah fell into a perfectly rehearsed pose at the edge of her zebra-print lounge chair. Smiling at camera one, Delilah morphed into her TV personality right before Athena's eyes as she introduced herself and the topic of today's show: "Life Decisions of Women in the New Millennium," trapping Athena on Planet Screwed.

Stunned at the abrupt start of the show, normally cool and collected Athena choked on her nerves as she looked back and forth between camera one and camera two, leaving her unprepared when the director pointed in her direction.

"Uh. My name is Athena Miles. I am twenty-eight years old, and h-h-h-happily single."

Good Lord. That did not sound good at all.

Athena sounded nothing like the cheery, self-satisfied single she wanted to portray. In fact, to her ears she sounded more like Gloria Steinem on crack or even worse, a guest speaker at a Lonely Hearts twelve-step program.

Remembering the exclamation points, Athena tried her best to level her gaze on the camera once more. She had come to deliver a message, and was determined to get it across regardless of her sticky mouth and the intimidating flashing red light above the camera lens.

"It has taken me a while to embrace being happily single without regret, Delilah," Athena said to the "audience," who responded with a pitiful, "Ahhh."

"But don't get me wrong," she continued, squaring her shoulders. "The only thing that I regret is deluding any of my ex-boyfriends into thinking that I was ever ready to get married." Feeling more in control, Athena relaxed for the first time since the cameras had begun to roll.

"You mean," Delilah asked, "you never want to get married?"

Seeing the exaggerated frown on Delilah's face, Athena bit her lip. From her expression, Athena realized she had not been expecting her response, and the undisguised look of disbelief made Athena want to laugh even more. She tried to be as gentle as possible because it was obvious that Delilah was one of "them."

"Them" were those women or people in general who believed all women spent their entire lives waiting to get married. In this case men were from Mars and women were from one of two Venuses, each with its own personal zip code. One was for the waiting women like Delilah, and one for women like Athena, who long ago had decided to get on with their lives.

"It's not that I'm against marriage," Athena said to Delilah, "it's just that I refuse to hold my breath waiting for a prince and a picture book 'happily ever after' ending because, as we all know, I could die before that happens."

Athena heard a few chuckles and murmurs of understanding from the women in the small group of employees who had gathered around the cameras.

Looking to her immediate left, Athena could see by the tight set of Delilah's perfectly glossed lips that she was not happy. A recently unhappy single woman herself, Delilah was not at all pleased with Athena's progressive stance. Feeling her own anger wane, Athena smiled at her host.

"I'm not by any means saying marriage is not a possibility. Finding someone to spend the rest of my life with is a beautiful idea. However, until then," Athena continued, "I have my health, a great house, a great car, great friends, and a career I love." Athena looked out at the audience, spreading her arms towards the camera, and said "Life is good. Besides, if the 'worse' thing I have to live with is the label of being happily single, I will gladly take that."

As the audience burst into spontaneous applause, Athena felt good about how things were going. If only she had taken her bow and exited stage right. As they paused for the commercial break, Athena sat back on the small couch and listened for Delilah's segue. She could tell Delilah was glad to be finished talking with her since the woman's left eye twitched every time she looked her way.

To be honest, Athena was glad to be done talking to her as well. Her pretentious attitude had worked Athena's last nerve. Settling back into the cushion of her seat on stage, Athena promised herself that she would not let Delilah put her on the defense again.

"Welcome back, ladies and gentlemen, to our program, *Delilah in the Morning*," Delilah chirped into the camera. "I am very pleased to have you with us today. We have been talking with Athena Miles, a twenty-eight-year-old executive, who describes herself as happily single." Delilah's eye began to twitch again as she was forced to pause when the crowd clapped their approval.

"Now," Delilah said, "I would like for you to meet Mrs. Tremona Banks, an Atlanta-born novelist who is happily married."

Elegantly dressed, a woman about Athena's age burst through the stage doors in an eggplant and fuschia-colored skirt suit with a mango-colored floral pin on her lapel. Although Athena was certain she, herself, could never pull it off, she had to respect the woman's over-the-moon style.

"Mrs. Banks is here to talk about a book she has written about the lives of single women in the new millennium, and since we are short on time, let's get started."

"Well, Delilah, I, of course, have been happily married for twelve months." Athena smiled as the audience broke into spontaneous applause.

Although she didn't really understand why a year merited the response, Athena still applauded. Now if it were ten, Athena could understand, in fact she would do the first cartwheel. Thinking they were probably just warming up from her segment, Athena decided she was being too cynical.

"Since I've gotten married, Delilah, I have begun to notice something very troubling," Tremona said with a delicate frown on her beautiful face.

"What is that?" Delilah asked.

"I've noticed a change in my friends, especially the ones who are single who want what I have—and they are everywhere."

This statement gave Athena pause and she looked at Tremona to see if she were serious.

"I recently had the chance to meet with a friend of mine and all we talked about, it seemed, was the large number of lonely, desperate, professional single women."

Frowning now, Athena turned the volume up in her head, wondering where Tremona was going with her conversation.

"My friend was going on and on about how her single friends claimed to be happy," Tremona crowed. "They claimed they really didn't have the time for a relationship."

A large cacophony of bells and whistles erupted in Athena's head as she tried to flex her hands in her lap to keep them from forming into tight little fists.

Desperately Athena searched the group that had gathered around the camera, and she tried to remember what she and Celina had talked about at Thea's restaurant. Tremona couldn't be talking about their conversation, could she?

Sure, the subject of men had come up, Athena thought. Really, what two women, single or married, would not eventually bring up the subject of men if they talked for any longer than 20 minutes? Whether it was to complain or to brag, relationship conversation just happened.

However, Athena did not think enough had been said to spawn all of this. Unable to remember the conversation verbatim, Athena continued listening for the point that Tremona was dancing around.

"Well," Tremona began, reaching over to take one of Athena's flexing hands and covering it with hers, "I'm sure Athena is without a doubt a successful, career-oriented woman, as my friend Celina, your show's talented producer, has told me."

Startled, Athena wanted badly to jerk her hand away, but instead fought hard to keep the smile on her face as the camera pivoted in her direction. What in the world had Celina told her?

"After talking with Celina," Tremona said, her forehead furrowed, "I went back to my hotel room with my husband, and I was haunted by what my friend had to say about her conversation with Athena!"

Wh-Wh-Whaatt?

"In my opinion the reason for Athena's 'enlightened' view is that she has all but given up on the dating scene because of her inability to find and keep a good man."

Oh my God. This chick was talking about her to her face. Reeling, Athena tried to settle with the fact that she was getting publicly dissed. All she could think was, "No, she didn't," and judging from the audience's response of gasps and a few drawn out "oooohs," Athena knew they felt the same.

Tremona had taken her by surprise, and being sucker punched was not a cherished feeling. In fact, it left Athena feeling slightly nauseous for the second time that morning.

"Athena . . ."

Stop saying my name.

". . . is a beautiful . . ."

Don't try to kiss up now.

". . . intelligent"

Maybe this was not going to be all bad.

". . . executive in social services, a very admirable field, but," Tremona continued, "what women like

Athena don't realize, Delilah, is all they are missing out on by delaying marriage and starting a family."

Athena sat back in her cushy seat digesting what she hoped were Tremona's final words and waiting for Delilah to do her thing and close the show. Unfortunately, Athena soon realized her hopes were wrong when Tremona let go of her cold hand, tossing her head to the side, neatly flipping back her razor-cut bangs from her perfectly lined, smoky-lidded eyes.

"That is why," Tremona exhaled, "I dedicated my book to all the women out there who are like Athena."

Athena held her breath as Tremona pulled out a thick hardback and held it up.

Sad and Single in the New Millennium.

CHAPTER 2

"Sad and single," Athena whispered with disbelief, as she watched the cannons rolling away now that they had taken their best shots. No, she wasn't sad and single, Athena thought to herself as she raised her head from her chest, but she was mad and seething.

I was set up. But why?

The last one to move, Athena watched as members of the crew approached both Delilah and Tremona to congratulate them on the show.

Feeling as if she had been poked with a jagged stick, yet still unable to get out of her chair to check for bleeding wounds, Athena was forced to bear witness to their smug grins.

Catching one furtive glance her way, Athena became lucid in one firecracker moment. Scanning the crowd, Athena searched for the woman who had caused her humiliation.

The crowd parted suddenly and Athena saw red—literally. Dressed like a demonic Santa Claus, Celina Figaro, executive producer for the *Delilah in the Morning Show*, and the cause of Athena' public humiliation, walked on stage.

"What did I do to you?" Athena wanted to ask. Obviously they must have met in a previous life for Celina to have gone to so much trouble to humiliate her.

Finding the strength, Athena rose from her seat as gracefully as she could since her legs felt like rubber in quicksand and her hands had tensed into arthritic claws.

Watching Celina's approach with her face distorted by a satanic-looking smile, Athena swore she could see two little pointy horns poking out of her Barbarella mound of hair. It was then Athena realized she had to choose.

She could A) maintain her professionalism by responding with a cool smile, all the time plotting her revenge; B) forgo the anonymous backstabbing and strangle the witch like she deserved, or C) find a bathroom and quick before the tears started to spill from her burning eyes.

After thirty minutes locked in a bathroom stall, Athena finally got control of her tears.

She felt so stupid. She was a grown damn woman. What the hell was wrong with her? On her way towards the bathroom, she had caught Celina with a smirk that had sent her over the precipice. Why had Celina set her up? Athena could not understand it. As she sat stunned on the toilet with her legs drawn to her chest, she heard the voices of two women dissecting her humiliation as they walked into the restroom.

"Did you see her face?" the first woman said in a nasally voice, giggling outside of Athena's stall.

"I know, I know," the second woman whispered, gasping for breath.

Athena knew they were talking about her but prayed helplessly it was some other pathetic hump. Listening to the glee in their excited voices, Athena had to ask herself if she knew them. They were enjoying her humiliation a bit too much.

"You know everyone said she was a wimp, but damn."

Wimp? Athena thought they definitely couldn't be talking about her.

"I know, I know. Athena Miles will not be showing her face anywhere anytime soon."

Damn, Athena thought as another sob threatened to escape her mouth.

"She just sat there. I mean, if someone had dissed me like that I would have at the very least walked off, but she sat there and took it. And you know that Delilah can't stand her," the first woman giggled.

"She said that she couldn't wait to show that mousy little girl's mother what an embarrassment she was. Can you believe that?"

Athena put her hand over her mouth, finally understanding why Delilah had done what she did. Determined to hear the rest, Athena forced the tears to stop, putting her feelings to the side. She wanted to know, she had to know everything. This had something to do with her mother, and she wanted to know what.

"Celina had been planning this for over a month, they said, but Delilah never expected Athena to go through with it."

"Unbelievable," the second woman added before the door banged shut behind their cackling laughs.

Slowly taking her feet down off the toilet seat, Athena exhaled deeply, feeling her heart thumping in her chest. Uh-oh. She knew what was coming. It had been a while but as she well knew, once you've had one panic attack you never forget it. It was coming on fast but she refused to give in, forcing herself to take in several deep breaths of air. She had to get out of there. Walking out of the stall, Athena was surprised when she heard a flush behind her. Turning quickly, she saw an older woman leaving a stall and walking towards her. Determined to look braver than she actually felt, Athena forced herself to look the woman in the eye. She was embarrassed but she refused to show it; she was tired of putting her head down. The older woman stopped in front of Athena, then reached past her to the sink, grabbing a tissue from the pink box. Turning, the woman held the tissue out to Athena. Confused, Athena just stared blankly at the woman. *Lord, please don't let her know my mother.*

"Booger bubble," the woman said, pointing at her perfectly powdered nose.

Athena moaned, grabbed the tissue and turned to the mirror, clearly seeing what the woman was talking about. She had officially hit her lowest point.

After taking care of her little problem in the bathroom and touching up her makeup, Athena went out the back door and made her way to her car, where the realization finally sank in, causing her hands to tremble.

If she had had the presence of mind, she would have pointed her car north and kept driving because although Biloxi was growing day by day, it was still very much a small town, and in all small towns secrets never stay buried long.

Putting her key in the ignition, Athena dug her phone out of her purse and called her best friend in search of a sympathetic ear and a voice of reason. Minutes into the conversation, however, Athena realized her mistake.

"And what did you do?" Mel snarled. "I know you snapped that woman's wig off," Mel said before bursting out laughing. It would take a best friend of more than two decades to see the humor in her situation, Athena thought as she drove down I-10. However, despite the attempt to joke away the situation, it still hurt even twenty minutes later sitting in stalled traffic. The shakes had finally left her stiff shoulders but the harsh reality of the situation was still with her.

Athena could put aside her lapse in judgment in deciding to go on television, but she could not forget what had been televised. The public humiliation could linger for weeks with VCRs, DVRs, and TIVO, not to mention the Internet. With that thought she couldn't help the moan that escaped from her full lips.

"Girrl, please. I would have strangled her and then I would have knocked the living 'ish' out of her, too, but really, you handled it right. If you had done any more it would have stayed in the press for weeks. At least this way it will all blow over quickly. I mean, really, how many people watch that rinky-dink show?" Mel said into the phone before adding, "What made you even agree to go on that stupid show? I never did like that stuck-up heifer anyway."

Confused, Athena's anger and embarrassment boiled over. "I thought she was your friend!" she yelled.

"Who told you that?"

"You did," Athena countered into her phone. "You said you knew her from some hospital program you did years ago."

"I said I knew her, but I didn't say she was a friend," Mel said. Then she added, "Ooh, what is Lee-Lee gonna say?" referring to their old nickname for Athena's mother.

If Athena could have reached through the phone at that moment she would have gladly strangled her best friend. She had it in her she was sure, but deep down she also knew Mel was right. Mel had told her that she knew the woman, and Athena had taken that for meaning they were friends.

She had known her best friend for so long that Athena sometimes forgot that Mel had lived in California for a time, L.A. to be specific, which put her on a whole other level of loony. In the South if someone was crazy, you would tell everybody and anybody to stay away from that person, not ever admit to knowing them.

"Look, I really don't want to talk about it right now," Athena murmured, suddenly tired at the thought of her mother finding out, which she would eventually. Her tentacles reached into every realm, and a local television show, albeit predawn, would be a snap. It was just a matter of time. Athena felt that the proverbial rug had been pulled from beneath her feet.

Proving why she was Athena's best friend, Mel said, "Okay, okay, let's start over." Then she disconnected.

Closing her phone, Athena didn't bother to check caller ID when it rang seconds later.

"*Que pasa, chica?*"

"*Nada,*" Athena lied. "What's up with you?" she asked, unable to resist smiling at Mel's antics.

"Well, as usual I had a fabulous weekend. Ask me what I did."

Obliging, Athena cleared her throat, then said, "Pray tell, Melanie, what did you do this weekend?"

As Mel launched into the tale of her weekend of lust, Athena realized quickly the question shouldn't have been what but who. However, none of the names that Mel threw out rang a single bell.

"Wait, who is Enrico?"

"Enrico, you know, *loca*. Ricky," Melanie shrieked.

Mel had recently taken up Spanish and now attempted to put it into every conversation, which Athena didn't mind since she had always been fascinated with learning the language herself. Nonetheless, she didn't appreciate being called crazy in any language, regardless of not remembering any Ricky or Enrico, for that matter.

"Clue me in, babe," Athena sighed, inching her car forward.

"Don't you remember that fine man that we met at Claudette's a couple of months ago? He came up to our table with a tray full of Sex on the Beach drinks and a tired line about getting in on a *menage a trois?*"

"Oh yeah, the dude with the lisp."

"That was not a lisp, that's his accent. He's Greek."

"Girl, please, I ain't never seen any brothas from Greece," Athena laughed.

"No, really, he said his mother was Greek and his father was from the West Indies."

"Right." Athena heard Mel huffing at her tone so she added, "Now you know I'm not trippin' about his looks, because from what I remember the boy had it going on in all departments, looking like Shemar Moore's twin brother, including an ass to crack walnuts with."

Hearing Mel's squeals Athena continued, "So we give much props for that, but please don't tell anyone else about the Greek thing unless you never plan on them meeting the dude, all right?"

She had to watch out for her girl, Athena thought. Mel was smarter than the average chick on everything but men. For any other woman's man she came correct with the advice, but her head got all cloudy when it came to her henhouse. She had been known to let some really shifty roosters into her nest. Still, Athena appreciated the break. Mel was the only person she knew who did not trip about her mother or her fame. Regardless of where her family lived or what her family's status was, she knew Mel would keep it real.

Despite her many faults, the girl was no chickenhead. Mel had graduated magna cum laude with her BS in nursing and got her master's before she turned 24. No one could say that Mel wasn't a super-sista with a plan.

Even though she had subpar intuition when it came to her love life, she more than made up for it in the rest of her life. She had done well for herself. If it wasn't for

"Melly" Mel Waters of the New Orleans Creole Waters, the black version of the *Beverly Hillbillies*, Athena knew that she wouldn't have experienced a tenth of the adventures they had shared and her life would be hundred times more boring. It depressed her just to think about the possibility.

Although her famous father had moved their family at will for the first six years of her life, Mel had spent the majority of her life in Mississippi. After Mel's dad, who was one of the original Zydeco kings out of Louisiana, had a couple of huge hits he had been convinced that because they had "made" it they should set roots in California. Mr. Waters had lasted all of six months, running back for New Orleans as often as possible until the whole family had eventually followed suit. Athena and Mel had been inseparable since the U-Haul had parked down the street from her house.

"`Thena, how about we meet up tonight?" Mel asked, probably sensing she was losing Athena.

"Sounds good," Athena said.

"How 'bout we meet at my place. I'll cook."

Perking up somewhat at that, Athena started looking forward to a good home-cooked meal. Even though she had grown up with a Class A chef in the house, most people would have been surprised to know how little her mother had cooked for the family. Once her mother acquired Thea's, the cooking at home had ended. In order to get a "home-cooked" meal, the Miles family had to go to Thea's.

Having relied on takeout entirely too much lately, to which her waistband could attest, Athena was tired of fast food. Besides, Mel could really burn and it had been a while since they'd had girls' night out.

"And I brought you some stuff back from my trip and I want to show you my pictures," Mel added, interrupting Athena's thoughts.

"You developed them already? They better not be nasty."

"You know they are. Come over tonight at seven, okay?"

"Bet. I'll bring the wine," Athena said quickly, realizing they had a lot to catch up on since Mel got back from Tahiti with her himbo of the moment. Besides, she needed every distraction possible to get through this day.

"Oh, and 'Thena," Mel said, "whatever you do, if Momzilla calls, do not pick up."

Athena wanted to say, 'Do I look stupid to you?' Instead she laughed off the comment.

If anyone knew how Athena felt about her mother it would be Mel. Hell, Mel was the one who had originally dubbed her mother "Momzilla" after her first sleepover at the Miles house. Not many people had seen the machine behind the curtain, but Mel had a long time before the "Happy Homemaker" had aged and mellowed out.

Mel and Athena had bonded on the first day of kindergarten, when both of them arrived at DuKate Elementary School in matching plaid outfits. By the end of the day they had each gained a new best friend.

Athena's hair was jet black, and just as now, had only one style, which was to hang unevenly down her back. In all of their childhood pictures, her bangs blended in with the rest of her shoulder-length hair, making her look like a miniature Cousin Itt, as her cousin Stacy so bluntly put it.

In contrast, Mel's wilder auburn hair, like her personality, had a mind of its own. One day it would be a pageboy, the next day an updo, and another day in tiny red braids down her back. Either way, Mel's hair was just as unpredictable as she was, whereas Athena's hair, like her personality, was consistent and as predictable as gravity.

CHAPTER 3

Athena's Benz lurched to a stop, narrowly avoiding the dirty, yellow Volkswagen bug weaving its way through the slow Monday morning traffic.

Cursing, Athena swerved into the right lane as traffic picked up. A wreck would be the icing to her mud pie this morning. Talking to Mel had helped a lot in putting things in focus, or at least taking her mind off the whole debacle. Trying to put the program behind her, Athena prayed once again that no one she knew saw it. Then her phone rang for the third time that morning.

"Damn, damn, damn," she mumbled, looking at her caller ID before groaning and flipping her phone open.

"Are you O.K.?" Athena's baby sister, Sheree, shrieked in typical diva fashion.

Athena didn't immediately respond.

"Athena, pull over, pull over, if you're about to have an accident!"

If she only knew, Athena thought to herself. However, even if she had lost the ability to control all limbs and was blind in one eye, Athena refused to give Sheree the satisfaction.

For the past year Sheree had morphed into Athena's caretaker, even though Athena was the big sister by three years. In addition to her dispensing unwanted advice at every opportunity, Sheree had also appointed herself as Athena's personal matchmaker. Unfortunately, Athena had not been consulted on this shift in roles. After her repeated attempts at stopping her sister's interference, Athena had finally resigned herself to the weekly updates disguised as sisterly chats where she would be hounded for a play-by-play of her dating life, which consisted of various blind dates set by Sheree and her crew of cohorts spread across the East Coast. Many she managed to maneuver her way out of while still saving face. However, every once in a while she threw her sister a bone and went out with her pick of the week. This morning's embarrassment made Athena all the more sensitive to her baby sister's interference and her single status.

Forcing herself to laugh, Athena greeted her sister in her most perky voice as she switched on the AC to stop her short sleeve khaki pantsuit from sticking in all the wrong places.

"No, I want the eggs scrambled—hard," Athena heard Sheree say in her slow drawl, which she had worked hard to perfect years earlier when she had first heard the term "Southern belle."

Even though her loud, eclectic family was not the family the creators of the term Southern belle had originally envisioned, Sheree had adopted the role wholeheartedly. If she could get away with wearing a hoop skirt and a big, wide-brimmed hat every day, she would. Luckily, everyone was spared from her visual interpretation of *Gone With the Wind*, at least until Halloween, when without fail she would find some store to ship her

S. R. MADDOX

a costume regardless of where she was and whether or not she actually had a Halloween costume party to attend.

Nonetheless, regardless of her eccentricities, Athena loved her sister, and without fail found herself on the Internet once a year searching for a dress for her that would outdo the year before. Hell, that's what family was for, right?

"No," Athena heard her sister correcting the poor waitress yet again. "I. Want. Two. Fried. Eggs." Only it sounded like, "Ah. Wont. Two. Fer-ried. Eggz."

Sheree had a way of enunciating each word in what she called "Southern girlspeak with attitude" that would make even Einstein feel like an idiot.

Athena had told Sheree on numerous occasions that one day she was going to get the wrong waitress on the wrong day and end up with a plate of food with some special "sauce" on it, if she hadn't already. Although Sheree still had lapses every now and then, like now, she really had improved. Being a Southern belle with diva tendencies was a hard habit to break. However, she came by it honestly.

Sheree had never had to have one of those spirit-breaking jobs like most teenagers. Being the baby and the princess of the family, Sheree didn't understand the kind of resentment caused by having to clean a public bathroom after it had been abused by other people who had at some point in time had to clean filthy bathrooms themselves and made sure to miss the toilet as payback.

The most labor Sheree had known as a teenager was the brain power needed to answer the most important

35

question: "What should I wear to the prom—the fuschia or the turquoise?" Sometimes Athena wondered how it could be that they had grown up in the same household. The only reason she had come up with was that after three years of raising her, Athena's parents were tired and decided to give in to Sheree's quirks rather than redirect her to normal behavior. In addition, she was beautiful.

Consequently, Sheree was able to get away with most of the things she did. Once most people experienced her wide-eyed, bubbly personality, not to mention her perfect skin, perfect hair, and perfect body, they could not fault anything she did. She had a way of smiling and making even the rudest comments not sound so bad. Sheree was used to getting her way, and no one had deigned to tell her differently.

"Can't you move, 'Thena?" Sheree wailed into the receiver, finally remembering she was on the phone. "That noise is making my ears bleed."

"Well, maybe you should hang up," Athena yelled only half-jokingly over the sounds of a jackhammer on the street. "It looks like someone might have had an accident, so I might be here a while."

Her sister and the nut jobs on the road made Athena wish the freaks truly did only come out at night, which would leave the road to the people who at least attempted to act normal.

Looking out her windshield, Athena balanced her phone between her shoulder and her neck, grunting, "Huh?" for the second time.

"I said," Sheree huffed, drawing out every word, "Mom thinks you should have worn that black dress instead of that tacky khaki outfit."

What? How does she know what I was wearing this morning? Athena thought to herself as she turned into the parking garage.

"Athena, are you listening?"

"How do you know what I was wearing?" Athena managed, hoping that she had misheard.

"I just got off the phone with Hector," Sheree said breezily. Athena still rued the day Sheree and Hector, her longtime neighbor and self-appointed personal gossip columnist, had exchanged phone numbers.

"I heard in detail how you looked and what happened," Sheree said matter-of-factly. "I don't know what possessed you to go on that little show. You used to always say that you couldn't stand talk shows."

Oh no, oh no, oh no. Sheree was right, and what was worse was that she knew it. "Call it a lapse in judgement." Athena wished she could at least get out of the car and pace to relieve some of the tension mounting in her chest.

"Truly," Sheree said in agreement. "Look, Athena, I still have that number for Ned," Sheree chirped into the phone. "You remember the guy I told you about?"

Just great. Athena sighed. It wasn't like Sheree needed an excuse to pedal some guy to her, but her pitiful showing this morning had just reinforced her cause.

"You know what her problem is, don't you?" Athena heard her mother ask since Sheree had not bothered to

37

cover her mouthpiece. Why did she have to be there now? Athena briefly thought about hanging up, knowing she just could not handle her mother right now.

"What?"

"Hey," Athena yelled into the phone, shocked and feeling betrayed that her sister was giving their mother license to continue.

"Athena's problem is that she is terminally single," Aileen said in an accusatory manner, as if she had solved the crime of the century. "Athena does not want to get married because it would actually mean that she would have to open up her little life to someone else, and she doesn't want to."

Athena started to nod her head. Hell, yeah, that about summed it up. Then her mother dropped her next bomb.

Matter of factly, Aileen added, "But what she won't admit is that she doesn't have a life, only a career that is masquerading as one." Silence followed the occasional clinking of silverware Athena heard from the other patrons in the restaurant on the other end of the line. *Damn.* Athena had to give it to her. She could deliver an effective sucker punch from over 400 miles away.

Athena waited for her sister to lash into her mother for her inaccurate portrayal, but quickly realized she'd wait forever for that. There was only silence, which in anyone's speak meant "ditto."

Too shocked to respond, which seemed to have become a pattern today, Athena sat in silence in her car. In one day she had been called not only sad and single, but now it looked like being single, according to her mother and Sheree, was a terminal disease.

Although this was by far not the harshest thing Sheree or her mother had ever said to her, and Athena knew she herself had probably said much worse, it just was not a good time. The familiar tightness in her chest let Athena know that it was time to end this torture.

"Look, Sheree, I'm going to have to call you back," Athena said, shutting her car off. Assuring her sister for the second time that she was fine, she disconnected. Despite her feelings being hurt, Athena could not really get mad at her little sister. Her mother, on the other hand, was a different story. That pot had remained on simmer since she was about eight and didn't take much heat to boil.

Regardless of this morning's events, Athena happened to like her life, and her outfit, for that matter. It was just that her mother was, well, her mother, and Sheree was so in love with Ronnie, her actor husband, that she wanted her sister to experience the same feeling. Although there was a conflict between her new brother-in-law's career description and the one he listed on his IRS form, which was full-time waiter, Athena knew that he was a good guy, and was happy for them.

Sheree had just gotten it into her head that it was now time for her sister to get married and have a family of her own, and because she was such a determined little thing, she would not stop until that happened.

Unfortunately, Sheree, at her mother's bidding, had resorted to launching a campaign to get Athena "hitched in 2006." Yeah, it rhymed, sort of, but it was embarrassing as hell, especially when her mother wore one of the pins she had made up last summer and passed out to family members as party gifts.

Her marriage campaign had even caused Athena to start screening calls last November after receiving one from a woman who said she had a brother who was single and looking. When Athena asked her how she got her number, she learned that her baby sister had apparently written her name on the bathroom stall at a restaurant in College Park, though she still wouldn't admit it. Athena had had to change her phone number and refused to give it to Sheree until Athena had gotten it in writing that it would never happen again. The only thing that saved Athena from ringing Sheree's petite little neck that day was that she lived in New York.

Despite their recent problems Athena and Sheree were very close—they'd had to be growing up. Despite the piano lessons, expensive gifts, and full time maids there were times when all they had was each other. There was also the fact that as kids their mother would dress them alike as much as possible just to achieve that extra level of cuteness and up the "ooh" factor she had come to expect. Their mother, having been cute all her life, expected nothing less from both her girls. She was unable to continue dressing her girls alike when Athena turned twelve and sprouted a foot taller seemingly overnight. Unfortunately, that growth spurt had continued all the way to Athena's senior year, when she finally stopped growing.

Because of her stature most people, including her mother, felt cute was not something Athena was ever going to be. As her mother put it repeatedly, "Think regal, think elegant," when Athena would mistakenly think "cute" in her clothing choice.

Athena soon found out that regal and elegant meant monotone colors of black and navy. No matter how much she balked, pink and frilly went to cute little 5'1" Sheree and boring and sturdy went to her. At least that's how she saw it, which was probably the reason for Athena's lack of interest in her looks.

Growing up "healthy," as her family used to put it, Athena had to learn to focus more on what was in her head than what her head actually looked like. Maybe if she had been reed thin, Athena could have been a model, but at 5'8" and 160 she'd realized long ago that was not going to happen.

"Cute in the face, but thick in the waist," one big-headed little boy used to say every time Athena passed in the hallway in high school. Although he claimed it was a compliment, somehow it just did not sit well with Athena's teenage mind, only adding to her warped body image.

It wasn't until her last relationship that those extra pounds were finally appreciated for being in the "right" places as Athena's ex, Kendrick Wright, liked to say. Tall, dark, and handsome, Mr. Right, as she dubbed him, was Athena's longest relationship, and he had the full package: the right education, the right career, the right car, and the right financial portfolio. Unfortunately, it just didn't work out, which Athena thankfully realized before they got married.

Rubbing her eyes effectively smeared her pitiful attempt at mascara. Athena peered out her windshield through the mess, giving her full attention to the road. At this point in her life she really didn't have the attention to give to a relationship. Athena could admit that Tremona had gotten that much right. Unfortunately, no one believed her when she told them she was all right with her single status for the time being. She was happily single. Besides, Athena thought to herself, it wasn't like she didn't date.

Although Mel and her sister might say she was overly selective, Athena had three rules of dating that she refused to budge on even an inch. Rule number one was that absolutely no inappropriate men were allowed. Inappropriate meant if he didn't have a full-time job or own a suit, he didn't get a date. Rule number two was a little trickier. Any man who was not fully classifiable as single was deemed inappropriate. This was tricky because sometimes the most taken men behaved the most single. Athena had never been interested in sharing her toys as a child, and as a grown woman had extended the idea to men.

Rule number three was a lot more simple: Never, ever, mix business with pleasure. Nothing was more difficult than running into an ex at an event and having to work with them after you had seen each other naked repeatedly. You still had to act as if you hadn't as you were introduced to the new girlfriend or God forbid, you had brought someone.

which was also why the engagement had lasted so long. It was a big shock to a lot of people when Athena called off the engagement the night before the big day.

Unfortunately, ever since that day she had been plagued with one blind date after another. Lately, it had been her mother's turn to trot out Biloxi's most eligible bachelors. Athena swore she had been introduced in the last year to every eligible and sometimes not-so-eligible bachelor in the Southeast.

Last September there was Orlando, thirty-four, single and very rich, no kids. Ideal on paper, but in person, as anal as they come. Orlando had invited Athena over for some gourmet cooking at his house. He had a beautiful four-bedroom Tudor-style house outside Slidell. When Athena walked into the house, she was surprised at how welcoming the home felt because of its rich color scheme throughout. All through dinner Orlando was the perfect host and the food was outstanding.

Everything was going great until Athena moved the salt and pepper shaker from their perch on his dining room table and made the mistake of not immediately putting them back in the correct slots. Orlando ranted and raved about the need for order for a good ten minutes, which was long enough for Athena to grab her stuff and hit the road. She hadn't heard from him since, for which she was grateful.

Next up was Eric. Eric was a party planner, or at least that was what her sister Sheree, who had arranged their date, said. However, when Eric showed up and passed her his card across the table, she found out the true nature of his business. Eric was a party planner all right, a party planner for freaks. In fact, the name of his business was Freaks 'R Us. He promised in two languages to provide any event with the hottest strippers of all sizes. Although he was an entertaining guy, Athena made sure to lose his number after that first date.

Unfortunately, he kept hers. For about a month, she received calls at the most inopportune times, late at night, or while she was in the middle of a meeting at work. When she picked up the phone, all she would hear was, "You got my Usher CD?" Athena finally purchased the CD and mailed it to Eric. He hadn't given her anything, but she was just ready to be done with him.

The final straw was back in November, right after Thanksgiving. Sheree had yet another "perfect match" by the name of Troy. Troy was not much to look at, but he seemed to have a good head on his shoulders. That is, until she refused to go away with him on a cruise. It wouldn't have been a problem if he hadn't kept pushing the issue and it hadn't been their first date.

Right before Athena walked out of the restaurant, leaving Troy at his table, she heard him say, "See, that's what's wrong with you black women. You don't know a good thing when you see it." Athena just let that comment roll off her back because she knew she would never see him again, thankfully.

Since then, Athena had refused all of Sheree's and her mother's attempts to introduce her to anyone. She was suspicious of her friends as well, since Sheree had begun to enlist them to introduce her "dates."

While Athena's recent dates had all been disasters, her career was flourishing, and she had decided to focus on that for the time being. Because she wanted for nothing, it wasn't that hard. Sure, sometimes there were some lonely nights, but she had her girls. Although being in a relationship would be nice, she had finally realized that she was not going to die because she was not in one. Also, after her last three dates, she had opted for voluntary celibacy until she came across a man who could hold her the way she liked to be held. Sex was the easy part; it was a connection that was harder to find.

Pausing in front of the entryway to her office, Athena stopped to admire the elaborate script of her company logo, her one office extravagance. When she first reopened Regent's offices, after she had bought out the contract from the original partners, the logo was the only thing that she'd allowed herself to splurge on. She had spent months deciding on the design. She had wanted it to be classy. Although her clientele probably did not expect it, Athena wanted anyone who walked through her door to not only take her seriously but also respect what she was trying to do. Although the logo was a small thing that probably went unnoticed by most, she felt better about it.

Image was important, and no one knew that better than Athena. She had been raised with a mantra about it since birth. She had behind her almost three decades of growing up in the South amongst the most stylish and image-minded people in the world. She knew how even the smallest of things, like the wrong shade of lipstick or, gasp, a run in your stockings, could stack a social wall so high that it might never be scaled. First impressions didn't just make you; they could literally bankrupt you. Besides, the clientele they served deserved to feel good about where they brought their family during times of trouble or illness regardless of what their income was. Athena knew how big that was in the recovery process as well, and also determined how well they participated in the self-improvement programs that were a requirement of their repayment plans.

Taking her seat at the enormous desk and looking out the picture window at the waters of the Gulf Coast, Athena leaned back in her chair, and closed her eyes a moment. Feeling the tension ease, Athena opened her eyes and looked at the neat stack of messages on her desk. Twila, her assistant, a thirty-one-year-old Vietnamese "sista" had stuck several messages next to her phone. Noting the top one had *urgent* written in red across it, Athena picked it up. Athena quickly remembered that Twila had phoned her about it over the weekend and thanked the gods once again for sending her such a capable assistant. Twila had been in America for at least ten years and had adopted the American way of life a long time prior to receiving her naturalization papers. From the top of her dyed blonde curly hair to the soles of her Jimmy Choo shoes, Twila was a dynamo of persuasion. Athena still remembered their first meeting.

"You remind me so much of my mother," Twila had said, stopping Athena in the hall at DeAblos, a law office Athena had briefly worked at prior to striking out on her own after grad school. Athena was mildly surprised at hearing Twila's surfer-girl accent, but smiled at the new mailroom clerk nonetheless. Back then her hair had been a fire engine red and so glossy it looked like a wig. She'd had black eyeliner thick around her eyes, exaggerating their almond shape. On anyone else it would have made her look like a deranged cartoon character, but it worked on her somehow.

"Excuse me," Athena had said, walking away quickly. Twila simply changed directions and matched Athena's steps heading towards the elevator.

"I said that you reminded me of my mother."

Not knowing what to say to this, Athena replied, "Thank you?" then pressed down on the elevator button.

"You're welcome," Twila said before rushing back the way she'd come.

At the time Athena didn't really think much of their first conversation, but it was soon afterwards Athena understood—Twila was looking to move out of the mailroom. Athena was all for helping her, but knew there really was not much she could do. Her business was only a plan in her mind at the time. She was leery about getting too close, because although she admired Twila's bold style, she did not know if she was reliable. Nonetheless, she was not stupid enough to turn down Twila's volunteering to help after hours.

It was because of her mixture of ambition and devotion that she later got the job with Athena as her executive assistant when Athena took her leap of faith and ownership of Regent's, but it was her ability to handle the unexpected and her exceptional organization skills, which bordered on obsessive compulsive, that earned equal devotion.

"Hey boss," Twila chirped. Slightly surprised, Athena looked up to see her walking through the door and flicking on the light switch. Immediately the room was lit to a blinding level.

"Well, Goldilocks, what someone has been sitting in my chair while I've been gone?" Athena said only half-jokingly.

"Sorry, I caught Barry in here last Friday before I left out," Twila said as she headed towards the dimmer near the venetian blinds. Dimming the lights she continued, "I think I scared the heck out of him, because he jumped ten feet when I busted in on him. I guess he thought he would be safe since it was past 8 p.m. and the only person who stays that late is you."

Ignoring the dig at her late hours, Athena continued questioning her. "What exactly was he looking for in my office? He had to have felt mighty comfortable since he touched my dimmer." Everyone knew how Athena liked natural light more than artificial, preferring to keep her blinds open.

"I'm not sure. When I came in he jumped, shrieked, then mumbled something about needing some report. He was out of here so quick that I couldn't even get a word in." Barely pausing to take a breath, she continued in her usual manic speech pattern, "Can you imagine a grown man shrieking? It wasn't cute. I tried to figure out what the deal was by looking on your desk, but nothing was missing or looking different that I could see."

Athena couldn't help feeling skeptical. Barry was ambitious and always had something up his sleeve. However, until this point, Athena hadn't seen him as a threat.

Barry Gorenflo, of the Biloxi Gorenflos, had been one of her first employees. She'd hired him for his many connections. His family tree reached even farther than that of the Miles's and the roots were much deeper. Over the years he had proven an invaluable source of growth.

Last year, Athena had even made him chief financial officer. It had been a really good decision. However, lately Athena had noticed a change in Barry's demeanor. He seemed to be attempting to usurp her control in small ways in her absence.

Fortunately, Athena had not witnessed the power trips, but she had heard reports of them. In fact, it was rare that Athena even heard from Barry, which was why this latest situation concerned her a little. However, if Twila hadn't sniffed out any foulness yet, Athena would give it a few days. Twila was better than the *Enquirer*. In fact, Athena suspected she supplied them with stories.

When Twila left to go make a pot of coffee, Athena allowed herself to breathe. She had not run into one person who had seen her crash and burn on television. Doing the breathing exercises her doctor had taught her, Athena leaned back in her chair. The last thing she needed was to hyperventilate her way into another panic attack on top of everything else.

After an hour of playing catch up and phone tag, Athena called out to Twila to take messages and headed to the restroom on the other side of the U-shaped floor. After taking care of business she decided to drop in on Vincent and Frank's offices in the center's education division. The two high strung, creative men had single-handedly changed the community's perception of Regent. They had not only increased their monthly clientele of patients, but they also had initiated an awesome education program in the local elementary schools to teach students about everything from hygiene to drug abstinence.

Walking into their office, Athena could see that Vincent was on the phone, but took a seat across from him when he waved her in. From the conversation, Athena suspected Vincent was talking to Tres y One. They were a new singing group he and his partner Frank had been working with in their part-time business as a fledgling promotions company.

Tres y One had effectively crossed the R&B sounds of Boys to Men with funky reggaeton music into a new sound all their own. They were a diverse quartet of young men who could harmonize, but looked liked a legal version of the Latin boy band Menudo. Frank and Vincent were working with them on a documentary to help publicize the center's programs. Hanging up the phone, Vincent turned his green-eyed gaze on Athena.

"Hey hot stuff, where ya been?" Vincent said in his best wise-guy voice.

"I've just been busy. You know how it is," Athena said, holding her breath for any telltale sign that he knew about her morning in hell. At Vincent's stare, Athena continued, "How did your show go last Saturday? Come on. Tell me all the juicy details. I know the kids must have been excited." When Vincent smiled, then rushed to talk about his latest success, Athena finally let herself exhale.

"First of all, it must have been a long time since you last saw the 'kids.' Otherwise you would know that the youngest is now twenty-one."

"What? I still remember when he was on breast milk." Athena laughed at Vincent's indignant act.

"Yeah, well, if you had seen him last weekend you would also know that he is still heavily reliant on the breast, sans milk," he said, smiling as Athena joined in on the laugh despite its grossness. She had opened the door to it. "Secondly, it went great."

Standing up, he walked around to the front of the desk and sat on the edge closest to Athena. "Too bad you didn't get to join us," he said, reaching behind his back for a jar of Gummi bears, offering them first to Athena before grabbing a few for himself. "So how is your Monday going?" he asked, popping a green gummi into his mouth.

Stopping midchew, Athena looked at her friend for a moment, wondering if she had been wrong, if he had seen her horrible performance this morning. "It's going well."

"You mean you didn't spend any time thinking about the spread we laid out in the conference room this morning?"

Oh damn! Shaking her head, Athena sank in her seat slightly, understanding Vincent's needling. She had forgotten all about the meeting he had invited her to this morning. It wasn't required for her to attend, but she had said she would. Exhaling, finally realizing the reason for his playful mood, Athena quickly apologized. Vincent laughed off her faux pas.

"What? What did I miss?" Frank said, walking into the office and hearing Vincent laughing. When he saw Athena, he let out a loud shriek. "Hey, girl, where you been? Where you been?"

"She's been hiding away in her office with the rest of the old folks," Vincent said.

Frank dropped into the seat next to Athena. Vincent and Frank had shared office space for the past five years and had been running the education and development department for just about as long. Although both of them could have individual offices by now, they preferred to share the loft, running it like a fraternity.

Frank was rarely at his desk, preferring to do his work via his cell phone, pager, and numerous other gadgets he carried in his "man bag," as he called it, although Athena called it a purse at every opportunity.

"I have missed me some 'Thena," Frank said, reaching for her hand. He had the habit of slipping Athena's nickname in from time to time. Unlike some of her other coworkers Athena couldn't begrudge him anything. She had known him since her college days in New Orleans when they'd practically lived in the French Quarter. Athena knew more of his secrets than she cared to admit.

As she gave the quick version of her weekend to Frank, Vincent took yet another phone call. Athena was pleased to know that her reputation was still fully intact, but before she could ask Frank about his weekend, their assistant and a dark-haired man dressed in some torn jeans and a dirty plaid shirt came in.

Seeing that Frank was about to begin their weekly meeting, Athena stood to walk to the door. Even though they were old friends, Athena still made sure to keep it professional because business was just that—business. Both Frank and Vincent were just as serious about their work as she.

"Mike, I have someone very important I want you to meet," Frank said, slapping his hand on the tall man's back. "Athena, this is my new best friend, Mike Thibodeaux."

"Hello," Mike said in a rich, deep voice taking her hand into his much larger, rougher one, "nice to meet you."

Athena immediately recognized the accent, having grown up with it most of her life. From the South she was sure, but the drag to it meant that he must be from Louisiana bayou country. Although it was impossible to designate which parish, it was also impossible not to recognize. That easygoing accent brought back all kinds of memories, most wickedly good.

However, now that she was only two feet away from the tall man with the deep voice and the slanted smile, Athena could see that style wise he truly was lacking because he looked as if he had just climbed out of a ditch. Still, she smiled at Frank's flattery. Holding her hand out, Athena said, "Hello," in her warmest voice.

Looking into his black eyes that were fringed with impossibly long, inky black eyelashes, Athena was rewarded with a wink, which he had no way of knowing Athena hated. She immediately shifted her guard into place even though she felt a disturbing pull towards the man. There was something about how he carried himself that made Athena want to take a second look. Nonetheless, just as quickly she doused the flame of interest. The last thing she needed was some wannabe player with dreams of being a star trying to shine at her with a smile that rivaled Dennis Quaid on his best day. *That's what it was!* Athena thought to herself. He reminded her of that actor, except his skin was a little more bronzed, like he spent a lot of time in the sun. He could have been Spanish, but walking closer, Athena could tell that although his hair was dark—almost black—he was definitely white. Now that she was standing next to him, Athena checked him out a little more as Frank continued to sing his praises. Lord, that smile could do things to a woman if she wasn't careful. Shaking her head to clear it of her wayward thoughts, Athena reached out her hand.

"Very nice to meet you," Athena lied cooly, pulling her hand back, working hard to stop herself from checking for scratches. She briefly thought about recommending a heavy cream lotion to him, but decided to leave that to Frank, since he was obviously close to him. Besides, Athena had decided that between the wink and the smile, she didn't like him, and this time she would trust her instincts.

"Athena," Frank said quickly, "I want you to remind me to get his group's CD to you. What he is doing is absolutely amazing."

"Whatever," was Athena's first thought, which she hadn't intended to say out loud, but did. Shocked and embarrassed at her rudeness, Athena started to apologize. That is, until she saw Mike's amused face. This was totally unlike her, but something about this guy annoyed Athena in the worse way. Looking towards Frank, Athena saw that he had turned to his assistant and therefore did not hear her comment. Pissed at herself for the lack of control, Athena forced herself to return Mike's gaze, immediately noticing his grin, which stopped the apology. It was then Athena realized what it was that was rubbing her the wrong way about him. He was cocky as hell and didn't care who knew it.

Athena wasn't sure about where this was going, but she decided to cut it short before she added him to her choke list. Turning back to Frank, Athena committed to a late lunch the next day, then excused herself, but unfortunately not quickly enough. As she reached for the door, Mike reached for the doorknob, covering it and Athena's hand with his much larger one. Catching a whiff of something delicious, Athena was surprised at her brief flare of lust. That is, until she heard Mike's New Orleans drawl in her ear.

"I saw you on Delilah's show."

Turning her head, Athena was stunned to see Mike flash another grin her way, transforming him from nice looking to lethally handsome in a second flat.

Momentarily dazzled, Athena worked to close her gaping mouth. However, before she could gather her wits enough to check both herself and him, he said, "I thought you looked fine then, but I didn't expect you to be this gorgeous in person."

Lord, it might have been the way he dragged his deep voice across the word *gorgeous* that had Athena's lust-filled brain working overtime with the various positions in which she would like to hear him say that one word over and over. However, refusing to let herself be sucked in totally, Athena pushed open the door before responding.

"Thanks," she clipped, "that really means a lot coming from you." She managed to check him out with a cool eye, getting for the first time a genuine response from the handsome man as he threw his head back to laugh.

Forcing her gaze away from his beautiful white teeth, Athena turned, refusing to look back at him to see if he was still watching. It took all of her legendary control to walk away, head high. She made each step deliberate as she walked towards her office and heard the door close finally as she turned the corner.

Both relieved and angry at the same time, Athena cursed both herself and the infuriating Mike Thibodeaux. She had just gotten to the point where she had forgotten about her earlier morning embarrassment only to have that playboy bring it all back with one sarcastic crack about how great she looked. Looking at her reflection in her office window, taking in the tacky tan pants and the old blouse that had seen better days, Athena cursed the man again.

Glad to have the distance between Mike and her own errant thoughts, Athena now fully understood the reason for Mike's initial challenging stare and amusement, which did a lot to cool her shell-shocked libido. She also no longer felt bad about the "whatever" comment she had responded with earlier. Obviously she had been correct in her initial assumption that Mike was not someone she wanted to get to know better, let alone listen to his demo. His teasing about her crash and burn on television was not cute. But sitting at her desk, Athena couldn't keep her mind from drifting from the papers in front of her back to Frank's new arrogant "best friend."

One thing she did know for sure was that the next time she saw Mr. I'm-So-Sexy ThiboDOLT, she planned to let him know exactly what she thought of him. However, thinking back to her initial reaction to the man, her head fell back against her chair. What the hell was up with her? Shaking her head and sitting up straight in her chair, Athena forced her thoughts away from that grin.

Athena knew exactly what to do if she encountered the jerk again. Run.

CHAPTER 4

"I wanna a freak"
"Someone good in bed."
"I wanna freak"
"Someone to give good . . ."

Disgusted by the lyrics coming from the radio, Athena reached for the remote and before the singer could finish his verse changed the station, only to hear yet another song about what the singer wanted to do to some girl, how he was going to do her, what time, and the place.

Not being able to bear another moment, Athena turned it off and switched back to the CD player. Sighing with relief, Athena tried to relax as the soft sounds of a saxophone filled the air.

Once again she'd been chased away from free radio, where bad taste was rewarded. Athena rarely ever listened to the radio anymore because it was usually a disappointment, especially on weekdays, where the morning DJs tried to outdo each other by pulling off the most disgusting stunts possible in a media with no visual effects.

Music used to be a way to lighten the mood, get people talking, dancing, laughing, or making love, Athena thought. What the hell happened? Now it seemed that every song was about getting over, getting paid, or getting off. The beats might be on point, but unfortunately Athena was burdened by the inability to tune out the lyrics. The majority of what she listened to was the music targeted towards the older listener, which was technically a world away from the canned beats that made up the majority of the top 40.

When she was looking to fill her CD spinner, Athena went on the hunt for the next Marvin Gaye or Sam Cooke of the industry, artists who could withstand the test of time. Her father was part of the reason for her quest for musical purity.

He had been a musician back in the 70s. Although it was the age of disco, he had always been a fan of rhythm and blues, even forming his own blues band back in the early 80s. They had been the house band for Thea's for many years until his duties as manager and owner took over the time needed for rehearsals.

Changing it up a little, Athena popped a new CD into the player. It had been sitting in the back of her drawer where she had tossed it before she left work last week, the weekend before Black Monday, as she now referred to her day of humiliation.

Twila had passed it on to Athena after she said Tony, the bouncer at her second favorite club, Claudette's, slipped it to her a few weeks back. The name of the trio was Who Dat. Their interesting name piqued Athena's attention.

"This is a new group that's coming up," Tony had said via Twila's message relay. "This guy is a cross between B.B. King and Jackie Wilson."

Athena was interested in all types of music, but rhythm and blues especially got her going. The smart lyrics, working with the body-tingling sounds of actual music instruments rather than a machine, did something to the pit of her stomach. Athena had grown to appreciate the effort that it took to pick a guitar into submission and play a piano until the keys opened up the wounds that made a person nostalgic to feel even the harshest hurt again and again.

There was a time when Athena had wanted nothing more than to be a talent scout for a big record company. While she was still in college she'd visited all the local clubs, promoting acts as a side hustle, and planning events to get exposure for talented people who had no way of showing what they could do. However, when Aileen learned of it, she had hit the roof. Although Athena had initially stood up to her mother, like most times, she had eventually backed down. Before long Athena found herself enrolled in law school with a summer job lined up at a local law firm in Biloxi, exactly what her mother wanted.

Although her mother didn't like that she eventually left the law firm to use her law degree to run a nonprofit specializing in providing health care services to low income residents, she accepted it because of the charity aspect of it. Aileen could brag on the "good" work her daughter was doing for the less fortunate people of post-Katrina Biloxi. Those bigwigs she dealt with in New York ate that stuff up, and as long as they didn't actually know about the heartbreaking situations that Athena contended with every day in order to provide services to people who had to work despite illness, Aileen could glamorize her glamourless daughter.

Athena was suddenly struck by the guitar solo that came from out of nowhere. It sounded like an electric guitar that could be called Lucille II. Whoever was playing really knew what they were doing, Athena thought, feeling a tingle work its way down her spine to her legs and bring her to her feet. Enraptured by the sound, Athena didn't hear the knock at her door.

"Athena, I just got—" Twila stopped in midsentence as she stared at Athena, openmouthed.

"What?" Athena responded, turning at the interruption.

"Were you dancing?" Twila asked, smiling.

Not realizing she had started grooving in the middle of her office, Athena responded, "Yeah, so what? It's not like it's the first time you've seen me dance."

"Uh, yes, it it," Twila said, now laughing.

"Uh, no, it's not," Athena said back to her, trying hard not to be offended. It wasn't like she couldn't dance. She had good rhythm.

"No, don't get me wrong," Twila said, catching herself and trying to fix the look on her face. "You looked good dancing, but I have never seen you dance like that in the office. It was just kind of funny walking in to see you standing there with your button-up suit on, slow dragging."

"Slow dragging?" Athena repeated.

"Yeah, you know, when you get with a guy and you slow drag."

"I know what it means," Athena said, interrupting, "I just didn't realize that was what I was doing." Walking over to her desk, Athena pressed the stop button on the remote, and the music immediately stopped, leaving only the sound of Athena's breathing. She had really let herself get swept away, Athena realized.

"Who was that? You really seemed to like them," Twila said, refusing to let it go as she walked to the CD player and took out the CD.

"That was Who Dat, the group Tony passed to you," Athena said nonchalantly, looking for a distraction. "Why don't you have another listen and let me know what you think about it."

After Twila left with the CD, Athena sat down at her desk and began separating the piles. For the next two hours she became so wrapped up in work that her morning passed quickly, and before she knew it Twila was walking back in with lunch. She laid out broccoli and cheese soup and half of a grilled chicken sandwich on the coffee table.

Grabbing her stack of telephone messages and taking them over to the couch, Athena looked through them as she dictated some contracts to Twila. Then Twila left, leaving Athena to her lunch.

Taking a few bites, Athena couldn't help thinking about the coming night. It had been a week since the "incident" and it was going to be nice to get out of the house and let her hair down for at least one night. She rarely went out and she was itching to do so, particularly tonight. She had a lot of tension and she hoped good music and good drinks would let her forget her worries some. Besides, she needed a reality check big time. Between her humiliating experience on that horrible show and the anxiety about who might have seen it, Athena had been on pins and needles all week long.

Although she was thankful that no one at work had mentioned Delilah and the show—at least not to her face—Athena couldn't help expecting someone to slip it in just when she finally let her guard down. Athena's mind instantly drifted to Mike and his sarcastic remarks last week. Then she cursed silently at her body's response.

Just thinking about the man with the infuriatingly sexy smile still made Athena's blood race, and not in a way she was completely comfortable with. She didn't know what it was about that man, but he kept popping into her mind at the oddest times. A few days ago she had been standing in line at Belk's about to buy a cute pair of shoes when she thought about that damn smirk of his, and it made her blood boil all over again.

Glad to have him and the whole incident behind her, Athena decided to just chalk it up as a learning experience and try to enjoy the rest of her evening. Tonight she and Mel were finally supposed to meet at her place for that dinner she'd promised her. They had mutually agreed to cancel their get-together the night of the "incident" and tonight they were supposed to make up for it. Taking a deep breath, Athena took a bite of her sandwich, as her mind drifted once again.

"Damn," Athena yelped around a bite of tomato. She had bitten her tongue. Not even wanting to think about where her mind had drifted once again, Athena cursed the image of a reclining Mike in a pair of speedos smirking at her from the belly of a canoe on Lake Pontchartrain.

What the hell?

"Hey girl," Mel said as she stood at the top of the steps to her two-story home on the east side of Wolf River.

"Hey," Athena said, returning the greeting and embrace.

"It's about time you got here." Mel took Athena's coat and pulled her into the foyer at the same time. "We've been waiting for you."

"What do you mean by *we?*" Athena said, catching on to Mel's pronoun usage a little late. She'd been admiring the redecorating Mel had done to her den. Suddenly having a flashback to her sister's matchmaking, Athena started to back towards the front door.

Mel grabbed Athena's hand and pushed her into the kitchen. "Ricky is here."

"Oh, girl, I'm not interrupting anything, am I?" Athena whispered, thinking maybe she would have to make a quick exit. She said in a low voice, "You should have called to tell me he'd dropped by unexpectedly."

Although she would never admit it, she was tired after having left late from the office. Even though she wanted to see her friend, Athena would have much rather have taken it to the house after the long day of catch up she'd had.

"No, Ricky is here," Mel repeated, sitting Athena down on a stool at the island and thrusting a glass of red wine into her hand before walking away mumbling, "and he brought a friend."

"Ooh, this is fruity," Athena said, not registering what Mel had said. "Is this Alize?" Sitting back in her chair, Athena got more comfortable before looking up to see Mel smiling at her. The smile was not a comfortable one, more like a please-don't-trip one.

"Wait, what did you say?" Athena asked as she took another sip of whatever Mel had given her, feeling the warmth immediately oozing to her toes. She never could hold her alcohol too well.

Mel walked to Athena, carrying a bowl of breadsticks. Looking in the bowl, Athena saw that they were the kind that she loved, the ones that tasted like those big, fat yeast rolls Quincy's restaurant used to have back in the day. It was then that Athena realized she had been set up. Plying her with alcohol so she couldn't drive and bread so she wouldn't leave, Mel had made her immobile.

"Hey babe," a voice called. "Are those rolls ready yet? You got a couple of hungry brothers out here."

In walked the finest man Athena had seen in about a week. Only he was model perfect, so perfect Athena had to gulp down the rest of her drink to wash down the piece of bread she had shoved in her mouth.

"Athena Miles, this is Ricky Matenoupoulos," Mel said, introducing the god who had walked into the room. This was not the guy that Athena remembered as she looked at Melanie, who just cheesed back. Remembering her manners, Athena took the hand that was offered and shook it.

"Very nice to meet you," she managed to say. Ricky smiled in response, picking up the basket.

"Marcus said he was about to eat the centerpiece if he didn't get something soon," pretty Ricky said to Melanie as he turned to leave.

Mel kissed him on the lips, then patted him on the ass, as he walked out the door. "Who is Marcus?"

"How's the bread?" Mel asked, ignoring the question.

"I said, who is Marcus?" Athena repeated, trying to keep a rein on her temper. It was one thing to have her sister, who was miles away, interfere in her love life, but now to have her best friend join in was too much, and Athena just wasn't in the mood for it.

"Isn't that man fine?"

Although she had to give her that, Athena refused to high five the hand in front of her face, but the responding grin she wore told the truth.

"Well, Marcus is even finer," Melanie said quickly.

"Don't even try and tell me that lie," Athena said just as quickly. "No one could be that fine."

"You're right, you're right," Melanie said, giving in as she went over to the pot of spaghetti and stirred it before taking it to the sink to dump it in a colander to drain. "But he is very handsome, and he works in the music business, too."

"Really," was Athena's only response. Purposely misreading the tone, Melanie launched into a quick sell on Marcus.

"Look Mel, I know what you're trying to do, and I appreciate it, I really do, but I am just not interested."

"Well, at least give him a chance, 'Thena," Mel said. "He has good manners and he speaks well. Besides, it's been a while."

Athena didn't bother to tell her that she was doing a horrible job if she was actually trying to get her to stay by echoing her own secret sentiments. However, when Ricky walked back in, Athena was again stunned by his beauty. She had never called a man beautiful but there truly was no other word for the six foot tall muscular man standing in front of her.

"Mel, is it about done?" Ricky whined, bringing down his hotness level. "Girl, we are starving out there."

"Five minutes," Melanie said, without even looking up from the pot as she stirred the sauce. Ricky, now satisfied with the dinner time, flashed Athena a smile, which she half-heartedly returned before he walked out of the kitchen rubbing his hands together.

"Come on, 'Thena," Mel said as she refilled Athena's glass.

"That's enough," Athena said, pushing away the bottle. Ricky was fine as hell, but he had started to irritate her, and if Marcus was a friend of his, things did not bode too well, buzz or no buzz.

"Just stay for an hour, okay?" Melanie said, pleading with her eyes. "Marcus has been here for the past two days and has not given us a moment's peace. I need some time to get Ricky alone to tell him to dump the boy." Suddenly Athena understood what was going on. She was the diversion.

"I thought maybe you could distract Marcus for at least thirty minutes for me to get Ricky alone. He's going to be here for two more days, and I need some more us time." Mel said this with a strong emphasis on need, and Athena could really feel her on this, so she decided to help her out because she had been in her shoes before.

No matter how tired she was, Athena was determined to help Mel out for at least the next sixty minutes, or however long it took for her buzz to wear off.

After introductions they sat down at Mel's brand new dining room table. Athena immediately noticed some new artwork on the wall.

"Yeah, we got it while we were in Tahiti," Ricky said, beaming at Mel.

Oh, he's got it bad, Athena thought to herself, turning to smile at Marcus, who was nice looking, but hadn't said too much. This was all right as far as Athena was concerned because she wasn't looking for a love match, not tonight anyway. She just wanted to do her time.

"I've never been to Tahiti," Marcus said, finally saying more than a few syllables. With a slight accent, he continued, "But from all that I've heard about it this past week I really need to make a break for it."

"Well, once you've seen one beach, you've seen them all," Mel said, then added, "Athena, Marcus is from the islands." Taking the not-so-subtle hint, Athena turned towards the island man.

"Really," Athena asked, "what part?"

"St. Ann's Bay," Marcus said with a little more lilt in his voice.

"I thought I recognized the accent."

"Are you from there?" Marcus asked.

"No, but I have visited the island before," Athena said before taking a bite of pasta and sauce. "Mainly Ochos Rios, but I did get a chance to go to St. Ann's on a day trip."

"So, did you like it?" Marcus asked, taking a sip of his wine.

Looking over at Ricky and Mel, Athena saw that they were deep in conversation, cheesing big grins at one another, and realized quickly that she was on her own and had to really dig deep for her good manners. The effects of the wine had long worn off, but Athena realized she was only twenty minutes into the sixty minutes she had mentally promised Mel.

"Yeah, I loved the island, and as a matter of fact, I would love to go back sometime." Athena took another bite of pasta.

"Really?" Marcus smiled at her.

Nodding yes as she continued chewing on the mouthful she had practically shoved in, Athena was unprepared for the hand that came to rest on her knee.

"Maybe the next time I go you could come along."

"Huh?"

"I said, maybe the next time I go you could join me," Marcus repeated, filling Athena's half-full glass with more wine, this time to the top.

No, this fool didn't. Athena put her fork down, and reaching for her water glass, she looked at him to see if he was serious. Yes, he was.

"Yeah, we could stay in my villa on the beach, and we could pick up seashells in the daytime," he said, reaching for Athena's hand and pulling it closer to him, "and skinny dip at night."

No, he didn't. Athena looked down at her hand, now in his lap, which had a lot of things going on down there. *Yes, this fool did.*

Seeing Mel stand up and begin clearing the dishes away, Athena yanked her hand away, almost knocking over her chair as she stood. Feeling sick to her stomach, she ran after Mel into the kitchen.

"So what do you think?" Mel said quickly as she took the dishes from Athena's hands and began scraping them into the trash can.

"Hmmm, what do I think?" Athena said out loud. "I think you have paired me with a pretty boy."

"You're welcome," Mel said, proud of herself.

"Did I say thank you?" Athena responded quickly. "I don't think I said thank you."

Melanie stopped scraping long enough to look in Athena's direction. "Is something wrong? Did he say something rude to you?" she asked, stomping towards the dining room.

Not wanting to start World War III, but not intending to return to the dining room, Athena grabbed her arm. "Your friend seems to have gotten me mixed up with the strippers down at the Bush Gardens." Athena relayed Marcus's offer for her to join him at his island get-away, then the journey down south he attempted with her hand.

Eyes bugged out, Mel said in the most menacing voice Athena had ever heard, "That is it, he is out of here. Now."

Athena wasn't sure what Mel did, but it was less than two minutes later that she heard a door slam and quickly thereafter the Hummer she had spotted in the driveway peeled out and raced down the road. It was the quickest exit Athena had ever heard. When Mel came back in the kitchen, she looked defeated.

"I am so sorry, Athena," she said, near tears. "I didn't mean for any of that to happen. I thought that we would have a nice night, and this is what happened."

"It's okay," Athena said, meaning it. "I know how it is when you are in a relationship and really want it to work. I've been there and will eventually be there again one day. Really, Mel," Athena said, grabbing for the plates to scrape, "I was happy to help out. It's not your fault he turned out to be an ass. Where did Ricky meet him anyway?"

"Girl, I don't even know," Mel said as she loaded up the dishwasher with the remaining dishes. "Like I said, he showed up a couple of days ago. He's been staying at Ricky's apartment, but spending most of his days with us," she said with a sigh. "And since he's been here, Ricky's been staying at his place. He said he didn't want to be a bad host, so we haven't been able to spend much time together. I feel awful for bringing you into this."

"Aww, don't even speak of it," Athena responded. She truly felt bad for her friend, and she could tell she was really hurting, although it surprised her how much, considering she had never sweated any of her other boyfriends this much. Trying to lighten the mood, Athena added, "Now, that he's gone, I can tell you what nonsense Sheree said to me."

"Uh, let me guess. She said you were uptight and repressed and needed to get laid."

"Uh, no," Athena said, frowning.

"Oh, my bad. That's what I say all the time."

"First, Ms. Smarty Pants, you're not funny," Athena said, laughing despite herself.

"If I'm not funny," Mel paused, laughing, " then why am I giggling my ass off over here?"

Ignoring her comment, Athena continued, "And secondly, I am none of those things you just said." Hearing Melanie howl at this, Athena couldn't help giggling. After they finished cleaning up, Mel took Athena on a walk through the house, showing her all the things she and Ricky had gotten on their trip, including their pictures.

Athena wasn't sure of when it had happened, but sometime in the last few months her best friend had started a serious relationship. It had been awhile since Mel had had a steady boyfriend. Usually it was the other way around: Athena with Kendrick and Mel with some flavor of the week. That was why Athena really could not begrudge Mel attempting to get some alone time with her man, even though it was at her expense. Mel deserved to have someone special in her life, and even though Ricky wasn't the brightest man he was fine as hell and Athena knew she had no room to judge.

On the drive home Athena couldn't help thinking that maybe it was time for them to switch places. For most of their adult lives, Athena had been in a serious relationship and Mel had enjoyed her freedom.

Maybe it was time for Athena Miles to just have some fun. She wouldn't be calling Marcus up anytime soon, but maybe she might start accepting some of those dates that had been thrown her way lately. For the first time in a week, Athena actually felt like smiling until her mind drifted once more to the last man she wanted to occupy her thoughts. And dammit, he was wearing those speedos again!

CHAPTER 5

"Barry just handed this to me," Twila said cheerfully, winking at Athena as she passed her boss the envelope. "He said it got mixed up with his mail this morning."

Looking at the envelope attached to the letter and seeing that it was from her onetime business associate, Trey Lister, a local radio personality and part-time talent agent dealing with wanabee pop groups, Athena opened it immediately.

Scanning the letter, Athena saw that he was having a show this weekend for a group that was looking for a deal. Feeling her heart begin to beat faster, Athena forced herself to calm down. This was not her business anymore. She was a respectable business woman now, not some star chaser looking for the next big thing. She was responsible now, as her parents reminded her repeatedly, as if that alone would keep her in check.

"Did you see his description of the group?" Twila asked at Athena's questioning stare.

Looking back through the letter Athena read:

"Who Dat is the next big thing! This group will do more for pop music than Destiny's Child did in the `90s or New Edition in the `80s. This group is the evolution of the pop groups of past years. Led by talented musicians/singers this group will bring the craft back to popular music."

Although pop was not Athena's thing, she couldn't help remembering the demo she had listened to not too long ago. The guitar soloist had potential. In Athena's opinion, it was the addition of the guitarist that raised the group from mediocre to good.

Those in the pop audience were not necessarily known for their good taste, in Athena's opinion. However, they were known for their buying power, and Trey was always looking for a new way to feed the beast in whatever form it came. None of the acts he had spotted on his own had exploded nationally other than one little local girl, who had a voice out of this world. Athena herself had brought the singer to his attention.

As a matter of fact, Athena thought with regret, she felt the girl's talent was now being wasted. Regardless, Athena understood business and the main focus with any business was to make money. Besides, she had turned her back on that life a long time ago.

She placed the showcase on the calendar and made a mental note to call Mel to see if she would like to join her. Athena knew with Mel by her side she would be more likely to enjoy the performances other than analyze them to death. She had given up the dream to work in the music industry a long time ago, but she couldn't give up her love of music. Yeah, she had made her decision, Mel would have to come. With Mel there, Athena knew she would keep her feet firmly on the ground.

Before she could change her mind Athena called Twila and told her to RSVP for the tickets.

Feeling good and positive for once, Athena felt she had finally fully made the transition back to her former self. She'd spent the week avoiding television and all other forms of media, just in case there was a snippet about her incident that some wise-ass newscaster just wouldn't let die. Unfortunately a copy of *Sad and Single in the New Millenium* had mysteriously found its way onto her bookshelf in her outer office. The joker who had set it up there never fessed up, but Athena made it clear to Twila that she did not want to be reminded of the incident ever again. Luckily for her staff, Twila had passed on the word.

Now that the jokes had all but stopped, Athena felt ready to take a chance on going out on the town. Hell, she desperately needed it. She had hung out in her hermit shell for too long. After spending all week in meeting after meeting, she was ready to cut loose, so when Athena's cousin Stacy called, Athena thought of it as a good omen because if anyone knew how to relax it was Stacy, the perpetually unemployed.

"Hey Athena, w'sup?" Stacy said.

Looking at the clock, Athena could see it was already 3 p.m. She had been trying to tie up loose ends before she made a dash home to change for the showcase tonight.

"Where you been, girl?" Stacy said with a laugh in her throat.

"Around." Athena didn't bother to elaborate, not liking Stacy's tone. "What you been up to?"

"Aw, nothing, girl, I just been wondering when I was going to hear from my favorite cousin again."

"Well, I am glad to hear from—"

"Yeah, that's good," Stacy said, cutting Athena off, and immediately sounding like her old self. "I was calling to see if you wanted to go out with me and some of my girls tonight. I know it's been a while since we kicked it."

Stacy had recently moved to Biloxi from Atlanta. Prior to that she was in Florida for a year before leaving her mom's house for the hundredth time, vowing never to return. She and her three kids had moved into a small apartment near Bay St. Louis five months earlier. However, it didn't take long for Stacy to get into the groove of things. As a matter of fact, within weeks she had made a few new girlfriends and had become a regular on the Coast's burgeoning club circuit.

According to Stacy, she had been to just about every club on the Coast, from the ones specializing in country line dancing to the ones with the heavy beat of salsa pulsating off the walls. She had done it all. However, it was rare that Athena joined her. Although she had to admit the last time they'd gone out, which had to have been over three months ago, she'd had a good time.

That's how it always was with Stacy. Excitement just seemed to follow her. Despite the fact that she usually paid for it in some way, Athena usually had a good time with Stacy and her crew of misfits, mainly because it was the one time when she didn't have to think so much. In fact, the less she thought about things the more fun she had. Wherever they went, it was a party and if Stacy wasn't known at the club, one of her girls was bound to be able to take the reins, so they usually ended up VIP all the way. Unfortunately, Athena also usually ended up sick as a dog the next day, and it usually took more than a week to recover.

Stacy had moved in with Athena's family back while both were in elementary school. Having attended a predominantly white school all her life, Athena was glad to have someone who looked like her in her classes, and that she was family was an added bonus.

It was the mideighties then, and Athena had been teased for just about everything, from her hair, which was always too thick, to her clothes, which were always clean and starched, but not the trendy clothing that her classmates wore. It wasn't so much her color or her size that made her stand out but her lack of cool. Athena was never the loudest or the funniest, and for the most part she kept to herself.

All of that changed when her cousin Stacy showed up. The first time Athena saw her she thought her older cousin should have been on TV. Cousin Stacy looked just like Denise on *The Cosby Show*. As soon as she walked into the school she practically owned it. From the principal to the teachers to the students, everyone knew and liked Stacy immediately, and because of her popularity they liked Athena as well. Athena came to be compared to her older prettier cousin, and unfortunately always fell short.

Athena was no fool. She knew that it was because of their family ties that Stacy allowed her to hang out with her and her expanding group of friends, but she didn't care. She didn't care because there were times, especially late at night, when they lay side by side in Athena's shared bed and talked about what they wanted to do with their lives and what they really thought or felt about different things.

"When I grow up I want to work with music people," Athena used to say all the time as they sat and listened to music under the covers, and she talked about her favorite artists she wanted to meet.

Stacy would then say what she wanted to be when she grew up. One week it was actress, another week fireman. Despite what she chose, Athena would lie there and listen, trying to help Stacy decide the best path to make it happen.

Everyone in her family had seemed to favor Stacy when they were growing up, sometimes even Athena's own mother. Her mother had included Stacy in everything she and her sister Sheree did. She would take her shopping, sometimes even leaving Athena and Sheree at home. Athena could never fault her for that. However, she did hate that she never received the same attention because wherever she went Sheree was bound to follow. Later she learned that her mother gave that extra attention to Stacy because Stacy's own mother did not seem to have time to spend with her.

"Girl, what time?" Athena heard herself saying into the phone, deciding to throw caution and sobriety to the wind. Usually she didn't go for anything stronger than a carbonated drink or a glass of wine, but tonight, Athena thought, she would give herself permission to drink at least one margarita. *Watch out world—wild woman on the loose*, Athena thought, laughing at herself as she hung up the phone. Closing up the office, Athena headed home after making plans to meet Twila at 7 p.m. at the Kit Kat Lounge, where Who Dat was to do a couple of sets. Unfortunately, Mel had had to back out at the last minute, but Athena promised herself to remain on her best behavior. Tonight was about entertainment. The frustrated talent agent in her would have to take a seat.

The plan was to meet up with Stacy at her place over in College Park at around 9 p.m. Stacy had yet to get a car and didn't have a license anyway. Therefore, she was always relying on someone to pick her up, but it worked for her when she went clubbing because it meant she was never responsible for being the designated driver.

"I would drive, but you know," Stacy would always say as they were heading back or about to take the party to another level, and Athena would be left standing to the side as shots were ordered all around.

Most of Stacy's friends were much like her, and when they got ready for a night out they held nothing back. Short skirts, perfect makeup, and "just done" hair and nails were all a must for the evening. Never considered a glamour girl herself, Athena never even tried to compete with them. In fact, she always felt in some way lacking, which was probably the main reason she usually felt worse walking back through the door at the end of the night than out it.

However, after pulling on a tapered black dress with ruffles at the hem that hit right below the knee, and pulling her hair into a tight ponytail accentuating her long neck, Athena looked in the mirror and decided modestly that she would get her fair share of attention that night even while standing next to her cousin and her video girlfriends.

After meeting up with Twila and being disappointed by yet another press release that overstated the talents of the next big thing, Athena left Twila at the club with her dreadlocked boyfriend. She was disappointed. There had been only one good thing about the group, the sole guitar player she remembered from the CD. Unfortunately Athena found out he was just a contract player hired to play for one song. Athena couldn't help thinking how infinitely better the small group would be if they hired the guitarist full time.

"Well, don't you look—nice," Stacy said as she walked towards Athena with her eyes staring her down.

"Yes, I know that is true," Athena said, smiling and laughing, pleased at her approval.

Stacy just had a way about her that always made her seem so pulled together. Whenever anyone was in her presence, compliments seemed inevitable, because she always looked so stylish. Athena doubted that Stacy had ever had even one blemish anywhere on her body her entire life.

Stacy walked over to Athena's car in the driveway, and as she was moving towards the passenger side she asked, "You don't mind us taking your car this time, do you?"

"Who needs a ride?" Athena asked automatically.

Unlocking the doors, Athena and Stacy both climbed in. When Athena started the car, music poured from the speakers. Turning the music down, Athena backed the car into the street and headed out, following Stacy's directions to pick up two more of her friends.

They ended up in downtown Gulfport after an hour of driving. The street was quiet in front of the building where they stopped. In fact, Athena wondered if Stacy had picked the wrong place, until they opened the door of the building and were flooded with a bright neon light leading down a hallway to another set of doors.

Neon was always a good sign of life, Athena thought, smiling to herself and feeling more optimistic. A club without neon was like a rapper without bling, it just didn't happen. A child of the `80s, she still associated neon with *Miami Vice* and Crockett and Tubbs, but welcomed it purely for nostalgic value.

Opening the next set of doors, the four were immediately bombarded with music that had the floor vibrating from the bass. All that was visible from the inside of the club were flashing strobe lights which illuminated a sea of bodies writhing in abandonment to the hard drumbeats pouring out of the speakers.

Stacy and her friends headed to the right and up a staircase leading to the second level with Athena trailing. They bypassed a second shorter staircase and followed the wall around the club to another staircase to a third level blocked by a black curtain where a tall man stood.

S. R. MADDOX

Stacy had a few words with the man, who broke into a face-splitting grin and then stepped back to open the door. Stepping through the curtain into a smoky room with dome lamps hanging from the ceiling over several pool tables, Athena was in awe. Only Stacy would be able to find the only VIP lounge in a club in under five minutes.

Upstairs the vibe was much more subdued. Athena could still hear the thumping through the floor, but it was not distracting. They pulled up some stools around a tall table to order some drinks from the bar.

After placing their orders, Athena and the other ladies checked the room. Athena couldn't help being impressed with the decor. This place was much more her style. Noting the small stage in the corner, Athena could only hope for some live music as their drinks arrived.

Taking a healthy sip of her first and only margarita, Athena promised herself once again that she would finish the whole drink and not just lick the salt off around the edge. She wasn't a big drinker, but Athena planned to let it all hang out tonight, and that meant drinking with the girls.

"This place is dead," said video girl number one.

"Yeah," Stacy and video girl number two agreed. Athena took another sip of her drink as she continued to look around. She thought it was pretty nice, but she kept her opinion to herself as she took in the mixed crowd of college students and young executives who still wore their ties or jackets.

Looking at Stacy's two friends, Athena was still having a hard time telling them apart. Their shoulder

85

length curls were perfectly coiffed and their M.A.C. makeup made them look like twins, although Athena knew they weren't. She noticed several young women in the room who had the same look: a cross between girl-next-door Ashanti and Ciara's round-the-way girl. Varying shades of hair color were the only differences between all of them. Athena decided then that she would keep track of Stacy by her short Halle Berry haircut.

After they all finished their drinks, Athena followed the crew downstairs. She was definitely feeling a lot looser now, so much so that she found herself holding onto Stacy's shoulder and the wall to keep up with the women. When they reached the bottom floor, Athena was left standing by herself as Stacy was led away by a nice-looking brother, who looked to be about as expensive as Stacy pretended to be. The other two women found their own targets. Athena was pleased when she felt a hand reach for hers and she was sucked into the crowd.

Letting the music guide her, Athena danced her way to the middle of the floor. A couple of songs had passed by the time she realized she was no longer with the guy she had started with. Seeing Stacy and the others nowhere, Athena followed her guy to the bar where she had the first beer she'd had in years.

After that Athena spent the next half hour upstairs with somebody named Cedric, and still there was no sign of Stacy or her friends, whose names she could not seem to remember. When her new friend got pulled into a heated conversation about Howard versus Harvard,

Athena left her dance partner to head back downstairs, determined to find her cousin.

Moments later, Athena felt a hand tapping her on the shoulder. Turning, Athena smiled at the trio, who were laughing as they sipped on cocktails. Stacy stepped close enough for Athena to smell Stacy's choice of drink— some fruity concoction—as she pulled a guy from the crowd.

Tony was tall and bright and had a smile that redefined the color white. However, before Athena could be introduced, the song switched, and Stacy yelled, "Ooh, shut up, this my song." She pulled everyone around her onto the dance floor.

CHAPTER 6

"Thump-a-thump-a-thump-a," was all Athena heard coming from the speakers as she tried to dance to the beat. With her thighs burning Athena made her way to the side of the club, leaving Stacy and her friends once again.

She was having a great time, but her body was about to give out. Looking at her watch, Athena quickly realized why. The little hand was way past the one. She hadn't been out this late in years for anything that didn't end with some sort of accident.

Like the time Mel and she crashed FAMU's homecoming and then got into an accident as they made their hasty exit for midterms back in New Orleans. Or a couple of years ago when Kendrick slipped and fell on the coffee table at a friend's house on New Year's Eve and had to be rushed to the emergency room for eight stitches.

Late hours had never signaled a good thing for "early bird" Athena—until now, it seemed. Heading back upstairs to the second level for something to drink—bottled water or a Coke—Athena saw Tony, Stacy's friend, at her side. He was smiling and Athena couldn't help smiling back as she wiped a trickle of sweat off her brow.

"God, it gets hot in there, doesn't it," Athena said, waving the bartender over. "I had to step out to get something cool to drink."

"Oh, allow me," he said as the bartender asked for their orders.

"Just a water for me," Athena said, yelling over the music and the chatter of the other clubbers around the bar.

Leaning forward, Tony spoke to the bartender. Minutes later the bartender returned with two glasses and Athena's bottle of water. Looking at the two glasses sitting in front of Tony, Athena assumed he was getting something for Stacy. Both glasses contained a pretty auburn-colored liquid and a cute little lemon on the side, which immediately made Athena smile. It looked good, but she knew she had reached her limit.

"Thirsty much?" Athena asked, raising her eyebrows.

Tony pushed one glass towards Athena.

"What is this?"

"It's just an iced tea," Tony yelled over the music.

Taking a sip, Athena didn't think to ask if it had alcohol, and after she tasted it she didn't care. It was so good and it hit a spot she hadn't even know was there.

"This is good," Athena said appreciatively, reflexively reaching for her pocketbook. "How much?"

"Oh, consider it on the house, pretty lady," he said. "In fact, once this gets low you just come back on up."

After Tony swaggered away, Athena learned from the bartender that Stacy's big baller was owner of the club, which explained Stacy's interest in him. However, Athena didn't have time to think about that. In fact, once she finished her drink she didn't care to think much about anything.

Suddenly tired, Athena went in search of Stacy. It was time to go. As Athena went up the staircase to the pool-room to look for her shady cousin she felt her stomach begin to roll. She knew immediately she was going to be sick and frantically searched for the restroom.

Running into the restroom, Athena went in the first empty stall she saw, barely making it to the commode before her stomach emptied. Oddly, Athena's first thoughts were that it had been about a decade since she had last thrown up. *God, I really was drunk,* she thought as she heaved one last time into the swirling water.

When her stomach stopped rolling and she finally felt that she could stand without falling into the walls, she stood up and leaned her forehead against the cool bath-room stall door, letting her stomach settle.

Athena could feel her temper unfurl. Normally slow to boil, Athena went from zero to one hundred in two seconds flat and cursed her cousin for abandoning her. Whether it was the alcohol or just built-up resentment she had reached her limit. *How had she sunk so low so fast?*

Gathering her wits and her resolve, Athena had her hand on the door to go find the girls when she heard a voice that made her stomach clench once more.

"Girl, this is the deadest I have ever seen it up in here," the voice said.

It was the same woman's voice from the studio. The one that Athena had vowed she would never forget. Peeking through the crack of the stall, Athena couldn't see the owner of the voice, but she already knew who it was. The voice had haunted her dreams since that awful day on Delilah's show.

"Yeah," a second woman's voice answered. "I'm about to go get my man and take him home for a little treat." Athena heard the door open and the sound of music poured in as the woman and her companion stepped out.

Hurrying out of the stall, Athena frantically searched for her tormentor. Walking into the dimly lit lounge, she saw her, wearing all red and green, of course. "Bitch," Athena hissed. Before she could think, Athena started towards the woman until she saw the man with her. For a moment Athena felt suspended like some wobbly marionette unable to control the direction of her floppy arms and legs. Blinking, Athena took in the scene. Celina was kissing her ex, Kendrick.

"Oh. My. God."

Suddenly it all made sense. Athena craned her neck to look around the spinning room for her cousin, someone to help her move, because the last thing she wanted was to run into either Kendrick or Celina. She had to get away. But as she stumbled towards the stairs, she heard her name.

"Athena, Athena," Celina yelled so loudly that Athena couldn't help hearing. To ignore her would be to admit defeat, but her mind was in flight mode, and all she could think was that she had to get away. Then she heard her name a third time. This time the voice was distinctly more masculine and seemed to offer compassion. She knew instantly it was Kendrick.

Looking over her shoulder she saw Kendrick leading the evil Celina towards her. Athena was attempting to turn towards the VIP lounge as if that had been her destination all along when her heel caught in the carpet, pitching her to the side.

Falling into the black carpeted walls, Athena suddenly realized that standing didn't seem to be the best idea. She willed herself not to faint.

"She's drunk," Celina said, barely hiding her grin.

"I'm not drunk," was what Athena intended to say, but instead it came out slurred even to her own ears.

"She's a mess."

"Quiet, Celina. Athena? Athena, are you okay?"

What an idiot. Does it look like I'm all right? Athena burped, gaining her equilibrium, sort of.

"Hi, Ken," Athena said.

"Hi. Are you all right? Athena, you look like you're not feeling—well."

No joke, Sherlock.

"I'm good, I just had a little bit too much." Tipping her thumb to her mouth she tossed her head back once, which was not a good idea, considering she was still sobriety challenged.

"Let me go get you some coffee or some water—something."

Athena felt so bad that she weakly nodded her head before fully realizing that left her with Celina to deal with—alone.

"Well, we had a little bit too much to drink tonight, didn't we?"

Athena was not in the mood for Celina and had every intention of walking away, but Celina was not having it.

Grabbing her shoulder, Celina held Athena in place. Seeing Celina's red-tipped talons on her shoulder caused the pulse in Athena's temple to throb.

"Don't you walk away from me!" Celina hissed, digging her talons in as she held on tightly to Athena's shoulder. This chick had caught her on the wrong day, a day where she was too liquored up to edit her thoughts, words, or actions.

Before she knew it, surprising even herself, Athena had pulled back her hand and landed the first punch of her life. The punch deflected off Celina's jaw, but it stunned her enough that she let go of Athena, and fell to the floor. Standing over her, Athena gasped for breath. What did one do after knocking someone's block off? The only thing she could think of was something she had heard on some seventies flick.

"You best to watch yo' self, sucka," Athena growled before limping away, having lost her shoe at some point in time. Unsure as to where she was going, she left Celina scrambling on the floor with her cohorts standing with their mouths hanging open.

Athena stopped to take one last look before continuing her victory stroll. Then she turned and walked straight into a wall. The bump sent her backwards and she twisted her ankle as she took a tumble all the way to the bottom of the stairs, landing with a smack to her face.

Half-conscious, Athena looked up to see people staring. Some were laughing and some were just shaking their heads. Dazed, Athena was considering warning them against the iced teas when she felt someone helping her up from behind. With the support of two hands under her shoulders Athena was able to stand.

Leaning into a much taller figure, and Athena was grateful for the support until she was outside in the alley.

"Hmmm," she mumbled. Then she said the first thing that came to her mind. "You smell good." Feeling the warm chest vibrate, she heard a deep chuckle. She was drunk, but it was true, he really did smell good.

Closing her eyes for a moment, Athena tried to ineffectively stop the spinning. Then she gave in to the floating feeling, vaguely aware of being placed in the front seat of a large truck before a big dark-haired man climbed in beside her. After that the world went black.

Opening one nasty, crusted eye, Athena stared at what had to be a ten-foot ceiling and immediately realized the situation was not good.

Waking up in a stranger's bed never was. Looking in the direction from where the singing was coming, she could also hear the sound of running water. Ignoring the pounding in her head, Athena attempted to roll herself from the bed, but instead barely moved a leg. Trapped in the bed sheets, she unraveled herself and put her feet down.

Tripping over some clutter, she fell to her knees. Still hearing sounds coming from the bathroom, Athena was spurred into action and started grabbing for her shoes and then her clothes. She had both on in record time.

"Shit, shit, shit," Athena cursed as she searched for her purse.

Ah ha. She saw it resting on top of some old dusty LPs on the dresser. Not pausing to check the contents, she bolted towards the door.

As she turned the doorknob, the night before came rushing back, including the foulness with Kendrick and Celina and the embarrassing fall down the stairs. For the first time since awakening she took inventory. She had not been molested in any way that she could tell, but who knew what perversion this guy with the smooth voice was into. Just thinking of all the different things the big guy she barely remembered could have done to her unconscious body spurred her into action.

She bolted out of the bedroom, briefly noticing her surroundings as she ran past a mantle full of photographs. As she ran towards the front door, Athena reached for her phone. Blinded by the light, she leapt out the door onto an empty street.

Confused for a moment, Athena spotted a bodega that she had passed a few times on her way to work. Having a general idea of her location, Athena limped up the block towards a busy intersection. As she neared the corner she heard movement coming up fast behind her, but refused to turn around.

Hailing a cab, she jumped into the backseat before the car completely stopped, telling the cabdriver to head towards Lameuse. Not wanting to look back but not being able to stop herself, she turned once the car was safely in motion. Her relief evaporated. Naked except for the towel wrapped around his waist, there stood Mike Thibodeaux. Even the increasing distance as the taxi sped away couldn't hide Mike standing in the middle of the street with both fists on his hips and the biggest scowl Athena had ever seen.

Athena groaned. Added to that, the knowing smirk on the cabbie's face as he turned the corner had Athena ready to scream. Great! Another witness to her shame! She let her hair fall forward in an attempt to hide her face.

All she wanted to do was go home and crawl under the bed. Her head was splitting and the humiliation was all too much. Unfortunately, she still had to retrieve her car, and to her further embarrassment, it took half an hour because she had forgotten where she had parked it.

After directing the cabbie through numerous back streets and alleyways, Athena finally got lucky. After paying the cabdriver forty dollars for taking her a total of ten blocks, Athena crawled into her car and turned the key. More than ever she wished she could make like Dorothy and click her heels three times and chant, "Home." Unfortunately, Athena had no ruby slippers nor a fairy godmother so she drove herself home, remembering the proverb, *Oh, how the mighty have fallen.*

When she finally pulled into her driveway Athena dragged herself into the house and fell into bed.

"Oh shit," Athena mumbled as she wiped the dribble from her mouth. Lightning flashed outside, followed by thunder so loud it echoed. Athena hated thunderstorms. They reminded her of hurricanes and she wanted no part of them. As memory of her mortification returned in graphic detail, she wanted to pull the covers over her head and press snooze for the rest of the day, maybe for the rest of her life.

Not only had she embarrassed herself in front of the entire club of God knows who, but she had done it in front of Mike as well.

"Jerk," Athena growled as she pulled herself out of bed and headed to the bathroom. After washing her hands she crawled back into bed again.

Yes, it would be one of those days, and boy did she deserve it. It had to be past eight, but Athena just could not get it together, and the scene in Mike's apartment just kept replaying like some bad ESPN tape.

Just thinking about the way she had dashed out of his condo like Deion Sanders running for a touchdown made her cheeks burn.

You would think she had never had a sleepover before. One night stands were not her thing, but it wasn't like anything had even happened. At least, she didn't think anything had happened.

Shaking her head, she tried to think back, but she couldn't. What the hell? Her mind was a complete blank after the—. Oh snap, Athena thought. She had actually punched someone. Athena sat for a second massaging her temple as she tried to remember. Celina, it was Celina! For the first time since waking Athena smiled. However, her grin turned sour as the memory of falling down the stairs came rushing back, as well as the memory of being carried out of the club.

God, she had really made a fool of herself. She never drank heavily, which confused her even more. She had only had a couple of drinks. Even if it was a hundred proof alcohol, which it wasn't, the small amount she'd drunk wouldn't have caused her to black out. Would it? God, please don't let becoming an alcoholic be the latest on her increasing list of screw ups. Shaking her head, she tried to think. She hadn't drunk anything straight. The two drinks she'd had were mixed drinks and tasted more fruity than alcoholic. She should have been able to handle that.

With increasing clarity, Athena became more and more sure of herself. The only explanation was that someone had put something in her drink. Thinking back to the night, she couldn't think of a time she did not have her drink in front of her. As a matter of fact, the only time she hadn't had it in front of her was when she was handed the drink.

Mind racing as she tried to figure it all out, Athena felt the beginning of a headache. Then she thought she heard pounding. Had she broken her brain? *Please Lord, don't let me have to call an ambulance.* Then she heard the pounding again, this time harder, and realized it was knocking.

Oh great, company. As the knocking continued, increasing in intensity, Athena pulled herself up. Obviously, this person was not leaving. As she felt her temper rise, she almost looked forward to the coming confrontation.

Briefly glancing in the mirror as she made her way to her front door, she ran one hand through her flattened hair and another around her eyes to clear some of the crust away so she could see her victim more fully. Without pity, Athena bypassed the keyhole and yanked the door open.

Oh, shit.

"Hello, Athena."

With those two words, Athena felt herself falling. Throwing a hand out to steady herself, Athena slammed the door closed.

Resting her cheek against the red door, she could feel the coolness and welcomed it as her face burned with shame. She must still be drunk on some strange residual alcohol hanging out in her liver, she thought. That had to be the reason for the hallucination. Then she heard knocking again.

"Athena," the voice said, concerned, "I'm not leaving until I know you're okay."

Don't run or worse, pass out, Athena told herself. God, what was happening to her?

"Open up, babe."

With that plea, Athena had no choice. Regardless of the mess her life had become, she could not bear to lose this man's total respect. Squaring her shoulders, Athena turned the knob.

"Hello, Kendrick."

Standing in her kitchen, Athena cursed herself for the tenth time that morning. Since opening her door to her ex, it had been one curse after another.

"Why, God?" she wondered to herself. What had she done that was so wrong? "Please tell me," Athena moaned as she peered at her reflection in the toaster. She raked her fingers through her unruly mop of hair and took a deep breath. Then she reached for her glass of juice, hoping to mask the fact that she had yet to brush her teeth.

"Athena," a voice called, "really, I don't need anything to drink." Athena let out another curse as she poured another glass of OJ. She had used the excuse of refreshments to escape out of the living room where she had seated Kendrick. Grabbing a box of Poptarts and the two glasses of juice, Athena prepared herself for her close-up with Kendrick.

Pushing the swinging door open with her backside, Athena closed her eyes once more to plead with God, despite His seemingly deaf ear. *Please help me make it through the next hour of my life, God, without embarrassing myself any more.*

As she turned to face Kendrick, Athena felt her foot take root underneath the carpet her mother had insisted she buy. Before she could stop herself, Athena felt herself falling flat on her face.

"No, no, no, no," Athena groaned with her forehead pressing her hands into the carpet. She truly did not want to look. However, she knew she had no choice when she heard Kendrick's words.

Clearing his throat, Kendrick said dryly, "Should I get a towel?"

Looking up at the man who could have been her husband for the first time that morning, Athena smiled a genuine smile. Covered in juice, Kendrick stood in her living room with a look she remembered too well. Suddenly, it was as if the year and a half had disappeared and they were a couple once again. Not just any couple, but that couple who knew all of their partner's faults and still chose to hang around.

"I see not much has changed."

Pulling herself to a standing position, Athena had to laugh. "No, I guess not."

Grabbing some towels and shepherding Kendrick into the bathroom to get cleaned up, Athena was amazed at how comfortable it was to have him there. He had not seen her newest place, but he was all too familiar with her. Kendrick was one of the few people who knew her for what she truly was—a natural born klutz.

In her professional life, most people perceived her to be a no-nonsense business type, but her family and friends knew what lengths she went to give that impression. In fact, Athena was not even half as together as many people believed her to be. In her downtime she was a walking time bomb of misfortune; she had just learned to hide it well.

However, Kendrick knew better. They had practically lived together most of the time they were together. Although the last year of their relationship they had spent less and less time together, Kendrick knew just about all of her secrets.

However, thinking about the fact that he was now dating the woman who had orchestrated her humiliation on live television, her guard was firmly in place. Regardless of the relationship they had once had, Athena knew that it wasn't enough to make her forget her humiliation at the hands of Celina.

"Athena," Kendrick called from her bedroom.

Walking to the door, Athena was shocked by the vision that greeted her. Kendrick stood wrapped in only a towel perched low on his waist. Before she could speak, Kendrick thrust a ball of wet clothes in her arms.

"You got something I can put on?" he asked.

Nodding her head, Athena forced herself to get a grip. "Back of door in bathroom." Once the door was closed, Athena headed towards the laundry room. "What the hell?" Washboard abs that would make Shemar Moore say, "Damn!" had Athena wondering about the other changes in Kendrick's life.

The last time she had been with Kendrick, the boy had been the picture of what not to do when it came to health. Thirty pounds overweight, a steady diet of fast food, and little exercise had caused him to go soft in more than one area. Smiling to herself, Athena threw the clothes in the washer and filled it with soap before turning the switch on.

She was being catty, she knew, but damn, the brother was fine. He had always been an attractive, if lumpy, man, but now Athena could only say, "Hubba hubba." She then kicked herself because who said "hubba hubba" now, really?

Walking through the living room once more, Athena had to wonder if she had been the dead weight in their relationship. Kendrick seemed to be doing so much better now, and she had even heard that he was up for partnership in his firm.

Feeling the tears return, Athena couldn't help questioning whether her leaving Kendrick was possibly the best thing to ever happen to him. It wasn't as if she had gained anything by the ending of their relationship. She was single, lonely, and she had been humiliated twice in the past month—both times her fault.

When they had parted she had blamed him for all that was wrong with her life. She had said some really hurtful things to him. Come to find out, it was more than likely her fault.

"Athena, can we talk?"

Athena kept her back turned as she heard Kendrick enter the room. Here it comes, she thought to herself as she stifled a sob that came from out of nowhere. The harder she fought against the tears, the harder they worked to make their way out. She didn't want to do this. Not now, she wasn't ready for it.

As Kendrick placed a hand on her shoulder, Athena forced herself to pull it together. She would not let him see her cry. Wiping the tears away, Athena fell back on anger to make it through the next few minutes.

Thinking about Celina, Mike, her mother, hell, there was a whole pile of rage in that one, Athena stoked the flame.

Why had he come over here anyway? She felt herself harden. He'd come over here to see his girlfriend's effect. *He thinks he's got the better of old, klutzy Athena. Well, I'll show him.*

"Athena, look at me," Kendrick said more forcefully for the second time.

I'll look at you all right, Athena thought, jerking away from his touch. However, when she turned ready for battle, Athena's plan, along with her defenses dissolved under his watchful stare.

Looking at the man that she had at one time loved, the man with whom she had spent hours, days studying, she saw he was staring back at her with nothing more than concern and sympathy. Without saying a word he took her into his embrace.

That was when she broke. She still loved this man, but she knew she was no longer "in love" with him. The guilt she hadn't fully realized she still carried broke and shattered, leaving her exposed and vulnerable. She let Kendrick lead her to the couch where he pulled her into his lap, never breaking contact, just rocking her the whole time. While he did, she let herself remember.

"You what?" Kendrick exploded. "Now, you tell me this? Now?"

At his sarcastic tone, Athena began to wish she hadn't insisted everyone leave the rectory of the church. Pressing her wet palms into the dress she had spent the last five months hunting for, Athena searched for words, any words. The only ones she could utter were, "I'm sorry."

"Sorry?" Kendrick yelled, bug-eyed with disbelief. "You're sorry? When did you decide this?"

Athena was about to respond, but Kendrick had gone into lawyer mode. As he started his interrogation, Athena suddenly felt empathy for any and every defendant who had had to withstand the barrage.

"You couldn't tell me this last week, or last night, Athena? You had to wait until the moment right before our wedding?" Kendrick yelled the last word as if realizing for the first time that he was dressed in his tux with his bride in the back of the church her mother had picked because it was the biggest and most sought after.

Kendrick hadn't even wanted a wedding, Athena thought to herself as she covered her eyes with her hands, wishing she could blink two times and find herself on an island far, far away.

If she had kept her mouth shut that would be where she would be headed—on her honeymoon. However, at the last minute her body had erupted in hives in revolt against the idea of going through with what she knew would be the biggest mistake of her life. Even then it wasn't until Kendrick had asked her if she was okay as she stood before the preacher and the entire church full of family and friends that she chose to acknowledge her doubts.

"I'm so sorry," Athena said for the hundredth time when her would-be groom grabbed her by the shoulders.

"I am sick of hearing your sorries," Kendrick said, his voice deep and tight. He released her and then hit the wall, leaving a small patch of blood before walking out the back door and her life.

"She's not pressing charges, Athena," Kendrick said.

Until their encounter at the club, Athena had not spoken to Kendrick since their wedding day. She had seen him around town. She knew for a fact that he had seen her as well. It was Biloxi, after all, not some metropolitan city that you could hide out in. In Biloxi you were just a second and a half behind everyone else. Forget seven degrees of separation. It was more like centimeters of separation. His arrival on her doorstep had her reeling, but she felt relieved to hear Celina wasn't pressing charges.

Athena regretted the way things had ended between them. Kendrick had been her lover and her best friend for almost ten years. It was the loss of that friendship that she had regretted the most.

"I hadn't realized how much I missed you until just now," Kendrick said, giving her a kiss on her forehead.

Hearing the whistles, Athena shifted to the side, out of his lap. Although she felt guilty about how things had ended, she refused to let her guard down. Ex-fiancee or not, Kendrick was sitting on her sofa in her robe—a very short robe. "Look, Kendrick, I don't think . . ." Athena began until she looked up to see Kendrick smiling.

"Whoa," Kendrick said, waving away Athena's comments. "That is the last thing on my mind."

Confused, Athena was embarrassed more by his tone than her thoughts. Damn, she knew she had just crawled out of bed, but she didn't look that bad, did she?

"Athena, I know it has been a while, but I am totally happy with where I am at right now. I came over here because after last night," Kendrick paused, "I was concerned."

Great, Athena thought. *Not only am I the loser, but I am the pitiful loser.*

"It was nothing," Athena began but she could tell by the look on his face that he didn't believe her.

"Look, I don't know what it was, but it was nothing that you or Celina needed to worry over." The room was silent except for the dripping of her air-conditioning unit as it tried desperately to cool the high-ceilinged rooms.

"About Celina," he began.

"Yeah, what about Celina, Kendrick?" Athena felt more comfortable on the offense so she continued. "What is that chick's problem? She obviously has it out for me, although I didn't fully understand why until the other night when I saw the two of you cuddled up."

"She's my fiancée, Athena."

The air flew out of her lungs leaving her gasping, "Your fiancée?"

"Yeah." He smiled ruefully, as if he half didn't believe it himself. "We got engaged about three months ago and we set the date a couple of weeks ago."

Looking guilty for the first time, he stalled. Fumbling with the strings of the robe he wore, he avoided Athena's gaze as realization sank in, and she saw red. Not only had that bitch set her up, but she had used her to gain a wedding ring.

One look at Kendrick's face, and Athena knew it was true. She knew all of his looks and this one said, "Busted," with a capital B. Hearing the washer's buzzer, Athena stood. Walking to the laundry room, she grabbed the wet clothes out of the washer.

So my humiliation was a well-hatched plan to kill three birds with one stone. Humiliate the ex, avenge her boyfriend's honor, and gain that all important ring. Unbelievable. Never in her wildest dreams had she believed that someone could do something so heinous. Walking towards the front door, Athena ignored Kendrick's questions. Opening the door, Athena drew back her bundle of dripping clothes, threw them as far as she could.

"What the hell are you doing?" Kendrick yelled, stalking towards the door.

Unfazed, Athena untied his robe and yanked. Too stunned to defend himself, Kendrick was disrobed within seconds. Wrapping the robe around her arm, Athena grabbed the door firmly with one hand.

"Thank you so much for your concern, Kendrick," Athena said, smiling sweetly, "but I really don't need it. You tell Celina," Athena paused, taking in Kendrick's tense posture at her mentioning of his girlfriend's name, "she has my condolences."

The look on Kendrick's face was priceless. The sincerity and concern dropped away, leaving the Kendrick she had almost forgotten had ever existed.

"You know you want this." Kendrick smiled arrogantly. With a sneer he placed both hands on his waist, striking a pose.

Taking a long, lingering look Athena smiled.

"Been there and done that, and from the little I remember," Athena paused, "it wasn't all that."

"You spiteful little—" Kendrick began, but Athena closed the door before he could finish, leaving him yelling on the lawn.

Locking the door firmly, she turned her back on her past. She felt lighter. Even the smugness Kendrick tried his best to hide could not destroy her buzz. She felt free—free of her own self-imposed guilt. For the past year she had been beating herself up for her treatment of Kendrick.

Now she realized that he had spent the last year seeking a way to punish her for leaving him. Celina had only been the linchpin. Amazingly, the fact that she had enemies out there who were plotting against her somehow decreased her fear.

The truth made her stronger. Now that she knew it, she could prepare herself for what might come.

She was no longer a sitting duck.

CHAPTER 7

Athena headed for the kitchen to forage for a Maalox and Tylenol shooter. She paused when the phone rang. Making sure to check for caller ID first, Athena picked up.

"Hey."

"Right back at you," Mel said. "What's going on with you today? I called you this morning two times and couldn't get an answer. Must have been some night."

You don't know the half of it. Athena decided then and there to not share her "kidnapping" with Mel. She wanted an image change, but did not need to hear Mel rant about the rules. The rules were a set of do's and don'ts both women had created when they were much younger. Back then, they had been limited in where their college IDs could get them into, but they had been around enough to have set limits.

At the top of the list was to keep an eye on who you came with, and secondly, never ever let someone watch your drinks, even the person you came with. Although Athena really didn't think Tony had done anything to her drinks, in hindsight it was a possibility. Decking someone and falling down entire flights of stairs were not Athena's usual M.O.

"So, tell me where you went, what you did," Mel said somewhat out of breath. "Better yet, who did you do, and where did you do it?"

Unable to stand her heavy breathing Athena asked, "Do you have company?"

"Huh?"

"What are you doing? You sound so out of breath."

"Oh, I'm just getting off my walker," Mel said before gulping, "and drinking some water to cool down. Girl, we have got to start back going to the gym. I looked in the mirror yesterday and I swear it looked like I had two asses."

"I know what you mean." Athena laughed for the first time in two very long days.

"I turned too quick and caught myself in one of those dressing room mirrors and my ass said, 'Find thee a gym, now!' "

"Oh, please girl, you know Ricky is happy with all that you got."

"True, true," Mel said, laughing to herself, "but I'm not happy. It's just getting a bit too much. How 'bout we start going to the gym after work?"

It didn't take much thought on Athena's part before she agreed, knowing that she had been needing to lose a few pounds to just make things a little tighter.

"Bet," Mel said in acceptance. "So, when you gonna tell me what happened last night? I haven't forgotten."

"Well, if you had showed up you wouldn't have to be asking," Athena said, still a little perturbed at Mel's sudden bout of flakiness. "I'm not gonna forgive you for leaving me hanging like that."

"What? Don't tell me Stuck-up Stacy showed out yet again."

"Actually this time it wasn't her fault," Athena said, automatically defending her cousin.

"Hold on, girl, I'll be right back. That might be my boo," Mel said after her phone clicked, signaling call waiting.

It wasn't long before she was back on the line and saying she had to go. From her giggling Athena knew who it was. They ended the conversation confirming their standing Sunday brunch at the Fifth Street Diner. After grabbing an ice pop, about the only thing her stomach could handle, Athena crawled back into bed and tried not to think about Stacy, her ex, Celina, or how good Mike had looked standing in that towel.

The next morning Mel didn't waste a minute getting down to the details. As soon as the waitress left with their orders she started.

"She didn't even bother calling you to see if you made it home all right, did she?"

"No," Athena said, "but then again, I really didn't expect her to."

"Yeah, after falling on your ass in the middle of the club. Did you drive them? I bet you drove."

Athena nodded, avoiding Mel's eyes.

"That just makes it worse. She dumped you and didn't bother to see if you made it home all right and you drove her," Mel said, disbelieving.

"You know what, I don't really think she meant to leave, but when she probably didn't see me, she just found another way home." Even to her own ears that did not sound right. If it had been Mel and her, or hell, anyone, Athena would have stayed until the club closed to make sure her friend was all right. Looking at Mel's crooked lips and raised eyebrows Athena knew that she didn't buy it either. Athena was glad when the waitress approached with both their orders.

"Alrighty, this here's for you," she said, placing the "loaded omelet" with a side of bacon in front of Athena. "And this hereey is for the diva."

Athena couldn't help saying a prayer for this chipper woman named Rita because she was able to do the impossible, erase the dark cloud that had just about devoured their table.

Even Mel couldn't help smiling at the woman using her nickname, which was proudly displayed across her ample chest.

Mel had gotten the cheap little T-shirt back as an undergrad, and tended to wear it on her ass-kicking days. Even though the shirt was made for the barely legal, even I had to admit she worked it.

"You are one bad ass woman, Rita," Mel said to the waitress as she laid out the "Heartland Special" order in front of Mel. It had three types of pork and two fried eggs with a buttery biscuit side meant to clog even Godzilla's arteries, thus its ironic name.

Rita smiled before turning, leaving behind a cloud of Jean Naté.

"First name basis, huh? When did that happen?" Athena asked around a bite of bacon.

"Don't try to change the subject," Mel replied, reaching for the ketchup. "I really don't understand why you let Stacy get away with what she does. I could understand back when we were kids, but damn, she's not the big city cousin we used to idolize. We are all grown ass women now and you don't have to be at her beck and call."

Athena knew what she was saying was true, but it seemed that when it came to Stacy, she just couldn't say no. Stacy was family, plus she was all alone. It was true that Athena was, too, but Stacy also had three kids to take care of, so what if sometimes Athena tried to help her out? However, no matter how many times Athena tried to explain this to Mel, she was just not accepting it.

"I *hear* you, but it's time to cut that out. She has friends here, she has a man. Why is she always asking you for money or dropping her kids off at your place and making you scramble to find a babysitter?" Mel asked as she picked her way through some eggs. "She can't keep on putting her problems on other people and running away from them."

"I know, but she has had it hard."

Dropping her fork, Mel said, "Oh please, Athena. We have all had it hard in our own different ways. Yeah, her mother and father divorced when we were all young, and her mother bounced around with Stacy with different men who kicked both their asses more times than not. She had it rough, but we all have to get to a point where we say enough is enough," Mel huffed before picking up her fork and beginning to eat.

"Besides, how is your bailing her out really helping her?" Mel paused to take a sip of OJ. "Have you ever thought that you might actually be hurting her by giving her an out whenever she screws up?"

Upset, Athena dropped her fork. "What the hell? After all I have done for Stacy, how can you say I was trying to hurt her?" Athena could feel her stomach start to roil and realized quickly that she would not be finishing her meal. Pushing her plate away, Athena leaned back in her chair. Dammit, she had just gotten her appetite back.

"You know I am not trying to upset you, but what she did last night is unforgivable," Mel said, reaching across the table. "You're my best friend. What if something really had happened to you last night?" she said.

Athena softened at her friend's sincerity and concern.

"You are always trying to help someone out and you have the best intentions, but you can't control her situation."

Athena knew this but there was a difference between knowing and believing. Athena knew that something had to change in how she dealt with Stacy, Sheree, her parents, hell, just about everyone in her life, but how?

Her doctor had warned Athena at her last checkup after she had described the anxiety she had been experiencing how it could evolve into something worse than mere panic attacks. The idea of something worse than her panic attacks scared Athena, but not enough that she would accept the medication he prescribed. Having a regular relationship with her doctor was not something she wanted. Despite the fact that she ran a health center that focused on community health, she herself was scared to death of doctors. For all her health insurance, Athena rarely used it. No, she would continue to manage her attacks. All she needed was some rest. Athena quickly decided it best not to share the rest of her night out with Stacy, especially where she'd ended up yesterday morning.

"Girl, everything will be all right," Mel said, finally letting the touchy subject of Stacy drop. Giving Athena a hug good-bye in the parking lot, Mel couldn't help taking one last parting shot. "Just pray that I don't run into that chickenhead cousin of yours on the street."

Athena, knowing her friend was dead serious, said a little prayer because she knew her friend always had been the one between them to quickly "knock a bitch out." Last night not included, Athena had always been the quiet one.

As she hugged her friend back, the two made plans to meet on Wednesday night, no excuses allowed. Both agreed it would be a girls' night only, going so far as to cross their hearts as they had when they were little kids.

"I'll call Shaundra too," Mel said before shutting her car door. Shaundra was a mutual friend they had both met soon after graduating and starting their individual careers. Shaundra hadn't joined them out on the town in years. In fact they hadn't seen her much since she'd gotten married to a gynecologist a few years earlier and started dropping babies every couple of years. They currently had three, but her husband was always trying for that fourth one.

Hopping into her car to run a few errands before heading home to get some much-needed rest, Athena found herself looking over her shoulder periodically. The more that she thought about it, the more she wondered if Celina might be thinking about pressing charges. Considering how she had gone out of her way to embarrass Athena on television, she couldn't imagine Celina would pass up the chance to put her behind bars.

Deep in her own thoughts, Athena screamed when she nearly ran over her neighbor Hector and his dog taking a walk outside her condo. She didn't bother apologizing despite his shrieking. She was still mad at him for cutting the roses off her bush for an arrangement he just had to have for his picture window last month.

"I see you, Athena Miles," Hector hissed as Athena turned the key in her front door. Refusing to give in, Athena turned a cool eye to Hector, who immediately stuck his tongue out at her. Before she could stop herself, Athena returned the favor, shutting the door as Hector burst out laughing.

Tomorrow she would go over and clip a few of his magnolias. Just the thought brought a smile to her face. Stripping her clothes off as she walked down her hallway, Athena threw herself on the bed.

God, just let today end, and I promise to be better tomorrow.

CHAPTER 8

"Damn," Mike said to no one in particular as he draped his muscular arms over the steering wheel. Turning his head, he caught a glimpse of a speeding red van in the outside mirror. "Man, you might as well slow down," he said, defeated. He leaned back in his bucket seat. Rolling his massive shoulders, Mike tried once again to work the kinks out. It had been a rough night and the crouching on the cement floor required for tiling had finally caught up to him. However, regardless of the toll it was taking on his body, Mike was pleased with the work he had done. Settling into the seat more comfortably, he put the truck in park and reached for his CD case.

It was times like this that Mike was glad he had bought a truck with some amenities. Popping in a CD, he prepared for the wait. Traffic jams had become a way of life in the months following Katrina. Everyone wanted to either rebuild or renovate their homes. For the past month he had been working between two separate jobs at two different houses on the same block. One was a cabinetry job in a half million dollar home in the exclusive SeaCrest residential area. He'd finished that one earlier that morning. The other was a contract job for a local company he had hooked up with for extra work. The latter had taken longer than expected because the woman of the house couldn't decide what color to stick with. After measuring twice, Mike had put in two carpets and she had yet to be satisfied. Although it meant more money for him, Mike hated the waste.

His thoughts moved on to other matters. He still did not understand what had made him take Athena Miles from the club to his home. He never brought women back to his house, not even the ones he dated.

He had met her at the office of his friend's brother-in-law, but he never would have expected to see the young put-together woman he saw like that in the club, especially one in that part of town.

He had always been a sucker for a woman in need, he thought to himself, smiling a wolfish grin. A dark frown replaced it as he thought about the uptight young woman. Her hasty exit the next morning from his bed might have been funny, but that look on her face had taken all the mirth out of the situation, had made Mike feel as if he were some kind of pervert rather than a good Samaritan. He hadn't expected her to cut and run as she had. So much for some appreciation for helping her out, and more importantly, missing out on his bed and sleeping on the couch.

Despite the hardship, Mike still did not regret taking her home with him. He had seen the way some of the men in the club were checking her out like wolves at a buffet where she was the appetizer, entree, and dessert all in one. He hadn't seen anyone with her, and there was no way that he could leave her in that situation.

As the cars began to move again, he pressed on the gas, eager to get to bed. He hadn't been able to go back to sleep after Athena made the forty-yard dash into the cab Saturday morning. Not because he wasn't tired, but because he had run out his front door without his keys, locking himself out. It took him an hour before he was finally able to climb the fire escape and work his way through the upstairs window and back into his apartment. He'd nearly broken his neck in the process, and he had no one other than Athena "I-don't-know-how-to-say-thank-you" Miles to blame.

As a matter of fact, the more he thought about it the angrier he got.

By the time he had made it back into his apartment all he had time for was to pull on some clothes and his shoes and then jump in his truck to head out to his first job of the day. Then he'd swung by his second one to put in some hours stripping carpet before he headed back for his weekend gig at Claudette's. He was a little late, but his friend and bandmate, Rick, had someone to fill in for him on stage. It wasn't until Sunday morning that he was free to return home, which was the cause for his being stuck in traffic once again.

At the ringing of his phone, Mike absently reached for it. Not recognizing the number he flipped it open. "Mike Thibodeaux," he spoke in a firm voice.

"Mike, I've got a problem," his work buddy said into the phone.

"When don't you have a problem, Ben?" Mike said back to him, wishing he hadn't even answered the phone.

Not that he didn't like Ben, but he knew at this time of the morning it could only mean one thing.

"No, seriously, man," Ben said, pausing only long enough to catch a breath. "You remember that house we did two weeks ago with that bitchin' deck?"

Mike didn't bother to answer that he remembered; he just waited for the punchline that seemed to have a running theme in his life—no sleep for him.

"Well, they had a really bad storm a few weeks ago and guess what?" Pause. "That lawyer guy, you remember how we told him to go over it with the varnish, since he didn't want to pay us to do it? Well, he didn't and now it has streaked something awful. I need your help, buddy."

"Man, I don't know, I'm existing on fumes right now," Mike said, interrupting his pleading.

Ben added, "He's willing to pay extra because he needs it done for next weekend. I promise two, three, hours top."

Mike knew this was a lie, but he could tell his friend was desperate. Ben had recently gotten married to a woman with three kids, two dogs, three cats, and five birds. Even though he had never been happier, he was paying out money hand over fist and was always looking for work. Mike didn't really need the extra work, but he agreed, figuring it would buy him some extra studio time.

After getting Ben to admit that it would take longer than three hours, Mike put him out of his misery and made his way over to the work site, which was outside the city once again. During the next four hours, Mike had to reroute the two children who poked their heads out the back door every thirty minutes. Getting tired of the distraction, Mike went into the house to find their mother, who was supposed to be watching them, and ask for a little help.

Unfortunately, that made the situation worse. It seemed the lady of the house was a little bored and decided he might stir up a little fun. After she popped her head out the door for the fifth time with an offer of some food or drink, Ben couldn't hold back any longer.

"Man, what did you say to her?"

Mike stopped what he was doing for a beat, "I didn't say anything except ask her to please keep her kids inside." Then he began spreading on varnish again.

"Come on, Mike, you had to have done something, because, man, she's looking like she could eat you up. I know that look. It's been a while, but that's the same look my wife hooked me with."

"Well, she's already got a husband, and that's all that needs to be said." Mike moved to the other side of the deck, away from the door.

He wasn't about to lose this job for getting too friendly with the wife while her husband was away. This wasn't the first time something like this had happened. He had this effect on many women. As a matter of fact, Mike couldn't think of the last time a woman had not responded to his dark looks. Except for Athena Miles, who it seemed couldn't be paid to give him the time of day. Just thinking about Athena, Mike couldn't help smiling at her buttoned-up image. If he had the time, he wouldn't mind loosening some of those over-starched clothes.

After finishing with the stain and varnish on the deck, Mike jumped in his truck, leaving the cleanup and the whole maintenance spiel to Ben. Making his way home, Mike got caught up in the afternoon Sunday church traffic and decided not to make his usual stop at the diner for his daily lunch but instead go home for some much needed rest.

The next two days were his to do as he pleased, and Mike intended to put everything out of his mind, especially Athena and her prissy attitude.

As he drifted off to sleep, however, he couldn't help thinking about how infuriating it had been to watch her run away like she had.

Eight hours later, and feeling a lot more rested, Mike grabbed his regular morning booth in the back of the diner on Fifth Street. Normally at night he would sit at the counter, but he wanted a little more privacy tonight to read over a few things in a new contract he was considering taking on in Florida.

Although he hated to eat alone, he had done it enough in the past year to get used to it. After eating his bacon burger and fries, he laid out his papers again and began looking them over for the fifth time, looking for mistakes in the figures or the agreed upon assignment. Not seeing any, his eyes drifted to the window and the scene outside. It was sprinkling, and he watched as the light rain gathered in little puddles on the hood of his truck and then ran in rivulets down the sides. Sighing, he looked at his watch, then picked up his papers, surrendering his booth for its next customer. He walked up to the waitress at the counter and pulled out a few bills. Waiting patiently for his change, he leaned his entire six-feet-and-some-change length against the counter. The waitress smiled brightly at him. Thinking to himself that he hadn't noticed her before, Mike commented on her nice smile. It was the kind of smile his aunt used to give to him despite whatever trouble he had just gotten into, which was a regular thing.

As a kid he was always breaking something just to see how it worked. She usually didn't mind as long as he put it back the way he found it. That skill had helped him a lot in his chosen profession. He probably could have gone to a trade school and done well, but school had never really appealed to Mike. He spent the years most kids were in college playing guitar in various bands, bouncing around the country from gig to gig. He had played in most of the blues dives from Louisiana to St. Louis and beyond, and he had loved every minute of it, although he didn't have a lot to show for it. He had recently settled in Biloxi and was able to make a decent living off the other skills he'd picked up along the way. It was in Houston that he'd learned cabinetry during the year and half he lived there playing the guitar in a good old honky-tonk band. Then in New Orleans he'd had a gig for two years playing saxophone, and there he'd learned all about masonry and carpentry. In between the laborers and the musicians he had learned from, he felt he had gained enough knowledge for six degrees.

S. R. MADDOX

Still, at the age of thirty-three he also realized that it was time to find a spot of his own and stop the nomadic lifestyle he had going. That was why he had bought the duplex he was currently in, to get a sense of permanency.

Through the jobs he had gotten through various friends, he had established a pretty good name for himself for skilled labor jobs in the mansions that had sprung up all along the Gulf Coast and on the outskirts after Katrina. Although music was still very important to him, he no longer relied on it to pay the rent. However, it was the reason he found himself burning the candle at both ends, trying to build his savings account while pleasing his band at the same time, who were still searching for their big break.

As the waitress handed him his change he took a look at her name tag. Holding her hand in his for a second longer than necessary he introduced himself and said, "I'll see you next time, Rita."

As he turned away from the counter she responded saucily, "I'll be waiting, shug."

Seemingly oblivious to the fact that he had just made a new fan for life, Mike sauntered out the door with his folded papers and jumped into his truck, headed to the club for his ten o'clock gig.

CHAPTER 9

"EEE! EEE! EEE!"

Slapping at the alarm clock for the second time, Athena rolled over to the center of the bed. Opening one eye, she saw that it was only 6:15. She was so tired and could really do with ten more minutes, but thinking of all she had to do, Athena dragged herself to the side of the bed.

Taking her first step onto the carpet, Athena caught a glimpse of herself in the mirror and shook her head at the sight of her backside.

"Yeah, I have got to hit the gym," Athena said out loud as she walked towards the bathroom making a mental note to pack a bag to meet Mel later for their bi-weekly workouts. They had been pretty regular for the past couple of weeks, but Athena was still waiting for the results.

After taking a shower and styling her hair in record time, Athena selected her clothing. It really couldn't be called a selection considering all she had to choose from was black, navy, white, and beige in plain styles. However, considering her decision to try to at least act as if she were interested in appealing to the opposite sex, Athena wished for the first time in a long time she had something cute to put on. "Black it is," Athena thought, selecting a black blouse, black tailored pants with a little lycra, and black shoes.

Athena scarfed down some cereal, then made a dash to her car to make the short trip downtown. Because she had a little extra time, Athena took the long route to work, meaning she stayed off Highway 90, crisscrossing her way through neighborhoods filled with green trees. The pretty neighborhoods made her a little more upbeat. After a quick stop at Starbucks she was ready for work.

Regent Way had been Athena's life ever since college. Her workplace was the one place that she felt most at home. In her college years she had put two summers in as an intern working in various mailrooms, running errands or filling in on administration jobs. Athena had watched other interns come and go. They found it too hard or too boring, but she always knew, even on her worst days as an intern, that no matter what, she could and would make it in the social program business. Helping people to help themselves was truly a passion for Athena. She believed it went all the way back to a church sermon Deacon John had given when she was still wearing patent leather shoes. He had preached the need for self-sufficiency in a changing world but also the need to extend a helping hand. His final words had stuck with Athena and become her personal philosophy.

Deacon John had said, "If you give a man a fish, he can eat today, but if you teach that man to fish then he can eat forever."

Athena believed that was what she and her employees were doing at Regent—they were teaching people to fish so that they would no longer need help—or at least that was the goal. Sometimes, no matter what they did, the client chose not to accept that help. When that happened, even though it hurt Athena to do it, she was the first to turn them away.

However, they also had some great success stories, their biggest being Shelly Ryans, or SheLe, as she was known to her fans.

Shelly's mother was a former drug addict when Athena first met her, back before she became administrative head of Regent Way. Shelly's mother had come to Athena's office in worn clothing, towing her ten-year-old daughter behind her. The two had been running from domestic violence and Athena had set them up with a social worker and several agencies to help them get on their feet. She had even dipped into her personal finances to help them. Athena learned very quickly that Mrs. Ryans was determined not to become dependent on anything or anyone ever again. Athena respected that, but at the same time she hated the idea of the little girl wanting. Even at the age of ten Athena knew the girl was something special. However, it took the world another six years to discover it.

At sixteen the onetime quiet teenager had become a hot musical talent. Once Athena and Trey Lister heard her sing, they swung into action. However, before Trey could even get contract papers for the teenager signed, legitimate record companies edged him out.

Athena and Trey had no hard feelings about it, however. Considering their background, Athena could not blame Mrs. Ryan and Shelly for making the most of their opportunities. In any event, the two had never forgotten their roots, and had done a lot to improve their old neighborhood, as well as making numerous donations to Regent. Athena was still amazed whenever she turned on the television and saw Shelly. She couldn't help remembering her as the little girl who used to steal jelly beans off her desk when she thought Athena wasn't looking and contrasting her with the poised young woman whose ambition had propelled her to international fame. It was enough to keep Athena going through even the toughest days, knowing she could actually make a difference in someone's life.

Her mother called her a workaholic. "You know it's going to catch up to you one day." Although she hated to admit it sometimes, some days Athena thought it already had. Although she loved her job, the feeling that something was missing had become more and more persistent. She hated to admit it, but Sheree, Mel and worst of all, her mother, might have a point. Maybe it was time for her to settle down, have a couple of kids. Become an adult.

Waking up alone was getting old, but the alternative, Athena thought, was probably just as disappointing. She wanted the love of a lifetime or no one at all. Hell, if she just wanted a warm body to occupy the other half of her bed she would have stayed with Kendrick. There just weren't too many men of substance who could satisfy her requirements. Being a control freak with a slight case of over-achieve-itis could do that to a girl.

"You've got to slow down," her doctor had said during her last visit two months earlier. "Your blood pressure is up, and you are showing signs of stress."

Athena had been on her way into work when her heart had started racing and her vision had blurred. Unable to continue the remaining three blocks to the office, Athena had pulled off the road onto a side street and lay curled in her seat. It had taken a good fifteen minutes of deep breathing before she was calm enough to call in to work. Even then she didn't tell Twila she wasn't coming in. She had just told them she would be a little late.

When she staggered into the hospital emergency room thirty minutes later, wet with sweat and gasping for air, Athena was treated immediately because they thought she was having a heart attack. Athena did, too, until the doctor diagnosed her as having a panic attack.

Athena had denied it until it happened again a few days later and she ended up right back in the hospital. This time she demanded they test to find out what was physically wrong with her. After the tests showed that nothing was wrong with her that a few weeks vacation couldn't cure, Athena vowed to do whatever it took to not have to see the inside of the emergency room again. It was soon after that visit that Athena scheduled a two-week vacation.

Athena never told her family or friends about the two episodes. They were already harassing her about her late hours and long work weeks, and she didn't want to give them any more ammunition. Especially since she'd had to cancel that vacation, and had yet to reschedule. Something just always came up.

Besides, there was no way she could duck out on her staff with the fall fundraisers coming up—not to mention the annual Christmas drive and ball. No, cutting back was not an option, at least not right now, no matter how much fun it would be to float down a river in a canoe with a dark-eyed, smooth-talking man—even if only in her dreams.

After checking her makeup, Athena put away her compact as the elevator doors opened. Even though the calendar said spring, it was already feeling more like summer—another blessing and curse of the South, year-round humidity.

Luckily Athena had a shawl around her waist that she could use to cover her shoulders once inside the club, where the air-conditioner would be set most likely below sixty-five. Athena briefly wondered what people had done before air-conditioning. Despite being a native she, like her fellow Southerners, did not tolerate heat well. In fact, in most homes Athena knew the A/C ran 365 days a year just to maintain a sense of homeostasis due to the unpredictability of the weather. Like most of her fellow brethren, she wouldn't trade the heat for anything.

Considering the other option of blizzards and power outages during the middle of a snowstorm, Athena would take the hurricanes and frizzy hair any day—at least with those she had a warning beforehand and could get the hell out of Dodge if she chose.

Walking into the Cadillac Lounge Athena noticed how her dress moved over her body. It even felt looser. Joining Mel at the gym was making a tremendous difference both physically and mentally. The dreams about her and Mike had even stopped and Athena was getting a full night's rest.

Athena heard her phone ring and knew instantly it had to be Mel.

"I'm here," Athena whispered into the phone before closing it. Searching the crowded club, Athena looked toward the stage and saw Mel standing there swinging her arms.

Walking closer, Athena saw Shaundra with her hand hiding her face. Athena could tell by her friend's slouch she was not happy. Athena waved at Mel, hoping it would make her friend stop her antics, but of course she continued to make a spectacle of herself, determined to make Athena pay for her lateness.

Athena briefly felt sorry for Shaundra, who was principal and owner of one of the most exclusive private elementary schools in Biloxi. She prided herself on maintaining the highest standards. Mel had met Shaundra ten years earlier when she first moved back to Biloxi. Back then Shaundra was not known for her dignified composure. A transplant from Chicago, Shaundra had a body made for trouble.

Both Shaundra and Mel had once been heavy into the night scene, closing out the clubs every weekend and

S. R. MADDOX

some week nights. However, in the past six years she'd married, earned a doctorate degree, and given birth to two children. Shaundra now projected a much different image than she had in her younger years. She still had a fierce sense of humor and an adventurous spirit that Athena admired, but Shaundra now expressed it mainly through the creativity with which she ran her school.

The Cadillac was one of the first places Shaundra had insisted on introducing Mel and Athena to when they were still low on money. The club had evolved since then to cater to those with bigger bank accounts. Now its patrons were mostly young black professionals who had moved to the Coast with their BAs and MBAs hoping to get in on the booming growth and limitless opportunities since Hurricane Katrina.

As far back as Athena could remember, the Cadillac had always been the best place to hear live music, which was the real reason she and her friends were there. Mel had been bragging about her boyfriend's band for the past couple of months, and Athena had also heard some really good things about them. Even her secretary, Twila, had raved about Thunder Road, Ricky's band, this morning when she heard Athena was going to see them.

As soon as Athena reached the table, Shaundra leaned over for a hug . Of course, Mel, who had taken a seat and abandoned her gesturing, just sat there.

"'Thena, it has been entirely too long since we saw each other," Shaundra said, smiling as she sat back in her seat.

Ignoring Mel's behavior, Athena replied, "I know. Have you and the good doctor added any more children to the fold?"

"Girl, it has not been that long," Shaundra said, trying to keep the smile off her face.

"Well, you've been such a hermit lately, I half expected you were going to skip out on us again," Mel said, fixing her gaze on Shaundra. "Not that I really care. If you want to dry up in that posh new subdivision on the hill that's fine with me. But when all the other little children start calling your son Norman, then I want you to forget my number."

"Whatever," Shaundra said back to Mel, then called the waitress over to take their orders. Patting Athena on the back, Shaundra smiled. "We've been waiting for you to get here before we ordered. Are you hungry?"

"Starving, but I'm not going to go crazy," Athena said, looking at the menu. "We've been going to the gym trying to get sexy, you know," she added, gesturing to Mel.

"Girl, please, I'm already sexy." Mel popped her gum. "And my sexy self wants some ribs, which I'm gonna get."

Once the waitress left, Shaundra leaned over to speak in Athena's ear, "How have you been doing? You know that you have to check in with your girls from time to time."

"I talked to you both yesterday," Athena said, taking a deep breath. She really was not in the mood for a replay of her recent exploits—not tonight. For one night Athena did not want to even think about her problems.

She just wanted good food, good music, and good company, although looking over at Mel, she began to wonder if it was possible. She didn't know what was wrong with Mel, but she would be damned if she would put up with her attitude for much longer.

"Yeah, you did, but that was after I left you two messages," Shaundra said with a laugh, although Athena could see it bothered her, which immediately made her feel bad.

Looking at both of them, Athena regretted not staying in closer touch with her oldest friends, but was not quite ready to admit even to herself that she just had not been feeling like talking to anyone. It was just easier that way. It seemed that lately she had been stacking up secrets, and it was hard keeping them all straight.

"Well, I'm apologizing now, and I'm here now. I'm ready to let loose, and you two witches had best keep up, because it's been too long since I kicked my heels up with my girls." Athena turned away when Mel just looked at her with a knowing expression. Thankfully she didn't get the chance to say anything about her adventure last weekend because the waitress returned with their order.

She filled their table with finger foods that each picked over as the warm-up band tried its best to keep the crowd interested. They were not faring too well. When the lead singer launched into some drawn-out poetry, Athena's mind drifted.

"You're looking sharp in that ensemble, girl, looking all businesswoman-like. Did you just come from work?" Mel asked before sipping on her rum and Coke.

"No, I did not come from work, I was going for high class tonight." Athena leaned back in her seat, not wanting to get into it with Mel. She didn't know what had gotten into her friend but she was getting on her last nerve.

"Oh, I thought you were going for uptight," Mel responded.

Athena was about to return fire when Shaundra shushed them both, which it was not like her to do. Feeling like a kindergartner Ms. Shaundra had caught eating glue, Athena glared at Mel as the house lights dimmed.

Feeling a change in the energy of the room, Athena sat back, not wanting to miss out on something special. She would find out what was going on with Mel later. The energy level began to rise in the room as a group of men in black suits walked onstage.

If they could quiet a room simply by their presence, Athena thought to herself, they must be able to do even more amazing things once they actually got started. Several of the men, Athena saw, were wearing fedoras or sportsboy caps, shielding their faces. Nonetheless, Athena picked Mel's boyfriend Ricky out of the group as he sat behind the drum set. With his broad shoulders and muscles that no jacket could hide, pretty Ricky would stand out in any crowd, even with a paper sack over his head.

Looking away from the glare of his shiny head, Athena turned to Mel, who was now beaming with pride. Suddenly she understood why her friend was so punchy. Crossing her fingers, Athena prayed that at the end of the performance she'd have something good to say because she knew that if she even attempted to lie Mel would catch her, and nothing good would come of it.

Draining her glass, Athena found that her mouth was still a little dry. If it weren't for Mel tapping the table next to her glass, Athena probably would have ordered another, but at her friend's reminder she ordered a bottled water when the waitress returned.

"Thirsty, are we?" Mel said, then leaned in closer to Shaundra, because even she knew there was a time and place for her loud-ass voice.

"This is them," she said to Shaundra, who had not yet met the mountain that was Ricky.

Shaundra smiled and gave a thumbs-up. Adjusting her red shawl over her shoulders, Athena noticed for the first time that Shaundra was definitely not wearing her usual garb. Although she'd always had a great figure, since starting a family, she no longer attempted to show it off. However, tonight she had on a sleeveless red dress that hit midthigh, which was the reason for the shawl, and she was even wearing makeup. Although it was a little surprising, Athena was happy to see a return of the Shaundra she knew from '98 when they first met.

"So you gonna jump him tonight?" Mel asked as the waitress walked away.

"What the—?" Athena gasped, choking. This was not what one asked Shaundra. Not reformed sinner Shaundra.

Athena was even more shocked when Shaundra responded, "If he's lucky."

Athena felt as if she had stepped into the Twilight Zone. Turning to Mel, Athena shook her head to warn Mel, who was smiling broadly at Athena's open mouth and big eyes, to stop.

"What have you done to her?" Athena mouthed over the sounds of the band as they warmed up their instruments. Mel's only response was to turn towards the stage and take a long sip of her drink as the show began.

The waitress put another plate of hot wings in front of Athena and despite her vow to watch her diet, Athena blindly reached for the glistening wings, trying to make sense of the last few minutes.

"You better close your mouth before you catch some flies," Mel said lazily before giggling once more.

That was when Athena realized that this night was definitely going to be the last night of the good girls. As the lights faded to black and the show began, she had a lot of catching up to do. Patting her almost full stomach, Athena reached in the dark to the plate and popped a fry in her mouth. Swiping at her lap and the front of her jacket with a napkin, she made a mental note to check her face when the lights come back on. The last thing she needed was to have smears of hot sauce on her face messing up her attempt at makeup.

"These guys are the best. That's why I asked you to come here tonight," Mel said in a hushed voice.

"The lead singer is amazing," Athena heard Shaundra say with awe. Athena could tell by the catch in her voice that he must be the reason for Shaundra and Mel's earlier exchange.

Mel had told her on the phone that Shaundra and she had attended a couple of shows together. From the expression on Shaundra's face, Athena had a feeling that there was more going on than just her liking his voice. Looking to the stage, Athena tried to get a look at the brother who had Shaundra all out of character, but when the guitarist took his solo, all thoughts about Shaundra and her mystery man vanished.

It was him!

It was the man that Athena had picked out weeks ago in the Who Dat sampler, she was sure of it.

Just then the lights took on an eerie blue glow, giving the club an even more intimate feel. No longer able to make out any band member's features, Athena closed her eyes as she listened to the intro of a beautiful rendition of Sam Cooke's "Change Is Gonna Come" by the guitarist, who had moved on to the saxophone. Opening her eyes, Athena was transfixed by his easy transition to a new instrument.

She was beginning to get irritated that she couldn't see his face. She wanted to make a connection somehow. However, admiration won out as the tall, lean figure at center stage enveloped the room in a sensual sound that swayed every soul present.

Although she had no clue as to who he was, Athena couldn't help thinking that something about him felt familiar. Athena looked forward to after the show when she could meet the man who had her working hard to keep herself from melting in her seat.

The songs that followed were a mixture of `50s and `60s hits with a couple of originals thrown in between. During the rest of the set, there was enough light for her to see that the five-member band was a virtual rainbow coalition. All that was missing was the Indian chief in headdress, Athena thought, laughing to herself.

It was rare to find this level of talent, and Athena could barely contain her excitement. It brought back the old days when she was heavy into the music scene. Never a musician herself, she had a great appreciation for those talented enough to create and perform in a way that spoke to people. It had been her dream to bring such people to the forefront. She had done it once, but since then her life had made a complete one-eighty. Still, the desire was there. She could tell it was by the rapid beat of her heart. She was glad "the rapid beating" was for a totally different reason than a panic attack. These were the artists that a talent manager or producer lived for. Although Athena was no longer in the business, her senses were ringing loud and clear. Now if she could just get backstage to pass them Trey's card . . .

CHAPTER 10

The band closed with an Otis Redding song, "Security," a melody so sweet that the crowd was literally begging for more, especially when the saxophonist put down his instrument and picked up a guitar again to rock it out during his solo. It was obvious he was feeling it as his hips swayed. He had Athena rethinking that old tale that white men had no rhythm.

Athena shook herself to clear her head when she realized the MC was on stage and the band was packing up. Noticing both Mel and Shaudra had grabbed their purses and were rising from their seats, Athena immediately cleared away her dirty thoughts about Mr. Saxophone Man. She had never gone there before, and was not about to go there now. Besides, she needed to focus on getting backstage. Business was business after all, and she had to follow through for Trey. Still, Shaundra had to repeat herself twice before Athena realized she was talking to her.

"Ready?" Shaundra said, leaning in closer so that Athena could hear her over the cheering audience. Athena grabbed her bag. She was about to tell them to meet her up front so that she could slip backstage for a minute when she noticed Mel and Shaundra were not walking in the direction of the exit, but towards the side of the stage.

"Athena, you don't mind going back for a few minutes, do you?"

Wiping the sides of her mouth, Athena tried to keep her cool. She was finally going to get to meet the man who had been haunting her CD player for the past weeks. Athena knew she was tripping but she couldn't help the fan in her that was catching the vapors for the guitarist with the magical fingers.

"Naw, girl, no problem at all," Athena responded, trying to keep her cool. She followed her two best friends behind the curtain, not letting on how excited she was.

"I just wanted to tell my boo bye before I leave him to all of these groupies," Mel said, giving the evil eye to one chick in particular wearing a white skintight minidress. She was in the corridor leading to the dressing rooms.

Showtime, Athena thought as her eyes adjusted to the darkness. Athena knew she was going to have to bring her A game, yet at the same time not appear too anxious or pushy.

So whichever member had been appointed leader, because there was always one, Athena would pitch Trey to represent them. Of course she would first work her way through the others because not gaining the consent of each one was not an option. Athena knew to lose even one would affect the sound and feel of the group.

Shaundra smiled at the large man at the end of the hallway. Athena assumed he had to be the bouncer by his size and scowl. There wasn't much room left between the walls and the man's humongous arms. However, once he saw Shaundra, recognition obliterated the scowl he was wearing.

"Hey, Ms. Shaundra," the big man said, like a big kid greeting his teacher at Kmart. He did his best to stand to one side to let her pass.

Shaundra patted his massive shoulder, then passed through the door he held open for her. It was amazing to see, but Shaundra actually had some pull. Mel and Athena followed Shaundra.

"How often do you and Shaundra come here?" Athena asked Mel. She was slightly irritated when Mel only shrugged her shoulders. Athena didn't know if she liked being on the other side of the secrets that were floating around, and for a moment forgot about her own agenda.

Making a note to talk with Shaundra later about her recent escapades with Mel, Athena followed both into another shorter hallway. Athena had been backstage at the Cadillac numerous times, but this was the first time she had seen what was behind these particular doors.

There were some drinks set up and some bags of unopened chips on the tables. The walls were painted a horrid puke green. Placing her card holder in her jacket pocket, Athena continued looking around the room for any signs of life. Spotting a mirror on the wall, she immediately walked over to check for hot sauce and smooth out her clothes and hair. Mel came up behind her to look at her in the mirror.

"We are going back to meet Shaundra's new man, not yours, wench," Mel said.

"He is not my new man," Shaundra smiled.

Ignoring her goofy smile for the moment, Athena turned to Mel. "For your information, wench," she drawled in the same sarcastic manner, "I was checking for crumbs before I met Trey Lister's newest clients."

"What?" Mel blinked a few times. "Are you for real?" she said, beginning to smile broadly. Brushing Athena's shoulders, Mel added, "Well, girl, do your thing. Ricky is going to be so happy. They were good, weren't they?"

For the first time, Athena really looked at her friend. *She really likes this dude.* Athena had never seen Mel this excited for a man. Moreover, excitement was over his success at something, not his looks, or money, or what he did for her. Smiling at her friend's happiness, Athena turned to Shaundra, who was now primping in the mirror.

"Excuse me, Ms. Devereaux," Athena said, walking behind Shaundra, unable to pass. "Excuse me, Blanche," Athena said again, this time using their code name for when something was about to jump off, "but it is almost midnight. Isn't it a school night?"

"Well, I thought you wanted to meet the guys," Shaundra said, finally turning from her reflection.

"The guys?" Athena mocked. "When did they become the 'guys'?"

"Look," Mel said, stepping between the two women. "Let Shaundra lead on this one, 'Thena. There'll be another time to fill you in."

Turning back to Shaundra, Mel added, "Look, it is a school night so let's just hurry up and introduce Athena."

Over the past few weeks Mel had been talking about Ricky wanting to get a label deal, and about his song-writing and his ideas for producing music. Athena knew that Ricky was interested in working a deal, but apparently not all of his band members were exactly sure. It was times like this that she wished that she was still in the game. Although she played it straight for her job as health care administrator, her love was still music. She would love nothing more than to help these talented men live their dreams, but for now she had to settle for just being the intermediary. She might not get them to the top, but she could have a hand in hooking them up with Trey, who had built up a name for himself in the Southeast as the go-to guy for up and coming musical acts. If a group or singer was hot, then Trey knew about them and was the man to go to with deal in hand. Athena was sure that he could do something for these guys.

Shaundra took the lead once more and knocked three times on the door.

The door squealed open and smoke billowed out of the room. Through the haze of smoke, Athena saw the figures of three very tall men. Shaundra immediately walked up to the one Athena recognized from the stage as the lead singer, who immediately embraced her in a big hug, which Shaundra returned with a big bear hug of her own.

Mel wasted no time finding Ricky and climbing onto his lap. Which left Athena staring into the smiling face of the last person she ever wanted to see again.

"Well, hello there," Marcus, the pervert, said.

Athena felt sick suddenly. She was conflicted. Although she wanted to slap his face for what he'd done at Mel's dinner party, she could not afford to show out in front of someone who was obviously in with the band. At least not yet.

Walking to the opposite side of the room to stand next to Shaundra, Athena immediately noticed the reason for Shaundra's fascination. Apparently, all six feet of the object of her desire was just as taken with Shaundra, considering it took several minutes for either to notice Athena's presence.

Once they finally did, she was thankful that he had the good manners to match the handsome package, although she was disturbed over what this meant for her friend's marriage.

Now this has to be the leader, she thought, pushing aside her negative feelings as dollar signs began dancing in her head, blocking out what looked like a burgeoning inappropriate affair. After all, business was business, and Shaundra was a grown woman.

"Good evening," the giant of a man said. "I'm Gregory." He took Athena's hand into his. For a moment she thought that she owed Mel big time. With this guy as the lead singer, with his smooth voice and even smoother personality, there was no way they wouldn't make it. America would eat him up.

Just then the door pushed into Athena as a short mass of attitude bumped into her and then planted itself firmly between Athena and Gregory.

"Are you ready yet?" the midget said, looking at Athena's hand still enveloped in Gregory's much bigger one.

Athena wondered momentarily who had let this little pointy-eared kid in. However, when the rude little person turned to her, she could see that the person was a she and most definitely not a child.

Gregory all of a sudden had nothing to say as all three women waited for his response.

"Uh yeah," Gregory said in a high-pitched voice. "Let me just grab my stuff." As Gregory made a quick turn-around in search of his "stuff," the imp turned on Athena with the most evil little eyes she had ever seen. Although she didn't say a word, Athena caught the gist of what her look said, which was, "Mine."

Athena would have pointed at Shaundra, but not wanting to draw out the scene any longer than necessary she kept her mouth closed and just stood there praying the little pixie didn't use her leprechaun powers on her as she watched Gregory scurry about finding his belongings.

It was at that moment that Athena remembered the reason she declined to get involved with musicians: She refused to be out in a club at two in the morning hunting her man down and fending off the women who were enamored from a steamy song or two and emboldened by alcohol.

As Gregory left with his better half, he said his good-byes, and even had the nerve to wink in Shaundra's direction, obviously out of view of his woman as he closed the door behind him.

For a moment Athena wavered on going further because she could sense messiness on the horizon with Mr. "Deep Voice" Gregory at the helm. Nonetheless, Athena decided to at least attempt to meet the three remaining members just to see what, if anything, was salvageable. They were just too good to pass on.

Seeing that Mel was still in deep conversation with Ricky, Athena recruited Shaundra to get the introductions. Following her out back into the greenroom, they crossed to another door that had two gold stars on it. Not knocking this time, Shaundra led Athena into yet another room full of smoke. As the smoke cleared Athena was able to see four guilty figures move apart. Not wanting to interrupt, Athena started to turn around, pulling Shaundra with her, reminding herself not to enter doors with double stars on them ever again. That's when she heard, "Hey, Shaundra."

Since when did Shaundra become such a regular? Athena wondered when she recognized the two men as two more members of the group.

Athena automatically moved to the side as the men walked by carrying a large equipment case on their shoulders. Shaundra and Athena followed them.

Shaundra introduced the two young men as Gary, who played the piano, and Stamps, who played the bass, harmonica, and anything else put in front of him, according to him. They both seemed nice enough, Athena thought to herself as the two left to load their equipment in the van outside. Leaving Athena by herself, Shaundra ducked through the third door of the greenroom to use the bathroom.

A million and one questions swirled in Athena's head as she waited for Shaundra to return. However, looking at her watch, she doubted she would learn the answers to them all tonight. Besides, she had one more band member to meet before she would allow myself to go home and catch some sleep.

While waiting for Shaundra to return, Athena pulled her cell from her bag to check for messages. She was just about to hit redial when she felt a tap on her shoulder.

"Excuse me, miss," a man's voice said.

Athena immediately recognized the voice, bringing an automatic groan of disbelief to her lips.

CHAPTER 11

Not wanting to turn around, but not being able to avoid it, Athena prepared for the worse.

"Uh, excuse me, miss, I don't know who let you back here, but we need a little privacy." Athena looked up at the man fearfully. Even though she couldn't see his face, she already knew who it was.

The fedora hiding his dark brown eyes luckily impeded his view of her as well. Additionally, there was the distraction of the petite brunette next to him who was trying to get her hands inside his shirt. Athena groaned in frustration. Why did this have to happen now? Here?

The woman looked like the stereotypical groupie, hair teased out to the max and a short skirt, short shirt, and most likely, Athena thought, a short intellect to match. Watching his fascination with the woman's spilling cleavage, Athena didn't budge. Although it took a minute, he finally tilted back his hat to give her his full attention.

"You!" Mike said, suddenly taking in her full frame through squinted eyes.

If it weren't for their history, Athena would have laughed because his immediate double take was comical. At least she was memorable, Athena couldn't help thinking to herself as the woman at his side stopped gig-gling long enough to notice another person was in the room. As the woman swept her icy gaze over Athena from head to toe, Athena reformed her opinion.

This one is not as dumb as she looks. She felt more than a little slighted when the woman immediately returned her attention to Mike, obviously deciding that Athena was not much of a threat. Athena also turned her attention back to Mike, who was no longer looking pleased.

So Mike Thibodeaux was the fifth member of Thunder Road. Athena felt her face go hot again. Summoning her professional voice and ignoring the tightening feeling in her chest, Athena held out her hand, hoping it wasn't sweating too badly.

"Hello, I believe we've met. I'm Athena Miles. I work with Frank and Vincent," Athena added.

The woman at Mike's side immediately gasped, reaching out to shake Athena's hand, making the quickest turnaround Athena had ever seen.

The fact that Mike hadn't attempted to raise his hand from where it was resting over the young woman's shoulder had not escaped Athena's notice. Well, Athena thought, so much for forgive and forget.

Although she knew she shouldn't expect too much, considering her hasty exit from his place, Athena still hoped for the best. It was no time to be a coward. Extending her hand once again towards Mike, she added, "I'm so glad to get to see you again."

"Really?" Mike said, lifting one eyebrow, which Athena briefly admired because it was a trick she had yet to master. "From the way you ran out of my apartment last Saturday morning I can hardly believe it." The three of them were suspended in silence for a beat until Mike broke the spell with a wink and grin that belonged on a Wheaties box, finally taking her hand in his.

"Trudy, this is Athena; Athena, Trudy," Mike said by way of introduction. Athena ignored the little flash of anger at his attempt to embarrass her with his reminder of their night together.

"So, you two have met before?" Trudy asked, directing her question towards Athena.

"Briefly," Athena responded, not offering further explanation.

"Hey, Mike, where y'at?" Athena heard as Shaundra opened the door. Athena was glad for the distraction until she followed with, "Hey Mike, have you met my girl, Athena?"

Both Mike and Athena looked at each other for a moment as she willed him to not mention Saturday. Athena was shocked when Mike let her off the hook by replying, "Briefly," again with one eyebrow raised.

Suddenly Athena wanted to rip that eyebrow off hair by hair, regardless of what he might say. She was stunned at the amount of anger she felt towards the man, who seemed to enjoy taunting her.

Before turning away, Athena saw that Trudy had cemented herself to his side. She wanted to scream at her that she was not in the least bit interested in her man although Athena knew that was a lie to the biggest degree. Nonetheless, all of this man-claiming was beginning to make her head hurt. Between the bimbo and the militant midget earlier, Athena had lost her patience and wanted to put as much distance as possible between Mike and herself as quickly as she could.

Athena could kick herself for not having made the connection sooner. It was obvious that Thunder Road didn't need her help. They already had an in with Vincent and Frank via Mike. As a matter of fact, Athena would be surprised if they didn't have a deal already in the works. Now that she had found out Mike was involved with the band, Athena doubted there was anything she could say or do to woo the group for Trey. Oh well, Athena thought as she prepared to leave. She was just glad she hadn't said anything to Mel getting her hopes up.

As Shaundra and Athena walked into the long, dark hallway, Shaundra was stopped by the bouncer. He asked the same question most parents with school-age children asked her: "Could you help my child get in your school?" It was then that Athena understood Shaundra's earlier pull. The bouncer was yet another eager parent looking to get his child into the best school on the Coast. Athena couldn't blame him for trying.

Waiting for Shaundra, Athena saw Mike and Trudy huddled together in a corner so close they looked like they were sharing clothes. Trudy had herself wrapped around Mike's body tightly with one hand on his neck and the other only God knew where. Suddenly Mike looked up, catching Athena's stare. Before she had the chance to even think about looking embarrassed, he winked one dark eye at her.

Instantly pissed again, Athena yelled, "Get a room," and stomped away.

Athena could feel Shaundra's stare, but she refused to look in her direction. She knew she was behaving strangely, but the last thing she wanted was to discuss it. Besides, considering all that Athena had learned about Shaundra tonight, there was no way Shaundra could judge her for her outburst. Athena realized suddenly that her chest no longer felt like it was about to collapse from the pressure. As a matter of fact, Athena felt nothing but relief.

Although Mike made her lose her temper more than anyone else she knew, Athena also felt pumped afterwards. Hmm, go figure.

Waking up Thursday morning was a chore, and each creak her bones made as she stumbled from the bed reminded Athena that she was no longer twenty-one with the energy of Richard Simmons on crack.

Unfortunately for her, it was the day that she had set aside to corral her staff for brainstorming and updating on projects, which meant that she would need to find some small pocket of residual energy to keep the meeting on task and lively.

"All right kids," Athena said as her last manager arrived at the early morning meeting in Athena's office and sat in his seat, "what have you got?"

For the next hour her staff related what they had been working on and the progress made on some of the more involved projects of community outreach they had planned.

The staff was relatively small. Not including support staff, it totaled eleven program coordinators and various supervisors, all in their late twenties and midthirties. Considering how young the staff was, the amount of knowledge they had about social programs and people was surprising. It was their love for what they did that impressed Athena the most. It was that characteristic, she believed, that brought them so much success in changing lives. For that reason alone Athena thanked heaven daily for the good fortune to have such a capable and lively group of people to work with. Some would say too lively, but the energy that the staff brought to work every day made for a very creative environment. As a matter of fact, Athena couldn't think most days where she would be without each of them.

"So, tomorrow, Kwame and May are heading out to Houston to the Sora City Convention," Athena repeated, reading from her notes. "Shyann and Jack are headed to the Rhythmn and Blues Showcase up in Jackson. And if I am understanding correctly," she paused momentarily to make a note on her long list, "the remaining staff will be manning the phones for publicity spots for our upcoming fundraiser for Helen House."

Helen House was a pet project of Athena's. Housing after Hurricane Katrina had become so scarce, especially for their low income clients, that Athena had decided to open Helen House, which had the capacity to house families in a community-type atmosphere. The home had stayed full since opening five months earlier, providing housing for at risk families in emergency situations. Overall, it was the one project that remained at the top of Athena's list for her attention.

Looking up from her notes, Athena checked the faces smiling back at her to see if there were any additions. When there were none she ended the meeting and sat behind her desk, willing her head to stop throbbing. Reaching into her desk, Athena took out an Advil bottle and popped two pills as Twila walked in carrying her clipboard.

"Late night last night, mmm?" Twila asked, smiling as she sat down.

"No, getting old, I think," Athena responded, trying for a smile, but not quite making it.

"Oh please," Twila said, "if you're old that makes me ancient, and I plan to kick my heels up for at least the next twenty years before I even think about getting old."

"Well, if you had the headache I have, you'd think differently." Athena grimaced, taking another sip of water.

Twila balanced her clipboard on her crossed legs, then tilting her head to the side asked, "When was the last time you went to get a checkup?"

Athena lifted her eyes to Twila, feeling a little paranoid. Forcing herself to calm down and focus on Twila, Athena realized she must have missed something. "Huh?"

Not missing a beat, Twila repeated, "I said sometimes headaches are a sign you're dehydrated or you're not getting a balanced diet." When Athena looked from Twila to her water glass, then back to Twila, she added, "Maybe you're not getting enough vitamins?"

Athena smiled at her. "Well, my mother has been trying to get me to take Geritol."

"Oh no," Twila yelled.

Alarmed, Athena asked, "What's wrong with Geritol?"

"Nothing's wrong," Twila said, "if you want to get pregnant."

Bursting out laughing, Athena took another sip of water while Twila remained serious.

"Seriously, my sister's two best friends who hated each other both started taking Geritol to cut down on the number of vitamins they were consuming, and within weeks they were both pregnant. Now they're living in the country in a duplex, carpooling every day like the Stepford wives."

Athena doubted that Geritol was the cause of their situations. If anything, she suspected a lack of proper use of birth control. Birth control was not the problem for Athena since you had to have sex before you had to worry about an unplanned baby.

The closest Athena had come to sex was the hand job Marcus tried to get out of her, and getting pregnant was impossible from that experience unless poor hygiene and some magic sperm were involved. A wayward pregnancy was the least of her worries. Ready to change the subject, Athena sent Twila for the quarterly report, which killed the next few hours.

The rest of the day passed quickly and before Athena knew it the workday was over. When the phone rang about six Athena was tempted to let the answering machine get it, but decided to take care of the problem now rather than later. "Hello."

"What's up, what's up, what's up," Stacy, her wayward cousin, said in her best Martin Lawrence impersonation. Athena would have smiled at her old school joke if it weren't for the fact that she was still pissed at her for flaking out on her at the club and being MIA for the past few weeks.

Feeling her temper rise, Athena tried to calm herself before her headache returned.

"Hello," Stacy said again. "Are you going to say anything?"

"Hello, Stacy," Athena said through clenched teeth.

"Hello, Stacy," she said, imitating Athena's tight voice perfectly. "What's wrong? You can't talk? What? Is someone in your office?"

"No one is in my office."

"What's your problem?" Stacy said, trying to sound offended. Athena wanted to say, "Well for starters, what happened to you the other week? Why are you just now calling?" However, Athena swallowed hard and did what she always did, acted as if nothing was wrong.

"Nothing's wrong, Stacy," she said, taking another deep breath as she swiped at a smudge on her desktop, "it's just been a long day."

"I know what you mean," Stacy said, sighing loudly. "I was calling you, wondering what happened to you last week. I looked up and you were gone." Before Athena could respond, Stacy went on, "I couldn't believe you just left me like that. We were all waiting outside for you, and when you didn't show we finally caught a ride with Tony over to Thea's. Girl, Auntie Aileen put her foot in that macaroni."

"Really?" Athena asked, not trying to hide her disbelief at what she was hearing, especially since she was still not sure if Tony had played a part in her getting so trashed.

"Really. I mean, why would we leave you? You were our ride," Stacy said. "As a matter of fact, it took me until today to call because I thought maybe I had done something wrong for you to leave us like that. Then you didn't even bother to call and check to see if I had made it home. It made me wonder if I had offended you in some way."

Athena couldn't believe it. Stacy actually sounded hurt, which was not common for her. She sounded so concerned that Athena found herself apologizing.

It was true that she had not thought about something having happened to Stacy, causing her to be unable to call. So in a sense she was just as wrong as Stacy in that she hadn't checked on her; that just wasn't what family did to one another. Instantly, Athena heard her mother's voice in her head saying that family had to stick up for one another. She had been getting that speech since she was ten, when Stacy and her mom had first come to live with them.

"Girl, you ain't got to say you sorry," Stacy said with a smile in her voice. "We fam, right?"

"Right," Athena said without hesitation, knowing that she had done the right thing to let it drop.

"But you had fun that night, right?" Stacy said, not giving Athena a chance to really respond. "We gonna have to do that again soon."

Before she could respond, Stacy filled in the pause, as usual.

"Tony was looking good that night, wasn't he? He had on his suit and everything," Stacy said. She paused long enough to take a breath. "You know, he asked me to move to Memphis with him."

"What? Say that again."

"Athena, girl, you heard me. He wants me and the kids to move with him to Memphis. He asked me to marry him and everything."

Not knowing what to say, Athena said nothing.

"What? You don't like Tony?" Stacy refused to let Athena get by without a response.

"No, it's not that," Athena said carefully. "I don't know Tony."

"Well you met him, didn't you?" Stacy refused to accept her nonanswer.

"I guess he seemed like a nice guy," Athena said, forced into a corner.

"Exactly. I wish you would call my momma and tell her that," Stacy said.

Athena immediately knew where this was going. Stacy's mom must have not taken too kindly to Tony's marriage proposal, which was completely understandable. As usual, Stacy was trying to get someone to cosign with her bad decisions. From previous experiences Athena knew that Stacy was as good as gone to Memphis in her mind. She had moved from Florida to Atlanta to Biloxi following a man, and three years later she still had not learned anything more.

Stacy's two sons were ten and eight and her daughter was just turning two. All of them had seen enough babysitters and boyfriends come and go in an endless cycle to have most adults' heads spinning. Yet Stacy was unable to see, or unwilling to see, how what she was doing was affecting them. After the last time Stacy had done this, her mother had threatened to call DHS and file for the children to come live with her.

Despite Stacy's dragging her children all over the country and dropping them off at a moment's notice to go to the newest club opening, she refused to give them up, even if it was in their best interest. Athena knew that Stacy loved her kids, but still didn't know if maybe they would be better off away from her.

"Athena, could you do me a favor?" Stacy began.

Athena could feel her head begin to swim again.

"Could you call my mom and tell her that Tony is a good guy?"

Athena wanted so badly to hold it in and keep it together. But the beginning pain in her chest and her conscience would not let her do it. Too much had built up.

"No," Athena said calmly.

"What did you say?" Stacy asked into the phone in disbelief that her cousin had actually said no.

"I said no. I can't do it this time, Stacy."

"You can't do it *this* time," Stacy said, mocking Athena's tone. "What do you mean you can't do it *this* time? Like I'm always asking you for stuff."

Letting her last statement go despite her obviously skewed grasp on reality, Athena continued. "Stacy," she said, trying to remain calm and stay true to her desire to help, "this may not be the best thing to do right now. You can't keep dragging your kids around and leaving them with people. You have to think about your kids. We don't even have family in Memphis."

Cutting Athena off, Stacy yelled into the phone, "I am always thinking about my kids. Who are you to tell me that I don't know how to raise my kids? Everyone always has an opinion about what I should be doing, how I should be acting. Let you be out here alone and see how you would do with them. But no, you sit up in your big office looking down on me."

Stunned at the acid dripping from Stacy's words, Athena tried to interrupt Stacy before she said something she would regret, but Stacy continued to talk.

"Who are you to judge me?" Stacy asked. "I can raise my kids perfectly fine despite what anyone has to say, and there is no way anyone is taking them away, you hear me? Besides, you should be happy that I let you take care of my kids sometimes, like you have anything better to do."

Stunned, Athena stared at the phone in her hand in disbelief at the insults her cousin hurled at her. However, she immediately snapped back when she heard Stacy repeatedly yell "bitch" into the phone.

Although they'd had arguments in the past, neither had ever called one another that. Later, Athena would say something in her snapped. Call it a recall of her run-in with Celina, but before she knew it, Athena had let go of what she thought about Stacy's ways, her boyfriend Tony, and the fact that she considered Athena her personal babysitter. Athena told her what she thought about her and her three baby daddies, and even touched on the state of public education in America today, which was when Stacy finally hung up the phone.

"Ask me if I care," Athena huffed out loud to her empty office.

She wouldn't bother to wait for a call of apology that Stacy usually followed up with after a tiff. Considering this was much worse than any other argument, Athena knew the wait would be much longer than a few hours.

Grabbing her bag, Athena stomped all the way to her car in the parking garage. By the time she had gotten on the freeway she was still hot, and all of it was directed at Stacy. It was because of her ability to sympathize with Stacy that she had allowed her to walk all over her all of these years. That made Stacy's current situation harder to witness, because now that Stacy's mother had finally gotten it together, Stacy seemed to be picking up right where her mother had left off.

CHAPTER 12

Athena breathed a sigh of relief at having made it to work without seriously maiming herself. She had already bumped her head once and her knee twice, all before she got in the shower. Dragging herself into the office, Athena avoided her coworkers, which was not her normal start to the day. She just couldn't handle dealing with anyone just yet. Athena had ended her mother's phone call just as she pulled into her parking slot. Her mother had called her shortly after Athena had left home, making her drive into work the longest twenty minutes of her life. Apparently her crazy cousin had called her own mother, who had gotten upset and in turn called Aileen.

"Athena, what were you thinking?" Aileen said in lieu of a greeting.

"Well, good morning to you too," Athena answered, sensing this would be one of *those* calls. One where the guilt would be spread thick, and she would end up apologizing and agreeing to do whatever her mother wanted. Settling into her car seat, Athena tried her best to mentally prepare herself, but nothing could have prepared her for what her mother said next.

"Athena, is it true you had a one night stand with a ditch digger?"

What the hell? Her sense of humor chose that moment to show itself, which was not the appropriate time.

"So you think this is funny, Athena Miles," her mother said between Athena's giggles. "You think this is acceptable; it is not. I will not have a daughter of mine embarrass me with some fling."

Unsure what her mother was talking about, she noted the hysteria rising in her perpetually perky mother. Only Athena and other close family members knew how the Southern Honeybee could pitch a fit, and Athena could tell by her mother's rising voice that she had gathered all the necessary tools.

"Athena, you listen to me," Aileen huffed. "Whatever you have going on with this ditch digger needs to stop now."

Uh-oh, Athena thought, the jig was up. Despite the number of years she had lived on the Coast, Athena forgot just how small it was. Nothing ever stayed hidden for long. She didn't know how much her mother knew but she knew it had to be damning for her mother to bother with a call this early in the morning.

"Stacy told her mother that you left her stranded at some god-awful nightclub to sneak out the back with a greasy-haired day laborer."

Athena understood suddenly. This was Stacy getting back at her for not agreeing to do her bidding. Athena was surprised at the tactic, although not at Stacy's retribution.

Athena hadn't realized Stacy had seen her, although that changed the whole situation. That meant that Stacy had seen how messed up she was that night and instead of helping her had let some stranger take her home. Athena hadn't thought her opinion of Stacy could sink any lower but it did.

"Mother," Athena interrupted. When Aileen did not stop her tirade, Athena tried again. "Mother, I know you probably heard some disturbing things, but let me assure you that nothing happened." Athena knew the best tactic was to stay calm and not feed into her mother's rant, but as her mother continued ignoring her comments, Athena began to feel that familiar throbbing in her temple. Uh-oh. She had to get off the phone and quick before she said something both would regret. Her track record of late had not been so great when it came to saying the right thing.

"You know how you are, Athena. You let people walk all over you, and this person you have let into your life is just going to use your kindness against you. What could he possibly want otherwise?"

Yes, Athena thought, *what could he want, other than me, perhaps?* Athena realized how silly that might sound to her mother's ears, but why shouldn't he? Not that she wanted anything from him. Athena felt a flash of something. Why shouldn't he want her? Did her own mother find her to be so unattractive that she couldn't imagine even a day laborer would find her attractive? *Well, damn.*

"Athena, you need to wise up," Aileen said in her winding-up tone, the same one she used as she closed out her television specials encouraging the audience to buy some product or use extra sprinkles or whatever. Athena could tell her mother was through with the subject, but she couldn't let it go.

"So, you don't think it's a good idea for me to date Mike?"

"Date?" Aileen yelled, "Who said anything about dating? I don't care who this guy is. Athena Miles, you end it and end it now. It is not acceptable."

"Okay," Athena said as she reached for her purse for her iPhone. As her mother continued talking, Athena tuned her out and scrolled through the phone book pages. When she finally hung up with her mother, Athena looked at the red circle on the screen. Apparently Mike had a listing in the white pages. *Hmmm, interesting.*

Outside her office Athena saw Twila busy on the phone so she quickly waved a greeting, glad to not have to say anything just yet. She still had not gotten over her mother's words.

As Athena got closer to the conference room, she was surprised to hear several loud voices coming from behind the door.

Noticing that the door was slightly ajar, Athena pushed the door all the way open. Inside, three young women lounged on the furniture.

All were attractively dressed in the latest hip-hop fashions only women under twenty-five could get away with wearing. They had also made themselves very comfortable. Not speaking, Athena slowly crossed the room, waiting for the girls to see her. Walking to the table, Athena pushed the feet of the boldest one off the tabletop.

"You know, some people actually use this for work," Athena said, not smiling.

"Imagine that," the young woman said, smiling back from behind a pair of dark owlish shades that covered half of her petite face. "Some people just don't know no better," she finished in a husky voice.

Pulling the girl out of her chair, Athena ignored her protest, waving a hand towards a chair on the other side of the table. Athena took a sip of her coffee, Twila came running in, having heard the younger woman's outburst.

"Oh, I didn't know anyone was back here," Twila said, apologizing to Athena as she openly glared at the young woman, not recognizing the famous face beneath the cap she wore.

Sitting down, Athena said, "It's okay, Twila," as Twila apologized again for the slipup. Athena assured her that calling security was not necessary.

"So to what do I owe this pleasure?" Athena said, brushing nonexistent dirt from a few papers where feet had recently rested.

"Quit trippin', girl. You knew I was coming."

"No, I didn't," Athena said to the young woman she viewed more as a little sister than a client after the long history they had shared. It was only because of this that Athena didn't bother to hide the bad attitude she was currently feeling. "You weren't on my schedule."

"Yes, I was, 'cause I checked about fifteen minutes ago when I first came in here. Look there. My name is in your handwriting, mind you."

Athena glanced at her appointment book where she had written in Shelly's name herself. It had been over a month since she had last talked to her protégée, yet she was surprised she had forgotten it. She had become the girl's mentor from the day she had begun helping her and her mother. They had an understood appointment once a month via phone at the very least to catch up with one another. However, three months ago, Shelly had called her to let her know she would be in town at this time, and they had scheduled a face-to-face meeting. Athena was surprised she had forgotten about it. It just wasn't like her to do that, especially since she actually liked Shelly.

Shelly, or SheLe, as she was known to her numerous fans around the world, had been with Athena from almost the very beginning of Regent's opening, and she always looked forward to seeing the young woman as she breezed through on tour stops in her hometown.

Each time she saw her, Athena was amazed at the changes she had made and the smart businesswoman she had evolved into. However, looking at her now sitting in front of her with a baseball cap covering her usually stylish coif, fresh-faced without need of makeup, she looked like the little girl she'd met seven years ago.

Embarrassed, Athena immediately apologized for her tardiness, and stood to look in her cabinet for the paperwork she had asked Shelly to come in and fill out. Shelly had agreed to perform a few numbers for their fundraiser next month. Fumbling for a minute or two, Athena sat back down in her chair and looked up to find Shelly and her two friends, whose names she could not remember, with confused faces.

"What?"

Silently the three young women just stared at her with their mouths hanging open. Wondering if she had sprouted horns, Athena just stared right back at them.

"What happened to you? Why are you acting so strange?"

"I don't know what you mean," Athena said to Shelly a little too quickly.

"Usually when I come in here, you are so together and prepared. But now you just—you didn't even know I was coming in. Now that just ain't right. You can't still be trippin' about that Delilah chick."

Athena forced herself to smile through the memory. "Of course not." After getting off the phone with Aileen and having her all in her business, not to mention what her cousin Stacy had laid on her the night before, Athena did not need a reminder of the sad state of affairs from a young multimillionaire. "Everything is perfect," Athena lied. Athena wanted nothing more than to change the subject and get Shelly and her hip-hop friends out of there as soon as possible. However, Shelly wasn't having it.

"No, really. What's wrong?" Shelly said with concern in her voice. "You can tell me. What? You about to get fired? Just say the word and I'll go tell them that if you go, I go." Shelly was no fool, and was willing to throw her significant top-selling record weight around for a good cause.

"Shelly, they are not about to fire me. I'm the boss, remember?" Athena said, laughing, flattered by her loyalty.

"Well," Shelly paused for dramatic effect, which she had always been good at, "why do you look like that?"

Athena's first response was to say, 'Look like what?' But she stopped herself, not knowing if she would like the answer. "Let's just drop it, nothing is wrong," Athena said, trying to get everyone back on track. Pushing the pen towards Shelly, she said, "Now all you have to do is read over this," Athena gestured to a page of the contract, "and sign at the bottom of each paragraph."

Shelly was having none of that. She was concerned and she wanted answers. "I mean, you never have been a fashion queen," Shelly continued, ignoring Athena's request.

"Thanks," Athena said sarcastically, realizing that Shelly was not going to let it drop.

Not stopping, Shelly continued, "But you have never looked this bad. Your hair, your clothes, but even more than that, you just look sad. Your eyes look sad."

Talk about her hair and clothes she could handle, but the part about her sad eyes got to her. She hadn't given herself much time to think about it, not really wanting to, but the truth was that she did feel sad. Between her fight with Stacy the night before, the pressure from her sister and friends and their constant interference, and even Mike, she was feeling pretty run-down. Add to that the unpredictability of her panic attacks, and Athena was not having the best of months.

If she weren't trying so hard to keep everything together and hadn't gathered so many secrets in such a short period of time, she might be able to laugh Shelly's comment off, but right now she felt that things had begun to finally catch up to her. What she wanted more than ever was someone to talk to, who could make it all better, or at least act as a sounding board. Instead, she did what she always did, tried not to pay any attention to the lump that had now formed in her throat and was aching to come out. Maybe, just maybe, it might go away.

"Adapt and keep going and never let them see you sweat," her father had always told her whenever things got rough.

But now, sitting in her office of all places, Athena found that despite her best effort to control what she was feeling, her twenty-four-year old client had her almost in tears.

When Shelly got up and came around the desk and put her arm around Athena's shoulder, she lost it. The next half hour was a blur as Shelly directed one or the other of the young women to the kitchen for some bottled water, ice, and paper towels. She then ordered Athena to sit down on the couch and breathe into a bag while one of her girls blocked the door, daring anyone to enter.

By the time she had calmed herself, Athena was lying back on the couch with her feet elevated and a cold towel on her forehead as she sipped from a glass of ice water.

The absurdity of the situation was not lost on Athena. Even though she and Shelly had known each other for years, having a panic attack in front of a former client was not the best way to do business.

Athena had known Shelly since her tenth birthday and she had always been proud of how seriously the young girl took her career. However, Athena remembered a time when Shelly's bright future was threatened. She was still a teenager, and like most other teenagers expected to have a social life. That social life, unfortunately for her, was centered at the time on a boy named Raymond who had put her through so much drama that her life could have supplied at least a year's worth of Lifetime mini-movies.

Of course, her mom put had up a strong effort to keep her mind focused on her future, but a teenager in love was an unpredictable thing, and the reasoning went in one ear and out the other. In fact, everything was filtered through her "man" Raymond. Surprisingly, though, she did listen to one person—Athena.

Shelly had known Athena was in a stable relationship with Kendrick. Drama free, Athena's life in Shelly's eyes was a blueprint for what she wanted. She actually listened to what little bit of help Athena was able to offer from experience. Probably because there was not much of an age difference between them, Shelly had looked at Athena as a big sister, or at least a cool aunt. Now, some seven years later, it was Shelly's shoulder that Athena was leaning on for support or a kick in the pants, something to put the curtain back in place to cover up Athena, the fallen wizard.

"It's a guy, isn't it?"

"No," Athena said, then repeated herself once again because it sounded weak even to her. "Actually I don't know why I'm crying. I really have no reason to cry."

"There has to be a reason. But if you don't want to tell me right now, I'll understand," Shelly said in a grown-up voice. The patience and understanding coming from Shelly surprised Athena. For all her kidding around and occasional diva fits, she really had grown up. When had that happened? Like a proud mama hen, Athena wanted to call Twila, anyone, in to witness this occasion.

Then Shelly took a deep breath and said, "Look, I realize you might be feeling a little down, but, uh, there's no sense in looking as bad as you do."

"Aw, there she is. I was beginning to wonder where you had gone with all that niceness you were extending towards me."

"Anyway," Shelly said, blushing, "there is absolutely no way anyone in my presence is going to look like this."

"Who says I am going anywhere with you?"

"I came here to sign the papers," Shelly said to no one in particular, "but I think that a service day is in order."

"A service day?" Athena repeated as Shelly picked up her purse and looked at her two friends, who both wore wide grins showing their agreement.

"Yeah, a service day for us," Shelly continued to explain. "You know—like when you get your car serviced. You take care of it, take it to the mechanic and make sure that it's working properly. We are going to take care of ourselves with the essentials—manicure, pedicure, massage. As a matter of fact," she said, taking one more look at Athena's ensemble, " I think we might need to have the works done."

Athena didn't really know what the works were, but after about ten minutes of Shelley's selling her on the day, and then pointing out the need for a wardrobe makeover as well, Athena didn't have the heart to ruin the girl's fun. Looking in the mirror and seeing her untamed hair, smudged makeup, and stained clothes cemented the deal.

Although she didn't like being railroaded, Athena allowed them to take charge of the day. She figured it couldn't hurt, and since being pampered was not an everyday occurrence for her—wait, strike that—a nonexistent occurrence, Athena thought it was time for her to make a change.

Sometimes it took a ton of bricks to bring a change, and Athena decided to take a half day and allow herself to be serviced, for once.

Immediately after she agreed to go with Shelly and her friends, Athena found herself given a pair of shades to put over her eyes instantly making her a member of the crew. Taking them down the back stairwell to her waiting car, Shelly ordered her assistant/trainer/chef named Drama to take Athena's car home so she wouldn't have to worry about picking it up later.

Although Athena was not too keen on anyone associated with the word "drama" handling her baby, she decided to go with the flow. Besides, anyone who wore that many hats had to be capable of managing the ten miles of road it took to make it to her front door.

CHAPTER 13

By the time Shelly was through with Athena, they had hit every department store on the Coast. As soon as her feet stepped through her front door Athena dropped the bags of new outfits the girls had helped her to pick out and ran to the hallway mirror. Stepping in front of the mirror with her eyes closed, Athena made a quick wish that she still looked the same way she had when she had left the salon. Counting to three, Athena prayed for the best, then opened her eyes.

It took her three blinks before she believed her eyes and let loose with a yell that surprised even herself. After doing a 360 looking at her new 'do from all angles, she couldn't help letting loose a second time. Athena didn't know how long she stood at the mirror admiring her new cut that gave her once one-length shoulder-length hair layers that framed her face and accented now-visible cheekbones. With the subtle makeup job, Athena literally felt like a new person. She was about to run to her room with the rest of her bags to begin sorting all of her loot when she was interrupted by loud banging on her door.

Looking through her peephole first, Athena was surprised to see Hector's eye peeking back at her as if he were trying to see into her apartment. Opening the door, she let her next-door neighbor have it. "What's wrong with you, banging on the door like the police?" Athena didn't even try to control her anger over being startled.

"What's wrong with you?" Athena repeated when Hector just stood in her doorway staring back at her with a spoon in his hand.

"And what's with the spoon?" Seeing that Hector was not answering her, Athena turned her back to him and waited for him to follow, knowing from past experience there was absolutely no telling what crazy story Hector had to tell. She had gotten used to his rants at all hours of the night less than a month after she had bought the place years ago. In less than two weeks Athena had met and learned about everyone in Hector's family and immediate circle of friends.

From his lover of the moment to his one-legged mother in Puerto Rico, Hector could not hold water. However, despite Hector's inability to focus sometimes, Athena enjoyed him as a neighbor and friend, except when he got a little too involved in her love life or lack thereof. She already had a nagging little sister, she didn't need a nagging big sister as a next-door neighbor.

It wasn't until Athena made it into her kitchen and was sipping on a glass of cranberry juice that she realized Hector had not followed her. Walking back into her living room, she looked at the front door and saw it was closed. Athena was about to walk across the lawn to Hector's to demand he tell her what his problem was for startling her when she heard wheezing coming from the couch.

Looking over her shoulder she saw Hector reclining on her couch with one hand over his forehead and the other pointed at Athena. "Who, who?" Hector sounded like a constipated owl. "Who are you, and what have you done to my Athena?"

Although Athena tried her best to stay mad, she failed miserably, bursting out laughing at Hector and his sorry acting. Looking at him panting and remaining in character despite her tears of laughter, Athena had to give him his props. Giving him a round of applause, Athena added, "Bravo, bravo. Encore, encore," before taking a seat on the couch next to him.

Hector finally broke character and reached out a hand to touch Athena's now feathered hair, then the lapel of Athena's flowery baby blue blouse that hugged every curve she had tried to hide her entire life. It wasn't until he attempted to pat her cheek that she slapped his hand away.

Immediately drawing his hand back to cover his mouth in mock horror, Hector yelled, "Oh, my God, you're actually wearing makeup."

"I always wear makeup, you nut."

"Liar," Hector said in complete disbelief.

Athena took another sip of juice as Hector continued his inspection.

"Athena," Hector said, "you look absolutely stunning. Beautiful."

Moved by his words, Athena almost teared up because for once she actually felt it. Not necessarily just because of all the decoration she now had on the outside, but because she now felt that her outside matched how she'd always felt on the inside.

She now felt cute. And like every cute person there ever was, she wanted to show it off. Grabbing her bags and then Hector, Athena pulled him into the bedroom to give an impromptu fashion show, and Hector, being the true divo and good friend he was, stayed until he had paired each and every outfit with the perfect shoes, hose and accessories.

Friends are great to have, but every girl needs a true divo to dress her from time to time. A couple of hours later, after Hector had called for mercy, Athena listened to her messages. There was a call from Twila about a showcase that night for a group called Holistic Soul. Considering how good she felt and looked, she could not see keeping all her sexiness to herself. No, she needed to get out of the house tonight. She called Twila to say she would be joining her.

Taking Hector's advice to "show off the cuteness," Athena let Hector pick something out for her to wear that night, but she stopped short at his suggestion to go braless.

"Baby steps," Athena said repeatedly as she pushed him out the door, reminding him about his dog needing to go for a walk.

After he left, Athena jumped in the shower once more and dressed in the outfit Hector had laid out for her. Before she hopped in her car she stopped by Hector's as she'd promised to show him her final outfit. Knocking on the door, Athena could hear Elian barking. When the door swung open she saw nothing but blond hair and red fabric as she was embraced in a bear hug by Andrew, Hector's boyfriend.

"Oh, Athena," Andrew gushed, "you look wonderful. Do you feel wonderful? Because you look wonderful."

Although she didn't get to see Andrew as often as Hector, considering his busy work schedule, Athena liked him just as much. Where Hector was in your face, and sometimes a bit too honest, Andrew had tact and reminded you of your kindergarten teacher, always full of encouragement. They made an odd pairing, but it worked, considering they had been together going on ten years now. They had seen each other through Blue Blockers and fanny packs and still managed to stay together. They were an inspiration because if two people who were so different could compromise and form a relationship, it gave Athena hope of one day learning to open the door at least an inch wider for someone to step in past her defenses.

After Hector and Andrew gave their approval, Athena made her way to the Skylark Bar where the reception and showcase Twila had mentioned would be held. Not wanting to run the chance of sweating out her 'do, Athena chose to valet her car, even though she had promised herself ever since she and Mel had started their gym workouts that she would work to get in 10,000 steps a day, as Oprah's trainer said she should. Promising to make up for it later, Athena stepped out of her car as the valet driver held the door open for her. Smoothing her skirt, she did not notice the look of approval the young man gave her as she walked away, leaving a cloud of her perfume in her wake.

Entering the building, Athena noticed an attractive woman in a plum-colored outfit similar to the one she was wearing and found herself frowning before bursting out laughing. She was seeing herself in a mirror. Athena kept walking towards the club, hoping that Twila had saved her a seat.

"Hey," Athena said to Twila, immediately after spotting her and her fiancé sitting at a table towards the back of the room, center stage.

"Oh, this seat is saved," Twila said, automatically smiling in Athena's direction.

"Well, I hope that you saved me a seat somewhere," Athena said, surprised that her feelings were hurt. For a second she felt as if she were back in middle school and the popular girls were excluding her again.

Twila took a second look and then realized it was her boss, Athena. "Oh my goodness," Twila said, standing up to embrace Athena. "What have you done?" Twila said loudly, holding Athena's hand out.

Not wanting any more attention directed her way, considering there was a performance happening onstage, Athena sat down in the empty seat next to Twila, who also sat.

"You look amazing, Athena," Twila said, hitting her boyfriend. "Doesn't she look amazing." Her boyfriend barely got a head nod out before Twila turned back to Athena. "So is this what you did after disappearing from work?"

Athena nodded.

Giving her another hug, Twila told Athena again how good she looked. "I'm so glad you're here. Ever since I got here people have been coming up to the table dropping off these CDs and cards for Frank and Vincent. I told them that we're not a record company, but they won't leave me alone."

Looking at the table in front of Twila, Athena saw three neat piles of CDs, cards, and some notes written on what looked like napkins. Looking around the club, Athena tried to see if she recognized any of the faces as those of record producers, radio personalities, and other media types that usually attended these types of events.

"I don't know who half of these people are," Twila said, mirroring what Athena was thinking because she couldn't make out most of the folks in the crowd either. Considering that the Holistics were relatively unknown, she was surprised that the club was packed. There were even people lined up along the walls.

Looking at her watch, Athena realized that she had missed about twenty minutes of their set, so she wasn't surprised when the band began to close up.

Overall, what she saw didn't impress her, but she clapped to be polite. However, from the lackluster applause, Athena didn't believe anyone else was all that floored by the group either.

The MC came on stage and tried his best to pump up the crowd, who seemed to have lost their energy, if they ever had it. He did jokes for about ten minutes before he asked the crowd if they were ready for another act.

He got a slightly more enthusiastic response. Then he started listing some of the awards the next group had received and some of the original songs they had produced and the applause began to grow.

Athena recognized the names of a couple of the songs, but hoped that she was wrong about who was about to appear on stage. When the MC finally got around to saying the group's name, the crowd was literally screaming for the blues band and some were on their feet as the men began filing on stage.

Not wanting to look but not being able to stop herself, Athena stifled a groan when she saw that it was indeed Thunder Road. Athena sat back in her seat and thought, "Oh shit," and prayed that she could just make it through this night without completely embarrassing herself.

The show ended on a high note as the group finished with their own rendition of "Down Home Blues." Athena had to admit that she enjoyed the show just as much as the last time she had seen it, particularly Mike's performance. She was still attracted to Mike, but unfortunately they were like oil and water. No matter how many times she dreamed about black eyes and a speedo, it just was not going to happen. Still, she wondered why his phone number had been seared into her brain. She hadn't remembered a phone number since 1996 when she had gotten her first cell phone. Remembering his phone number was big—how big, Athena refused to think about.

After the band left the stage following three encores, Athena found herself in the center of a group of coworkers who had descended on her as soon as word spread about her transformation. Athena at first was flattered, but soon grew embarrassed by all the attention.

When it came down to it, she hadn't really changed. All that had changed was a little paint and polish, and the fawning kind of made Athena wonder about what they had all thought of her looks before the transformation. Had she been a hag then, but no one had bothered to tell her?

After getting bumped from one corner of the venue to another as people vied for her attention, Athena was glad to finally be clear of the crowd and able to watch from the side of the venue. Before long, some chairs and tables were cleared out of the crowded room and the space was set up as a makeshift dance floor. Then Frank pulled her onto the floor to dance to some salsa the DJ had put on.

When that song ended, Athena found herself paired with a Latino man, whose hands showed interest in getting to know her better during a slow dance. Athena had a workout trying to keep her partner's hands from straying too far south. His footwork was another story. She did her best to keep up.

After a couple of dances with some coworkers who did not challenge her as much, Athena returned to her table to cool down, only to see Twila gathering her stuff up.

"Athena, we're going to call it a night," Twila said, smiling at Athena.

"I hear you," Athena said, fanning herself. She'd had fun tonight, but she had to agree that it was time to turn in. "Let me just give my ticket to the valet."

Athena made her way to the valet counter. Handing her ticket to the lady behind the counter, Athena heard someone walk up behind her. Looking at the partition in front of her she froze when she saw the reflection in the glass.

Damn.

Taking a deep breath, Athena turned to see Mike grinning at her. However, before Athena could even speak, she heard a familiar voice to her right. Turning in the direction of her friend and mentor, Athena put a smile on her face.

"Bill," Athena exclaimed as he swept her into his arms for a hug.

"It's been a long time," Bill admonished, "too long. I barely recognized you. If it weren't for Lee, I wouldn't have noticed you."

"Lee is here?" Athena asked, referring to Bill's wife. She hadn't seen her in a while either, and wanted to say hello.

"Oh, she went outside to put her mother in the car. We finally got her to come out. It was her birthday and we tricked her into coming here. She loves that new group, Thunder," Bill said, muddling the name.

Amazed by the scope of the band's draw, considering Bill's mother-in-law was in her 70s, at least, Athena looked over Bill's shoulder and saw Mike still standing in the same spot, now smiling back at her. Athena wished that he would just leave, but realized there would be no such luck when he stepped forward to correct Bill's mistake.

"Thunder Road," Mike interjected.

Surprised by Mike's interruption, Bill finally noticed the younger man, and seconds later placed his face.

Reaching out a hand, Bill apologized and introduced himself and excitedly told Mike how much he'd enjoyed seeing them onstage.

The valet returned with Athena's car, and although she knew it was childish, she prepared to walk out with Bill and avoid Mike altogether. Although being rude went against her upbringing, Athena felt the need to get away fast.

"Bill, it was nice seeing you again," Athena said, reaching for his arm. However, her plan to cut and run was foiled by her friend Bill.

"Have you two met?" Bill asked, ever the gentlemen and businessman. Athena didn't respond, hoping that Mike would not embarrass her in front of her former colleague and mentor. Besides, she didn't know what to say.

"How could you forget someone you shared . . ." Mike began, but was interrupted by Athena before he could finish his sentence.

"Of course I remember you." Athena smiled broadly, clenching her hands to keep from strangling the man across from her.

"Yes, we share a similar love of music." Mike continued, "Athena came down to the Cadillac a few weeks ago and we met backstage. We exchanged cards but unfortunately I haven't contacted her since, which I deeply regret."

She tried not to stare openmouthed at Mike and his crazily eloquent lie about their last meeting.

"I have to say, it is a pleasure to meet you," Bill said to Mike, then turned towards Athena. "You would be very wise to catch this one." He winked and pointed at Mike.

Athena gasped, then saw that Mike was grinning at her. Athena dared not ask Bill to explain himself; she just prayed that the floor would swallow her whole. Glancing at Mike once more, she swallowed a curse, wanting nothing more than to smack the grin off his face.

Laughing to himself at his attempt at matchmaking, Bill hugged Athena once more, promising to stop by the office for lunch soon. Even though he had been retired for the last year, Bill still sat on the board of Regent, and kept a busy schedule. Athena felt honored that he would even consider going out of his way to have lunch with her, but she also knew that the topic of conversation was most likely going to include Thunder Road.

When Athena turned to find Twila, hoping to leave Mike to his games, he fell into step right beside her.

"Don't we look different tonight?" Mike said to Athena once they were out of range of other people.

"Look," Athena said, stopping abruptly and squaring off toe to toe with Mike. "I've had enough of the innuendos you keep throwing around. I'm sorry I left like I did that morning, I'm sorry I didn't thank you for helping me out, and I'm sorry that I didn't call to say I'm sorry. Okay?" Athena said, stopping long enough to let that sink in. Keeping her voice low, she added. "That means that you can stop playing your little games every time we run into each other. I don't know why every time I look up you're right there anyway, but I don't want to have to worry about you telling everyone that I stayed over at your apartment, because nothing happened."

Trying to control her breathing, Athena stopped and waited for Mike to respond, hoping that this would finally be the end and she could stop feeling tense every time he popped up. Looking up at Mike, she waited for his response, any response.

"First of all," Mike began, staring into Athena's eyes, "only little boys play games." He took a step closer to Athena.

Athena refused to take a step back, despite feeling the effect of being so close to Mike's much larger frame. Staring up at him with a challenge of her own, Athena waited for him to make his next move.

"Secondly," Mike said through tense lips, "I like your hair."

Athena blinked in confusion momentarily, before she recognized the wicked gleam in his eyes and the smirk that played over his full lips.

Athena wanted to kick him, to scream, but instead she turned and walked away. She made it all of five steps before Mike was at her side once again.

When she didn't stop or slow down, he moved to get in front of her, causing Athena to stop or bump into his broad chest, which to her shame she wanted more than anything. In order to not cause a bigger scene, Athena tried hard to calm her raging thoughts as she stood once again in front of Mike.

Judging from the fit of his clothing, she imagined walking into him would be like walking into a wall anyway, and ending up on her ass did not appeal to her. Especially since she was trying her damndest to be cute tonight.

"Look Athena," Mike began, "I am not trying to embarrass you."

Realizing he didn't have much time to win her over before she walked around him and away once more, Mike continued with, "I was just having a bit of fun."

Seeing Athena's jaw set even harder, he rushed to finish. "At your expense, and I know that it wasn't right. I admit I was angry when I saw you run out of my apartment as if I was some kind of rapist, but I understand in hindsight." Mike looked away for a moment, then added, "Look, I don't want you tense every time you see me. Despite how we started, I would like to try again, so that we are not going at each other like this every time we run into one another."

Athena looked into Mike's eyes and tried her best to see the lie in all that he said, but could only see heartfelt sincerity, or at least she hoped that's what she saw.

Holding out her hand, she said, "Agreed." Mike took her hand into his to shake and once again Athena was reminded of their initial meeting when she first noticed how rough his hands were.

"How do you play your instruments with your hands like that?" Athena couldn't help asking, despite their calling a truce.

Confused, but still smiling, Mike said, "Like what?" He looked at his hands, trying to figure out what Athena was talking about.

Holding his hands palms up, Athena gestured to the scabs and dry skin. "Like that. They're so rough."

"They're so rough," Mike mimicked, sounding more prissy then Athena had intended.

"I'm sorry," Athena apologized once again. Taking a deep breath she rolled her eyes. "I don't know why but every time I'm around you I say the wrong thing, do the wrong thing." She looked into Mike's eyes. "I'm not usually like this."

"Oh, don't tell me that," Mike said, smiling. "I like you like this."

Blinking, Athena was speechless for a moment. Taking Mike's hand in hers she couldn't help taking one more dig before he figured out how much he shook her up.

"Can you say Vaseline Intensive Care?" Then she walked away.

However, before she could make it two steps, Mike ruined her exit by growling, "Believe me, baby, I've never had any complaints before."

Athena didn't doubt that. But she was not like any of his other women and was about to tell him this when Twila spotted her and came over to drag her to where her boyfriend was standing impatiently.

Athena couldn't help looking over shoulder to where Mike had been standing. She was surprised he had yet to move. He waved a hand before disappearing into the crowd. In her mind, Athena was glad that they had resolved their issues and decided her mother just might be right—it was best to put Mike out of her mind. He was far too dangerous and besides, they really had nothing in common.

As she drove home that night she figured that if she ever did see Mike Thibodeaux again it would be across a smoky club, separated by a throng of willing women and a stage. That would keep her life just how she liked it—comfortable. However, as she drifted off to sleep alone in her king-sized bed, she couldn't help the regret she felt.

CHAPTER 14

Athena awoke abruptly as if a switch had been thrown and bing! She was up. Instantly the previous night flooded her racing mind and she couldn't help the smile that came with it. Just the thought of all the pretty clothes waiting for her made Athena beam with anticipation. Usually, the first thing Athena saw that was not stained and wrinkled would make the cut, but not this morning. She actually had a choice, and she was looking forward to opening her closet to pick an outfit from the new clothes now hanging inside. Before what she wore didn't matter as long as it projected with the image Athena had formed of herself as a capable executive and spoke of responsibility.

However, as she left her house dressed in a lime green skirt and jacket set with a floral top that accented the narrowness of her waist, plus the fierce alligator shoes that Hector had paired with the outfit, she was excited for a whole other reason.

Several of her coworkers participated in an unofficial fashion show every morning, wearing the latest fashions in an attempt to win the "best dressed" award daily. In the past Athena had never even acknowledged the competition. She felt as long as they looked like professionals, it didn't matter whether they shopped at Nieman Marcus or Kmart. Because she normally lived in beige, black, and navy, regardless of the season, Athena expected to get a little attention when she showed in a spring ensemble.

After getting a round of applause from her neighbor upon stepping out of her front door, Athena waved at Hector on her way to her car, as if she were Miss America. Because she was in such a good mood she even called out a greeting to Elian, who immediately lifted a leg and peed on the flowers she had planted last year.

Pulling into Regent's parking garage, Athena parked in her usual spot, but upon leaving her car she was stopped by a security guard that she had spoken to every morning for the last two years. Although the older man did not seem completely convinced Athena was who she said she was, he let her on the elevator, following behind her and talking the whole time. Once they reached her floor, Athena thought for a moment that he was going to actually follow her into her office, as he told her about his plan to retire in a few months.

"Really, Mr. Gutman," Athena asked stopping in the corridor. "Congratulations!"

As Mr. Gutman attempted to follow, Athena asked him if he had locked up his office at the bottom of the stairs. Reminded that he was still on the job, Mr. Gutman tipped his hat once more to Athena, then sputtered that he hoped to see her later.

"Looks like you have an admirer," Twila spoke from behind her.

Athena turned to her assistant. "I don't know what got into him," she said, walking with Twila towards her office. "That is the most words I have ever heard from him."

"Athena, I do believe he was willing to sign over his check to you, the way he was looking at you," Twila said, smiling the whole time. "As a matter of fact, he was looking at you like you were a lime and he was thirsty for some limeade."

Both Athena and Twila barely made it into her office before bursting out with laughter.

After calming themselves down, Athena and Twila sat down to start going through the day's agenda. By the time lunch rolled around, Athena had returned several calls she had received from people she'd run into the previous night. Many complimented her on her new makeover. She had one call from a man named Alexster she'd spoken briefly to at the club the night before and had given her card to. From the smoothness and deep timbre of his voice on her answering machine, she identified him as possibly calling for more reasons than just networking. She put his number aside, still not sure if she wanted to go there yet.

Picking up Alexster's note once again, Athena amended her earlier decision. Although she might not be ready to have a serious relationship, Athena decided that if he asked, one date couldn't hurt. She would definitely return his call.

After going out to a late lunch with Vincent and his assistant, Athena returned to the office to finish up some of the loose ends. She had kept to her plan to take in more greens and had only had a salad. She now regretted the decision as her stomach grumbled for something more. Slipping out of her jacket, Athena made herself comfortable on her couch in the corner and spread out several of her staff's agendas. Sipping on bottled water, she began the long process of checking in with some of her staff members who were out of the office on assignment and had called while she was out of the office. At three, Twila briefly stuck her head into Athena's office to remind her that she would be leaving early for a doctor's appointment. A little later Athena heard the door reopen and assumed that Twila must have forgotten something.

"Twila?" Athena called out to the foyer. Looking at her watch and noting it was after five, Athena continued, "Twila, can you make sure to lock the outer door when you leave?" She didn't want to be surprised by some wandering manager or client who might sneak past security into the upper offices despite the hours posted. At least twice a week without fail, someone, thinking Regent meant free money to any hard up person, would pop in demanding help for a light bill, rent, or even gas money. Usually they would get stopped by someone who realized that they did not belong there. However, every once in a while random people managed to roam the halls.

Still not getting a response, Athena cautiously stood, trying not to ruffle the papers that she had strewn all around her on the couch and the table. Then the heel of her brand new shoes caught on the rug and she found herself falling.

Unfortunately, as she stopped herself from getting hurt, she inadvertently pushed all of the papers on the couch and table into one big mess on the floor. Although they had been scattered about her while she was sitting, they had been organized. Looking at the pile on the floor, Athena let a curse rip, knowing it would take another thirty minutes to get them back in order.

Getting down on all fours, Athena began gathering the papers. Cursing at herself, and the time she was wasting, Athena bent down to reach under the couch where a message had lodged itself almost out of reach. That was when she heard someone knock. Imagining the picture she must be making, Athena prayed that her butt didn't look unflattering perched in the air and high-lighted in bright lime. Grabbing the paper, Athena raised herself back onto the couch, pushing her hair out of her eyes.

"Need some help?"

"No, I don't need your help," Athena said, standing up and walking towards Mike in the doorway. Looking over his shoulder, she saw that Twila's desk was empty and realized she'd have to deal with him on her own.

This was the first time that she and Mike had actually been alone. Heretofore there had been some interruption to keep them from exploring the tension between them. Athena never looked forward to confrontation, yet it seemed that every time she ran into Mike she felt her temper start to flare, and she had an unexplainable need to have the last word. More troubling, she enjoyed it entirely too much.

"Are you sure?" Mike said, looking at the big pile of crumpled papers that she had deposited on the table.

"Do you not need help, or do you just not need my help?" Mike asked with a knowing look.

Ignoring his question altogether, Athena walked to her desk to get her keys, planning to lock the outer office doors after she put Mike out. She decided to try friendliness and keep her temper in check, so she smiled at Mike as she approached him.

Seeing that Athena was going to leave his last comment alone, Mike asked, "What are you doing here so late?"

Keeping the smile on her face, Athena said, "Oh, I just had a few things to tie up. With tomorrow being Friday, I didn't want to wait until the last minute and find myself taking work home this weekend." As she went to the outer door, Mike followed, as she'd hoped.

"What? You gotta hot date this weekend?" Mike asked in a tone that Athena did not like too much. She stopped short to turn and look at him. Mike, who was right behind her, bumped into her, knocking her a couple of steps forward.

"Oh, I'm sorry," Mike apologized, grabbing Athena by the waist to stop her from falling for the second time this night. Her shoes, although cute, seemed to be hazardous. "Are you all right?"

"If you hadn't been all up on me I wouldn't have tripped," Athena said. When Mike's hands continued to rest in crook of her waist, she said, "I'm fine." After he finally let his hands drop, Athena pushed the door open for Mike to pass. "I'm going to be closing up soon. Were you looking for Vincent or Frank?" Athena said, assuming that Mike wanted to leave a message for one of them for the next day.

"No." Mike began smiling. "Actually I popped in to see you."

Stunned, Athena forced herself to listen. Though she had found him attractive before, she hadn't thought that it was mutual. Besides, attraction did not mean she wanted anything to happen with him. She had just earlier decided to possibly date.

Mike walked back into Athena's office, leaving Athena no choice but to follow him. "I'm sorry to stop by so late," Mike said, sounding more businesslike, "but I wanted to ask your opinion about a business matter."

Mike waited as Athena walked behind her desk and sat down. At his reference to business, she couldn't help being curious. She was a little disappointed but felt more in control now that the conversation was not turning romantic. Still, she did not like the feeling of being led around.

"What can I do for you?" Athena found herself asking, regretting her words when that sexy smirk appeared once again on his lips. Forcing herself not to respond, Athena rephrased her question. "How can I help you?"

Pulling a document from his jacket pocket, Mike opened it. "Last night before I left from the show," Mike began, "Frank approached me with a possible deal. Now I know you are his colleague, but I don't know much about the business end of producing records. I've always been in the studio or onstage and that was as far as it went for me. As long as I was paid, it was all cool." Mike turned more serious as he said, "But last night when I talked to some of my boys, they jumped at the opportunity to actually put a demo together, so I agreed to meet with Frank for lunch today."

Athena quickly remembered that Frank had been missing from their usual weekly lunch. Now she knew why.

"Well, I walk into lunch with Frank today," Mike continued, "and he pulls out a bunch of contracts and papers." Pulling another wad of documents from his pocket he started unfolding them. "I didn't realize how much went into getting a deal," Mike said with a lopsided grin that was both endearingly masculine and boyish at the same time. "Frank said I could take some time to look it over with a lawyer if I wanted to, but I have never had a lawyer," Mike said, laughing, "and I wouldn't know how to go about picking one either. I was hoping that you might help me out."

Athena badly wanted to ask, 'Why me?' The question was probably written all over her face.

"I came to you because after last night and our conversation, it seems like you really tell it like it is."

Thinking back on her comment about the lotion, Athena smiled.

Relaxing visibly, Mike said, "I know with you being a president and all you're really busy."

He said it comically, as if she went around boasting about her title. It made Athena laugh.

"But I hoped you could help me out this one time."

Lord, Athena thought, he is pushing all the right buttons. Briefly, she wondered if she was being conned. Between his ridiculous flattery and her own guilt over her past behavior, Athena found herself agreeing to take a look at Mike's papers.

As soon as Mike got her agreement, he stood up and got her jacket and said, "Great, I know a great restaurant that is quiet enough for us to talk and has great food. I haven't eaten all day and I'm starving."

Although Athena had no reason not to join Mike, she didn't know if she liked the new Mike, the polite one with the gentleman's demeanor. A girl could almost forget he was an asshole. Still, Athena had offered her help, and since there didn't seem to be any of Mike's usual taunting going on, Athena found herself agreeing.

After taking one last look at the pile of papers, Athena did something that shocked even her—she decided to leave them for the following morning and slipped into the jacket that Mike held for her. Then she locked up.

They took separate cars at Athena's suggestion. Even though he seemed to be on his best behavior, Athena wasn't quite ready to be in an enclosed space with Mike just yet. They agreed to meet at a restaurant that was a few blocks away. Parking on the street, in front of Luchesi's, Athena remembered an article she'd read a few weeks ago in the *Sun Herald* about great restaurants of Biloxi and this was one of them. She was surprised that this was where Mike was taking her, considering that they were very popular and seated by reservation only. Athena didn't really care where they ate, as long as it wasn't Thea's, which had been listed, not surprisingly, at the top of the local paper's list. He was probably still too new to the area to know about the hot spot, Athena thought with relief. Nonetheless, Luchesi's was the second nicest restaurant, and almost as hard to get a good seat. She rarely went in, but she knew of the family. How could she not? Every restaurant owner and wannabee owner had graced Thea's front steps to find a way to emulate what she had in hope of finding the same success. None so far had been quite that successful.

Walking up to the door, Athena hoped that with her new 'do no one recognized her. She really didn't want to talk about her family, especially her mother, in front of Mike, and it seemed that on the Coast anything food-related eventually led to her mother. She definitely did not want to find out that Mike was a fan of the Southern Honeybee. She liked him enough that she didn't want to have to compete with her mother's larger-than-life image. Regardless of where she went, when people found out who her mother was, it was no longer a conversation but an interview about the Honeybee.

After quickly deciding that if they were unable to be seated, she would gracefully bow out of the impromptu meeting and get back to him by phone, Athena was sur-prised to see Mike greeted warmly by the hostess. Despite their lack of a reservation, she immediately sat them in a corner of the restaurant with plenty of privacy, exactly what Athena dreaded. A waiter arrived, took their order, and left.

"Will you or won't you sign the contract?" Athena asked after she'd had a chance to glance over it, explaining the high and low points quickly.

"Yes," he said.

Before he could continue, Athena said, "Good, then you can just sign the letter of agreement and I can leave you to enjoy your meal."

"Yes," he said, adding, "I think."

Athena settled back into the plush booth seat.

The waiter arrived with their order, placed their food on the table with a flourish, and when he backed away, Athena imagined that she heard a "ding" go off in her mind. Sitting back in the pocket of the seat like a boxer, Athena sized up her opponent. However, her opponent was calmly eating his calamari. After getting a whiff of her pasta with shrimp and lobster alfredo sauce, Athena lost interest in anything that did not involve her fork and her plate.

Damn, Athena hated to lose her temper, but it seemed that whenever Mike was around she did it quickly and readily. He didn't even have to try to irritate her. Taking one of the buttered rolls from the bread basket, Athena tried to hold onto her frown despite the wonderful flavors that were popping in her mouth. However, after taking one bite of the toasty, buttered roll, she had to let it go. A low moan of appreciation erupted from her, which brought a sexy smile to Mike's lips.

"You like that, don't you?" Mike said in a deep voice, pleased at her visible sign of enjoyment.

"Mm-hmmm," was all Athena could manage. She closed her eyes and took one more bite, smiling because it had been such a long time since she had allowed herself bread. Mel had her on a crazy diet that was working in bringing back her muscles, but was depriving her of pleasure like this.

Looking up at Mike, who had put down his fork and was now looking at her intensely, Athena reached for her napkin, embarrassed. It was so wrong that she was enjoying her food so vocally. Wiping her mouth, she noticed that he was still staring at her.

"What?" Athena said after she had finished chewing.

Shaking his head as if he were trying to clear it, Mike said, "Nothing."

"No, what?" Athena wanted to know what was wrong. "Do I have something on my face?"

Mike looked at Athena's face and into her eyes for a moment too long before saying, "Nothing's wrong with your face at all."

Athena was thinking about Mike's last statement, feeling that she'd missed something, but the waiter returned and she decided to let it drop.

The waiter asked if they would like dessert, and Athena automatically declined. Besides, they had just about finished going through all the paperwork and it was getting late.

"But you have to get some dessert to end your date on a high note," the waiter said adamantly.

Athena wanted to tell the waiter that this wasn't a date, and that he needed to mind his own business, but when Mike began speaking, she decided to let him handle it.

"I think we will have something," Athena heard Mike saying. She was about to stop him, but he seemed so happy to be getting dessert that she just smiled back at him and waited for him to order.

"Well, order whatever you want," Athena said. "I'm stuffed." She sipped coffee and reached for some papers.

"There must be something that the missus would like."

Athena looked at the waiter, thinking, "You really need to mind your business."

"I think I know what the missus would like," Mike said, mocking the waiter and smiling at her. Ready for the waiter to be gone, Athena ignored Mike until he beckoned the waiter to bend down towards him.

"What in the world?" Athena said, laughing. Disbelieving that Mike was actually whispering in the waiter's ear, Athena was once again charmed by his playful side.

"So you think you know what I want," Athena said addressing Mike after the waiter hurried away with his order.

"I'm sure of it," Mike shot back, leaning back in his chair, challenging Athena.

"All right," Athena said, "let's bet."

Immediately interested, Mike leaned towards Athena. "Whatcha got?"

"Well," Athena said, smiling, and thinking about what the stakes should be. "If I don't like it, then you

have to build me a shelf for all of my CDs and records."
Athena smiled to herself because Mike had no clue as to
how big her CD collection was. She had taken to storing
her CDs in her basement in egg crates after she had filled
a closet and her pantry with them. Since he had described
himself as a master carpenter earlier, Athena decided to
take full advantage.

"Now what do you want?" Athena said, sounding like
a kid who was trying to trade lunches.

Mike sat up straight, smiling. "I want a kiss."

"What?" Athena said, sitting up straight in her chair.

"I said I want a kiss," Mike repeated.

"No," Athena said with a slight frown, not taking
Mike seriously.

"What, you can't hang?" Mike said, baiting her once
again.

"Look, I have to tell you that I never mix business
with pleasure."

"So you think what would happen between us would
be pleasurable."

"What?"

"Admit it."

"See, this is what I'm talking about. I don't get
involved with clients. We should be sitting here talking
over the specifics of your contract rather than what you
are suggesting."

"Bull."

"Bull?"

"Bull," Mike began, then added for clarification,
"shit."

"I don't think . . ."

"See, that's your problem. You think too much."

Athena felt her face getting hot, but stopped herself from negating what Mike had said. She hated that he always made her feel this way, especially since she had begun to enjoy his company. It would serve him right if he won, and that was a big if, and she could show him just how uninterested she was in him. Athena was sure a man as sexy as Mike was used to women throwing themselves at his feet. It would be fun to see the look on his face when she simply yawned. As a matter of fact, Athena thought to herself she might lose the bet on purpose just for that reason. Accepting the bet, Athena enjoyed Mike's surprised look when she agreed to his terms.

"Just one more thing," Mike said quickly, holding onto Athena's hand.

"Oh no, no amendments," Athena said, already thinking about her set of shelves and where she was going to put them.

"Yes," Mike said stubbornly, "you have to take a bite of the dessert."

"What?"

"That's the only way I'm going to be able to find out if you like it or not," Mike said, sitting back in his chair.

Doubting that, Athena said, "You think that you know me, huh?"

"I know what you sound like when you like something," Mike said suggestively. Then he added, "The way you enjoyed the meal earlier, I think I have a pretty good idea."

Still not convinced, Athena shook his hand once more on the rule change and sat back to wait on the dessert.

They both sat in silence until the waiter returned with a covered dish. Waiting until the waiter had left, Mike put his hand over the lid. "Now, remember the rules, one bite first." Nodding her head in agreement, Athena prepared herself to not laugh too loud in Mike's face after she'd won.

As Mike slowly removed the cover, Athena was surprised to see a bowl of the most beautiful banana pudding she had ever seen.

Closing her eyes, she willed herself to keep her face impassive. Looking up at Mike's expectant face, she said, "Banana pudding." It had to have been a lucky guess that he'd picked her most favorite dessert.

Mike just grinned and put the lid down. "One bite," he said, lifting that one irritating eyebrow.

Preparing herself, Athena picked up a spoon and stifled an inward groan when she dipped it into the firm yet soft cookie and banana pudding mixture.

"Bigger," Mike said when Athena tried to get by with eating just a bit at the tip of her spoon, "and get some bananas too."

Glaring at Mike, Athena got another spoonful. This time the fragrant, golden pudding spilled over the sides of the spoon. Putting the dessert into her mouth quickly, Athena tried her best not to react to the rich taste of the pudding that, God help her, was just as good, if not better than her Grandma Miles's.

Licking her lips and trying to just swallow without tasting, Athena felt her eyes closing as her taste buds popped. Before she knew what was happening she had let loose with a moan that even she hadn't heard in a long time, a moan that had the hairs on Mike's arm standing up. Once she had finally finished swallowing the dessert in her mouth, Athena opened her eyes to stare at Mike, who was looking at her with a mixture of awe and shock.

Smiling in amazement, Athena asked, "How did you know?"

At first he looked a little puzzled until she motioned to the dessert. He cleared his throat to say hoarsely, "Oh, you said a lot of things that night on the ride to my house, in the car, in the kitchen, on the bathroom floor, in the bed. One of those things was a little song about your grandma's banana pudding. I guess I just got lucky that my hunch was right, huh?" He added the last comment with a little wink.

Unfortunately, that wink just about did it for her temper, "Well, I'll have you know this is not my favorite. I doubt you know as much about me as you think you do. In fact, you know nothing."

Realizing her voice had risen quite a bit, she put down her spoon and took a sip of water. Lowering her voice, Athena leaned across the table towards him a little to make sure he heard what she had to say next.

"But let me tell you this," she said through her teeth. "This act, this whatever this is, is not going to happen."

"Act—what act?" he said, laughing.

"What you are trying to make happen between us. It's not."

"It's not what?"

"It's not going to happen," Athena said, tired of his game, whatever it was.

She sat in silence as he grabbed his spoon and took a bite of the pudding. Pausing for a second, enjoying the pudding, Mike said, "You know, you are a very high-strung woman." He smacked his lips. "Lucky for you, I like my women sassy." He laughed and took another big bite of pudding.

"Would there be anything else?" the waiter asked hesitantly as Athena openly glared at Mike.

"No, we're ready for the check," Athena answered. The waiter turned quickly to leave to get their bill, obviously not wanting to stay any longer than necessary.

Mike stared back at her for a moment and the tension that had all but disappeared between them earlier returned in a flash.

"What is not going to happen, Athena?" Mike said slowly.

"We are not going to get together—ever. The only relationship we will ever have is a business one, if that."

"From what I understand that won't happen unless I agree to do business with Vincent and Frank," Mike said plainly, "And I need your help—or I walk."

"What?" Athena asked.

Smiling, he just wiggled his eyebrows. Quickly, Athena stood to leave.

"Calm down, I'm just kidding," Mike said, suddenly serious as he held onto her wrist. "Please," Mike said apologetically.

Sitting down, Athena decided not to cause more of a scene then they already had.

"Look, Athena." Mike pushed the now empty dish to the side, and put his hands on the table. "I trust your opinion. I don't want to be a star. I'm not interested in worldwide tours or anything like that." Mike paused when he saw her skeptical look.

Laughing, he continued, "Now don't get me wrong. When I was younger it was a different thing, but now I'm a grown man. I know my time has passed. I enjoy the music, that's why I play. If I'm not heard outside the state of Mississippi, it makes no difference for me."

"That's all well and good, Mike," Athena said, shrugging her shoulders, "but I don't know how I fit in this."

"Even though I may not have big dreams for this group, some of my boys still do. Marcus is twenty-five and the other two are younger than him. Gregory is about my age but he still is playing the rock star game, wanting to make the girls scream. Either way, he's in it for what he can get for as long as he can get it."

Mike leaned in closer, trying to make his point. "What I'm trying to say is regardless of what I want, I don't want to destroy their chance of making it. I went after my dreams, I don't want to do anything to ruin theirs."

Athena had been ready for any explanation except this particular one. Mike had done the impossible and increased her level of respect for him, and that did not sit well with Athena. She wanted to continue thinking of him as some playboy no deeper than a puddle of water. No, she didn't like this one bit.

"Well, I don't know what you want me to say, but as far as signing with Vincent, I honestly cannot give you a reason not to after looking at the contract. However, you understand I'm by no means an insider." Athena paused, looking into Mike's eyes.

"No, no, I understand that," Mike said, putting down his napkin before taking another sip of water. "Still, I respect your opinion, Athena Miles."

After hearing Mike speak so passionately, and judging the sincerity in his voice to be true, Athena began to look at the situation as a business relationship. She wondered if she could help him in some way. Athena knew that Thunder Road was a rare find. They would have some success regardless of whether they went with Vincent or not.

"I understand your hesitancy, Athena," Mike said, looking into Athena's eyes, "but I promise you that if we agree to go with Vincent I won't hold it against you if it doesn't work out. I also promise there will be nothing but the most professional behavior, if that's what you want, after tonight."

It took only a few seconds for Athena to catch his meaning. She rolled her eyes. But she didn't want to ruin the temporary truce, so for the third time that night Athena and Mike shook on an uneasy partnership.

"We have just one more issue to cover," Mike said as Athena reached into her purse for her keys.

Looking up once she had her keys in her hands, she laughed.

"What now?" she said, not knowing if she could take much more tonight. She felt as if she had been on an emotional roller coaster. It seemed that way every time she was around Mike. All she wanted now was to go home and rest.

"Our bet," Mike said, smiling.

Athena burst out laughing, thinking Mike was playing again. When she looked at him closely, she realized he was serious.

"Oh shit," Athena said, "are you serious?"

It was Mike's turn to burst out laughing. When Athena looked at him strangely, he said, "You said *shit*."

Gathering her purse, Athena walked to the door with Mike close behind. Once they were out into the cool night air, Mike gently took her hand. "Look, I'm sorry. I don't know what it is about you, but it seems like every other minute I'm apologizing to you."

"That's because you're a jerk."

Mike just laughed at her comeback.

"I thought we had agreed this was going to be business only, completely professional."

"I said after tonight," Mike reminded her. He leaned in closer to her as they stopped at her car.

"Tonight's not over with yet." Then he leaned in closer still, giving Athena no time to brace herself for the touch of his lips to hers.

Athena could feel the stubble as he deepened the kiss, then gentled his pressure when she made no move to stop him. Athena could feel her bones melt as her head began to roll back into the cradle of Mike's hands.

When he finally pulled back, Athena noticed that his harsh breath matched her own. Surprised that her hands were now linked around his neck, Athena found herself shaking her head.

"Just as I thought," Mike began when Athena's phone began to play "Black Magic Woman."

"Oh, I have to take this," Athena said, still trying to clear her head. Mike backed off slightly as Athena tried to regain her composure.

Smiling, Mike said, "Okay, Athena. I'll stop by tomorrow to finish the paperwork, partner." Mike reached out his hand to shake hers.

"Good," Athena said after a beat, finally catching her breath. Getting into her car, Athena left Mike standing on the curb and pulled away. It took her three blocks before she realized her phone was still ringing.

"Hey," Athena said immediately into the phone, already knowing who it was. "What's up."

"Well, don't sound too excited to hear from your best friend," Mel said pretending offense.

Athena listened, distracted by what she was feeling. She didn't understand how one kiss could completely short-circuit her mind. For a minute there, she admitted to herself, her mind for once had been completely clear of all thought.

A known multitasker, Athena had never known a moment when she was not thinking about the long list of things that had been done, needed to be done, or had yet to be thought of to do.

Although it had been a while, Athena remembered that sex with her last boyfriend, Kendrick, had not completely quieted the constant litany of activities. In fact, that was what one of their final arguments had been about.

The phone had rung in the middle of sex and although she didn't answer it, Kendrick had figured correctly that her mind was more on the possibility of some new work development than his lovemaking.

Athena couldn't help thinking what it would be like with Mike. If just his kiss could stop the noise in her head and so focus her attention that the need to get closer was the only thing that filled her mind, what would it be like to actually make love with him?

CHAPTER 15

"Earth to Athena, earth to Athena."

Realizing that her friend was still talking to her, Athena snapped out of her thoughts. "Hey, I'm here."

"Girl, you must be really tired. Where you at?"

"I'm just on my way home."

"Don't tell me you're just now leaving work."

Deciding to let her think that, Athena changed the subject. "Mel, what are you doing on the phone with me? I thought you were supposed to be out with your honey."

"Girl, we have gone out, celebrated, eaten, come home, and celebrated again," Mel said with a smile in her voice, "if you know what I mean. And now he is doing what all men do, sleeping."

"Don't tell me you wore him out?"

"Girl, I rocked his world."

They both laughed until tears were coming out of their eyes. Glad to have something else to think about besides her new problem, Athena stayed on the phone all the way home. At her front door, Athena said good-bye to her friend.

It was past midnight. Not worrying about messages on the phone or the dishes in the sink from that morning, Athena pulled off her clothes and was asleep soon after her head hit the pillow. Her last thought was that she would put Mike and his tempting propositions behind her. Business, that was all that would be between them.

The next day at work, Athena made a concerted effort to forget about Mike and his deliberate effort to let her know of his interest. Since they had come to a truce, Athena was determined to maintain a business relationship, proving it by suggesting the band for the benefit party Regent had planned for next month.

By the end of the day Athena was more than ready to make her way home. She brought contracts home with her to keep her mind busy and off Mike and his obvious interest. As soon as she got home she stripped and took a long hot shower, then put on her favorite pj's, some cutoff jersey shorts and an old matching sweatshirt a` la Jennifer Beal in *Flashdance.* Shelly had forced her to buy several nightgowns and other lingerie, but she just couldn't imagine wearing that stuff for only herself.

When her doorbell rang, Athena grabbed for the money she had sitting on the television to give to the pizza delivery man. She had been looking forward to the supreme from her favorite Italian restaurant. Although she had been invited to celebrate with Mel and Ricky over the impending record deal, Athena had turned them down in favor of a much-needed night at home.

Athena didn't even bother to look through the peep-hole, making her more than surprised to see a visitor sans pizza.

"It's okay, I'm not dangerous," Mike said. He held a bottle of champagne up for her to see when she continued scowling at him.

"Well, you can just take that back."

"I promise you won't be ending up in any strange beds from this, not unless you want to." He wagged his eyebrows suggestively, in such an over-the-top manner that Athena had to laugh.

"Give it a rest," Athena said, suddenly wide awake, but not feeling like a fight right now. She just wanted her pizza.

"No, really," Mike said seriously, "I told you I would meet with you today to go over the contracts."

Athena was about to say that she didn't expect him to show up at her house when she saw the pizza man coming up her driveway. Why hadn't the pizza gotten here just a few minutes earlier? She paid the man and took the pizza. Athena closed the door, then looked for Mike, who had disappeared.

Glancing around her living room she spotted him sitting on her couch with the bottle in his lap. Following his line of vision, Athena saw that Mike was looking at the fireplace in the far corner of the living room. Music was softly playing from her speakers.

Mike asked, "Am I interrupting something?"

Slightly confused at first, Athena laughed finally, reassuring him that he was not interrupting anything that could not be finished later. "I was just looking over some work that I had no business bringing home with me in the first place. So the answer is no, you are not interrupting anything." She walked into the kitchen to put down the pizza.

Following her into the kitchen, he asked, "Where are your glasses?"

Recognizing the bottle as one of those that she had sent to Mel's party, she didn't bother asking how he had learned her address. Since Mel hadn't called with a heads-up, she decided not to worry about it until she was face to face with her.

"I thought since you were so nice to splurge for our celebration, you at least deserved to have a taste," Mike said, smiling.

Athena gave in, surprising even herself. Despite their inauspicious start, Athena found that she actually enjoyed Mike's company, which was saying a lot. She didn't enjoy the company of too many people, especially people who went out of their way to annoy her. Nonetheless, it was somehow different with Mike.

Athena pointed to the cabinet, and Mike reached in to get glasses. Despite all the back and forth they participated in, Athena couldn't help liking Mike. He was just a likable guy. However, looking at the dark curls on the top of his head, and the way his inky eyelashes framed the most intense eyes she had ever seen, she wasn't stupid enough to not realize she needed to be careful.

"One drink," Athena said, smiling back at Mike. This relationship was going to be strictly professional if it killed her.

"Just one glass?" Mike playfully whined. "You mean I don't get any pizza?"

Laughing, Athena reached into the box and picked out the smallest piece and gave it to Mike.

"Now that's cold," Mike said, laughing before taking one bite of the pizza and being left with only end crust.

"Come on, grab the box," Athena said as she got some plates, glasses, and a Coke from the refrigerator. Her mama didn't raise a fool, so she left the rest of the champagne in the fridge for some other time when she wasn't around temptation.

Mike bared his teeth in a big smile that was potent. Turning to walk into the living room Athena shook her head, wondering how it was that she was actually smiling about her former nemesis.

Sitting on the floor in front of the couch, they balanced plates in their laps. Athena turned on the TV and while they ate their way through the pizza, Mike asked a few questions about other thoughts Athena might have had about the contract. Athena admitted she was still going through the thick document with a fine-toothed comb, but she also recommended a lawyer for Mike and his group to have peruse the papers as a second party. Impressed by Mike's insightful questions, Athena found herself enjoying their conversation before she realized it. She also appreciated his respect for her knowledge of the music business.

When they finally put their plates to the side, Mike popped in one of the DVDs that Athena had stopped to get on her way home. She didn't even question his audacity in assuming she would want to watch the movie, which surprised her even further.

It wasn't just how comfortable Mike had made himself; it was also that Athena was surprised at her willingness to share her space with him. She was actually enjoying his company. It was just so easy. Choosing not to think about what that meant exactly, Athena focused on the movie. Before long both were laughing.

Athena heard her doorbell ring halfway through the movie. For the first time that night she felt irritated, but only because of the interruption. In the movie, Chris Tucker was just about to get the girl, and Athena was sure something funny was about to happen.

Looking through the peephole this time, Athena smiled, recognizing her neighbors on the other side of the peephole and opening the door slightly. "Hey, 'Theena," both Hector and Andrew said cautiously with smiles on their faces as Hector tried to look over her shoulder. Moving her face in front of his, Athena forced him to make eye contact.

"So, what's up?" Hector asked.

Not fooled, Athena figured quickly that they must have spotted the activity outside of her house, that two men came up and only one left. The only surprise was that it had taken them this long to make the trip across their adjoining lawns.

"*Nada,*" Athena said, leaning in her doorway. She decided to make them admit to the fact that they were nosy, that the reason they were here was to find out who her company was. Unfortunately, Mike ruined her plans by sauntering up behind her. Athena realized he was behind her by the way Hector's eyes bugged out and he put both his hands over his mouth.

Athena prayed that Hector would not embarrass her by letting Mike know the lack of dates coming through her house in the past year.

"Sorry to interrupt, Athena," Mike said now with a heavily accented New Orleans drawl that made Athena's knees go weak. "I was just wondering where your napkins were."

Athena was stunned at her reaction to just his voice. Lord, if his voice could cause this reaction, what would she do if he actually tried something?

Finding her voice, Athena said firmly, "Try the kitchen."

Mike just smiled at Hector and Andrew, who simultaneously gasped and waved back before Mike swaggered off to the kitchen to find the napkins.

"Who. Was. That?" Andrew said, almost as excited as Hector looked. She didn't really want to get into this right now, especially since Mike was feeling like playing games and no doubt would be back any minute.

"That's just a client of a friend of mine," Athena said, closing the door an inch.

"Really," Hector said, putting a hand up to stop Athena from closing them out completely. "Where did you find that cowboy?"

"He's not a cowboy," Athena exclaimed, just imagining all of the fantasies Hector was probably concocting and adding a few of her own. "He's just a musician, and he will be leaving very soon."

"Awww," Hector said to Andrew. "If that were me, I wouldn't be letting him loose if you paid me, at least not walking."

"What's that supposed to mean?" Andrew said, now angry. "You mean you would let somebody you just met set up house with you?"

Athena knew very well the answer to that, but she chose to stay out of it and said goodnight, closing the door as Andrew stalked back to their apartment.

When she walked into the living room, Mike had napkins stacked on the table.

"Found the napkins," he said, wiping his mouth.

"Good."

"Who was that?"

"My neighbors," Athena said, reaching for her glass, "who will probably be up arguing for the rest of the night."

"What?"

"Let's just say they have a complicated relationship, and your appearance tonight just added another dimension."

"Me?"

"Yes, you," Athena said firmly, not wanting to talk about her neighbors anymore.

"Where are you really from?" Athena couldn't help asking, her curiosity getting the better of her.

"Louisiana, but I lived in Texas long enough to get at least an honorary citizenship."

Curious, Athena asked, "When were you in Texas?"

"I moved there about ten years ago. While I was there I actually worked on a cow farm, although we called it a ranch," he said.

"Oh really?" Athena replied. "You must have been twenty, twenty-one?"

Turning to face Athena, Mike smiled, "Nineteen. You sure are asking a lot of questions." Reaching for the remote control, he turned down the volume. "Okay, what else do you want to know?" he asked, holding his arms out in the air. "I'm an open book. Ask me anything."

Surprised but pleased at Mike's willingness to answer her questions, Athena stared at him. Most men weren't willing to answer questions freely. Then again, maybe it was her choice of men that was the problem and not the men. Either way, they didn't like answering her many questions. That could be because curiosity was her middle name and her questions were so deep that they exposed even the most cautious player. Most men ran for the hills at first chance. Mike's complete openness was refreshing.

There were so many questions Athena had now that Mike had pulled back the curtain just a little bit. Over the next hour she found out that Mike had done more in his thirty-three years than most people had done their entire lives. Although he didn't graduate from college, in fact never attended, he had a lot of knowledge about a lot of different things.

Athena, who didn't know too many people who didn't go to college, or at least didn't have regrets over not having gone, was amazed at all that he had learned and done.

"I had the chance to go, once," Mike said, "but I just knew that for me, it would have been a waste of time. As soon as I got my high school diploma, I left my parents' home and headed for New Orleans. I stayed there for a while playing in some of the clubs in the Quarter. Then when that got old, moved on to Texas."

Athena just listened, not being able to imagine having the guts to do what Mike had done. It sounded as if his family believed in a very laid-back form of parenting that Athena couldn't imagine since her parents were very hands-on her entire life. Her father had always been big on plans. From the day she and her sister had been born, it was planned that they would go to college and law school. In fact, Athena never knew a time when she didn't think she wouldn't be going to college. She didn't regret going because she loved what she did, but she also envied Mike for his freedom.

"How did you end up in Biloxi?" Athena asked.

"A friend of mine had a business and said he had a lot of work for me if I decided to come because of the number of new houses he was building. I had kind of gotten tired of the road. Every week I was somewhere new. Had an apartment in Houston, but the band I was in traveled four out of seven days and I only ended up with enough money to pay for the apartment I rarely slept in."

Looking at Athena, Mike added, "After a couple of years doing that, it was time for a change. Since moving here a year ago, I have finally been able to put down some roots." Smiling that lopsided grin that Athena was getting more and more used to, he said, "Besides, I get to meet so many nice people, such as yourself."

Athena couldn't help smiling back, but when he reached out to touch her chin, she forced herself to pull back.

Ignoring the awkward silence, Mike pulled back as well. "Now that I've told you my life story, you have to tell me something."

"You did not tell me your life story," Athena said, protesting. "You just told me a few bits and pieces."

"That's more than you've told me," Mike countered.

Thinking about it momentarily, Athena held her hands out in imitation of the move Mike had made earlier. "Okay, what do you want to know? Ask me anything," Athena said jokingly, but instantly regretted it when Mike smiled and raised one eyebrow at her.

"Oh Lord," Athena groaned when he sat back and put one hand under his chin as if in deep thought.

"Where are you from?" Mike asked as if were interviewing someone for a job.

"Mississippi."

"Is your family in Biloxi?"

"Yes," Athena said, trying to maintain her smile as she thought about her family, in particular her mother. She realized she did not want to discuss her with him.

"Are you close?" Mike asked, smiling back.

Thoughts about her extended family and in particular her cousin and their last conversation brought a slight frown to her face. "Yes," Athena said, trying not to let the knot form in her chest.

Seeing the change on her face, Mike asked, "Man, what did they do?"

"No," Athena said quickly, "the question should be what didn't she do?" Not one to talk poorly about family, Athena was surprised to hear herself say that out loud, to

Mike of all people. Athena tried her best not to talk bad about Stacy, even to Mel. Yet when he asked her if they were close, Athena found herself telling him how far back their conflict went.

"Before I went away to college, there was a boy," she told him after a few moments.

"Aahh, a boy," Mike said, teasing. When Athena didn't respond he wisely stopped smiling and waited for her to continue.

"No, this boy was special. We had dated all through most of high school, and he was so smart. He was the smartest boy in the school," Athena said, remembering her first love. "My cousin and I used to share everything. We shared clothes, secrets, even the same bed until we turned sixteen. When it was time for graduation, Tyrone, that was his name, and I had made all of these plans. He was going to go into the army so he could get money for school and I was going to go to college at Dillard. We were going to graduate and then get married and move to New York," Athena said, smiling because of how naive they'd been.

"The weekend before both of us were to go away, I found out that I had to drive down to Louisiana to sign papers that would guarantee my financial aid. It was mandatory. I didn't want to go," Athena said sadly, thinking about what came next.

"When I got back a couple of days later, everything seemed normal. Tyrone said good-bye that Sunday as he got on the bus to go to basic training. Stacy even came with me to take him to the station." Smiling, but without humor, Athena said, "I didn't find out until six months later, when Stacy was showing, that they had done more than share a couple of drinks at his going-away party."

"Whoa," Mike said. "Your boyfriend got your cousin pregnant?"

"Yeah," Athena said, not smiling. "Sounds like something off Jerry Springer, but it's the truth."

"So that's the reason you don't talk to your cousin," Mike said more as a statement than a question.

"No," Athena corrected him, "no, that doesn't have anything to do with us now. It was hard, but I forgave her a long time ago. She's family, after all," Athena ended with the now familiar phrase.

"Yeah, but she slept with your boyfriend." Mike shook his head with disbelief at her lack of emotion. "There are just some lines you don't cross."

Athena agreed with him, but she hadn't had much of a choice at the time. Tyrone was gone, and she was in school. Her cousin, who'd had a difficult pregnancy, gave birth while she was away.

After all the complications, her family encouraged her to forgive her cousin, and to be honest, she'd just willed herself not to think about what she felt, tried to forget about it all and concentrate on her work. In a way she realized she had been doing that ever since: Concentrating on her schoolwork, now job, to not think about what she was feeling.

"So what happened to the boyfriend?" Mike asked disgustedly.

"He was killed."

"How?" Mike frowned.

"Like I said, he joined the army, and shortly after the Gulf War began he completed basic training. Soon after he was sent to the Middle East. During some practice maneuvers he was shot by 'friendly fire.' "

"Damn," Mike said, running his fingers over his head.

"He didn't even get to see his baby," Athena said, tearing up for the second time since she was initially told of the whole affair. Placing his hand over hers Mike squeezed it slightly, offering some support. Even though what Tyrone had done was foul, she remembered him to have been a gentle boy who always tried to do the right thing. Regardless of what he and her cousin had done, she had never wanted to see any harm come to him.

"And you forgave your cousin after all that?"

After having finally talked about it with someone, because she hadn't even talked to Mel about it all, she understood why Mike sounded so surprised. However, she was even more surprised at how readily she had forgiven Stacy for her disloyalty. She felt more anger towards Stacy now over her more recent behavior than she did for taking away the dream she had shared with her first boyfriend.

"Has your cousin always dated your exes?" Mike finally asked seriously after Athena had calmed down enough to sip from her Coke.

Surprised to find herself laughing she said, "No, but Stacy has definitely always got what she wanted. At the time she thought she wanted Tyrone, but a few months after he died she was married and pregnant by someone else."

"What happened to the baby?"

"She had it. He turns eight in two months."

Athena found herself watching Mike more and more. She had never really had any close male friends, other than the ones she had dated, and usually that ended once she had decided to stop seeing them.

She couldn't help wondering about Mike's history because she had never thought of having a white man as a close friend, let alone dating one, and even though she was determined to keep her relationship with Mike about business, she couldn't help wondering about his history.

"Have you ever dated out of your race?" Athena asked after Mike came back from throwing away the pizza box. Considering how he had made himself at home, Athena felt comfortable asking him this question.

"You mean have I ever dated an alien?" When Athena didn't laugh, Mike asked, "You mean black women? Does it matter?"

"Yes," Athena answered without hesitation.

"Why?"

"Because looking at you—it's just . . ." Athena paused, not knowing exactly how to put it into words. "Most people wouldn't expect you to be the rainbow coalition dating type."

"Oh, there's a type? I didn't know that."

"You know what I mean."

"Explain it to me," Mike said, looking down. Athena had the feeling he was disappointed with her.

"Well . . ." Debating whether to take on this topic, Athena tried to formulate exactly what she could say to him to get him to understand. "The thing is, growing up in the South, especially in Mississippi, whites would go with whites and blacks with blacks when it came to dating. Although things have changed somewhat, that fact has mostly stayed the same. Now every once in a while you might see a black man with an Asian woman or a white guy."

"A white guy with a black guy?" Mike asked, confused

"No, a white guy with an Asian—you know what I mean. Black women just were not one of the options for white men. In fact, until fairly recently that was how I viewed it. White men and black women just didn't happen."

"I doubt that," Mike replied.

"Yeah," Athena agreed knowingly, "there has been some, but it was always done in secret." Mike smiled at this understanding of what Athena was saying.

"Now if you do see a black woman with a white man, usually it seems that the dude usually has a Justin Timberlake, Jon B vibe going on with him," Athena said, laughing along with Mike at her observation. "Whereas you," Athena paused, looking at Mike from the top of his head to his work boots, "have more of a blue-collar Bruce Springsteen vibe going on."

"Do you always describe people in terms of music styles?"

"No," Athena answered matter-of-factly. "It's just that I see how recently there are more couples of black men and white women rather than vice versa. Not a lot, in fact it's very rare, but enough to make me not so shocked when I do see it."

"I can see you've studied this a lot," Mike said jokingly. "So, I guess this means that you have never dated a white man before?"

"No," Athena answered immediately.

"Have you ever been attracted?"

After a brief pause, Athena answered quietly, "Of course."

"Are you attracted to me?"

"Oh my Lord," Athena said, laughing out loud. Mike joined in, knowing that he had gotten about as far as he was going to get tonight, especially since they both already knew the answer to that question.

CHAPTER 16

"Here," Twila said, walking into Athena's office, carrying a small paper bag and a mug of coffee. Athena glanced up, and was shocked speechless. Twila had obviously decided it was time for a makeover herself. Considering the change was so glaringly obvious, Athena couldn't help wondering whether she should comment or wait for Twila to say something.

"So what do you think?" Twila asked when Athena remained silent. What could she say, Athena thought, when a person suddenly showed up with hair the color of cotton candy, only pinker? Other than the change in hair color, Athena did not see much of a difference. Although Athena still didn't understand exactly why, she had to admit that it looked more natural on her than some of the other colors Twila had tried in the past year.

"Nice," Athena said truthfully. Most bosses would have attitude about the change, but Athena couldn't complain, considering the girl worked the pink better than some more conservative people worked their look. Also, the girl was the best damn assistant this side of the Tallahatchie River. Anyway, Athena figured it wasn't worth it to make a big deal out of something that was likely to change in a week.

"Thank you," Twila said to Athena as she placed the mug on her desk.

Taking a sip, Athena patted herself on the back again, grateful that her assistant knew her better than she knew herself sometimes. "Oh, this is good, Twila, thanks. I didn't have enough time to get something this morning," Athena said as she tugged open the bag to see a gorgeous-looking chocolate muffin inside.

"Oh," Twila said, correcting her, "don't thank me. Your boyfriend just left it."

For a second Athena was confused. Boyfriend? Then suddenly she pictured Mike, realizing Twila had misunderstood what she had seen between them. Even though technically he was a friend, he was not her boyfriend. Nonetheless, she couldn't help that her stomach did the little flip-flop thing at the mere thought of him.

"Yeah, he said they were made fresh this morning in his kitchen."

Athena felt even more confused now. Although she didn't know Mike well, he just didn't seem like the muffin-baking type. She could be wrong, but she doubted it.

Seeing the confused look, Twila said, "You know, Mr. Gutman?"

Instantly, Athena remembered, laughing to herself. Lord, where was her mind going? Not wanting to think about the answer, Athena pushed the thoughts of Mike to the side, and made a note on her desk to remember to thank Mr. Gutman later.

If it were anyone else, Athena would have been concerned at the attention Mr. Gutman was suddenly paying her. However, she knew just how harmless he was. As a matter of fact, she knew his wife and knew well enough that their relationship was very much secure. Mrs. Gutman did not play and Mr. Gutman was not going anywhere. Although he hadn't said anything to her this morning about his treat, which tasted heavenly, she was sure it was his wife who had baked it for her.

As she took a bite, she brushed at the crumbs that landed on her brand new sweater. She had paired it with a pair of white slacks which Mr. Gutman had praised repeatedly on the ride up the elevator. Ever since he had followed her up the elevator over a week ago, Mr. Gutman had gone out of his way every morning to speak and compliment her on her daily outfit.

Mel and Shaundra had also been impressed by her new look. They had finally been able to get together for another night out. This time Shaundra's husband, Will, and Mel's boyfriend had come along.

Athena was glad to see Shaundra and Will together again. She'd been a little worried about them ever since that night at the club when Shaundra had seemed stuck to Gregory's side. However, since then, Gregory and the rest of the guys had become focused on their work, not to mention his wife had become very focused on Gregory. After two weeks of intense studio time, the group had some really good recordings which Athena had listened to almost nonstop since Vincent had given her a sample CD. Athena was very excited for Mike and the rest of the group. Although she'd rarely seen him since that night in her apartment, she treasured their late night phone calls. There was only one thing that sort of bothered her.

Although she had gotten used to her style change, she still enjoyed the compliments, and she had received a lot of them. In fact, she had received them from everyone she knew with the exception of Mike. At first, Athena hadn't noticed. In fact, the only way she had to tell that he even noticed her as a woman was that one incredible kiss.

After he'd made no more attempts kiss her, Athena began to wonder. Mike had been to her apartment a few times since their unplanned movie night, but he had not broached the subject. Athena felt relief at not being pressured, but still strangely felt a little bummed about how easily he had given up.

"Athena, you've got a call on line one," Twila said via intercom, stopping her troubling thoughts.

"Athena Miles," Athena said, holding the phone to her ear.

"Long time no see, or hear . . ." Sheree huffed into the phone.

"Well, hello to you," Athena said, smiling. Even though her sister could work her last nerve, she still looked forward to hearing from her. "What's up?"

"What's up?" Sheree mimicked. "That's all I get?"

In the past Athena would have been writhing in her seat with guilt, but instead this time she just smiled at Sheree's best effort to make her suffer.

"I was just calling you to let you know that your baby sister is doing big things," Sheree said.

Athena couldn't help smiling. She could hear the gloating in her sister's voice, and she could tell she was pleased.

"Your one and only fabulously intelligent and beautiful . . ."

"Sheree," Athena began, hating to interrupt, but she didn't want to be on the phone all day.

"Okay, okay," Sheree said, laughing, "I got beauty editor at *Tawny.*"

"You got the promotion," Athena screamed. She clapped her hands, mouthing, "She got it," to Twila in the hallway, who simply nodded her head in acknowledgment. Realizing she was not the first one to get the good news, Athena smiled at her sister's inability to keep a secret. She would probably call everyone in her Blackberry, which held the numbers of everyone she had met since she was probably three years of age, if she hadn't already. Still, Athena was proud and happy for her. This had been her dream since starting her job there.

Sheree, who had always been more sociably adept than most, had gone to Spelman University and majored in English. A lot of her friends had never even seen the inside of their local newspapers, let alone the inside of one of the most popular African American women's magazines in the country. Not Sheree. She had kept plugging away after graduation until she found a position that would allow her to get a foot in the door.

Even though she played the helpless Southern belle to a T, people who really knew Sheree knew that she was a force to be reckoned with, especially when she wanted something. After getting an internship in New York, she'd moved there and worked as a waitress part time until she could parlay her way into an entry-level position. After that she was off and running. Making beauty editor was just an inevitable next step. Athena was filled with pride over her little sister's accomplishment.

"Well, I hope that Ronnie took you out to celebrate," Athena said, still smiling into the phone.

"Girl, with as much money as I'm making now, I was able to take Ronnie out," Sheree boasted. "Hey, how long has it been since you showed your face at Thea's?"

Groaning, Athena didn't respond. It had been about two weeks, if she remembered correctly, which was not at all like her, but she didn't want to tell her sister that. Anyway, Athena thought, Sheree couldn't talk. She lived in New York so she didn't have to deal with their mother on the level Athena did. Although she was sure Aileen would be delighted to see the new and improved Athena, she just didn't want to see her. At least not yet. Their last conversation still burned in her brain. That, paired with the fact that she was seeing Mike, would not make the meeting easy. Her mother could read her like no one else, except maybe Mike. Smiling at just the thought of Mike, Athena wondered if maybe she had bitten off more than she could chew, but pushed that thought to the side as her sister continued.

Sheree reminded Athena to get ready for the upcoming family reunion. She was the only one who knew how difficult it had become for Athena to deal with the pressure coming from even their eight-year-old cousin for Athena to "get a man." She asked Athena if she had called Ned back. Athena instantly regretted having said anything about the man she had met at the club that first test run of her new look. She was sure the piece of paper with his number on it was still rattling around in the bottom of her briefcase, along with that of Alexster, whom she had never called either.

"Did you call Alexster?"

"Yeah, of course I did," Athena said.

"No, you didn't," Sheree said, busting her sister, "because I talked to him last night."

Athena just sighed into the phone.

"Girl, you better call that man. I'm telling you if you don't you'll regret it."

Athena doubted that very much, but to appease her sister and get off the phone, she promised she would. However, minutes after she hung up, she regretted the promise. Still, thinking about her commitment to herself to at least consider dating, she decided to actually follow through—eventually.

Sitting side by side in front of the fire later that night, Athena and Mike finished off their drinks as they listened to the latest of Thunder Road's creations. Athena was impressed. It had been a while since she had joined them in the studio. Other than a quick peek in, usually when Mike was there alone with the producers, she hadn't really known what to expect.

As the last bar of the group's cover of "I'm Feeling Good," an old Nina Simone song, played, Athena couldn't help glancing at Mike. This was the only song on the CD in which he sang lead, and it was the most passionate thing she had ever heard. She knew that if he could hold onto that level of energy while he was in front of a crowd of people, it would become the group's signature song.

"So, what did you think?" Mike asked, smiling easily. It was obvious he was proud of the work he and his friends had accomplished.

"It was all right," Athena said, trying for cool, which lasted all of a second. Then she said seriously, "It was absolutely beautiful." Sharing a moment where eyes caught and lingered, Athena found it hard to keep enough air in her lungs.

Keeping to his word to keep things light, Mike was the first to break the stare. "Well, I guess that's that. I just wanted to drop our recording off to you first to see what you thought," he said, trying to bring back the camaraderie they had come to share. "Frank said he would have the final contract ready soon and I told him to just give it directly to you since you are officially our counsel."

Athena nodded her acceptance, regretting that their night was coming to an end.

Standing, Mike said, "It's getting late, and I should be going."

Still sitting on the floor a little stunned at Mike's abruptness at leaving, Athena slowly stood. In a matter of seconds he'd caused a chill in the room that even the fire couldn't bring back. However, trying to recover, she rationalized that it was probably for the best as she walked Mike to the door.

Mike apologized once again for coming over unannounced, and said that it wouldn't happen again. Kissing Athena on the cheek, he turned away, walking quickly to his car.

Closing the door, Athena went back into her living room to put the fire out and then finished up the dishes she'd left soaking hours ago when Mike first arrived. Looking at the clock, she couldn't believe it was so late. It just didn't seem that he'd been there that long.

As she pulled the covers over her head in her big bed a little later, she couldn't seem to shake the feeling of disappointment that had come over her. Before closing her eyes she came to a conclusion. Mike Thibodeaux was definitely a nice guy. "If only," she sighed as she drifted off to sleep.

As the days passed and she didn't hear from him, Athena began to really miss his unexpected visits. For the first time she felt lonely as she sat in her house. No amount of videos, pizzas, or other distractions could make up for the loss of Mike's company.

To compensate, Athena did what any independent, career-minded, results-oriented young woman would do: She made plans for a service day and a date. In the interim she let her loneliness drive her into making the mistake of stopping in at Thea's on a particularly slow night. "Long time no see," Aileen said as soon as Athena stepped through the archway. If it were possible to turn tail and run, Athena would have, but she knew her mother would only chase her down.

"Hello, Mother," Athena said with her best smile, hugging her mother's neck. The two walked into the dining area and sat at the bar. Athena hated dealing with Aileen when she was "on" as the television star she had become. However, it was a way of life, and it occurred any time she was not in the sanctuary that was her home. Her fans were everywhere, and this was especially true for Thea's. People came from all over to see the same woman they saw daily on their TV screens, and Aileen was ready to give her to them.

"Athena, you've been hiding from your mother," Aileen said through lips that barely moved as she waved at a customer. "I've been hearing things."

Athena took the opportunity when yet another fan came up to hug her mother's neck to ask for a rum and Coke from the bartender. He smiled as he made it a double, placing it before her with a wink. She always had liked Tim. He was one of the few workers who had stayed at Thea's for longer than a few months. After they realized working at Thea's was not like what they saw on television, most employees left quickly, unable to keep up with Aileen's detailed demands.

"I heard you were still hanging around with that ditch digger."

"He is not a ditch digger, Mother," Athena interrupted, surprising both herself and her mother. "Mike owns his own carpentry business, and he's a musician."

Leaning back on her stool and crossing her long legs, Aileen replied, "A musician, huh. Tell me what musician digs ditches."

Athena shook her head, but because they were interrupted yet again she could only sit quietly as her mother greeted a new customer, the mayor of Biloxi. After the mayor was seated, Aileen picked up right where they had stopped.

"Marilee Muching called me and told me that my daughter, my soon-to-be spinster daughter, was seen at Luchesi's with the man who worked in her backyard last summer."

Athena only returned her mother's gaze when Aileen stopped talking. There was really nothing she could say.

"Well, Athena?" Aileen prompted.

"What do you want me to say?" Athena said louder than she intended.

Her mother put her hand on her daughter's arm.

Whispering, Aileen said, "I want you to tell me its not true, that you are not wasting your time and energy on a ditch digger."

"First, he is not a ditch digger, and what if he is? So what?"

"Do you really think that he would be dating you because of your personality, this ditch digger? Come on, Athena, a man like that? He's a beefcake, isn't he?"

Still stunned at her mother's dig at the improbability of Mike being interested in her for herself, something she had wondered about as well, Athena did not bother to respond.

"Look Athena, you should be with someone who is more like you, someone safe and dependable, not some drifter that we know nothing about. He could be a serial rapist or killer for all we know. He could even be getting kickbacks from someone to see what behind-the-scenes information he can get on the family."

There it is, Athena thought. It was about her mother once again. Athena had to admit she'd had that thought as well, but after spending so much time with Mike she didn't believe it. However, doubt in his interest in her for herself, new wardrobe or not, weighed on her mind. That had always been Athena's Achilles heel, and her mother knew it.

"I think it wouldn't hurt if you gave Barry Gorenflo a chance. You know, his mother was talking to me about how he was still single."

"Mother, he works for me."

"Oh, please," Aileen said, taking an olive out of her glass with long red polished fingernails. "He's a man and you're a woman. A date wouldn't hurt. Mrs. Gorenflo also told me how much they all admire you, especially Barry."

Although Athena was surprised to hear that Barry would have any interest in her, Athena found herself agreeing to consider seeing him just to end the conversation. She was just too tired to fight anymore. However, a couple of days later when Barry popped into her office to ask her for a date, Athena regretted her inability to stand up to her mother yet again.

"What's wrong with you?" Mel asked after Athena snapped at the waitress that her orange juice was warm.

Looking up, Athena said, "I'm supposed to just drink it just because she couldn't do her job right?"

"I know there must be someone behind me, because I know you didn't just snap at me," Mel said, getting indignant. When Athena didn't respond Mel continued, "Who did you wake up in the bed with this morning that has you all puffed up?"

Laughing at her friend, Athena couldn't hold onto her frown. "No one, girl," Athena said quietly, choosing to not talk about her date with Barry the previous night. Discussing it would be a waste of time, just as the entire date had been.

"Well, maybe that's the problem," Mel said, laughing now and picking up her fork again. "Now tell me what's your problem, because you have been walking around lately with a big ole bug up your butt for some reason. Did I do something wrong?"

"No," Athena said, wishing she had canceled on her friend this morning when she woke in a foul mood. However, their Sunday ritual was so ingrained that the thought didn't last long enough for her to pick up the phone.

"I didn't think so," Mel said. Gesturing with her fork, Mel added, "I know you're all cute nowadays with your hair and nails and junk, but you're not cute enough to get away with the frown 24/7. So tell me, what's the problem?"

Athena didn't really know what to say. She realized she had been unfair to Mel, and Shaundra as well, who had noticed how distracted she was and had commented about it last night on the phone. She had even had to apologize to Twila last week for snapping at her unfairly over some small task that was late getting done.

Overall, her attitude stunk and she knew it, but she couldn't seem to let it go. She knew what the truth was, but just didn't want to believe it. However, sitting across from her friend of twenty years, she wanted badly to tell her how much she missed Mike, but she couldn't. Mel had no clue how personal her relationship with Mike had become. She knew that Mike had spent a lot of time with Athena from what Ricky and the other guys had told her, but she had no doubt figured it was business. However, Athena knew better—her bad attitude started when Mike left.

"How do I get myself into these messes?" Athena whispered into the mirror. She had spent the last hour getting ready for Mel's party. Mel had decided to throw a surprise birthday party for Ricky's younger sister as a way to get "in" with his family. Athena understood Mel's thinking, and she'd promised to come and lend her support for her best friend's campaign to get that ring. Athena thought she was going a little over the top, but she had to admire Mel's chutzpah. Mel had rented the entire club for a night, and had planned a jungle theme. At first Mel had decided that everyone should come in grass skirts or bathing suits.

However, after numerous returned invitations, she reconsidered and changed the theme to supermodels, which she told Athena meant to think sexy and go big or stay home.

It had been a while since her makeover, and Athena went shopping for a little something new in which to do it "big." Staring at her big hair and professional makeup job, she barely recognized herself. Barry was meeting her at the party and she wanted to at least appear to be trying to make a good impression, but she wondered if he would get the wrong idea from The Dress. It was skintight and red and looked like it belonged on some runway in Paris. Although she wasn't interested, she had to at least act like this was a real date. She was sure she would never hear the end of it from her mother if she didn't. Besides, Barry seemed to just be grateful to be going out and had not shown any interest in her either. He had told her he had just had a bad breakup, relieving Athena's guilt since she was doing him as much a favor as he was doing for her by keeping her mother off her back. Still, as far as Athena was concerned, the sooner she got this over with the better.

Since agreeing to go out with Barry, they'd had a few conversations outside of work. Although she was sure she would have enjoyed herself a whole lot more if she had gone with Mike, she chose to not go there. Besides, she didn't know if Mel was even inviting the band to the function, although she would be very surprised if she didn't. It had been a while since she'd seen Mike, making Athena even more anxious about the party because of the prospect of seeing him again.

Athena rushed towards her front door trying to make up for lost time. Looking at her watch, she prayed she was not late. Running to her car, Athena heard whistles coming from across the lawn. "Hi, boys." Athena smiled and waved, not breaking her stride as Hector, with Elian in a makeshift fanny pack, joined her.

"Where are you two headed?" Athena asked, pushing her shades to the top of her head to hold her hair out of her face.

"The V-E-T," Hector spelled out. Athena didn't see the reason for trying to hide their destination from the devil dog, since it didn't take much to set him off anyway. In the past, Athena had found that if Elian wanted to a throw a fit, he needed no reason or cause.

Opening her car door to get in, Athena could see that Elian was not looking his usual self, and for a moment, despite their past history, she felt sorry for him. His ears, which were usually pointed up with malice, were flopped to the side, and he didn't even have a leash around his little neck. Usually anytime Elian left the house he had to have a leash; otherwise he would run. He wouldn't run away because he wasn't a stupid dog, and knew a good thing when he had it. No, he would run just for the hell of the chase until he was caught or decided to give up, which usually was the case.

Athena actually felt bad for the dog, and told Hector to hurry him to the vet. Surprised that she actually hoped he felt better, considering all the damage the dog had done to her house, not to mention her shoes, Athena took this as a good sign. If she was capable of feeling compassion for that demon pooch, then she might actually be able to enjoy herself tonight on her date with Barry. She definitely decided she would give it her best.

Athena felt pretty good stepping into the club that night. Immediately seeing Mel, Athena joined her and a couple of mutual friends at the bar to wait for her date. Getting a case of nerves, Athena allowed herself a drink. Taking a sip of her drink, Athena felt a tap on her bare shoulder.

"Hello, Athena?" a deep voice said behind her.

Athena turned to see Barry dressed in a navy suit that actually made him look like the grown man he was. This couldn't be, Athena thought before saying, "Hi, Barry." Nodding, he held out his hand to Athena. Expecting a handshake she was pleasantly surprised when he brought her hand to his lips. *God, what a suit can do for a brother.*

With an admiring glance, Barry said, "I hardly recognized you."

"Yeah, I clean up well," Athena said quickly, thinking the exact thing about him. Normally, Barry had the trendiest garb on and it just never seemed to look right, possibly because he was as prep school as you get. The suit fit his frame very well, and relieved her concern that he would stand out at the party tonight for all the wrong reasons.

"No, you look gorgeous tonight," Barry said, not catching her sarcasm. "Have you been here long?"

"Oh no," Athena said truthfully. "We're still waiting for the party to get started. Trina hasn't gotten here yet."

Sitting next to Athena on the seat, Barry ordered himself a drink. Athena noticed a flash of movement over Barry's shoulder and looked up to see Mel giving her a thumbs-up in approval. Although Athena wanted to tell her friend she had the wrong idea, she decided to let it pass. It was just a date, after all. It wasn't like they were getting married or anything. However, a moment later when Barry's hand caressed her knee for a moment, Athena began to wonder if Barry had different plans. After a couple of margaritas, though, they were laughing like old friends.

Feeling good after a couple of dances around the floor and mingling with the other guests, Athena led Barry back to their table, where a waiter immediately came up to take their order. Ordering hot wings and fries, Athena raised her eyebrows when Barry ordered a salad and grilled chicken.

"So you like to eat healthy," Athena said, making light conversation.

Barry turned to her and said, "Well, I believe in eating to live and not living to eat." Thinking he was joking, Athena laughed out loud, but stopped when she realized that he had not joined in, but was sitting there simply staring at her, confused.

"So, did you like Atlanta?" Athena asked, deciding to just let him talk about the only subject they truly had in common, work and his recent business trip to Georgia. As Barry launched into all the things he had learned about Atlanta, Athena found her mind drifting to the dessert menu.

Looking at Barry's handsome face, she wondered if he enjoyed banana pudding, and how he would react if she took home an extra slice of the gooey, chocolate birthday cake. In the middle of figuring how she was going to pass a message to Mel to save some cake for her, Athena looked up to see a familiar pair of dark eyes staring at her.

As soon as she saw Mike's smiling eyes, Athena found herself exhaling a long breath before smiling back.

"Do you know him?" Barry said, following her gaze.

"Uh, yeah," Athena said, turning quickly, embarrassed at her reaction. "He's one of Vincent's new artists."

"Oh," Barry said in a disappointed voice. "So, he's a musician."

Athena understood immediately that Barry was having a hard time accepting Mike's blue jeans, plain white t-shirt, and workman boots, the wardrobe of a hip blues man. She was disappointed at how much he was like her mother. Athena assured him that Mike was indeed a member of one of the Southeast's fastest rising groups and expressed surprise that he had not heard about them, considering the whole office had been abuzz with their music for months now.

Over the next hour Athena kept finding her gaze returning to Mike. Her eyes unconsciously followed him as he made his way around the room, catching his return gaze from time to time. When he finally made it to her table, Athena was on pins and needles, wanting to hear his voice. Standing next to Mel, who sat on Athena's left side, Mike greeted everyone.

"Well, well, Mike," Mel said, greeting Mike with a smile. "Who is this you have with you?"

Looking behind Mike, Athena saw for the first time a pretty young woman holding his hand. Athena hadn't noticed her at Mike's side the whole evening because she was so petite, but Athena could see that she was very attractive. With her dark brown hair and striking green eyes they made a very attractive couple. Athena did not like her, and once introductions were made all around, Athena had the feeling that the woman, named Emily, did not like her either.

Mike and his date sat down in the chairs next to Mel and although she wanted badly to look at Mike and find out how well he knew Emily, she couldn't without being obvious. Attempting to let go of her curiosity, Athena turned her full attention to Barry, who seemed to never run out of things to say.

As the night began to wind down, Athena pulled Barry back on the floor for one more dance. Not being able to enjoy sitting at the table with Mike and the girl, who seemed to laugh constantly, Athena had asked Barry to dance on a slow song.

For the first time in her life, Athena could not even enjoy the music, although it was one of her all-time favorites, one she normally would be singing along with.

She couldn't keep herself from looking back at the table every time Barry spun her around.

When the dance finally ended, Athena walked with Barry to the door, then made an excuse that she needed to say good-bye to Mel. Barry said that he would call her. All Athena could think in response was that she was sure her mother and sister would be happy. She made a bee-line to the cake table. Cutting a piece of cake, Athena could not resist the temptation to lick the gooey choco-late cream on her finger. She closed her eyes, savoring the rich taste. When she opened them, Mike was standing in front of her.

"Good?" Mike said.

"Mmm-hmn," Athena responded, smiling.

He took her index finger and licked the remaining frosting off the tip quickly, mimicking her perfectly. This was the Mike she was used to seeing, and after softly gasping, Athena immediately started laughing out loud at his audacity.

"Long time no see," Athena said.

"Well, I have been busy this week."

"Oh, so it was just this week you were busy," Athena said, not being able to stop herself. What about last week and the week before that? Athena thought, getting angry.

"So, what happened with your date, Larry?"

"Barry," Athena corrected, "and he left, which I am about to do."

"Yeah, we're about to leave out too," Mike said, pointing over his shoulder but keeping his eyes on Athena.

"Really? Emily seems nice," Athena said as she grabbed a plate to cover her cake to make sure that it got safely home.

"Yeah, she's good."

For a second neither had anything to say and the silence grew. Suddenly Mike stepped closer to Athena and put his hand to her chin, raising it so their eyes met. He was just about to say something when they were interrupted by an incredibly chirpy voice.

"Here you are," Athena heard someone say. Blinking to focus her eyes, Athena was aware that Mike had moved away. Once her mind came back, she found herself cursing whoever had picked that moment to notice the two of them. However, when she looked over she could see Emily with her friend Mel behind her. Judging from the way Mel's eyes were darting back and forth between Mike and Athena, she could tell her friend had seen their moment. *Oh shit.*

"We have been looking for you all over," Emily said, grabbing onto Mike's arm. "The fellas have a request to sing a song," she said. Her other hand touched the curls on the side of Mike's head. Briefly, Athena wondered what it would be like to pull the girl's hair out strand by strand.

Looking a little confused, Mike allowed himself to be pulled away, leaving Athena alone with Mel.

"Ooooh," Mel said as soon as they were out of earshot.

Athena just looked at Mel, then picked up her cake plate.

"What was that?"

Deciding to play dumb, Athena said, "I don't know what you're talking about."

"Don't you dare," Mel said laughing. "He was about to kiss you."

Not bothering to deny or confirm, Athena shifted her purse on her shoulder and just shook her head.

"Don't even try it, Athena Diche Miles."

Just then Athena heard Mike's voice coming from the stage as he introduced his bandmates and sat on a stool with his guitar in hand. After a guitar intro, the rest of the band started playing their now signature song set to a slower dragging beat, and Athena was rooted to the spot.

"Athena," Mel said in her ear, "Athena, you can't be serious."

As close as Mel was Athena couldn't ignore her comment anymore without her eventually causing a scene if she knew her best friend correctly. Besides she was tired of denying what she felt for Mike. Although she wasn't sure yet what that whole thing earlier meant, she was sure of what she felt, and until she found out what Mike was thinking, she was not ready to admit to anything, especially since Emily was in the picture, and obviously was determined to have Mike to herself.

Saying good-bye to Mel, she promised to meet her for their usual lunch date. As Athena walked out the front door to her car, she listened to the music drifting from the hall, and she envied Mike for the next words he sang about new beginnings. She longed to walk on stage and take her chances. Instead, she turned her back on the chance, opting to keep playing it safe.

CHAPTER 17

"I don't understand," Mel said for the fifth time since the three women had sat down. Shaundra tried to shush Mel, but she would not be stopped.

"I just don't see the attraction." Grimacing at Athena, Mel asked, "Why? Why?"

Unable to not laugh, Athena put her menu down and sat back, waiting for Mel to stop her ranting.

"I can see what the attraction is," Shaundra interrupted, causing Mel to turn on her.

"What?"

"Yeah, he's tall, he's handsome in his own way." When Mel just shook her head, Shaundra continued. "Now, if you put him in a suit and gave him good shave, haircut, and got him some lotion for that dry skin . . ."

"You noticed that, too?" Athena asked, finally saying something.

"Yeah," Shaundra agreed. "He could be very handsome," Shaundra said optimistically.

"But what about that fine cho-co-loto man you were with?" Mel asked, "I couldn't believe it when you let that man leave alone. Girl, if it were me I would've . . ."

Cutting Mel off, Athena said, "Look, not that it's any of your business, but Mike and I are business associates and friends at the most."

Seeing disbelief on Mel's face still, she said, "Look, I'm not trying to convince y'all." She took a sip of water.

"Now hold up, little girl," Mel said, "I'm trying to help you out." Calming herself , she said, "Athena, you know I love you, but this would not be a good thing." Seeing Athena about to say something, Mel just held up a hand. "Hear me out. He is uneducated. He is a day laborer. He is a musician, for God's sake."

"So is Ricky," Athena yelled.

"That's me, not you. My family doesn't take issue with every little thing I do, but Ms. Honeybee is a different thing altogether. What would Momzilla say about this, Athena?"

Athena didn't want to admit that her mother had already been on her case and had handpicked Barry to solve the situation. Nonetheless, what she was feeling was too strong for her to deny. She couldn't let this go.

"What? Is it because he's white?" Athena asked, interrupting Mel's laundry list.

"No," Mel said, exasperated. "I mean yes, but that's not what I have a problem with."

Surprised, Athena found herself interested in what she had to say.

"What I was saying is that he's not stable. He doesn't have a regular job. Yeah, now he has a contract for an album, but what's going to happen a year from now, two years from now? What if, God forbid, this album doesn't do anything once it drops? Then what? You'll be with a man with a background so different from yours it's not even funny."

Unable to respond, Athena looked to Shaundra, who despite her desire to see the bright side of the situation, had nothing to say. It wasn't that Athena hadn't thought of all the things that Mel had just said, but that had been when she was still trying to keep things from getting complicated romantically. Now that she was actually considering pursuing a relationship, she found it hard to admit to the fact that they were very different. Where Mike worked at not having ties and being independent, Athena liked the predictability of a steady job with benefits and a 401K plan. These little things in the beginning didn't matter, but when you got down to a serious relationship, they could be a deal breaker.

"Athena, I know this is hard to hear, but we don't want you to get hurt," Mel said, reaching for Athena's hand.

Athena smiled at Mel's light squeeze. "I know. You're looking out for me, and I appreciate your friendship."

"But?" Mel said, causing both Shaundra and Athena to laugh. She hadn't meant for there to be a *but,* but there it was.

"But I have to see where this is going. I've been running away from relationships and conflict for so long that I've missed out on a life. It's time for me to stop using my brain so much and just go with my feelings," Athena said more to herself than to her friends.

"That is so beautiful," Shaundra said, sniffing.

"And the Academy Award goes to . . ." Mel added, laughing. Once they had all quieted down, Mel soberly said, "We're here for you whatever you do, Athena, but I have to say that I am surprised that you're taking a chance with Mike Thibodeaux, of all people." Before Athena could show offense, Mel added, "It's not because he's poor, whatever to that. What I'm talking about is that he has such a stick up his ass."

Athena couldn't help laughing out loud at that because that was the total opposite of the man that she knew. If anything, Mike was the more outgoing person of the two of them. To hear the way Mel described him, he sounded like a totally different person.

"What? Mike is the most interesting man I have ever met, and he's not poor, he's average middle class. Just because he doesn't own a million dollar mansion doesn't make him a deadbeat."

Looking at Shaundra, Mel said, "Well, it's official, she's in love."

Athena didn't think in the slightest bit that love was what she was feeling. It was more like camaraderie, even lust, maybe, but love—definitely no. At least not yet. She had to admit that being around Mike made her happier than she had been in a long time. However, she had not deluded herself into believing that Mike was Mr. Right and they would get married and live happily ever after. The fact that she couldn't even pick up the phone to call him had to be a strong indication of her complicated feelings towards him.

It had been five days since she had last seen him, and the loss was becoming more and more pronounced. Yet she couldn't do anything about her feelings. It wasn't that she was against a relationship with Mike, but there were too many things that stood in the way. She was just beginning to feel good about herself, and finally her outside reflected her inside. She had friends, her career was going well, and the panic attacks had all but vanished. She didn't know if she was ready for the feelings that were so strong whenever she was in the same room as Mike. Even now sitting at her desk, just thinking about Mike and his smile caused her midsection to feel all warm and oozy. However, thinking about how Mike would fit into her chaotic life, Athena really didn't know. Aileen alone was enough to stop that train of thought. She hated to think what it would be like to have those two in the same room.

It was because of this that she felt the need to stay away a little longer until his album was released which was two days away. She knew that her professional involvement would be minimal. There was talk of a second album already, but Athena knew you could never predict how customers would be attracted to a new group. Regardless, she no longer felt comfortable working as the band's consultant. The album's release would free her from conflicting roles. Feeling good about her plan, Athena began working.

"Hey, buddy," Ben said. "I need your help."

Mike groaned into the phone and rolled over to take a look at the clock on the wall. Seeing that it was just ten past twelve, Mike groaned again. He'd had another late night at Claudette's and had expected to sleep in until well past noon. Kicking himself in the butt for picking up the phone, he sat up on the side of the bed. The past two weeks he'd had late nights and early mornings doing press promoting the album in the southeastern regional market. He and the fellas in the band had even made a commercial that ran in the evenings on several local channels. Because of the promotional work, paired with his regular gigs at the clubs and contract work he had scheduled, he had been dragging lately. The only reason he even bothered to keep the ringer on was because he was hoping that Athena might call.

For the past three weeks he had been trying to give her space, hoping that maybe she might show some indication that she cared or even spared him a thought. Instead, it had been three weeks of silence until last Thursday when he saw her at the birthday party, which ended up being a big mistake. He had been about to tell her how he felt that night when Emily had interrupted them. Mentally smacking his head, he thought to himself what a big mistake it had been bringing her with him to that party. He and Emily had gone on only one other date, but since then it seemed that he ran into her on a weekly basis, and she always alluded to a future date. When he had found out about the party, he knew Athena would be there and like some love-struck adolescent he had thought that maybe she would get jealous seeing him with a date and admit that there was something between them. Regardless how ridiculous Mike sometimes felt, he

S. R. MADDOX

knew that they had to see where this was headed because he knew Athena felt the same way. Although she was trying her best to deny it, Mike knew it was just a matter of time. Pushing himself off the bed, he promised himself it would be soon, despite her stubbornness. However, until then, Mike was resigned to wait it out. He would give her some more time.

After a quick breakfast at the diner, Mike headed to Gulfport for the second time that week to help out Ben. It seemed that more and more Ben was calling him. However, his inability to predict ahead of time whether he would need him was beginning to wear on Mike because he would end up having to change his plans. Besides, with the increasing number of gigs and the money for the record deal, he really didn't need the extra jobs with Ben.

Mike had always prided himself on his ability to walk away from any situation. It was something he had learned at a young age from his father. Unfortunately, he had learned it by seeing his dad walk away from his family. That day Mike had become a man. He hadn't had any other choice. With a mother who had been a stay-at-home mom and two younger sisters who each had been brought up believing they were princesses, Mike had learned to hustle at an early age.

His father had grown up on the wrong side of the tracks, and had both admired and scorned his mother's silver-spoon background. Mike remembered the day he left. He had come home from school early to find his mother and father in yet another argument. He was supposed to have gone on to baseball practice, but because of a sprained ankle early on in practice he was sent home. Mike heard the yelling when he turned off the ignition of his old beat-up Ford truck. Limping into the yard and up the front porch, Mike could only think about getting to his mother. He didn't notice the woman sitting in the swing on the porch. When he got upstairs, he hesitated, not wanting to interrupt what was obviously an argument between his parents, but when he heard a slap and the sound of a fall, he ran into his parents' room ready to defend his mother.

She was on the floor, holding her face. He saw red. If his mother had not pleaded with him to let his father go, he didn't know what he would have done. At sixteen, Mike had long ago matched his father's height and build. However, twenty years of sitting behind a desk had turned his father's once-toned body to flab. Mike had a body filled with muscle from the many sports in which he excelled.

After his mother assured him that she was all right, Mike finally noticed the suitcases his father had packed. Staring in disbelief, Mike watched his father walk out the door, cursing in Cajun about the crazy woman who was his mother. The woman on the porch, his girlfriend, was the new checkout girl at his father's grocery.

Mike watched his once beautiful mother begin to fall apart that day. Five years later she had died from years of prescription drug misuse and embarrassment over becoming a laughingstock in the town she had called home all her life.

It was soon afterwards that his sisters, still in middle school, went to live with his father, who worked overtime to spoil them after the years of neglect while they lived with his mother. The price was that they could not speak of their mother, effectively wiping out any memories of her. Regardless, Mike remembered the laughing woman, who had spent her whole life being protected and therefore was all the easier to destroy. Where most women would have picked themselves up and done their best with their circumstances, his mother had fallen apart. The worse part for Mike wasn't her death, it was watching her deteriorate day by day. As a result Mike had spent his whole life trying to make sure that he could take care of himself, at all costs.

At twenty-one, when a lot of his old classmates had already graduated from college, Mike, with a hundred dollars in his pocket, set out on his own, determined to enjoy his freedom. For thirteen years, he'd done exactly that.

It had been a while since he had thought about his family, but it seemed that it went hand in hand with his thoughts of Athena. Whenever he thought of Athena he couldn't help but comparing her to the earlier women in his life, specifically his mother. Although they were both beautiful, Athena and his mother were as different as night and day. Although Athena was sheltered in a lot of ways, Mike saw stronger stuff in her than even she probably knew she had. It was what he had found himself attracted to—her independence. Although it was what kept her out of his reach, it was also something he admired in her because he treasured his own independence so much. He remembered how comfortable it was the last time they had spent time alone together. More and more, he kept thinking how nice it would be to be able to put down roots.

CHAPTER 18

The week of the fundraiser arrived, and the excitement had reached a feverish pitch. Athena and her staff worked nonstop the night before to make sure that the fundraiser/release party went off without a hitch.

Since it was to be a red carpet event, Athena had Twila call around about getting a car service donated for the members of the band to arrive in style with their dates. This had Mel thanking her for at least an hour on the phone. Athena figured she would just take a cab.

The afternoon of the event, Athena called in the big guns. She asked both Andrew and Hector over to help her choose between gowns. She was looking for sexy, yet not too slutty. She knew that she was going to see Mike, and whether he brought Emily or not, she wanted him to notice her. When they finally decided on a dress, Athena was very pleased and knew that she would leave a definite impression on Mike. The question was, would he be able to handle it?

The dress that she ended up wearing was a basic black that accented her caramel skin tone and complemented her hourglass figure. Looking in the mirror, Athena silently thanked her trainer and Mel for helping her out in the gym, because it surely showed. She wore her hair down with soft curls and no jewelry except for a gold watch with a matching pair of golden hoop earrings. Slipping into the high-heeled shoes that perfectly suited her dress, she felt like a queen.

"Girl," Hector said glowing, "you look gorgeous."

Looking at her heels, worrywart Andrew frowned slightly. "Now you're gonna be all right in those heels, right?"

"Stop it," Hector said, playfully swatting at the negative vibes around him. "She's going to be fine."

Checking herself in the mirror one more time, Athena hoped that Mike would think she looked good. She knew she looked good, but she wanted to hear Mike say it. He had yet to say anything about the way her look had changed. She wondered if he'd even noticed.

"Now," Hector said, already knowing what Athena's plan was, "when you see that man I want you to walk by him and ignore him." He strutted across the room in illustration. "Wait for him to come to you."

Andrew sat in his chair, shocked. "Don't you listen to him, Athena. You better go to him and not play those games."

Hector, not liking that his advice was being challenged, immediately told Andrew what he thought of his advice, which was not at all nice and involved a few blue words.

Not wanting things to get any uglier in her house, because she liked her furniture the way it was, Athena grabbed her purse and led the couple outside. Waving good-bye to the pair, Athena left them to their bickering, knowing that it would eventually lead to their making up later. Either way, Athena had too much on her mind. She had some making up of her own to do.

When Athena arrived, she immediately checked in with Twila, who had spent the last hour checking items off the list that Athena had given her. By the time Athena caught up with her everything was under control, which never happened at these events. Athena thought that the hand of luck must have been placed on her forehead because everything had been falling into place perfectly. She and Twila made rounds through the crowd of press and their Regent coworkers. Everyone complimented them on the event and the "great new find" also known as Thunder Road.

Athena also had several admiring glances from men, who wanted to get closer, and women, who wanted to know where she now shopped. She was actually enjoying the party so much she almost forgot she was supposed to be working, which was not at all like her. Just as the band was about to make their entrance, Athena went with Twila to stand at the end of the red carpet, where they would be able to greet the band members after they had their pictures taken.

Ricky and Mel were the first to arrive, and looked fabulous in coordinated baby blue outfits. After having her picture taken on the carpet, Mel was on cloud nine, finally living out her celebrity fantasy.

Next came Gregory and his wife. Athena barely recognized the small woman because for the first time she did not have a scowl on her face. She looked stunning. Although they were not matching, they made the perfect couple with Gregory looking tall and lithe in his black Armani suit, and she in a flowing, pale pink dress that made her look completely feminine, not the bulldog Athena remembered.

Having a car of their own, Gary and Stamps stepped out of the next limousine. She noticed that neither had dates, but was sure that it was calculated. By the end of the night they would have plenty of numbers, if not a date accompanying them in their limo home. Athena was surprised when a third man stepped from the back of the limo. Looking closely she saw that it was Mike, and she felt her heart lurch at the sight of him. Then he disappeared into the crowd of flashing lights. He was alone, Athena thought, smoothing her hair unconsciously.

"God, he looked good," Twila said with longing. Looking at her from the corner of her eye, Athena had to hold back the comment that danced to the forefront of her mind. Remembering that Twila was very committed to her fiancée, Athena ignored the longing she heard in Twila's voice.

Lord help me, Athena thought at her spark of jealousy. The man wasn't even hers yet but she had most definitely claimed him.

As he came toward her Athena noted his well-cut black suit. He'd also had a haircut and his usual stubble was nowhere to be seen. Athena had to remind herself to breathe when she felt herself getting light-headed. Feeling stupid, she turned to Vincent to distract herself.

"Looks like it just might be a success," Athena said, smiling.

"Might be a certified hit."

Looking at Vincent, Athena felt a twinge of worry over her plan. Although she wanted Mike and the guys to be successful, once they made it, her involvement and excuse to be in Mike's life was over. There would be no more late night drop-bys on her front doorstep with a contract in one hand and a pizza in the other. Athena didn't know if she could handle losing Mike's friendship. For the first time she had doubts about Thunder Road's deal, and she hated what that could mean because she wanted them to be a success—didn't she? Not liking the negativity, Athena did her best to push away those thoughts, and by the time Mike reached her she had a smile for him, and was ecstatic when he smiled back before embracing her in a big hug.

"Glad to see you," Mike said.

"Me, too." Holding on to his broad shoulders, Athena wanted to stay in the pocket of warmth, but dared not to. This was, after all, a business event, and she didn't want there to be any talk in the office. Lord knew there was already enough gossip going around about her one unfortunate date with Barry. Athena had crossed herself repeatedly about that one, thankful that she had made it out of that sticky situation with both of them maintaining their self-respect. It had been a little iffy there for a minute. Barry had seemed to pop up every time she turned around, asking for a repeat of their first date, even though it was obvious there had been no sparks between them. There was one brief second when Athena thought Barry might try to start trouble from the look on his face. He had actually scared her, but a second later his face had cleared and he had apologized and walked out her office. They hadn't spoken much since, which was how Athena preferred it. Even though their families had known each other her entire life, Athena had never had many dealings with Barry, and beyond work had no cause to. She was glad that they had come to an understanding. Now she just had to wait out the gossip-mongers at work who hated to let things die.

For the next couple of hours, Athena worked the crowd, gaining several pledges as Thunder Road entertained the attendees throughout the fundraiser's events. After several songs, the band set up a press line where they went into serious schmooze mode, signing CDs and taking pictures with anyone who asked. Athena couldn't help marveling at the band's natural ability in handling the press and their fans. They were so sincere and honestly grateful for the attention. It made Athena all the more thankful that she had been able to help them realize their dreams. Nonetheless, the evening did have to end. Looking at her watch, Athena noted it was way past ten o'clock and there was still a long line in front of the stage where the fellas were set up.

"When do you want me to stop the autograph signing and get them back to the interview rooms?" Twila asked Athena.

Looking up to the stage and seeing that the line was moving very slowly, Athena said, "No, what we can do is get a list of the stations that have not been able to get a personal interview and schedule them later for a one-on-

one. We'll make sure everyone here who wants an autograph gets some face time. Tell the stations that
tomorrow someone will set up personal interviews."

"Athena," Twila said, looking serious, "a lot of people
are asking just for Mike."

Vincent had already discussed the possibility of Mike
being thrust to the front despite his not being the lead
singer, but Athena knew for a fact that Mike had no
intention of going solo. They'd had many discussions
before about the subject and he'd said he was not interested in playing lead. Athena told Twila that would not
be possible, even though she knew refusing requests such
as this was a risk so early into their fame.

Athena continued to circulate, spending some time
with her friend Mel, who had spent a good deal of time
waiting for Ricky. Nonetheless, she seemed to be having
a ball every time Athena stopped by to talk. Athena also
got a chance to sit down with Shelly, who had accepted
her invitation to perform. After seeing Thunder Road
live, Shelly was excited about speaking with the band
about a possible collaboration, which she had never
mentioned doing before to Athena's knowledge. No,
Ms. SheLe was a solo artist with a capital S. Since she
was making an exception, Athena knew that she
thought Thunder Road was something special. This
alone piqued Athena's interest because she knew that
Shelly and Thunder Road would create an awesome
sound. Both their influences were more contemporary,
even though both held on to the traditional blues
makeup.

It wasn't until after midnight that things started to wind down. The people with children at home began to file out, even though they did so regretfully. The people who were left were raring to keep the party going, but Athena called for a last round, unwilling to make her staff stay any longer. Many were volunteering their time and she didn't want to take advantage of them. The Saenger had been rented until midmorning so they would be able to remove all of their equipment, and Athena would need them back first thing in the morning.

Athena told the head of security to keep the lights on for another hour, than start clearing people out. Work time was officially over once Athena called for a toast to the night's success. Both Regent personnel and the band joined in on the toast.

Preparing to leave, Athena made sure to say good-bye and thank each staff member personally. Then she went in search of the band members to do the same. She had a hard time finding Stamps, but said good-bye to Mel and Ricky and Gregory. Then she saw Gary with Mike. Although she wanted to talk to Mike alone, she approached both to give her congratulations and good-byes. Halfway through her speech, Athena saw Gary's attention wane as he spotted a young woman in the crowd.

Watching him walk away without a word, Athena started laughing. "Well, I guess he saw someone he knew." As Mike joined in on the laugh, Athena wanted so badly to brush his hair back off his forehead. Any excuse to touch him.

"I'm about to leave," Mike said. "You want me to wait to walk you out?"

"Uh yeah," was what Athena was thinking, but instead, trying to hide her surprise and enthusiasm, she said, "Can you just give me a moment?"

When he nodded his head yes, Athena forced herself to walk when what she wanted to do was sprint to tell Twila, who had now joined her boyfriend since she was off duty, and tell her that she was leaving. She then did her best to avoid getting in any conversations with other partiers on her way out. She didn't want to keep Mike waiting. When she saw him, she found herself feeling a little peeved at the group of giggling young women around him. Athena was pleased that he immediately excused himself once he saw her walking up. Stepping into the cool night air, Athena approached the valet to ask for a cab.

"You didn't drive?" Mike asked. When she said no, he smiled and suggested, "I can take you home, unless you just have to ride in a cab."

For a moment Athena was stunned at just what his smile did to her, briefly thinking about what Mel had said about Mike's scowl.

"Stamps and Gary are catching a ride, so I have the limo for the rest of the night," Mike said, explaining.

"I would love to ride in the limo that I ordered."

"Oh yeah," Mike said, looking down. "Did I not thank you for that?"

"No." *Not yet,* Athena said to herself.

"Thanks," he said, draping Athena's shoulders with his jacket. For a second Athena thought he was going to kiss her, but he simply adjusted the coat. Remembering where they were and that it would not be wise to start something at a business event, Athena squelched her disappointment.

The car pulled up and the valet opened the door for them.

Following Athena into the back of the limo, Mike sat as close as possible to her. So close that she could smell the freshness of his cologne, and felt his warmth against her thigh.

He had tried his best to play it cool during the whole soiree, and keep his distance. He knew that if he got too close to her tonight that he would end up holding her and never let go.

Walking down that red carpet and seeing her at the end had almost killed him, and his self-control was at the breaking point now that he was alone with her. Tapping on the partition he told the driver the address, but also told him they were not in any hurry and to take the scenic route. As soon as the partition closed, Mike turned to her and his hands took on a will of their own as they dove into her loose curls.

Athena tensed, momentarily surprised at his touch, then immediately softened as Mike ran his thumb along the fullness of her bottom lip.

Without a word, never breaking eye contact, Mike gently cradled her face, holding her mouth in place so that he could have his way with her pouting lips.

"Mike, I . . ." was all she could get out.

He descended on her with his mouth's warmth, using his tongue to taste her and feel what he had been waiting on for the last two months. After what seemed like hours, Athena gasped and he finally pulled back, leaving her shivering from the lack of his body heat.

As Mike stared into her eyes, Athena was hypnotized by the almost feral look in his eyes. Athena imagined the same look was in her eyes. Suddenly Mike reached for her again, pulling her to sit in his lap. As she traced her fingers along his strong jawline, Athena pressed herself firmly on his lap, causing Mike to gasp in response. Smiling at his body's response to hers, Athena felt out of control but safe at the same time. It was a dangerous but powerful feeling she had never experienced before but she reveled in it, wanting more. She groaned as he ground against her.

Suddenly, there was a knock on the door.

"Already?" Athena asked, feeling dazed and very frustrated.

Mike looked at Athena and then through the tinted window at the driver, who was standing on the other side of the glass patiently waiting to open the door for them to exit the car. When he looked back at her, Athena knew instantly that Mike was not going anywhere tonight, and as she fixed her clothes, she couldn't think of one reason why he should.

"So?"

"So what?"

Exasperated, Mel yelled, "Oh, come off it. You've were MIA all day Saturday and you're two hours late today. Something is up." Mel had already ordered her food, so when the waiter showed up to take an order from Athena, Mel sat back, squinting her eyes and wrinkling her nose at Athena as if she were sniffing for a secret.

Once the waiter left with the order, Athena saw Mel's face brighten before she said, "Ewww," so loudly that their neighbors turned to look.

"Sshh," Athena said, trying to quiet down her friend.

Whispering Mel laughed, "You got some, didn't you?" Frowning, Athena just looked at her friend.

"You so nasty," Athena said in her best prissy voice, trying to give Mel the stink eye.

"I bet you were really nasty all yesterday and last night, too," Mel said, laughing. "Don't lie."

Athena tried her best to keep up the frown, but couldn't help remembering all the hours in which Mike had worked her body in ways she had forgotten, creating some ways as well. She couldn't help it if she had been grinning ever since she had awakened next to Mike this morning with the phone ringing in her ear.

Mike had stayed over Friday night, really Saturday morning, and Saturday night, and it wasn't until Mel threatened to come over with her key that Athena finally decided to skip out for just a couple of hours to meet her friend for their traditional Sunday brunch.

"You are just glowing." Reaching for her purse, Mel pulled out her shades, "Lord, someone turn down the lights, I can't see for the glare."

Athena coughed on the sip of iced tea she was trying to swallow.

"Girl, I saw the way y'all were looking at each other Friday night. Un-huh, Ricky said you had probably forgotten we were there, but we spotted you getting in the limo. Groupie! Groupie!" Mel sang.

"Mel," Athena said slowly, trying to change the direction in which Mel had taken the conversation. "Your imagination has gotten entirely too wild since you got with Ricky. Just because I'm single doesn't mean I'm having all of the freaky-deaky liaisons you keep trying to accuse me of."

"Wild and freaky-deaky," Mel repeated, making it sound dirty. "Right."

"Right is right. All I did was get a ride home with the guy."

"Then what?"

"I went home."

"And then?"

"To bed—by myself." Athena hated that she'd lied to her best friend once she saw how disappointed Mel was by the news. She actually looked sorry for Athena.

"Why didn't you tell me that in the first place?"

"You're not my mama, I don't have to tell you everything."

As the waiter returned with their food and placed it in front of them, Athena began to think how much she really wanted to tell Mel the truth, but at the same time this was new territory for her, and she didn't know if she was ready to discuss this with Mel because, hell, she didn't even know where this was going to lead with Mike yet. They hadn't really talked that much in the last few hours, she thought, smiling.

"Okay, see right there," Mel said, pointing at Athena's smiling face.

"What?" Athena said, denying it again but not fooling Mel.

"Okay, just know this. Two weeks from now when y'all are hanging on to each other like a starving man on a cracker, I am going to be so pissed that you didn't share this with me."

"You are being melodramatic, Mel," Athena said in a exhausted voice. "It is not even that serious."

"Yeah, I just know that when that first tiff happens, when you realize that he is not the next best thing since sliced ham—"

"That's bread, Mel."

"Whatever—hell, when y'all have your first fight," she said quickly, "don't you come running to me then. You hear?"

"Yeah," Athena said, rolling her eyes.

"Huh?"

"Yeah, I heard, Melanie, " Athena said, unable to stay mad, letting a chuckle unwisely escape, which immediately set Mel off.

Laughing until they both were holding their bellies, Athena forgot what had set her off. That is, until Mel spoke, changing the subject only slightly.

"Just tell me this, Athena," Mel said seriously. "Hypothetically, this isn't going to cause you problems?"

Because she had been thinking the same thing, Athena had a hard time playing off her own concerns. Nonetheless, she was determined to see how this played out, whatever "this" was. Her mother would not be happy, nor would Mrs. Gorenflo or Barry, most likely, but Athena was willing to deal with them all when the time came, because she was happier than she ever thought possible. It was time to stop worrying about other people's happiness and start going for what made her happy. What a concept, Athena thought to herself, to actually live her life with her own happiness in mind. Most people should only be so lucky.

"What if we did start a personal relationship?" Athena asked. "What would you think about it?"

"Oh, please," Mel said dryly. "That's coming from someone who hasn't dated any one person steadily in over a year. I'm just glad you are out with someone. It could be Jabba the Hut." Then after thinking about it she said, "Well maybe not Jabba, but some other half-decent human with a penis and two legs and I would be."

"You had to specify the penis part, huh?" Athena said, reaching for her sweet tea.

"You know what a difference that makes," she said with a smirk, then added in a whisper, "doesn't it?"

"Yeah," Athena said, laughing at her joking.

"You sure now?" Mel asked again as if she weren't too sure herself. "Because child, it's been so long for you I wasn't too certain anymore."

"Oh please," Athena hissed. "You're too crazy."

"Yeah, you're right," Mel said, steering the conversation back to Athena and Mike. "Whatever he is, Athena, there's only one thing that matters. Is he good to you?" she asked softly.

Thinking back to the first moment they met and how since he had come into her life literally rescuing her from herself, she had to say a definite yes. Nodding her head, Athena could feel tears coming to her eyes just thinking about the tenderness and thoughtfulness that she had come to know from Mike's words and more importantly, his actions.

Putting her fork down, Mel said with finality, "Well, that's all that needs to be said." Holding her eyes, Mel added seriously, "Look, I'm going to be honest with you. There are a lot of people out there who will probably not agree with whatever it is the two of you have going. I understand you not wanting to tell me all the scandilicious details for now, and I forgive you," Mel said, smiling. Then more seriously she added, "The fact of the matter is that you will probably catch more hell than any other couple out there." Mel let that sink before asking, "Is he happy with you?"

When Athena nodded, Mel asked, "Are you happy with him?"

All Athena could do was nod yes again.

"Then tell all those other people I said to mind their own business." She grabbed her fork and dug into the rest of the rice and vegetables on her plate as Athena took a napkin to dab at the moisture of her eyes. "Although I doubt too many of them will have the guts to say anything to you, and if they do that shows their lack of class. So just say what my granddaddy used to say whenever things weren't fair: 'Tough titty said the kitty, but the milk's still good.' "

Leaving lunch feeling a whole lot better, having finally shared with Mel some of what she was going through, Athena felt relieved. Once Athena promised to not keep everything to herself in the future, to stop the superwoman act, as Mel put it, all things were definitely back on track between them. Athena's only worry as she entered her condo a few minutes later was where exactly Mike and she were going with this.

However, despite her lingering worries, Athena's mind went blank as she walked into her bedroom to see Mike standing in nothing but a towel, still wet from his shower. Drinking in his muscular build and the way the dark hairs curled on his still damp chest, all Athena could think about was how he made her feel and decided then and there to let this thing play out, no matter where it ended. That was the exact moment that she knew. The old Athena was no more. In fact, it made her wonder why she had ever been holding herself to some antiquated Southern fried standard that required she forgo pursuing what fed her soul. She had been imprisoned in a web of denial her entire life.

CHAPTER 19

"Wake up, Athena," Mrs. Trace, Athena's fourth grade teacher said, tapping on her forehead with a ruler.

Opening her eyes, Athena realized that she had been having a very drawn out dream concerning a spelling bee that she was failing miserably at in front of her entire hometown while wearing a polka-dot bunny suit.

Pushing her hair out of her eyes, Athena touched her tender forehead. Her first thought was she was going to have to teach Mike another way to wake her up in the morning. Then she heard, "Get up, nut."

Athena's whole body stiffened at the voice, a very familiar voice. *It can't be.* Athena knew that voice and it was definitely not Mike's. In fact, it belonged to her younger sister, who was supposed to be hundreds of miles away in New York City. Opening her eyes, Athena looked up into the face of her younger sister, Sheree.

"What are you doing here?" Athena asked, mortified that her little sister had walked in on her with Mike. Damn, why had she not taken her key back from her sister?

"Well, that's a nice greeting," Sheree said, sitting back on her legs on the bed. Athena looked around for Mike and didn't see him anywhere.

"Where's—" Athena began only to be interrupted.

"Come on, girl," Sheree said, getting off the bed. "I'm starving and you've got to get up. If you hurry, we'll have enough time to go to breakfast before you go to work," Sheree said, walking over to the closet.

Frantically, Athena listened for signs of Mike as Sheree continued talking about how she had just gotten off a plane and how she had been stuck for three hours in a seat next to a collicky baby.

Not hearing any noise outside her bedroom, Athena gathered the sheets around her naked body and slid off the bed. As the sheet came with her, a piece of paper fell to the floor.

"Hey babe, I had an early job," Mike's neat handwriting said, "but I'll see you tonight." Smiling at the directness of his note, Athena was glad that her tactless sister had not shown up to find them in bed together.

It wasn't that she was ashamed of Mike, but the fallout from that scene would have been too *Three's Company* for her. Just imagining how Sheree would have cherished letting fly in the middle of the family reunion that juicy piece of gossip about Athena finally having a man made Athena a little nauseous.

"What the—" Sheree shrieked as she caught sight of Athena's backside. "Since when did you start sleeping in the nude?"

Not responding to Sheree's outburst, Athena dragged the sheets with her into the bathroom. Before she closed the door, she heard Sheree say, "Well, it's about time you let go of those tacky pajamas."

Athena couldn't help smiling as she looked in the mirror at her tousled, wild hair. *If letting go leaves me feeling this good, then call me Ms. Freakiness, queen of the freaks.*

After a shower and serious work with her comb and brush to tame her hair, Athena stepped out of the bathroom in her robe to see her sister looking at a pile of clothing on her bed.

"Dang, Athena," Sheree said in disbelief, "what did you do? Buy out the whole store?"

Smiling at her sister's comments, but pleased at Sheree's admiring glance, Athena said, "I hope you know you gonna be putting all those clothes back in my closet." She sounded very big sisterly.

"No, really, Athena, did you hire a personal shopper or something?" Sheree said in awe. "And what did you do to your hair? It's be-yoo-ti-ful."

Laughing at her sister's disbelief, Athena said as nonchalantly as she could manage, "I just went and updated my wardrobe a little bit."

"A little bit?" Sheree said as she turned to look at Athena. Her eyes widened and her mouth opened in a wide O before she clamped a hand over it. Smiling, Athena guessed correctly that she liked her new hairdo and color, now that it had been properly styled.

Reaching out a hand to poke at it, Sheree said, "Is it real?"

Swatting her hand away, Athena went to the bed and grabbed a pair of jeans and a peach silk blouse to change into. Then she disappeared back into her bathroom to put on the finishing touches of makeup and add jewelry.

When she stepped back out minutes later, all her clothes were back in the closet, and Sheree was giving her a standing ovation. Even though she had worn the outfit a few times before, she was still pleased by her sister's response.

There hadn't been many times in her life that Sheree had said anything encouraging about her looks. For the first time Athena felt that her sister actually saw her as a person with style instead of her frumpy older sister.

Nevertheless, over breakfast Athena decided to hold off on telling her sister about her new relationship, opting instead to talk about the upcoming Miles family reunion that weekend.

"Is Ronnie going to come down for this weekend?" Athena asked as she ate from her bowl of buttery grits with gravy, still wondering about Sheree's unexpected visit.

"No, his job couldn't let him go."

"Really?" Athena said, "so the restaurant just couldn't find a single other person to bus tables?"

"Watch yourself," Sheree said, eating her biscuit. Even though Sheree was now twenty-five years old, with her hair in a long ponytail as her lip stuck out, she looked like a twelve-year-old who had been grounded.

"Sorry. Well, it's not like you're not gonna have any fun. I heard *Tawny* has a great lineup. Shelly's even appearing on one of the stages. And get this, she's donating her proceeds to Regent," Athena said, smiling, hoping to lift up Sheree's plummeting spirits. Shelly was her baby sister's favorite performer, next to Beyonce.

"If I wasn't going alone, then I might be a little more peppy, but as it is, there are only coworkers allowed and their immediate family member. Everyone else I know is bringing their boyfriend or husband. I'm going to be there as a third wheel the entire time that I'm not working," Sheree said, frowning as she bit into her biscuit. "Unless, of course you come with me," Sheree said suddenly, brightening at the idea.

"I can't go with you," Athena said, "I have to work." Athena knew it would be fun, because she had gone a couple of years ago with Kendrick, and knew there would be plenty of good music and food, but there was no way she could take off two days for the festival in addition to leaving early Friday to go to the reunion.

"Come on, you could," Sheree said, pleading. "You said last year at Mom and Dad's house that you had a lot of leave even after taking that week off. If you wanted to come you would come."

Athena knew this to be true, but wasn't going to admit it because she had already decided what she was going to do with those days. She planned on spending the nights with Mike. Her Monday, Tuesday, and the rest of the week were already taken as far as she was concerned. Still, she told her sister that she would try to get away Saturday night to take her to New Orleans and drop her off. After they finished breakfast, Athena let Sheree drop her off at work and keep the car so that she could have some freedom until Athena got home.

"What time do you want me to come back to get you?"

"I'll make sure to be off at five today," Athena said determinedly. "So just meet me in the parking garage on the second floor." Waving good-bye, Athena walked into her building and then to her office.

"Good morning," Athena said, greeting her now black-headed assistant.

Removing the mirror from in front of her face, Twila looked up at her boss, who was holding two cups of coffee.

"I got you one of those chocolate macchiatos you like so much," Athena said before placing it down on the desk when Twila didn't move.

"Good morning?" Twila said, sounding perplexed.

After one final smile, Athena left Twila at her desk and headed to her office. Before she could even put her briefcase down, Athena heard her door close behind her.

"Did you just bring me a beverage and then skip into your office?" Twila said, imitating Athena's arrival by placing her drink down on the desk with flourish.

Athena laughed at Twila. "What? You didn't want the drink?"

"Thank you for the drink. I appreciate it, but your mood . . . You are downright . . ." Twila paused, waving her hands in the air as she searched for the right word, "scary." Looking at Athena's horrified face and remembering that she was her boss, Twila added, "I mean, very happy."

Athena walked behind her desk and sat down. She knew what Twila was talking about because she couldn't seem to stop the smiling. Downstairs when she stopped at the coffee stand she could have sworn the entire staff stopped and stared at her the entire time, as if she were a stray dog they weren't sure they could pet without getting bit.

"Well, Twila, I am happy, very happy. Considering we pulled off a coup Friday night," Athena said, putting her feet up on the desk, "I'd say I was ecstatic."

Smiling, Twila sat down. "Are you sure that's all? Are you sure something else isn't going on here?"

For a second Athena felt her throat constrict as she wondered if someone had found out about her and Mike. Furiously thinking back to the weekend Athena tried to remember. She wondered if they had been spotted making out on the street when they left the restaurant.

"I mean, did you find out that because of the great success the department had this weekend that you're going to be able to send the entire staff on an all expense paid vacation to Hawaii?" Twila said with hope in her eyes and a goofy smile on her face.

Relieved that her secret hadn't been discovered, Athena burst out laughing in genuine amusement. Even though the fundraising had surpassed their goals, with the way the financial books had been looking lately, Athena doubted she even had enough pull now to get them back into Thea's, let alone pay for a trip to Hawaii.

"You are so crazy," Athena finally said once they had both calmed down.

"Well, there's always hope." Twila stood. "So, boss, do you want me to go ahead and call everyone in to your office, or will we have the meeting in the conference room?"

Athena glanced at her watch and told Twila to give her thirty minutes before calling the staff for their weekly meeting in her office. After Twila left, Athena noticed some notes by her phone, each marked urgent. Two messages were from Vincent and one from Barry, which was not normal, considering both usually came in much later than she.

Deciding to return Barry's call first, Athena picked up the phone, wondering what was so important. Even though he was down the hall from her office, she preferred to call instead of walking down.

"Barry Gorenflo," Barry answered on the second ring. Surprised to hear him answering his own phone, Athena said hello.

"Well, hello, Athena," Barry said with a smile in his voice. "Congratulations on your event. I was just talking with Frank and Vincent and we were saying how great it was, really the most fun we've had in a while."

Feeling strangely suspicious, Athena sat up in her chair. "Well, I just have to say thank you for all of your help. I couldn't have done it without—everyone's help," Athena said, doing her part in the schmoozefest that was playing out.

After a pause she heard Barry say, "About that, Athena. We really need to talk. How about we meet for an early lunch?"

Though slightly concerned at Barry's tone and his use of "we," Athena pushed her worries to the side. She was sure it was nothing. Nevertheless, she called Twila and told her to cancel the morning meeting. Grabbing her purse, Athena headed to the lobby where she was to meet Barry to drive together over to Fiesta, a Mexican restaurant that Barry loved.

After ordering their food and getting their appetizers, Barry asked Athena about the fundraiser figures. Athena didn't have to embellish the amazing numbers. It was the most Regent had ever received at a fundraising event.

Despite his accolades, however, Athena couldn't help feeling uneasy with Barry's attempt at being charming. She had a feeling that he was about to drop a bomb. He was just smiling too much.

Despite her attempt at maintaining a positive attitude, Athena found that when their main course finally arrived that she had lost her appetite. Taking small bites at first, Athena finally gave up and began to just move the food around her plate as she waited for Barry to finally get down to business.

"Athena, Vincent has done an amazing job with Thunder Road. I could tell Friday night that the band was really open to the both of you and that you have really hit it off."

When Barry paused, Athena could feel her stomach begin to roll and a familiar feeling began to creep into her throat—the way she felt at the thought of going to Thea's. All Athena could think was that somehow Barry had found out about her personal relationship with Mike. She didn't think it was really any of his business, but her credibility, which she had worked so hard for, could be destroyed in a matter of minutes.

"You're aware that Vincent is the group's manager?" Barry asked, putting down his fork and steepling his fingers in front of his mouth as if he were finding it hard to find the right words. "Are you aware if he has plans to continue managing the group now?"

Not completely understanding why Barry was asking her this, she did something her mother had taught her a long time ago whenever she didn't know what to say.

"Excuse me," Athena said, then took a sip of her iced tea, so that she wouldn't be expected to respond. Athena hated to be manipulative, but she was working hard to make it through the lunch without having a panic attack.

"I mean," Barry said pointedly, "Thunder Road is a popular group, right?" Continuing, Barry said, "What I'm trying to say is that after hearing Thunder Road last week, I'm beginning to wonder if they can be managed only part time. As it is, Vincent and Frank have missed several days of work over the past few months. Are you aware of that?"

Athena felt it was a trap, but she was getting tired of Barry's attempt to lead her through whatever agenda he had. She wished he would get to the point. "Yes, and I approved every one of those days." It was times like this that Athena wished she had banished the board of supervisors at Regent. When she became head of the company she had thought about it, but she had been of the mind then that if it wasn't broke don't fix it. The oversight of the programs at Regent by the board gave the company credibility that the money that was brought in was used on the community. However, it also made things more difficult for Athena, and it made situations like this one very awkward, because although Barry was technically her employee, as Chief Financial Officer his position was also protected by the board. Therefore, he was totally autonomous and free to make Athena's life a living hell if he wanted. Luckily, until now, that hadn't happened. Athena hoped things would not change.

"After their performance Friday night, which by the way I thought was amazing, I heard from several board members who were concerned."

Athena closed her eyes for a second as what Barry was saying sank in.

"Board members?"

"Well," Barry responded, smiling contritely, "they were concerned about some information brought to their attention about the band and the amount of time being given to them by the staff, particularly Frank and Vincent." Barry ended with a head bob to the side.

"Brought by whom, may I ask?" Athena put her napkin down on the table, done with acting as if she were enjoying the meal.

"Does it really matter when we have a bigger problem of clients not being cared for and an allegation of embezzlement?" Barry said.

"What? I can't imagine anything of the sort."

Barry sat back in his chair, "Well, it's true and there are records to prove it. Apparently Vincent and Frank have been dipping into funds and have been doing so for the past five years. In the past couple of months they've really upped the embezzlement. I've already talked with the board and they have advised that an outside party, someone who is not *personally* involved, should investigate the situation."

Athena watched as the bastard stabbed a carrot and placed it in his mouth. She didn't know how, but she was certain Barry had a hand in this. There was no way Vincent and Frank could be involved the way Barry said they were. The charge had to be bogus. She was also sure that Barry knew that she was seeing Mike and this was payback. She knew him to think highly of himself, but she hadn't taken him for an egomaniac. Either way, she did not like the idea of Barry going behind her back to the board—which she was sure he had.

"Barry, I understand what you are saying," Athena said, trying her best to be diplomatic, "but I'm having a hard time believing it," she added, not liking his answering smirk. "However, I would like to help out in any way possible, because I do agree with you on one point, which is that this band has talent. Regardless of any false allegations—and they are false—the group should not be affected."

"I am so glad to hear you say you want to help," Barry said, not commenting on her statement about not agreeing with his decision. "However, this has everything to do with the group. In fact, the board is wondering if your judgement has been skewed concerning this rock and roll band. They're learned that you have a personal relationship with one of the band members," Barry said, playing his hand. Sweeping his eyes down to her chest suggestively, he added, "Funny, Athena, I never would have taken you for a groupie. Neither did your mother when I talked to her this morning."

Standing up, Athena refused to stay any longer.

"Thank you for lunch, Barry, but I've heard enough," Athena said in a controlled voice. "The concerns you have will be investigated and proven wrong posthaste, and once they have been, I will have questions of my own, such as whether someone who has to sneak around behind coworkers' backs to discredit them has a place at Regent."

As she walked away, Athena heard Barry's laughter but did not give in to the urge to go back and punch him in the face. She got in her car, then cursed when it took her three attempts to get the car started. When her phone rang, Athena automatically reached for it. However, she stopped herself when she checked caller ID and saw her mother's number. Staring at the phone as if it were a snake about to strike, Athena let the phone ring until it finally stopped. With her hands shaking, Athena grabbed the steering wheel. What the hell was going on?

Pissed and still in shock, Athena briefly thought about going directly to the chairman of the board, but quickly realized that really wouldn't help until she saw the so-called records. For the first time, Athena regretted not appointing herself chairman. However, she had not considered this particular situation. Now she wished she did have autonomy. Then she wouldn't be freaking out.

Reaching for her phone, Athena called Frank and Vincent, but neither picked up. Driving back to her office, she tried her best to keep her cool. As she got off the elevator, Athena no longer had a kick in her step. All of the energy she'd had this morning was gone, and she wished more than anything she could go back to Saturday morning when she woke up in Mike's arms feeling warm and safe. How had her world changed so much in a matter of hours?

"Athena," Twila whispered, "you have a visitor in your office." Athena briefly wondered why Twila was whispering and looking so fearful, but when she opened her door to see Mike staring out her picture window she understood.

Walking into her office, Athena closed the door behind her, and breathed a sigh of relief. She wanted nothing more than to wrap her arms around this man who was so strong.

Putting her purse down, she went to stand behind Mike. When he didn't turn around or respond, Athena broke the silence.

"I guess you heard," Athena said, trying to lighten the mood. When Mike turned, Athena gasped at his dark expression. She had never seen him look so serious or dangerous.

Scowling, Mike said, "I don't know what to say, Athena." Moving away from her, he went to go sit on the corner of her desk, folding his arms over his chest. "When did you make the decision that I wasn't good enough for you, 'second best' as your mother put it? Better yet, why did you decide to lower yourself and sleep with me?"

Shock was the first thing that Athena felt. Confused at what he was saying, Athena was speechless.

"According to one Aileen Miles, it was from the very beginning. To quote her, this—what we have—was a diversion, and that was it."

At the mention of her mother, Athena instantly saw red. She felt her control quietly slipping. How dare she!

"Yeah," Mike continued, seeing understanding in Athena's eyes and taking it for collusion, "she called this morning—on my home phone." Mike began to pace. "She told me that I should walk away now because we would never last, but you didn't have the guts to tell me yet. Were you intimidated, Athena, with me being a ditch digger and all?"

Athena couldn't find any words. The only thing running through her mind was too foul to express. Her mother had crossed the line.

"I didn't say those things," Athena began, "that was my mother." Grabbing on to Mike's shirt Athena pleaded, shaking her head, "That's not me, you know me."

"I thought I did," Mike said, prying her hands off him as if he couldn't stand her touch, then moving away. "I didn't even know you had a mother. Tell me something," Mike said, pausing at the door. "When she was saying all of these things to you, did you once tell her it wasn't true—anything about me?" When Athena didn't respond, Mike opened the door and went out, closing it quietly behind him.

Watching Mike walk out the door wasn't the hardest thing that Athena had to do in her life, but having him leave without even a second glance definitely tied with it.

Moments later Twila came into her office, not bothering to knock.

"Tom Buckley is on his way up, and he has requested a meeting with you."

Meeting with the chairman of the board was the last thing she felt like doing, but she knew it had to be done. Knowing he was a very no-nonsense person, Athena forced herself to sit. The fight had been drained out of her with Mike's cruel words. They only proved everything her mother had always told her. She was incapable of being loved; it was simple as that. Happiness was not in her cards.

Athena got all the way down to the car garage before she remembered that her sister had her car. On the verge of tears, she was thankful when Mr. Gutman offered his assistance and called her a cab. She was even more grateful that he left her alone to cry in peace.

Once she arrived home, Athena walked in the front door to see Sheree sitting on the couch with Hector, sipping piña coladas even though it was not even two o'clock. Athena frowned at the giggling pair, then went to her bedroom where she got under the covers, shoes and all. It took Sheree all of two seconds to come in after her.

"Athena, what's going on?" Sheree asked. "What are you doing home so early, and why didn't you call me?" she drawled out with genuine concern in her voice.

When Athena didn't answer, Sheree pulled the covers back. When Athena pulled the covers back over her head again, she got up and went back out to the living room. Minutes later she returned.

Yanking the covers back, Sheree prodded Athena until she opened her eyes. "Drink this," she said loudly.

Not wanting to wear what was inside the juice glass, Athena sat up to take a sip. Expecting water, Athena was surprised to find the dark-colored glass was full of piña colada. Coughing, Athena recovered. Because it tasted good, Athena drank some more, and didn't stop until it was empty.

"There you go," Sheree said, taking the glass away from Athena. "Now tell me what's wrong."

Athena could feel the alcohol two-stepping in her brain already, but was not so far gone that she was ready to tell Sheree her problems.

"You might as well spill it," Sheree said in her usual twang. "I already know that this," pointing at Athena's disheveled clothing, "has to do with a man."

Athena just blinked at her.

"Don't even try to wait me out. Hector told me already about the man sneaking out your front door this morning before I got here. He told me that he had been here since Friday night when y'all were dropped off by a limo."

Adding Hector to her piss list, Athena swore softly.

"Athena, are you pregnant?" Sheree asked seriously.

"Now you ask me after you ply me with liquor," Athena mocked. "Not likely," she said, frowning, thinking about Mike and the possibility of never having sex again.

"Okay," Sheree said, trying to go another route. "Who is the guy that you've been hiding from everyone?"

"Nobody," Athena scoffed, refusing to go there with her sister right now. Sheree got up, took the glass with her, and minutes later was back. She handed a full glass to Athena.

"Drink it."

Athena couldn't help smiling at her sister's attempt to get her drunk enough to tell her what her problems were. She wanted to tell her how alcohol was what had gotten her in the current mess. Alcohol and her need to handle every situation herself. Deciding for once not to play the role of superwoman, Athena placed the glass down on the bedside table and started talking.

CHAPTER 20

"Who de hoo."

Athena heard the call, knew what her response should be but just couldn't get it out. Where was Sheree when she needed her?

"Who de hoo," Hector's voice was much closer.

Turning around, Athena walked towards her bedroom.

Then she heard jangling of keys at her front door, letting her know that someone had just entered her home. Groaning, she cursed the day she had given Hector a spare. Up until now he had never dared use them. It was going to be a bad day.

"Excuse me, miss?" A voice called out.

What the hell? Hearing a deep, familiar voice Athena ran for her door. *What was he doing here?*

"Kwame?" Athena said, as she opened her door. Walking into her living room, she saw the hulking manchild standing in the middle of her foyer alone. He seemed nervous and uncertain, which placed Athena even more on alert. *This can't be good.* Craning her neck to look into his eyes, Athena searched his face for an answer as to why Hector had dumped him in her living room.

If it had been any other day, the puppy dog hurt in Kwame's eyes would have had her melting and backpedaling faster than Lance Armstrong, but Athena was beat. Not only was she beat, but her head and her heart hurt. Thinking about all her problems made her eyes tear. The last thing she wanted to deal with was work. Didn't "pending further investigation" mean she didn't have to deal with this crap?

"Kwame, whatever it is you are in need of, please put it in memo form and turn it in to Twila," Athena said in a clipped tone. Silently, she added a please, but she dared not show weakness. The floodgates were leaking as it was and she did not need a breakdown on top of everything else. She was the boss, dammit, albeit in name only. The boss could not show weakness. Kwame refused to back down.

Closing the door, he followed Athena into her living room, sitting down on the edge of her chaise lounge. He looked ridiculous perched on the ultrafeminine chair.

"Kwame," Athena said with force. "Sit there." She pointed to a more appropriate chair on the opposite side of the room.

Realizing that something was weighing heavy on his mind, Athena put her feelings to the side. As usual, her needs last. She cringed at the pity party, but at the same time felt she deserved it more than anyone. She took a seat opposite him.

"What's the problem, Kwame?"

"Ms. Athena," Kwame began, and Athena cringed again. With Mike she was never Ms. anything. He saw through the no-nonsense mask she had to wear 24/7. With him she was just a woman.

No more. Athena forced herself to stop thinking about Mike and what could have been to focus on Kwame.

"I was just trying to do my job," Kwame continued, growing more and more agitated.

"What happened, Kwame?" Concerned now at Kwame's manner, Athena gave him her full attention. This was not like him. Kwame was one of the more cool-headed people on her staff. No matter the problem, Athena was able to trust his judgement. Now looking at the way the oversized man was fidgeting in his chair, Athena felt a sinking feeling in her stomach.

"They're bringing up charges."

Driving to the Regent offices, Athena forced herself to breathe. She felt sick to her stomach and her shoulders were tense with frustration. She hadn't been able to get anyone on the phone since Kwame dropped the bomb in her lap fifteen minutes ago, probably because it was a Saturday. Athena still could not believe what Kwame had told her. It was Barry who was to blame for her firing; in fact, he was to blame for everything.

"The weasel" had really earned his title. Unknown to them, he had been using Frank and Vincent to do his dirty work, giving them the go-ahead on ventures not legally allowed by policy. He had duped them into breaking the law with funds that only he had access to by funneling money from fake accounts. However, unless she could find the paperwork that Kwame said was there, she would never be able to prove it, and Frank and Vincent would take the fall.

Braking, Athena turned into the parking garage. Athena was glad the garage was mostly empty. The last thing she needed was to be arrested for trespassing. Her mother, she was sure, would have a heart attack and die instantly. As soon as she stepped off the elevator she made a beeline for the office doors, searching for her key as she walked.

"Please let them not have changed the locks," Athena whispered. When the lock clicked open, she breathed a sigh of relief. Quickly walking into Barry's office, Athena remembered what Kwame had said earlier.

"Barry keeps a separate filing cabinet in his office. That's where he keeps a ledger of transactions from his slush fund. I think he has been moving monies around for years, just not enough for anyone to notice."

Athena had always felt leery about the amount of power Barry had as the Chief Financial Officer, but she would never have suspected this of him. Since he came from money, he seemed above reproach. But background obviously wasn't enough. He apparently planned to obtain control by bringing Athena down. He was actually willing to use her mother's desire for her to marry their families together to get it.

The thought of going with him on a date to appease her mother made her sick. Athena swallowed hard. She had work to do right now and vomiting on Barry's desk, although appealing, would not help get it done.

Athena spied the cabinet and ran over to it, not bothering to close the door behind her. Opening it, Athena searched for the ledger that Kwame said contained the documents to expose Barry.

Just as she spotted it, the room flooded with light.

"You know what?"

"What?" Mike asked, taking a sip of his rum and Coke. He really didn't want to know, but then again, he didn't want to be sitting across from Athena's baby sister either. How she had found him, he would never know, but once the little minx set up shop in the middle of his rehearsal set, there was no budging her. It didn't take an Einstein to realize he'd either talk to her or try to sing around her incessant chatter. She seemed determined to say her piece.

"My sister is a stuck-up, bourgeois fuddy-duddy," Sheree began, daring Mike to agree, "but she is my sister. I know her better than anyone."

Not wanting to draw any more of her ire, Mike sat quietly, hoping she would talk herself out.

"The last few months I have seen that woman go from cold to hot and back again more than once. Now you may not know how strange that is for her, but my sister does not let things that don't matter shake her. She's always calm, cool, and collected."

At that Mike couldn't help choking on his drink. She obviously didn't know Athena as well as she thought, because the woman he had grown to love was anything but calm on most days—at least not when he was around.

"Even with Kendrick," Sheree said, "Athena always held a little something back, and they were together for years." Looking up from her glass at Mike, Sheree caught his expression before he was able to let the mask slip back into place. It would have been obvious to a two-year-old that Mike had it bad for her sister. Sheree felt certain she was doing the right thing. She'd had her doubts when she first saw Mike, who in her opinion had only two expressions: pissed and more pissed. When she barged onto his stage he had shown her both.

"You do know about Kendrick?"

"Yeah."

"Yeah," Sheree mimicked. "Do you ever say more than one word?" Sheree was proud of herself when a third expression arose on Mike's face—frustration.

Suddenly Mike wished that he was anywhere but sitting in front of this little woman with eyes that didn't miss anything. She reminded him a little of his aunts back home. They'd never let him get away with anything, badgering him to death, forcing him to speak when it was the last thing he wanted to do.

"I know all about the fiancé. I heard about him from Athena, and then the little bit she left out was filled in by your mother." Downing the rest of his drink, Mike stood to leave.

"My mother?" Sheree said, following in Mike's footsteps as he began to walk away. "My mother doesn't know anything about that two-faced Kendrick."

Mike stopped short at her words, causing Sheree to collide with him. Rubbing her shoulder, Sheree swore she had hit concrete. Her sister had gone and gotten herself a hardbody. Smiling to herself, Sheree grew more determined to get the man Athena loved back in her arms where he belonged.

"Athena, what the hell?"

Breathing a sigh of relief when she looked up to see Twila standing in the doorway, Athena told her to turn the light out and close the door.

"What are you doing here?" Athena asked, pulling the folder out.

"I should be asking you the same thing," Twila said. "I just came in to clear out the leftover pizza from yesterday."

Any other time, Athena would have made a joke, but she was too busy looking for the ledger.

"Why so secretive?" Twila asked, turning off the lights.

Athena launched into the charges Kwame had stated against Barry as she continued rummaging in Barry's cabinet.

"He did what?" Twila yelled, angry. She immediately pulled out her phone and punched in several numbers.

"Get off the phone and help me look. We don't have much time."

"Actually you have no time," a voice said from the doorway.

Suddenly, the lights came on. Both women turned to see Barry standing in the doorway.

"Why do you care?" Mike asked, adding a fourth expression, surly, to Sheree's short list of Mike-isms.

"Why do you care?" Sheree couldn't help mimicking. However, at Mike's glower she composed herself. *This is important, don't screw it up, Sheree*, she told herself.

"My sister is very important to me. My entire life she's looked out for me, and I can be a little . . ."

"Snot."

"Well, damn," Sheree said, frowning at Mike's description. However, she pushed her feelings aside and continued.

"Difficult was what I was going to say," Sheree finished, squinting at Mike before continuing. "Still, my sister has always supported me. Now it's time for me to pay her back. Look, Mike, for whatever reason, my sister likes you." Sheree was stunned when Mike repaid her insult with a smile straight out of a Colgate ad. Suddenly she got what her sister saw in him. The man was fine. Not model fine, but oh-what-a-mighty-fine-man fine.

"She may even love you, for all I know, but regardless," Sheree paused making sure she had his full attention, "I have never seen my sister more miserable over a man before. For that reason alone I would walk through fire to make sure things work out."

Watching for a reaction, any reaction, Sheree grew more and more discouraged when Mike continued to stare off into space.

"Well?"

"Well what?"

"Call her," Sheree yelled in frustration.

"No."

"No? Didn't you hear me," Sheree yelled, standing up as if to do battle. "She quite possibly loves you."

"And?"

Sheree felt like her head was going to explode. This was not how it was supposed to go. She had begun to wonder if Mike was right for her sister when he actually provided some information.

"She never said that to me."

CHAPTER 21

"What exactly are you looking for, Athena?"

Athena felt a shiver crawl down her spine to her legs. She couldn't move, that is, until she remembered it was Barry. The same Barry who at day camp got so scared watching *E.T.* that he peed on himself. Barry who had asked her out for the prom and cried when she said no. Unfortunately, that same Barry was now calling the police.

Oh shit.

"What, are you crazy?" Twila asked. "This is Athena, not some burglar."

"This is a trespasser," Barry said, reaching into his pocket and pulling out a pistol.

"Oh. My. God."

"Shut up, Twila," Athena growled.

"He has a gun."

"Hush," Athena whispered.

"Oh. My. God."

"Shut up," Barry yelled, pointing the gun at Twila. "Yes," Barry said into the phone. "I would like to report a burglary in progress. I don't know who it is. I'm trapped in my office."

After giving the address, Barry shut off his phone abruptly.

"They should be here at any moment. There's just enough time for me take care of the both of you."

Flicking the gun towards the couch, Barry indicated for them to sit. Then, reaching between the wall and the cabinet, he pulled out a ledger.

"Is this what you were looking for?"

With a demonic smile, Barry cackled. "So you found me out? You can't possibly think I would let you win, Athena."

"Barry," Athena spoke slowly, "it doesn't have to go down like this."

"It doesn't have to go down like this," Barry mimicked bitterly. "What are we down to now? Dating a white boy? How could you? I cared for you!" Barry yelled across the room with the gun pointed at her.

"I care for you," Athena said slowly.

"Right," Barry said, gesturing wildly with the gun. "You cared for me by treating me like a pariah for the past twenty years. And then you go out with him? That—that trailer trash?"

Athena heard Twila's gasp but she ignored it. She didn't want to take her eyes off Barry, realizing how far gone he was. The embezzlement scheme was just a symptom.

"You know what's in here?"

Athena didn't bother responding; she thought it best to keep him talking.

"This is a file of every transaction for the past three years," Barry laughed, "every transaction that I didn't place on the books. No one ever suspected a thing. That is, until your pet, Kwame, started snooping around."

Athena forced herself to focus on the situation at hand. She had to keep him talking. As long as he kept talking she might be able to reason with him.

"Good ol' reliable Barry's not so stupid after all, huh?" Barry continued, giggling to himself.

Athena wasn't touching that comment with a ten-foot pole.

"You know, accounting is more than just numbers. It requires dedication, intelligence, organization, loyalty. Things that you can't even begin to understand!"

Despite his yelling, Athena kept her cool. She didn't want to force him into confrontation.

"All these years, and none of you had any idea about what was really going on. You were just so ready to 'let Barry handle it.' Right?" When Athena didn't respond he yelled again, "Right?"

Athena nodded her head, praying that was the right answer.

"It's not like I spent all the money on myself. A lot of it was donated. The rest," Barry grinned, looking almost boyish, "was spent on a little fun."

Athena quickly understood what he was talking about. All those trips to Brazil, sometimes five, six times a year. She'd assumed his trust fund took care of everything. Athena could only imagine the cost, and what he had used the money for. She mentally cringed at her thoughts.

There was a noise suddenly, and Barry looked to Twila. Frowning, he took a step forward.

"Stop," was all Barry said, but Twila was too far gone to obey.

Athena placed one hand on Twila's knee, which had started jumping, causing the entire sofa to shake. Twila was not going to make it much longer, Athena thought to herself. She just hoped she wouldn't do anything stupid.

Then the phone rang. It sounded so foreign in the silence of the building that all three of them jumped. Barry automatically reached for it.

"Good afternoon. Yeah, I just came in for a few minutes to get a file," Barry said into the phone. He sounded normal even to Athena's ears. It made her wonder just how long Barry had been hiding the craziness.

"Yeah, you were lucky to have caught me," Barry said, sounding as if he didn't have a care in the world. "What can I do for you?"

Athena kept her eye on Barry and the gun, grimacing when he used the butt of it to scratch his brow. Just as she wondered if the thing was even loaded, it went off.

Athena hit the floor. She tried to bring Twila with her but the girl had plans of her own and ran for the door. Scared and feeling vulnerable, Athena covered her head as her mind went strictly into survival mode. When she heard scrambling footsteps, she peeped to see what was going on. There were uniformed men everywhere. Three were wrestling Barry to the floor, and another was holding his gun. She jumped when a hand touched her shoulder.

"Ms. Miles?" a young police officer said gently.

Athena nodded her head and he helped her to stand.

"You bitch," Barry shouted, "you did this. It's all your fault."

Athena cringed in disgust at the madman who was now directing the officers to remove her from the premises for trespassing even as they handcuffed his arms behind his back.

"Are you okay?" the officer asked.

Athena patted herself. She knew that sometimes gunshots could cause shock. She quickly realized that she was not the one who had been shot. She saw bloody footprints leading to the door and immediately thought of Twila.

"Oh God, Twila!" Athena started toward the door, dragging the policeman with her.

"Athena," Twila said, meeting her at the door.

The two women hugged as the officer moved away.

"I was going for help," Twila whispered against Athena's shoulder.

"Right," Athena said, glad to see she was safe. Then she remembered the shot.

"Well, if you aren't hurt, where did all the blood come from?" Athena questioned.

"Apparently," an officer with a heavy Southern accent drawled, "the perp shot himself in the foot by accident."

If she hadn't been a hostage for the past hour, Athena might have seen the humor in it all, but all she could think about was the fact that Barry had been waving a real gun with real bullets at her only minutes ago. Her knees threatened to buckle. She wanted out—now.

The officers questioned both Twila and Athena, but let them go as soon as possible. Before Athena could make it to her car, her family descended. Her sister was the first to see her and Athena fell into her arms. Then her father scooped her up in a bear hug that left her weak. She was glad to see them, but at the same time, Athena knew someone was missing. The tears started to flow as she realized that Mike truly was gone.

"We would like to inform you of a hostage situation at the local . . ."

Mike tuned out the television. He really didn't care about hearing anyone else's drama after the morning—hell, the week he'd had.

Taking his suitcase out of the closet for the fifth time in the past hour, Mike finally had the willpower to throw some clothes into it. He had the art of leaving down to a science, and little thought or effort was required to gather enough clothes for the next couple of weeks. However, unlike in the past, he did not feel that old excitement about finding someplace new or different. For the first time, he actually dreaded it. However, he refused to let that stop him. Closing the suitcase, Mike took it and his guitar out to the truck.

The band was pissed at him for forcing them to leave a day ahead of schedule, but it was either leave or say or do something that would ultimately lead to couple of cracked ribs and a busted-up face. Mike was angry and frustrated, two things that in the past had led him to do far worse things than pick a fight with whoever was closest.

Why did she have to show up? Mike thought back to the conversation with Sheree earlier. Until she showed up everything had been simple. His woman had done him wrong, had betrayed what they had built together. If no one else, he expected Athena to have his back. Hell, he'd definitely had hers.

Cursing once more, Mike walked back into his home.

"Home," he said aloud, wincing at the echo. Some home, he thought. It was his, all right, but it looked as if a squatter lived there rather than a grown ass man. He had a beanbag chair, for chrissakes.

Grabbing his keys, Mike refused to think about it. He pulled out one of his old tricks and started thinking about what was ahead of him. There were plans to make and gigs to hit. Closing the door behind him, Mike refused to look back. It would only give credence to the hurt he felt in his heart, and he did not have the strength for that.

CHAPTER 22

Athena tried to push the childhood memories out of her mind and psych herself up about the reunion that she and her sister had returned home for. They both could have stayed at Athena's condo, but the reporters had caught wind of the Regent scandal and had camped out on her front lawn.

What a difference a week made, Athena thought to herself. Just last week she had been cuddling in her bed with a man she thought would be the love of her life. Now he couldn't be bothered to call her though she'd nearly been murdered. It was official: her choice in men sucked.

"Forget about him," her sister had said adamantly. Athena didn't quite understand her sister's dislike of Mike, but at the same time she didn't discourage it. What could she say? It made her feel better to have someone on her side.

Athena went to the refrigerator to get lunch started. This, she was sure, would be the first and last time she would be allowed in the kitchen this weekend. This weekend relatives who were first-class cooks would be cooking anything and everything. Although her mother had made a lot of money cooking for people, everyone in the Miles family knew that all of Aileen's famous dishes originated in the kitchens of Aileen's aunts', mother's, grandmother's, and mother-in-law's. Just thinking about the variety of dishes had Athena practically salivating. She was going to find it hard to exercise restraint. Her family loved to cook and eat and Athena was looking forward to it and the company—anything to keep her mind off her problems.

Thinking about last year this time, Athena smiled. Someone had had the bright idea to forgo cooking for the first night of the family reunion, and go to one of Biloxi's famously massive casino buffets. The Miles clan had gone en masse. They had almost single-handedly closed the restaurant down.

As Athena assembled ingredients, Sheree came in and pitched in to get lunch started. The two sisters were working on preparing sandwiches and soup. Their mother found them hard at work twenty minutes later when she walked in through the back door.

"Yo, Ma," Sheree said loudly, knowing how much her mother hated slang talk.

"Hello girls," their mother said, dropping bags on the kitchen table. "How long you been here?"

Frowning Athena didn't respond. So this was how she was going to play it. Well, if her mother didn't say anything, she definitely wasn't saying anything.

Seeing Athena turn her back to their mother, Sheree did her usual mediating. "Almost half an hour, Mother."

"Why didn't you call me on my cell?" their mother asked, refusing to acknowledge the tension within the kitchen. She went to the sink and began to wash dishes.

Sheree laughed nervously before glancing at Athena, signaling her to say something—anything.

Walking up behind the older woman, Athena imagined what it would feel like to tell her mother off. She was beyond tired of her interference in her life, and the anger she felt about her mother's need to control everything had just about consumed her.

To avoid erupting, Athena turned tail and hurried to the sanctuary of her old room. Lying across her childhood bed, she thought about the number of times she had done this exact thing. When she was an emotionally freer teenager, however, there had been a lot of slamming of doors and yelling.

Then, however, her mother had never followed.

"How could you . . ." Athena began when she heard the door open. She had no need to look to see who was there. She'd caught the scent of Chanel No. 5.

She wasn't surprised when her mother's cell began to ring; however, she was surprised when her mother didn't answer it.

That's different. Curiosity stirred, she turned to face her mother. "What did you think you were doing, calling my boyfriend?"

"Boyfriend," Aileen cackled. "Really, Athena, a couple of nights do not make a boyfriend."

"What? Do you have spies on me or something? How dare you?" Athena said, standing to walk over to Aileen. "How could you go behind my back and call him like that and say those things to him?"

"I just said the truth, 'Thena," Aileen responded. "The boy has no career, no degree, and spends most nights in one dive after another. He is a three out of ten and that is based solely on his looks." Walking to the window, putting distance between them, Aileen stared out. "He's nothing more than what they used to call in my day a gigolo, girl."

Before she could stop herself, Athena reached out to grab her mother's shoulder. Spinning her around, Athena looked her straight in the eye. "You overstepped yourself. Mike is a man. A man that I care about. I am a grown woman, and who I sleep with or don't sleep with is no concern of yours." Athena watched as her mother's eyes widened and she took a step back.

Athena took a step forward, causing her mother to look at her as if she had grown two heads. But Athena didn't care. She had something on her chest and it was time to get it out. Past time.

"You will not interfere in my life from this point on, do you understand?" Athena did not wait for her mother's response. "I came here today to let you know that. This," she said, waving her hands over her body, "is my life," Athena yelled. "And this," she waved towards her mother, "is yours. You are not to intrude in my life again. Understand?" Athena could feel herself breathing harshly as she waited for her mother's response this time.

"Well, do you?"

"Yes, Athena," Aileen said swallowing.

Taking a step back, Athena turned to walk out the door, but stopped before opening it. "And you will apologize to Mike," Athena whispered.

"Athena?"

Although she wanted nothing more than to walk away from her mother, she couldn't ignore the plea in her voice. Still, she refused to turn around.

"Are you all right?"

Now she asks, Athena thought in disbelief. Then she felt her mother's hand on her shoulder for a brief moment.

"Are you okay, Athena?" Aileen asked again.

Athena turned to her mother. If she weren't seeing it with her own eyes she wouldn't believe it. Her mother, the legend, the mogul, the queen of commercialized domesticity, was crying.

Blinking, Athena could only nod.

"I understand that you probably don't believe me, but I was trying to look out for you. I just want the best for you. You deserve it."

"Barry was the best?" Athena couldn't help rubbing it in. However, when her mother responded as if she had physically struck her, Athena felt bad.

"Mother," Athena said slowly, "you can't make everything perfect. My life, your life, our lives were not meant to be perfect. I like my life. Yes, I'm okay. Don't you understand that?"

Aileen nodded before letting her head drop heavily onto her chest. "I'm sorry."

Athena felt worse than she did when she was yelling at her mother moments earlier. This was not what she wanted. She did not want to see her powerful, self-assured mother broken, just humbled for once.

"It's not all yours or anyone's fault," Athena said, looking at the crown of her mother's head, wishing she knew the right thing to say. "You were only being you. It was my job to be me, and not allow you to dictate my life. I accept that my life is screwed up because I didn't have the strength to fight for it," Athena said fiercely. "Besides, no one could have known Barry was the whack job that he turned out to be."

"I should have."

"What?"

"I should have."

Athena looked at her mother, wondering if crazy was catching.

"His father was the same way."

"Oh Lord," Athena groaned, sitting on her bed. It was too early for this *Dynasty, Knots Landing* type stuff.

Why can't I have a normal family? she wanted to shout to the sky.

"I just thought," Aileen continued, sitting next to her daughter, "that it most likely would have skipped a generation."

"You mean to tell me that Barry's father held a gun on a woman who had spurned him?"

"It wasn't a gun, but yes, and the woman was me, about thirty years ago."

"And?" Athena prompted when her mother didn't continue.

Oh," Aileen said, as she'd forgotten she had been talking. "He took me up to Camp Wilkes and refused to bring me home until I said I would marry him. Of course I just hopped out of his Thunderbird and hitched my way back home. He was too embarrassed to show his face after that."

"And you wanted me to marry into that family?" Athena asked incredulously.

"Well, they do have a long history on the Coast."

Athena cut her off. "Jesus Christ."

"Don't you swear, Athena Miles," Aileen said, standing with her shoulders straight. She walked gracefully to the bedroom door and opened it. "Now get yourself cleaned up and come on back downstairs. You know how your daddy gets when he doesn't eat."

Athena watched as her mother closed her bedroom door.

"Well," Athena said aloud, "I guess I told her."

CHAPTER 23

Driving along Highway 90 to her parents' house, Athena was reminded of the past. After she'd learned to drive, she had particularly loved driving along the coastline from Biloxi to Gulfport to Bay St. Louis. She remembered well her first car, an old Toyota with a stick shift. The first time she had taken the thing on Highway 90 she had been so nervous she had almost wrecked. However, it wasn't long before she had become an old pro.

Her thoughts returned to the present. She didn't know what she would have done if it hadn't been for Twila's quick thinking a few days ago when Barry had held them hostage. It was because of her that the police had arrived when they did. When Twila had dialed her phone she had called her boyfriend, who had overheard the entire conversation and fortunately had called the police.

After the police had taken Barry away, Athena at first hadn't really cared about anything other than the fact that she was still breathing. The idea that he had been carrying around so much hate for her was so bizarre. Although they had grown up together, Athena realized now that she hadn't really known him. It would never have occurred to her that he was obsessed with her. When Mike came into the picture, he'd totally lost touch with reality.

Fortunately, he was now getting the help he needed at Whitfield Hospital in Jackson. During the course of the investigation Athena had learned that although Vincent and Frank had been using work hours to promote their bands, the embezzlement had been Barry's alone. He had tampered with the books to make it appear it was Vincent and Frank who were embezzling. Although Vincent and Frank were innocent of criminal activity they had allowed their personal goals to overshadow their responsibilities and had resigned.

Athena was sad to see her friends go but the shift in personnel looked to be good for the organization. Athena looked forward to working with the promoted employees in their new positions. She had heard that both Kwame and Latonya had already taken possession of their new offices and were developing program ideas for local communities.

Looking out her car window, Athena still couldn't believe the devastation that still remained from Katrina. Even though it had been two years since the storm there were still empty concrete slabs where there used to be businesses and homes. Still, she was optimistic that the Coast would be even better in a few years. It might take some time, but she was sure that the Miles family and the Coast would be all right.

Athena's mind drifted to Mike. She hadn't heard from him since their argument. The old Athena would have tracked him down, but the new Athena decided to let fate handle it. If it was meant to be, then it would happen. Besides, there were only so many times she could attempt to get Mike to listen to her explanation. If he wasn't ready to hear her, he wasn't ready.

Athena couldn't really blame him. If his mother had contacted her and talked the trash that her mother had done, she wouldn't be trying to hear him right now either. Since her mother lived in the same town, any man in her life would forever have to deal with Aileen, who was a force of nature. Mike would have to deal with Aileen if he was to be a part of her life. Hell, she would demand it. Athena needed someone running interference.

Her mother had been walking on eggshells ever since their confrontation, as well she should be. She'd caught her mother looking at her strangely a couple of times, no doubt thinking her daughter had lost her marbles. Athena shook her head. She wasn't crazy but she would no longer allow anyone to dictate to her how her life should be lived. Mike had been right in his assumption that she had not defended him to her mother. She did feel guilty about that. Hell, she hadn't even offered to introduce him to anyone in her life. If she were in his shoes she would have felt the same way. The hardest part for Athena was taking the blame for this whole situation. It had never been her mother's prejudice that had threatened to destroy her relationship; it was Athena's weakness.

Mel had offered to talk to Mike, but Athena had told her to leave it alone. She wasn't quite willing to let him totally off the hook. Even though she accepted that the blame was hers, Athena did not like how Mike had handled things. She didn't like that he'd showed up on her job the way he had or the fact that he hadn't deemed it important to call and see if she was still breathing. There was no way he hadn't heard about Barry. Biloxi was growing, but it wasn't that big.

Even though she loved her job, Athena had begun to realize in the past few weeks that it was just that—a job—and she wanted more, lots more. But for the first time in her life practical Athena was at a loss as to what to do next.

Where am I? Athena thought as she rolled over in her childhood bed, trying to wake herself up. Hearing an unfamiliar beep, she began digging her way out from beneath the covers, and reached for the noise. Picking the phone up from the nightstand, Athena heard her mother outside the bedroom door fussing about early morning calls. Rolling her eyes, Athena looked at the caller ID first, smiling when she recognized the number.

"Hey, Mel," Athena said, smiling, and looking around her room.

"Hey, girl," Mel said. "How are you doing?"

Still with a smile on her face, Athena said, "I'm better now."

Noticing the choppy static every once in a while coming from Mel's phone, Athena asked, "Mel, please tell me why you sound like you're in a tunnel."

"Girl, after this past week, I decided to take it easy today. I'm in my car now and I'm going to get me some breakfast in a few minutes."

Feeling her stomach grumbling, Athena asked what she was going to eat.

"Oh, I don't know, I'm gonna have to see what they got once I get there." After talking for a few more minutes, they said good-bye and promised to talk soon.

Smelling breakfast cooking, Athena made her way downstairs after brushing her teeth and her hair. As soon as she got halfway down the stairs she heard a familiar voice. Stepping into the kitchen, Athena immediately spotted her Uncle Pete and had to stifle a groan.

"Well, I'll be a monkey's uncle." Uncle Pete got up from his seat to come towards Athena for a hug. "You look just like that girl Beyonce, uh-oh, uh-oh, oh-oh." Even Athena couldn't help laughing hearing her uncle do his impression of the young woman. Laughing still, she grabbed a plate that her mother prepared and joined Sheree and her dad at the table.

Athena and Sheree joined in as their parents and Uncle Pete talked about all the relatives that were supposed to be coming in tonight. They had people from California and Florida who were flying in and then a mass of people coming from northern Mississippi and Alabama. All in all, they were looking at close to two hundred relatives who would all gather over the next two days.

Athena was really looking forward to seeing everyone tomorrow. She wouldn't be surprised if by the end of tomorrow she was ready to put a bag over her face after hearing all the comments from everyone about her new look, if Uncle Pete's response was any indication. After breakfast, Sheree and Athena got dressed to head over to their grandmother's to help out with the preparations. Their mother had already left. Their mother and their grandmother had a love-hate relationship. They loved to irritate each other and hated for one to outdo the other. Despite this, or because of it, they worked well together.

Athena had just put her shoes on when she heard a knock on her bedroom door. "Come in," Athena said over her shoulder. When she turned around, she saw her sister smiling a big smile, and then behind her, she saw Mel.

"I thought you were going out of town," Athena said, hugging her friend's neck. "Why didn't you tell me you were coming?" she asked once they all calmed down.

"Girl, I just wanted to surprise you. Besides," Mel said hesitantly, "I didn't know if you would tell me to turn back around or not."

Realizing that her friend still didn't believe that she wasn't upset over her initial disapproval of her relationship with Mike. Athena just gave her another hug. Finally accepting Athena at her word, the three of them laughed all the way down the stairs. Making sure that their dad and Uncle Pete were comfortable, the three young women said their good-byes and headed out to Grandma Miles's place to lend some extra hands.

The next few hours went by in a flash and by the time the three made it out of the small kitchen that evening they were beat. They had chopped, boiled, sauteed, and fried until they didn't want to even think about food. Calling it a night, Athena and Sheree dropped Mel off at her parents' house, then headed back to their parents' home and straight to bed.

Saturday morning everyone in the house woke up early to get ready to head out to the family reunion. Wearing shorts, both Sheree and Athena put their luggage into the back of her car for their overnight stay in New Orleans. Athena, Mel, and Sheree planned to leave out later that afternoon before it got too dark so that they could drop off Sheree to check in for the evening shows, and Mel and Athena could catch the Bombastic Players, Mel's second favorite band, on one of the side stages.

Leaving the house after their parents, Athena, Mel, and Sheree locked up, then headed over to the reunion. As soon as they pulled onto their grandmother's road they heard the music. It was so crowded that they had to park a little away and walk back to the house. When they got to the house, there was so much activity it took them thirty minutes to make it inside. Athena felt her head spin at all the names and faces that sort of looked like hers. There was kin everywhere. Athena couldn't help thinking that the Miles family sure was a fertile lot.

Once they made it into the kitchen, Athena immediately spotted her Aunt Ollie standing in between her mother and grandmother. Seeing that something not so pretty was about happen, Athena walked over to her grandmother to say hello. Immediately engulfed in a big hug, Athena was grateful to see Aunt Ollie take the opportunity to pull her mother away.

"I just don't know what is wrong with your mama," Athena's grandmother said. "That woman was about to use turkey in my greens."

Athena decided to not waste her breath telling her grandmother how much healthier it was to use that than the ham hocks she had set to the side. She just nodded and pitched in to help, laughing to herself. Her grandmother was the only person she knew who had no problem telling off Aileen.

The next few hours passed quickly as groups of people came in to fix plates. Everyone figured out very fast that turns would have to be taken in order for everyone to eat. First the kids were called in and given plates to take outside where they would end up playing in a few minutes anyway. Then the elders were given first pickings. After that it was a free-for-all.

With all the cooking they'd done and the covered dishes brought in, there was enough for everyone to get full and even take home a little something for later. Just as the mosquitoes started to come out, Athena, her sister, and Mel began making rounds to say their good-byes until Sunday. Promising to try to get back early on Sunday, Athena and the other two women headed out to Mel's SUV to hit the road.

Minutes later the three women were on I-10 with nothing but road in front of them. Raiding Mel's collection, they listened to Bonnie Raitt first, Athena's choice; then Macy Gray, Mel's choice; and finally the soundtrack to *Living Out Loud*. By the time they made it into New Orleans, the three were hoarse from singing at the top of their lungs to their favorite tracks, but in good spirits. It was just what she needed, Athena thought to herself as they pulled into the valet parking at the Beauchamps Hotel. Luckily, Athena had been able to get a room at the same hotel as Sheree, so as soon as they unloaded their luggage they went to check in.

Standing at the front desk, Athena and Mel both jumped when Sheree started screaming at the top of her lungs, before running at full speed through the lobby. Worried that her sister had lost her mind, Athena attempted to follow her, until she saw the cause of Sheree's screaming. Athena spotted her brother-in-law, Ronnie, standing by a humongous potted palm seconds before Sheree launched herself at him.

"I guess she's happy to see him," Mel said when Athena stepped back in line. Smiling, Athena looked back at her sister and couldn't help smiling at her enthusiasm.

"Yeah, I guess we won't be seeing her again this weekend," Mel said as the desk clerk called both of them up to the desk. While they were checking in, Sheree made it back over with Ronnie in tow, who Athena immediately hugged, having to reach up.

The first time Athena had met Ronnie she'd thought he was a basketball player, but she quickly learned he hadn't played a day in his life, and actually resented the assumption. Come to find out, he'd gone to school to become an accountant and over the years had become very sensitive about people's assumption that he wasn't in the classes for a degree, but for something to do when he wasn't on the court. However, by the time he graduated with honors, he had changed his mind about accounting, and had decided to make his hobby, acting, become his full-time job.

Unfortunately, in the past three years he hadn't received his big break, and therefore had been taking any kind of work that allowed him time for auditions. Most of the time it was work as a waiter. Both of his parents and all of Sheree's relatives, Athena included, were just waiting for him to come to his senses and get a job as an accountant, which would increase his income fifty times over. However, Ronnie, despite his being a whiz at numbers, had yet to see this.

Athena and Mel left Ronnie and Sheree in the elevator as they went on to their room three floors up.

"Can these beds get any smaller?" Mel said upon seeing the room. Although Athena agreed, she knew that they were lucky to have gotten the rooms on such short notice. Although she would have preferred a luxury suite like Sheree's, she did not begrudge Sheree and Ronnie. Hitting the showers, Athena left Mel to raid the bar. After they had both gotten dressed and were ready to head downstairs, Athena decided to at least call her sister to see if she wanted to walk over. Ronnie picked up the phone.

"Hey, brother-in-law," Athena said after hearing Ronnie say hello. "I was just calling to see if my sister wanted to walk with us over to the Superdome," Athena said, laughing.

"Uh," Ronnie said, stalling.

Athena heard whispering in the background and immediately knew it was a bad time. Before Ronnie could make an excuse, Athena said, "Well, just tell her we'll see her when we see her, okay?" Hanging up the phone, Athena said, "Alrighty, let's pray for my sister that she doesn't lose her job this weekend." Mel immediately burst out laughing, then followed Athena to the door.

The next two hours Mel and Athena went from one stage to another, trying to catch as many musical acts as they could and keep Athena's mind off her troubles. They stopped by Shelly's show first, flashing their VIP badges to get backstage. Seeing the excited faces, Athena was so happy that she was there to share the moment.

Although Athena and Mel couldn't get front row center they still were able to dance to the music as Shelly and her band brought the house down. When they finally left the Superdome, Athena and Mel were starving. It was 11:00 p.m., but they were not ready to call it a night, especially after Mel told Athena about a new club on Bourbon Street that she had heard another concertgoer talking about. When Athena said she was game, both of them jumped into a cab and headed down to Bourbon Street.

On the way over, Mel couldn't help reminiscing about the time when they were college students and entirely too young to be let loose in New Orleans. "Do you remember that time we got lost downtown?" Mel said, laughing. "We got separated from our group, and were so turned around that we couldn't even remember the address of our school."

Athena nodded her head, laughing at the memory. Nervous about missing curfew, it had taken them forever to flag down a cab. When they finally did get one, the cabbie had ended up leaving them in the middle of the street when they couldn't give him an address. Because they had never been in a cab before, they hadn't thought to just tell the man the name of their university.

"Do you remember," Athena said, still laughing, "the time we left the campus on a bus and came back in a limousine?" Both of them shouted at the memory, scaring their driver so much he actually swerved the car, then looked angrily in his rearview mirror. Athena thought the cabdriver probably thought they were drunk, but he just didn't know that when Mel and she got together, alcohol was never needed for a good time.

When they finally reached Bourbon, the cabdriver sped off as soon as the two stepped from the cab, obviously glad to be rid of the two hysterical women. By the time they made it to the club Athena was in the best mood she'd been in for days. Willing herself not to think about what was waiting for her back in Biloxi, Athena focused on the music spilling out of the club.

Then she heard Mel shout and start shimmying to the music. Athena immediately recognized the song. Although she was rusty on her zydeco, she remembered the song from the many that Mel played before they would go out clubbing on weekends.

Shimmying with her friend towards the club, both women noticed the stares from some of the men lining the street. Athena started walking a little bit faster. Although it was a well-lit street, she knew how quickly things could turn around for two women alone on

S. R. MADDOX

Bourbon, no matter how well dressed they were. Passing the bouncers at the entrance, Athena could smell the beer in the air, and the music got louder. The energy level was ridiculous and even though Athena wanted to join the people on the dance floor, her stomach was disagreeing with her feet, so they moved over to the bar, where there were some tables set up for service.

From their table they couldn't see the stage, but she knew that she liked what she heard. After they ordered they didn't have to wait long for their food, but Athena was disappointed when the band left before they had a chance to dance. As Athena worked on the last of her catfish and fries, the MC walked onstage to introduce another band. Athena saw Mel put down her drink, then look her way before turning back to the stage. Because the floor had emptied, Athena had a good view of the stage as some bar workers went on the stage to do some setup.

Leaning towards Athena, Mel said, "Fix your hair."

"Huh?" Athena asked, confused.

"Fix your hair and wipe your mouth," Mel said, repeating herself.

Feeling like a pig for her friend having to tell her to wipe her mouth, Athena didn't notice the band as they filed out onto stage.

"Oh great," Athena said, her head still bent as she recognized the first few bars of another Cajun song. "They have another zydeco band coming on."

Lifting her head she was shocked speechless when she recognized the singer as he sang the first few lines in perfect Cajun. She was even more stunned to see him staring right back at her.

Seconds later the audience jumped to their feet as the song took an up-tempo beat and the dance floor was suddenly crowded, once more blocking Athena's view of the stage.

"Athena, are you okay?" Mel asked getting off her stool to stand next to Athena.

Taking a deep breath Athena tried to stop her heart from beating so fast. What was Mike doing there? At the same time she wondered how the hell he'd learned to sing like that. And was that Ricky on the stage with him?

Looking over at her friend, Athena saw a smile spread on Mel's face.

"Surprise," Mel said hesitantly.

"Surprise," Athena mocked before jumping off her stool and heading outside, pissed at her friend's deception. She had told her not to interfere. When Mel finally caught up to her, Athena was still pissed.

"Athena," Mel said, "I thought you wanted to see Mike."

"I did last week," Athena said, "but now I don't."

Confused, Mel just looked at her.

"Why didn't you tell me that he was going to be here?" Athena asked angrily. "Why does everyone think they can just jerk me around?" Yes, she wanted to see Mike, but dammit, she wasn't prepared to right now, and of course there was the righteous indignation she had built up over the fact that he hadn't called her after she'd been held hostage.

"Athena," Mel said, grabbing her shoulders, "it's time to grow up. Yes, Mike was wrong, but you were wrong also. He did try to call you."

"What?" Athena asked, more confused than ever.

"He called your house, but you weren't there," Mel practically yelled. "You haven't spent a night at home since the night after you two broke up," she said more softly.

"We didn't break up," Athena said petulantly.

"All right, had an argument," Mel conceded. "When he couldn't get in touch with you, he called me."

Athena was surprised at that.

"Yeah, me," Mel said again, "and it wasn't easy for him. When he called he hadn't heard what Barry put you through. He had already left Biloxi."

Athena smacked her head. She had forgotten all about the tour.

"So he's been out of town."

"Exactly."

"Athena," Mel said, holding both of Athena's hands in her own, "I admit I was wrong about him. I was also wrong for discouraging you about seeing him. You have to do what's right for you. Forget your family, forget me. Do what's right for you. Give him a chance at least to make it up to you. He knows he was wrong, and believe me," Mel said, smiling, "it'll be a lot more fun to make him work for it."

Athena was still in shock from what had just happened. She wanted to both run to Mike and run away at the same time. Just a minute ago she'd had a face full of coleslaw and was feeling good for the first time in about a week. Now she felt that she could throw up.

"Lord knows what I must look like," Athena said, laughing to avoid the tears.

"You look beautiful," Mel sniffed, "as always."

"Thanks," Athena smiled, "you liar."

"Hey, that's what best girlfriends do," Mel responded without missing a beat.

Athena pushed at Mel's shoulder before grabbing Mel's purse, and taking out her compact.

Mel wiped away her tears and started laughing as Athena attempted to primp in the tiny little mirror. Finally she said, "Athena, you look fine. Since when did you become so prissy about your looks?" Mel asked, pitching in to help Athena with her hair, and holding the mirror as she reapplied some lipstick.

"Since I started caring about me."

They both walked back into the club, arm in arm, to find Mike waiting at the table they had left minutes before. Looking at the stage, Athena saw Gregory at the center microphone singing one of Thunder Road's original songs. It was rocking the house.

"Hi," Mike said, smiling at Athena and reaching up to brush her hair out of her eyes.

Athena heard Mel gasp behind her and say, "It smiles," before walking away.

Mike took Athena's hand and wordlessly led her backstage to a tiny dressing room. Although Athena followed willingly, she had plans of her own.

As soon as he closed the door, Mike pushed Athena back against the door, and kissed her until she felt her toes curl. Once he pulled back, releasing her swollen lips, Athena couldn't speak.

She wanted to say, "Where have you been the past five days?" Instead, she said, "May I have another, please."

Being the gentleman of Athena's dreams, Mike complied.

CHAPTER 24

When Athena awoke for the third time the next morning, she was alone in the bed. She could hear Mike showering in the bathroom. Normally Athena was an early riser, even on weekends, but looking at the clock next to the bed, to her surprise she saw that it was already ten.

Thinking back to the night before, she smiled at the memory of how quickly Mike had gotten her out of the club. For the first time Athena forgot about her "club rules" and left her friend Mel without telling her she was leaving. However, she was sure that her friend had gotten over any saltiness pretty quick, if there was any, considering she was standing at the stage in front of Ricky when Mike dragged her backstage.

Hearing Mike singing now in the shower, Athena thought about joining him, but she was still reeling from the question Mike had asked earlier. Athena was hesitant to go anywhere near him until she could trust herself and what she was feeling. Ten minutes later, Athena pretended she was still sleep when Mike finally emerged from the bathroom. After a kiss on the cheek and a playful swat at her bottom, Mike promised to return in a couple of hours. As soon as he left, Athena ran for the phone to call Mel's cell.

Finding out they were actually in the same hotel, the girls decided to meet in the downstairs restaurant as soon as possible. By the time Athena got downstairs, Mel had already ordered a bowl of fruit for the table.

"He wants to meet my parents," Athena said as she sat down. She felt spacey.

Mel barely stopped chewing to counter with "What's the problem?"

Athena looked around the restaurant, opening and closing her mouth, not knowing where to begin with listing the number of problems there were to bringing someone home to meet her parents during the middle of the biggest family reunion ever.

"Of course he would want to meet Mr. and Mrs. Miles," Mel said as if she were explaining the concept of one plus one equals two.

Seeing that the prospect still freaked her out, Mel sighed, saying, "Really, Athena, your parents are the most civilized and well-mannered people I know. I doubt that meeting Mike would change any of that. At least not with your father." She'd barely finished her statement when the waiter came to the table to ask if they were ready to order the main course.

Mel ordered two omelets for them. When the waiter left, Mel continued, "Now if they were coming to meet my momma and daddy, then I would be saying something different. My parents will not even be meeting Ricky until after a ring is bought and the wedding paid for, and even then I'm gonna have to think about it."

Surprised to hear Mel talking about marriage, Athena couldn't help staring in shock.

"Oh, don't look at me like that," Mel said, smiling and holding out her hand. "No ring yet. But yes, if he asks, I think I just might say yes."

In a perfect imitation of her assistant Twila, Athena said, "Oooh," before she was able to stop herself. After Mel shot her a look, Athena stopped laughing. Then remembering her earlier conversation with Mike, she rolled her head from side to side.

Mel said in an aggravated manner, "Please tell me you handled the situation better than this when Mike was standing in front of you."

Thinking back to what they were doing when Mike told her he wanted to meet her parents, she was about to say she didn't have time to say anything. However, not wanting to be guilty of TMI (too much information) Athena just told her that it didn't come up. However, thinking about why Mike was late to the interview that had been scheduled with a local radio station this morning started her beaming.

Seeing that smile, Mel said, "You love him, don't you?"

Surprising herself, Athena let out a wail and the tears flowed. She looked up to see Mel with an expression of near terror on her face. She probably thought her best friend had gone mad, Athena thought, which was what Athena would have thought if the tables had been turned and Mel had suddenly been transformed from super-woman to wimp.

Mel whispered, "Are you pregnant?" which made Athena start wailing even louder as she shook her head from side to side.

Though knowing she was a mess, Athena just couldn't seem to stop. It seemed that the stress and drama of the past week had finally hit her like a ton of bricks. Things were just happening too fast.

Suddenly Mel grabbed a handful of napkins and pulled her chair closer to Athena's. Putting her arm around Athena's shoulders, Mel said in a low voice,

"Look, I've known you for almost three decades, right?" At Athena's nod, Mel continued, "During that time you have had five boyfriends, including Mike. Two you were engaged to, and only one you never took home to meet your parents—this one. And only three of them you slept with, including this one," she said, raising her eyebrows.

After listening to her recite the history of her love life, Athena moaned, "Jesus, I tell you too much." She looked around to see if anyone else had overheard.

"Both you and I know you don't take this sleeping around lightly," Mel said emphatically, "no matter how I have tried to change your mind. Which means that you have to really care for him to let it get this far."

After hearing Mel break it down so easily, Athena realized she had been making entirely too much out of this. It was just that it had been really hard getting used to all the changes that had occurred in the past few months.

The Athena who had existed a month ago was no more. Hell, the Athena who had existed a few days ago was no more. Although it had taken a long time to realize it, Athena understood she had been changing all along, and it was possible that she would change a lot more. By the time the food arrived, Athena had made a clear decision.

After finishing lunch, Athena waited for Mike at the hotel. As they packed up the car, Athena found out that the band was gearing up to go on tour in a month. Surprised that Mike hadn't said anything, Athena decided not to push the subject with him, just let him tell her in his own time. Sheree and Ronnie had rented a car for the ride back to Biloxi, as had Mike. Mel and Ricky trailed in her car, but they all made it back to Biloxi in record time. Everyone was excited to get to the barbecue at Hiller Park on the bank of the Back Bay. The park was rumored to be a haven for alligators, but the two swimming pools and tennis courts kept the visitors coming.

Although no one said anything about it, everyone wondered what the response was going to be once they arrived. Even Mike was feeling the pressure as he pulled at his shirt collar. When they all got out of the car, Sheree immediately went in search of their parents.

Athena was really surprised at how readily Sheree accepted Mike. When Athena had asked earlier what she thought about Mike, she had been surprised by Sheree's lack of response.

"You don't like him, do you?" Athena had asked, having realized earlier that her sister's opinion was important, which was weird.

"I didn't say that, Athena," her sister said, confused at Athena's persistence.

"Well, say something." Athena was exasperated. "Tell me what you think. Should we go see everybody?"

Finally realizing what Athena was asking her, Sheree said, "Athena, it doesn't matter what anyone else thinks. All anyone ever wanted was for you to be happy. All of this time we have just been hoping that you would find someone. Whether you decide to see Mike or not see him, that's your decision, nobody else's. You don't owe anyone here anything," Sheree continued, "and believe me, everyone is going to be happy once they see how happy that man makes you."

For the second time in the past week Athena was leaning on her sister for strength. She hadn't been asking for permission, however, just some perspective, and her younger sister seemed to be full of it today.

Grabbing Mike by the hand, she led him the direction Sheree had gone minutes before. Walking through the crowds of members of her family, Athena could feel a few stares coming her way, but both Mike and Athena just smiled in response.

Some people smiled back, but Athena noticed the faces of a few couples just stayed confused. However, she was pleased that none were out-and-out rude. She'd half expected the confusion, more for the fact that she had brought someone, rather than showing up alone as usual. As a matter of fact everyone was cool, not that Athena no longer cared what anyone thought about her and Mike, with one exception.

"Hey, Daddy," Athena said, a little confused by the frown she saw on her father's usually smiling face. "I have someone I want you to meet." Making introductions, she watched her father as his good manners kicked in and he shook Mike's hand. Athena was surprised to see that the frown on her father's face never completely left. As a matter of fact, when Mike put his arm around Athena's shoulder it seemed to deepen.

"Very nice to meet both of you," Mike said, smiling the whole time.

Athena's mother smiled back readily when introduced, then offered to show Mike to the buffet table. Mike didn't miss a beat as her mother placed her hand in the crook of his arm, leading him away from Athena and her dad. She allowed herself to exhale.

When her mother returned, Athena forced herself to smile as her mother's sing-song voice, which lulled even the most cynical person into a false sense of security, chirped in her ear.

"So you brought him?"

Athena didn't bother responding to the obvious. Of course, she had brought him. She was staring right at him as he chatted with her father over a huge bin of baked beans.

Turning back to her mother, she saw a troubled expression on her usually wrinkle-free face.

"What," Athena asked, "are you sick?" She was actually enjoying her mother's discomfort. That's all it could be, slight discomfort, because she would never dare show anything more in public.

"No," she said gruffly before reaching behind her for a chair to sit down. After a few moments of silence,

Athena sat on the ground next to her mother's chair. Her mother said nothing about her dress and possible dirt stains, which caused Athena to begin to worry. Although she didn't want to, Athena found herself asking her mother what she truly thought about Mike now that she had actually met him.

"I don't know Mike, so I can't rightfully give my opinion about someone I don't know," Aileen said sharply.

So this is how its going to be. "Mother," Athena said slowly, knowing that she probably didn't want to hear it, but unable to stop herself, "admit it, you were wrong."

"Really Athena, I just don't get it. Why him? Why now?"

"Because Mother," Athena said, standing, "I love him."

Shooting out of her chair, Aileen shouted, "But you don't know him!"

Athena was more shocked by her mother's response than her words.

"No, Mother," Athena spoke gently, "you don't know him." Suddenly Athena realized her mother's response was born more out of fear than anything else. She had a messed up way of showing her love, but that was what she was doing. As loony as her behavior had been, it was because she felt she was protecting her daughter.

Athena watched her mother closely, Aileen appeared to be looking not at her daughter but through her, lost in some memory.

"Athena," her mother said slowly, "I just hope you don't set your hopes up in that boy because I can tell you now, you're just going to get disappointed." Looking over her shoulder, Aileen shook her head. "I just don't get it."

"Mother, it's not for you to get."

Nodding, Aileen looked back at her daughter and her shoulders slumped. "I guess not."

Looking at the ground for a moment, Athena did a victory dance in her head. She had finally defeated the queen. However, her mother quickly dashed her hopes when she squared her shoulders, placing one hand on her hip.

"What did you say he did for a living again?" Not giving Athena a chance to respond, her mother marched straight for the buffet table to where Mike stood.

Athena watched long enough to see her father shrug before making a dive for cover at a nearby table, leaving Mike to hold his own with her mother.

Athena thought for a moment she should rescue her man, but then decided if he was serious about giving them a try, it was time for him to fully understand what he was dealing with as an honorary member of the Miles family.

Whistling, she walked away—in the opposite direction.

After about an hour of making rounds, Athena ran across Mike, who was sitting with Uncle Pete and Cousin Bobby from Michigan. Mel, Sheree, and their beaus soon joined them, carrying plates to take home for the ride.

The sun was setting as Athena snuggled up to Mike as they sat listening to Uncle Pete talk about some card game back in 1966 and a car he had lost because of it. He had everyone in stitches as he related how he'd tried his best to hold on to the car.

"Man," Uncle Pete said, "after I lost that damn car, I did everything in my power to get it back. I even went to the police."

"What good did that do?" Bobby asked.

"Absolutely nothing. They said that I had to just try to work something out with that crook Jimmy who got in the card game. I told the police he took advantage of me."

"How'd he take advantage of you, Unc?" Ronnie asked, ready for the punchline.

"That fool knew I was drunk when I put those keys down, and he let me bet it anyway." Everyone started laughing at this, even Uncle Pete. "Man, that was the best car I ever had," he said, taking a sip of his beer.

"That must have been some car," Ricky said, beginning to feel sorry for Uncle Pete and his lost car. "What kind of car was it?"

"A '64 Pinto," Uncle Pete said with pride.

"A Pinto," Ronnie and Ricky said at the same time. Everyone started in laughing. Sputtering, Uncle Pete tried his best to act offended.

"Come on, Unc, a '64 Pinto?" Ronnie said. "You should be glad that he took that off your hands." Everyone kept laughing despite Uncle Pete's claim that it was a classic. "You young folks just don't know nothing about well-made vehicles. Y'all all about the hippety hop and junk like that. Well, let me tell you something." Pointing at them, Uncle Pete said, "Ronnie, Bobby, Ricky, and Mike, I don't care what you drive, I know what I like," then walked away as they all fell out at Uncle Pete's impromptu rap.

After packing up several plates of the home-cooked food and saying good-bye to everyone, the three couples prepared to head out.

Mel and Ricky took off first, followed by Ronnie and Sheree, who planned on taking their rental car back to New Orleans from where they would later fly back home to New York. On her way to the car Mike had rented, Athena was stopped one last time by her Aunt Ollie.

Bracing herself for another round of, "Your clock is tickin'," Athena waved Mike on to put their goodies in the car.

"Athena," Aunt Ollie began, "I'm so glad to see you again, and I wanted to tell you how much I enjoyed meeting your young man."

Here it comes.

"I just wanted to tell you how proud I am of you and all that you've accomplished."

Huh?

"I just heard from your cousin Stacy. You know she moved to Memphis last month?" Aunt Ollie asked. "I wish that she could have learned something from you. I was hoping with her coming back here on her own that she would finally find that confidence in being independent that she never got with me."

Athena reached out to take her aunt's hand when she noticed her tearing up.

"I know how much you looked out for her, and I just wanted to tell you how much I appreciated it."

"That's what family's for, Auntie. You don't have to thank me."

Athena pulled her aunt into an embrace. This woman had been in a lot of ways more of a mother to her than her own mother. Athena would never understand why her relationship with Stacy was so difficult. Still, she hated to see her aunt in pain.

After getting her aunt to promise to call so they could get together more often, Athena walked slowly back to the car where Mike was standing. She was sure that she would one day see Stacy again, but Athena knew that the next time would be different. One thing she had learned in the last few months was that the only person she had control over was herself.

All her life Athena had tried to live her life within a world of structure. If something didn't fit in with her goals, then it was unacceptable. However, as she approached another birthday she'd begun to realize that not everything was controllable—especially when it came to life. As a matter of fact, Athena thought to herself as she looked at Mike, being happily married might or might not be in the cards, but for the time being she planned to just enjoy.

"Your mother doesn't like me," Mike said, looking out at the road ahead as they entered I-10 heading east.

Athena remained quiet, not really knowing what to say.

She was not surprised at her mother's reaction, but she was surprised at how much her mother had tried to get to know Mike in spite of it. She was actually proud of her mother.

"Admit it," Mike said, now taking a look at her sitting to his right.

"Mike," Athena responded, "you're right, she doesn't." Looking over at him she saw that he was frowning, and grew worried. Wanting to be done with the conversation she said, "I'm sure she will come around."

"Yeah," Mike said dejectedly. "Who would have thought that she would be so opposed to you dating a three out of ten?"

Looking up from her hands, Athena saw that familiar grin back on Mike's face and couldn't help laughing. Her mother really shouldn't be allowed around people because she had absolutely no couth.

She didn't know what she would do if her mother didn't come around, but there was not much she could do to change her mother. Aileen was Aileen—take her or leave her. Reaching across the seat, Athena placed her hand into Mike's outstretched one.

"You know what this means," Mike said, looking intently into Athena's eyes.

Nodding her head, Athena smiled and countered in a breathy voice, "No."

And she truly didn't, but from the wicked gleam in his eye, Athena looked forward to taking the time to find out.

THE END

ABOUT THE AUTHOR

S. R. Maddox is a native of Biloxi, Mississippi. She earned a Bachelor of Science degree in Education, a Masters in Public Administration, and is currently working to obtain a Bachelor of Science in Nursing. *Southern Fried Standards* is Miss Maddox's first novel. If you would like to contact the author, please write to kiwinene@yahoo.com

2008 Reprint Mass Market Titles

January

Cautious Heart
Cheris F. Hodges
ISBN-13: 978-1-58571-301-1
ISBN-10: 1-58571-301-5
$6.99

Suddenly You
Crystal Hubbard
ISBN-13: 978-1-58571-302-8
ISBN-10: 1-58571-302-3
$6.99

February

Passion
T. T. Henderson
ISBN-13: 978-1-58571-303-5
ISBN-10: 1-58571-303-1
$6.99

Whispers in the Sand
LaFlorya Gauthier
ISBN-13: 978-1-58571-304-2
ISBN-10: 1-58571-304-x
$6.99

March

Life Is Never As It Seems
J. J. Michael
ISBN-13: 978-1-58571-305-9
ISBN-10: 1-58571-305-8
$6.99

Beyond the Rapture
Beverly Clark
ISBN-13: 978-1-58571-306-6
ISBN-10: 1-58571-306-6
$6.99

April

A Heart's Awakening
Veronica Parker
ISBN-13: 978-1-58571-307-3
ISBN-10: 1-58571-307-4
$6.99

Breeze
Robin Lynette Hampton
ISBN-13: 978-1-58571-308-0
ISBN-10: 1-58571-308-2
$6.99

May

I'll Be Your Shelter
Giselle Carmichael
ISBN-13: 978-1-58571-309-7
ISBN-10: 1-58571-309-0
$6.99

Careless Whispers
Rochelle Alers
ISBN-13: 978-1-58571-310-3
ISBN-10: 1-58571-310-4
$6.99

June

Sin
Crystal Rhodes
ISBN-13: 978-1-58571-311-0
ISBN-10: 1-58571-311-2
$6.99

Dark Storm Rising
Chinelu Moore
ISBN-13: 978-1-58571-312-7
ISBN-10: 1-58571-312-0
$6.99

2008 Reprint Mass Market Titles (continued)

July

Object of His Desire
A.C. Arthur
ISBN-13: 978-1-58571-313-4
ISBN-10: 1-58571-313-9
$6.99

Angel's Paradise
Janice Angelique
ISBN-13: 978-1-58571-314-1
ISBN-10: 1-58571-314-7
$6.99

August

Unbreak My Heart
Dar Tomlinson
ISBN-13: 978-1-58571-315-8
ISBN-10: 1-58571-315-5
$6.99

All I Ask
Barbara Keaton
ISBN-13: 978-1-58571-316-5
ISBN-10: 1-58571-316-3
$6.99

September

Icie
Pamela Leigh Starr
ISBN-13: 978-1-58571-275-5
ISBN-10: 1-58571-275-2
$6.99

At Last
Lisa Riley
ISBN-13: 978-1-58571-276-2
ISBN-10: 1-58571-276-0
$6.99

October

Everlastin' Love
Gay G. Gunn
ISBN-13: 978-1-58571-277-9
ISBN-10: 1-58571-277-9
$6.99

Three Wishes
Seressia Glass
ISBN-13: 978-1-58571-278-6
ISBN-10: 1-58571-278-7
$6.99

November

Yesterday Is Gone
Beverly Clark
ISBN-13: 978-1-58571-279-3
ISBN-10: 1-58571-279-5
$6.99

Again My Love
Kayla Perrin
ISBN-13: 978-1-58571-280-9
ISBN-10: 1-58571-280-9
$6.99

December

Office Policy
A.C. Arthur
ISBN-13: 978-1-58571-281-6
ISBN-10: 1-58571-281-7
$6.99

Rendezvous With Fate
Jeanne Sumerix
ISBN-13: 978-1-58571-283-3
ISBN-10: 1-58571-283-3
$6.99

2008 New Mass Market Titles

<u>January</u>

Where I Want To Be
Maryam Diaab
ISBN-13: 978-1-58571-268-7
ISBN-10: 1-58571-268-X
$6.99

Never Say Never
Michele Cameron
ISBN-13: 978-1-58571-269-4
ISBN-10: 1-58571-269-8
$6.99

<u>February</u>

Stolen Memories
Michele Sudler
ISBN-13: 978-1-58571-270-0
ISBN-10: 1-58571-270-1
$6.99

Dawn's Harbor
Kymberly Hunt
ISBN-13: 978-1-58571-271-7
ISBN-10: 1-58571-271-X
$6.99

<u>March</u>

Undying Love
Renee Alexis
ISBN-13: 978-1-58571-272-4
ISBN-10: 1-58571-272-8
$6.99

Blame It On Paradise
Crystal Hubbard
ISBN-13: 978-1-58571-273-1
ISBN-10: 1-58571-273-6
$6.99

<u>April</u>

When A Man Loves A Woman
La Connie Taylor-Jones
ISBN-13: 978-1-58571-274-8
ISBN-10: 1-58571-274-4
$6.99

Choices
Tammy Williams
ISBN-13: 978-1-58571-300-4
ISBN-10: 1-58571-300-7
$6.99

<u>May</u>

Dream Runner
Gail McFarland
ISBN-13: 978-1-58571-317-2
ISBN-10: 1-58571-317-1
$6.99

Southern Fried Standards
S.R. Maddox
ISBN-13: 978-1-58571-318-9
ISBN-10: 1-58571-318-X
$6.99

<u>June</u>

Looking for Lily
Africa Fine
ISBN-13: 978-1-58571-319-6
ISBN-10: 1-58571-319-8
$6.99

Bliss, Inc.
Chamein Canton
ISBN-13: 978-1-58571-325-7
ISBN-10: 1-58571-325-2
$6.99

2008 New Mass Market Titles (continued)

July

Love's Secrets
Yolanda McVey
ISBN-13: 978-1-58571-321-9
ISBN-10: 1-58571-321-X
$6.99

Things Forbidden
Maryam Diaab
ISBN-13: 978-1-58571-327-1
ISBN-10: 1-58571-327-9
$6.99

August

Storm
Pamela Leigh Starr
ISBN-13: 978-1-58571-323-3
ISBN-10: 1-58571-323-6
$6.99

Passion's Furies
AlTonya Washington
ISBN-13: 978-1-58571-324-0
ISBN-10: 1-58571-324-4
$6.99

September

Three Doors Down
Michele Sudler
ISBN-13: 978-1-58571-332-5
ISBN-10: 1-58571-332-5
$6.99

Mr Fix-It
Crystal Hubbard
ISBN-13: 978-1-58571-326-4
ISBN-10: 1-58571-326-0
$6.99

October

Moments of Clarity
Michele Cameron
ISBN-13: 978-1-58571-330-1
ISBN-10: 1-58571-330-9
$6.99

Lady Preacher
K.T. Richey
ISBN-13: 978-1-58571-333-2
ISBN-10: 1-58571-333-3
$6.99

November

This Life Isn't Perfect Holla
Sandra Foy
ISBN: 978-1-58571-331-8
ISBN-10: 1-58571-331-7
$6.99

Promises Made
Bernice Layton
ISBN-13: 978-1-58571-334-9
ISBN-10: 1-58571-334-1
$6.99

December

A Voice Behind Thunder
Carrie Elizabeth Greene
ISBN-13: 978-1-58571-329-5
ISBN-10: 1-58571-329-5
$6.99

The More Things Change
Chamein Canton
ISBN-13: 978-1-58571-328-8
ISBN-10: 1-58571-328-7
$6.99

Other Genesis Press, Inc. Titles

A Dangerous Deception	J.M. Jeffries	$8.95
A Dangerous Love	J.M. Jeffries	$8.95
A Dangerous Obsession	J.M. Jeffries	$8.95
A Drummer's Beat to Mend	Kei Swanson	$9.95
A Happy Life	Charlotte Harris	$9.95
A Heart's Awakening	Veronica Parker	$9.95
A Lark on the Wing	Phyliss Hamilton	$9.95
A Love of Her Own	Cheris F. Hodges	$9.95
A Love to Cherish	Beverly Clark	$8.95
A Risk of Rain	Dar Tomlinson	$8.95
A Taste of Temptation	Reneé Alexis	$9.95
A Twist of Fate	Beverly Clark	$8.95
A Will to Love	Angie Daniels	$9.95
Acquisitions	Kimberley White	$8.95
Across	Carol Payne	$12.95
After the Vows	Leslie Esdaile	$10.95
(Summer Anthology)	T.T. Henderson	
	Jacqueline Thomas	
Again My Love	Kayla Perrin	$10.95
Against the Wind	Gwynne Forster	$8.95
All I Ask	Barbara Keaton	$8.95
Always You	Crystal Hubbard	$6.99
Ambrosia	T.T. Henderson	$8.95
An Unfinished Love Affair	Barbara Keaton	$8.95
And Then Came You	Dorothy Elizabeth Love	$8.95
Angel's Paradise	Janice Angelique	$9.95
At Last	Lisa G. Riley	$8.95
Best of Friends	Natalie Dunbar	$8.95
Beyond the Rapture	Beverly Clark	$9.95

Other Genesis Press, Inc. Titles (continued)

Blaze	Barbara Keaton	$9.95
Blood Lust	J. M. Jeffries	$9.95
Blood Seduction	J.M. Jeffries	$9.95
Bodyguard	Andrea Jackson	$9.95
Boss of Me	Diana Nyad	$8.95
Bound by Love	Beverly Clark	$8.95
Breeze	Robin Hampton Allen	$10.95
Broken	Dar Tomlinson	$24.95
By Design	Barbara Keaton	$8.95
Cajun Heat	Charlene Berry	$8.95
Careless Whispers	Rochelle Alers	$8.95
Cats & Other Tales	Marilyn Wagner	$8.95
Caught in a Trap	Andre Michelle	$8.95
Caught Up In the Rapture	Lisa G. Riley	$9.95
Cautious Heart	Cheris F Hodges	$8.95
Chances	Pamela Leigh Starr	$8.95
Cherish the Flame	Beverly Clark	$8.95
Class Reunion	Irma Jenkins/ John Brown	$12.95
Code Name: Diva	J.M. Jeffries	$9.95
Conquering Dr. Wexler's Heart	Kimberley White	$9.95
Corporate Seduction	A.C. Arthur	$9.95
Crossing Paths, Tempting Memories	Dorothy Elizabeth Love	$9.95
Crush	Crystal Hubbard	$9.95
Cypress Whisperings	Phyllis Hamilton	$8.95
Dark Embrace	Crystal Wilson Harris	$8.95
Dark Storm Rising	Chinelu Moore	$10.95

Other Genesis Press, Inc. Titles (continued)

Daughter of the Wind	Joan Xian	$8.95
Deadly Sacrifice	Jack Kean	$22.95
Designer Passion	Dar Tomlinson	$8.95
	Diana Richeaux	
Do Over	Celya Bowers	$9.95
Dreamtective	Liz Swados	$5.95
Ebony Angel	Deatri King-Bey	$9.95
Ebony Butterfly II	Delilah Dawson	$14.95
Echoes of Yesterday	Beverly Clark	$9.95
Eden's Garden	Elizabeth Rose	$8.95
Eve's Prescription	Edwina Martin Arnold	$8.95
Everlastin' Love	Gay G. Gunn	$8.95
Everlasting Moments	Dorothy Elizabeth Love	$8.95
Everything and More	Sinclair Lebeau	$8.95
Everything but Love	Natalie Dunbar	$8.95
Falling	Natalie Dunbar	$9.95
Fate	Pamela Leigh Starr	$8.95
Finding Isabella	A.J. Garrotto	$8.95
Forbidden Quest	Dar Tomlinson	$10.95
Forever Love	Wanda Y. Thomas	$8.95
From the Ashes	Kathleen Suzanne	$8.95
	Jeanne Sumerix	
Gentle Yearning	Rochelle Alers	$10.95
Glory of Love	Sinclair LeBeau	$10.95
Go Gentle into that Good Night	Malcom Boyd	$12.95
Goldengroove	Mary Beth Craft	$16.95
Groove, Bang, and Jive	Steve Cannon	$8.99
Hand in Glove	Andrea Jackson	$9.95

Other Genesis Press, Inc. Titles (continued)

Other Genesis Press, Inc. Titles (continued)

Last Train to Memphis	Elsa Cook	$12.95
Lasting Valor	Ken Olsen	$24.95
Let Us Prey	Hunter Lundy	$25.95
Lies Too Long	Pamela Ridley	$13.95
Life Is Never As It Seems	J.J. Michael	$12.95
Lighter Shade of Brown	Vicki Andrews	$8.95
Love Always	Mildred E. Riley	$10.95
Love Doesn't Come Easy	Charlyne Dickerson	$8.95
Love Unveiled	Gloria Greene	$10.95
Love's Deception	Charlene Berry	$10.95
Love's Destiny	M. Loui Quezada	$8.95
Mae's Promise	Melody Walcott	$8.95
Magnolia Sunset	Giselle Carmichael	$8.95
Many Shades of Gray	Dyanne Davis	$6.99
Matters of Life and Death	Lesego Malepe, Ph.D.	$15.95
Meant to Be	Jeanne Sumerix	$8.95
Midnight Clear (Anthology)	Leslie Esdaile Gwynne Forster Carmen Green Monica Jackson	$10.95
Midnight Magic	Gwynne Forster	$8.95
Midnight Peril	Vicki Andrews	$10.95
Misconceptions	Pamela Leigh Starr	$9.95
Montgomery's Children	Richard Perry	$14.95
My Buffalo Soldier	Barbara B. K. Reeves	$8.95
Naked Soul	Gwynne Forster	$8.95
Next to Last Chance	Louisa Dixon	$24.95
No Apologies	Seressia Glass	$8.95
No Commitment Required	Seressia Glass	$8.95

Other Genesis Press, Inc. Titles (continued)

No Regrets	Mildred E. Riley	$8.95
Not His Type	Chamein Canton	$6.99
Nowhere to Run	Gay G. Gunn	$10.95
O Bed! O Breakfast!	Rob Kuehnle	$14.95
Object of His Desire	A. C. Arthur	$8.95
Office Policy	A. C. Arthur	$9.95
Once in a Blue Moon	Dorianne Cole	$9.95
One Day at a Time	Bella McFarland	$8.95
One in A Million	Barbara Keaton	$6.99
One of These Days	Michele Sudler	$9.95
Outside Chance	Louisa Dixon	$24.95
Passion	T.T. Henderson	$10.95
Passion's Blood	Cherif Fortin	$22.95
Passion's Journey	Wanda Y. Thomas	$8.95
Past Promises	Jahmel West	$8.95
Path of Fire	T.T. Henderson	$8.95
Path of Thorns	Annetta P. Lee	$9.95
Peace Be Still	Colette Haywood	$12.95
Picture Perfect	Reon Carter	$8.95
Playing for Keeps	Stephanie Salinas	$8.95
Pride & Joi	Gay G. Gunn	$15.95
Pride & Joi	Gay G. Gunn	$8.95
Promises to Keep	Alicia Wiggins	$8.95
Quiet Storm	Donna Hill	$10.95
Reckless Surrender	Rochelle Alers	$6.95
Red Polka Dot in a World of Plaid	Varian Johnson	$12.95
Reluctant Captive	Joyce Jackson	$8.95
Rendezvous with Fate	Jeanne Sumerix	$8.95

Other Genesis Press, Inc. Titles (continued)

Revelations	Cheris F. Hodges	$8.95
Rivers of the Soul	Leslie Esdaile	$8.95
Rocky Mountain Romance	Kathleen Suzanne	$8.95
Rooms of the Heart	Donna Hill	$8.95
Rough on Rats and Tough on Cats	Chris Parker	$12.95
Secret Library Vol. 1	Nina Sheridan	$18.95
Secret Library Vol. 2	Cassandra Colt	$8.95
Secret Thunder	Annetta P. Lee	$9.95
Shades of Brown	Denise Becker	$8.95
Shades of Desire	Monica White	$8.95
Shadows in the Moonlight	Jeanne Sumerix	$8.95
Sin	Crystal Rhodes	$8.95
Small Whispers	Annetta P. Lee	$6.99
So Amazing	Sinclair LeBeau	$8.95
Somebody's Someone	Sinclair LeBeau	$8.95
Someone to Love	Alicia Wiggins	$8.95
Song in the Park	Martin Brant	$15.95
Soul Eyes	Wayne L. Wilson	$12.95
Soul to Soul	Donna Hill	$8.95
Southern Comfort	J.M. Jeffries	$8.95
Still the Storm	Sharon Robinson	$8.95
Still Waters Run Deep	Leslie Esdaile	$8.95
Stolen Kisses	Dominiqua Douglas	$9.95
Stories to Excite You	Anna Forrest/Divine	$14.95
Subtle Secrets	Wanda Y. Thomas	$8.95
Suddenly You	Crystal Hubbard	$9.95
Sweet Repercussions	Kimberley White	$9.95
Sweet Sensations	Gwendolyn Bolton	$9.95

Other Genesis Press, Inc. Titles (continued)

Sweet Tomorrows	Kimberly White	$8.95
Taken by You	Dorothy Elizabeth Love	$9.95
Tattooed Tears	T. T. Henderson	$8.95
The Color Line	Lizzette Grayson Carter	$9.95
The Color of Trouble	Dyanne Davis	$8.95
The Disappearance of Allison Jones	Kayla Perrin	$5.95
The Fires Within	Beverly Clark	$9.95
The Foursome	Celya Bowers	$6.99
The Honey Dipper's Legacy	Pannell-Allen	$14.95
The Joker's Love Tune	Sidney Rickman	$15.95
The Little Pretender	Barbara Cartland	$10.95
The Love We Had	Natalie Dunbar	$8.95
The Man Who Could Fly	Bob & Milana Beamon	$18.95
The Missing Link	Charlyne Dickerson	$8.95
The Mission	Pamela Leigh Starr	$6.99
The Perfect Frame	Beverly Clark	$9.95
The Price of Love	Sinclair LeBeau	$8.95
The Smoking Life	Ilene Barth	$29.95
The Words of the Pitcher	Kei Swanson	$8.95
Three Wishes	Seressia Glass	$8.95
Ties That Bind	Kathleen Suzanne	$8.95
Tiger Woods	Libby Hughes	$5.95
Time is of the Essence	Angie Daniels	$9.95
Timeless Devotion	Bella McFarland	$9.95
Tomorrow's Promise	Leslie Esdaile	$8.95
Truly Inseparable	Wanda Y. Thomas	$8.95
Two Sides to Every Story	Dyanne Davis	$9.95
Unbreak My Heart	Dar Tomlinson	$8.95

Other Genesis Press, Inc. Titles (continued)

Uncommon Prayer	Kenneth Swanson	$9.95
Unconditional Love	Alicia Wiggins	$8.95
Unconditional	A.C. Arthur	$9.95
Until Death Do Us Part	Susan Paul	$8.95
Vows of Passion	Bella McFarland	$9.95
Wedding Gown	Dyanne Davis	$8.95
What's Under Benjamin's Bed	Sandra Schaffer	$8.95
When Dreams Float	Dorothy Elizabeth Love	$8.95
When I'm With You	LaConnie Taylor-Jones	$6.99
Whispers in the Night	Dorothy Elizabeth Love	$8.95
Whispers in the Sand	LaFlorya Gauthier	$10.95
Who's That Lady?	Andrea Jackson	$9.95
Wild Ravens	Altonya Washington	$9.95
Yesterday Is Gone	Beverly Clark	$10.95
Yesterday's Dreams, Tomorrow's Promises	Reon Laudat	$8.95
Your Precious Love	Sinclair LeBeau	$8.95

Order Form

Mail to: Genesis Press, Inc.
P.O. Box 101
Columbus, MS 39703

Name _____
Address _____
City/State _____ Zip _____
Telephone _____

Ship to (if different from above)
Name _____
Address _____
City/State _____ Zip _____
Telephone _____

Credit Card Information
Credit Card # _____ ☐ Visa   ☐ Mastercard
Expiration Date (mm/yy) _____ ☐ AmEx   ☐ Discover

Qty.	Author	Title	Price	Total

Use this order

form, or call

1-888-INDIGO-1

Total for books _____
Shipping and handling:
  $5 first two books,
  $1 each additional book _____
Total S & H _____
Total amount enclosed _____

Mississippi residents add 7% sales tax